"You are practically naked under that jacket. A man's jacket." Huw's growl started low in his chest and increased in volume and power. He fisted his hands, clenching and unclenching them. He would kill the man or men who had touched her, looked upon her beautiful breasts.

"Stop the growling and tone down the emotional tantrum." Nadia shrugged away from A'tem and Bram, who'd pay for touching her, later in the training room. She started to approach him. "I was shot. My jacket was shredded." Glaring, she stopped less than an arm's length away and jabbed her finger into his chest as if to punctuate every word. "A'tem gave me his. End of story."

Her explanation and obvious anger directed solely at him did nothing to halt his rumbling. In fact, it became worse. So much so, the other Prime in the area stiffened and began to match him growl for growl.

"I order you all to stop growling." Nadia shouted the order in a voice that clearly said do-not-mess-with-me.

It was all Huw could do not to laugh and growl at the same time. She sounded like a furious she-cat. He'd always liked she-cats.

REVIEWS FOR PRIME SELECTION:

PRIME SELECTION

BOOK 2
THE PRIME CHRONICLES SERIES

MONETTE MICHAELS

Print Version, Published by CreateSpace, 2014.

ISBN-13: 978-0-9862730-1-8
ISBN-10: 0-9862730-1-5

E-Book, Published by Liquid Silver Books, imprint of Atlantic Bridge Publishing, 2012.

Editor: Allie Hart
Cover Artist: April Martinez

DEDICATION

TO LINNEA SINCLAIR

ACKNOWLEDGEMENTS

Holly, Valy, and Michelle, thanks so much for commenting on early versions of this book. Georgia, thanks for talking me off the ledge when I was ready to chuck half the book away. Cherise, your critique of Huw was what I needed to make him worthy of Nadia's love. And, finally, to Ezra, thank you for all the line-editing, critiquing, and just being there while I struggled to make this book a worthy successor to the first one. You are the best critique buddy ever. Thanks to my editors, Allie and Rory. And a final thanks to my cover artist, April Martinez for another wonderful cover.

Adapted from The Official Prime History, Volume MMXX

A SHORT HISTORY OF THE PRIME

In the Perseus arm of the Milky Way lay the Cejuru solar system, home to the Prime, the oldest known hominid species in the galaxy.

After millennia of galactic exploration and colonization, the Prime had become isolationist as other Milky Way populations initiated their own space explorations and migrated to uninhabited planets.

The Prime did not seek membership in the Galactic Alliance formed by the new explorers, but still felt duty-bound to protect the Milky Way from the Antareans, an ancient enemy from the Andromeda Galaxy. The Antareans were a militaristic, pseudo-reptilian species, and their all-consuming goal was to eliminate all hominid species.

The Antarean invasion of the Milky Way was held at bay for more than a thousand years. But this feat was accomplished at great cost to the Prime.

The female Prime population had been targeted by the Antareans, and many women were murdered or abducted during frequent enemy raids. The remaining Prime females on the chief planets of the Cejuru system suffered from low fertility. The women who did manage to become pregnant and carry to term produced a disproportionate number of male offspring. A girl child was a rarity and considered a great blessing.

Fearing the loss of even more of their women and female children, the Prime Council evacuated the majority of the female population during a fierce Antarean siege.

After the Prime dealt the Antareans a severe blow and forced them back to Andromeda, many ships carrying the evacuated women and children never returned.

The missing were referred to as the Lost Ones.

With the loss of the majority of the female population, many Prime males could not find and "mark" their optimal mate. This mating mark was an unusual genetic adaptation that allowed a Prime man and a Prime woman to find the mate with whom they would have the best chance of producing healthy children.

When this marking process first appeared in Prime culture is unknown, but the cultural significance of it could not be denied. Men and women who did not mark could not mate.

With the loss of so many women and children, the Prime Council faced the reality of extinction for their species within the next two generations.

They voted, by a narrow majority, to join the Galactic Alliance.

The Council's reasons for abandoning the Prime's isolationist policy were twofold:

One, to join forces with the powerful Galactic Alliance Military to address the Antarean threat. The enemy had recovered from the last conflict and now ventured farther into the more populated arms of the Milky Way. And two, to locate compatible females with whom their males could mate.

Though the marking ritual was ingrained in the fabric of Prime society, biologically the Prime had mated with non-Prime hominids in the past during the time of space colonization. The theory was they could do so again.

But a small, vocal minority didn't wish to pollute Prime bloodlines with the DNA of other hominids. This contentious rebel faction, calling themselves "Pure Blood," caused discord on the Prime home planet—and in space.

Shortly after becoming a part of the Galactic Alliance, a miracle occurred. One of the Lost Ones was found.

Captain Melina Dmitros, the sole survivor of one of the ships bearing the lost women and children, was found to have a *gemate* mark. Her *gemat* was Captain Wulf Caradoc, the heir of the Prime Cejuru leader.

Adding to the miracle, Melina brought with her data on altered routes the Prime ships had taken to escape the pursuing Antareans, routes none of the Prime had known about.

The information gave hope to another Prime male with no mate—Huw Caradoc, Wulf's brother. Huw now had a chance to find his Prime mate still alive.

As long as there was a chance Huw might discover her, his honor wouldn't allow him to act on the attraction he had for Commander Nadia Petrovich, a Terran, with whom he had an unusual psychic connection.

And, thus, Huw and Nadia's story begins…

CHAPTER 1

Sunrise, Cejuru Tarn

Galactic Alliance Commander Nadia Petrovich, recently appointed science officer of the *Starship Galanti,* scanned the flat plain upon which the Prime Military had built their fortifications. She hunted for movement, for anything out of place, to clue her into the enemy's position.

The "enemy" in this instance was the Prime Elite squadron that had been selected to challenge the battle-readiness of Gold Squadron and its newly merged Prime and Alliance soldiers. The real reason for the joint exercise was to test whether Prime soldiers could work effectively with the female soldiers of Gold, which was why Nadia was in charge of this particular session and her equal-in-rank Prime counterpart, Commander Aeron Ard, was not.

Nadia took in a deep breath of the thin, cool morning air, appreciating the fact Tarn had enough oxygen in its atmosphere that they could do away with head-to-toe survival gear. Then something in the air made her stiffen. She looked around and saw nothing to cause the uncomfortable feeling. Her skin prickled and the fine hairs on the nape of her neck stood on end. Her pulse increased as adrenaline flooded her bloodstream. Her body's fight-or-flight response had kicked in big time—but over what?

Something wasn't right on Tarn. This feeling of impending danger had been there in one way or another since her Gold Squad team had been dropped off on the planetoid two standard hours earlier. She'd written the feeling off as nerves for the upcoming training session, but now, with her scouting partner alongside, it forced its way to the forefront of her mind.

For the second time in as many minutes, she swept her gaze over the flat, dry land toward the octagon-shaped compound built of the gray limestone found on the planet. It was built for optimal defense with three of its sides abutting the foothills of Tarn's main mountain range and the other five facing the stark, flat plains of what was once an ancient sea. The compound's perimeter was fully lit, but the military facility inside looked abandoned. Her empathic senses told her that was a lie.

The buildings teemed with the emotional auras of sentient beings—a chaotic cloud of emotions that created the anxiety she felt.

But where were the perimeter guards? Where were the Prime scouts who should have been scouring the land and gaining intel on her team for the war games? Was this part of the Prime squad's plan?

For over the last standard half hour, she and her scouting partner, Commander Joen Dakkin, Communications Officer for the *Galanti*, had made their way from the mountain cave system where their team had secured a base of operations. They'd seen no one. Something was very wrong, and her heart rate elevated another notch or two.

"It's been too easy," she muttered. "Do they think we're stupid? That we'll just waltz in because it looks abandoned?"

"If it makes you feel any better, Aeron agrees. It's wrong. All wrong. Has been since we landed without anyone attempting to score points on us." Joen's voice was flat, emotionless.

Nadia glanced at him and instinctively used her empathic ability to test his mood. He was boiling mad under the calm demeanor, a volcano ready to erupt at a moment's notice.

"Shit. I knew something wasn't right." Mentally, she kicked her own ass for not going with her gut. "Our landing wasn't challenged. When we secured the cave system as our headquarters, Aeron seemed happy, but as we set up base operations he grew more and more concerned. I should've confronted him then."

She'd treated Aeron with titty fingers since she'd been given command of the op. She hadn't wanted to challenge him overly much, since that might damage his stupid Prime male machismo. All the Alliance female soldiers had been tiptoeing around the Prime males—and the Prime males, around the women. It had been like watching a nature video of skittish she-cats and a bunch of alpha-cats scenting each other out, testing each other's limits.

Both races still had a long way to go before they understood the other. But then, this training session and others like it had been arranged for that very reason.

Lesson learned—next time her gut told her to challenge the big Prime male, she would.

Since Aeron wasn't here, she only had the Prime male next to her to obtain the information she needed. Her sense of dread was increasing exponentially now—something bad was coming down. "What do you think is going on?"

Joen scowled and shook his head. "Not sure. But something's awry. Our empathic feelings are connected to our fellow Prime during battle situations—and that would include the Prime stationed here. Aeron and I sensed nothing on landing. No excitement or anticipation of the war games to be played out. We should've sensed *something*."

And wasn't that odd? She sensed all sorts of emotions, so many she had a hard time singling out any other than Joen's. But unlike the Prime, Nadia's empathic abilities worked with all sentient beings—and there were sentient beings out there. She just didn't see them—yet.

Joen stared at the empty plain. The only thing visible out there was scrubby foliage and dust devils as the heat of the early morning sun met the chilled air of the night. He turned to look at her. His eyes glowed with the intense emotions roiling within him. "Aeron chalked the lack of emotional readings, other than our own Prime team members, up to the fact no other Prime were nearby when we landed and set up base camp."

He scowled and rubbed a hand over his dark, close-cut hair. "But that read wrong also. Any Prime soldier worthy of the name would have, at the very least, established perimeter alarms on the cave system we chose and had spotters in the mountains."

The caves had turned out to be a storage area for excess supplies and munitions for the military facility and would've been a coup for any invading force.

"Plus, why didn't our opponents challenge our predawn landing?" Joen frowned. "They knew we were coming sooner or later. Prime are always vigilant."

"We're on the same page. I had the same thoughts and feelings." Nadia clenched her jaw. "And there are other intelligent beings on this planetoid—and the emotions I'm picking up aren't particularly friendly. Call me overcautious, but we need to send our scouting teams back to base, regroup, and figure this out. It smells like a clusterfuck in the making."

"That's not overly cautious. It's a very wise call." Joen's golden eyes darkened with his concern. "You'll find Aeron has arrived at the same conclusions."

Nadia didn't particularly care if Aeron had or not. This was her op, her responsibility. If something bad happened, it was on her. There were too many science, engineering, and medical personnel and officers on this particular operation, crew members who normally didn't get exposed to battle situations. This training was supposed to be not only a test of the newly merged crews, but also a refresher training for skills some hadn't used since basic training. She refused to risk her people. The situation was feeling more and more explosive.

Nadia switched her com unit to team-wide communications. "All team members are ordered back to base. Code Foxtrot-Uniform-Bravo-Alpha-Romeo. Proceed with caution. Commander Nadia out."

If it wasn't FUBAR yet, it soon would be. Her gut was doing backflips at the increasing sense of danger.

"Ard, here. Logistics officer is in total agreement." Aeron sounded grim. "My teams are securing base camp. Suggest switching to alternate Com Code Tango-Tango-Two-Four."

"Agreed. All team members switch to Com Code Tango-Tango-Two-Four." Nadia sighed with relief. Aeron was thinking along the same line—regroup and defense. Maybe, between the two of them, they could figure out what was wrong.

"Let's pull back, Joen."

Nadia rose to a crouch behind the boulder where they'd taken shelter. They'd gotten as close to the Prime facility as they could and were about thirty meters away from a side entrance to one of the buildings that did not back up to the foothills. She hadn't been overly concerned about being seen since their uniform jackets and pants changed colors to blend with the desert and mountainous landscapes surrounding the military facility. Even the laser target sensor vests, which registered the low impulse laser fire for war gaming, had the same ability to merge into the background.

Between their camo and the large rocks scattered on the flat land from some past tectonic activity, she and Joen should be able to retreat as easily as they'd infiltrated. Once they made it into the foothills and the thick forests that grew there and up onto the mountains, they would be home free.

Empathic senses blaring and movement on their right had Nadia tackling Joen to the ground as a stream of laser fire streaked across where his torso had been. If Joen had been hit, it would have registered on his vest as a kill shot.

Instead, the stream hit her arm, and she hissed in pain. The searing burn of a fully powered laser blast shot up and down her dominant arm. Her eyes watered as she inhaled the smell of her burnt flesh and jacket sleeve. Her nerve endings screamed. She called upon every iota of her warrior forebears' strength to stay alert and aware and not succumb to the bowel-burning pain.

One hundred Gold Squad members relied on her command decisions, and no laser burn would stop her. Only death could do that—and she didn't intend to meet death today.

"Live fire! Live fire! Code Red. Code Red," she screamed into her com unit as she shoved Joen behind a boulder.

While she listened for chatter in response to her call, she pulled her laser sidearm. Thank God, her hand still worked. The laser hadn't cut any major nerves, just all the little painful ones. She rearmed her laser for live fire.

Nadia glanced at Joen who'd rolled out from under her once they were behind cover. He was dirty, but uninjured, and was arming his laser for live fire also.

"Nadia…" Joen's voice was a low snarl. It reverberated over her skin like a swarm of stinging insects.

His aura glowered in her mind's eye. The heat of his anger danced and burned its way along the edges of her empathic senses as if seeking a connection, warrior to warrior. *And isn't that strange?* The energy flowed from his body in churning waves. *So, this is what a Prime male's battle rage, his* batel rabia, *felt like.* The man could power a transport shuttle on the energy coming off his body.

"Nadia…" Joen touched her hand.

She flinched and pulled her hand away. His touch had disrupted her ongoing sensory scan of him, of their surroundings. She focused on his grim face.

"We have no intrateam communications," he said. "I can't raise any of our squad. We have no off-planet communications either."

"Fuck!" she muttered, testing the air around them for any hint of a further attack. "Can you fix the problem?" As Joen opened his mouth to answer, Nadia motioned for quiet.

The shooter approached their hiding place. He was very close. His eagerness for the kill was palpable; it tasted like day-old meat and copper.

She pointed one finger in the direction from which the would-be killer approached … no, wait … there were two of the fuckers. She added another finger. At this point, she could care less who the shooters were; they'd used live, full-stream laser fire and had attempted to kill Joen. They were the enemy. They needed to be eliminated.

Joen nodded, raised his weapon, and indicated with an angling of his head that he'd go right.

Nadia mouthed, "Go" and went left as Joen dove right; they let loose killing streams at the same time. She nailed her target in the torso and knocked him on his back. Joen's man was down also.

Joen checked on the two assassins. He turned and sliced his hand across his neck. Both were dead. He hurried to join her as she headed away from the Prime installation.

"Prime?" she asked in a low, noncarrying tone as they used boulders and dips in the land to hide their retreat.

From her quick glance, neither man had the look of a Prime male—who were almost uniformly tall, very muscular, dark-haired, and bronze-skinned with golden or amber eyes—even though they wore the Prime uniform. Some really bad juju was going on. She and her officers would try to make sense of it later—once all her people were safe and their base camp secure.

Nadia only hoped her order to return to base camp had been received. But in case it hadn't, she headed south to where another scouting team would've set up for surveillance of the military facility. She wouldn't head back to base until she was sure all her scouts were heading in and weren't under attack. As she and Joen moved swiftly, she listened for the high whine of laser fire.

"Not Prime," Joen finally answered. A sense of urgency poured off his aura.

She glanced at him from the corner of her eye. His normally bronze skin was more of a pale gold. He was scared—almost sick with it. "What's wrong?" She looked around searching for the enemy and saw and felt nothing. They were alone for the time being.

"Lia is out with one of the scouting teams." Joen's voice held more than concern for a fellow officer; it held gut-wrenching anguish. "She's a doctor, a healer. She shouldn't be here."

"Lia's a trained Alliance soldier. This is exactly where she should be. Give her some credit." Nadia would question what was going on between Lia and Joen later. "Stay alert, soldier. We have to get *all* our people to safety."

Joen's lips firmed and his color returned—but underneath, his emotions stirred and reflected rage and determination.

Laser fire sounded ahead of them. They increased their speed. As they sprinted from the cover of one set of rocks to the next, Nadia shoved away the pain of her wound and her worry. This was war—and her soldiers needed her.

Sunset, Cejuru Tarn

WHIRLING DUST CLOUDS DANCED ALONG the valley floor. The setting sun's rays created weird optical illusions through the haze, casting shadows over the arid land. Visibility was deteriorating at a time when the watchers on the cliff needed it most.

Nadia selected a different colored filter on her goggles and upped the magnification to get a clearer view of the wadi. Sorting through the wavering shadows among the large rocks that littered the dry creek bed, she located the two humanoid-shaped figures she'd lost for a few seconds in the glare of the day's last gasp. The duo slunk from rock to rock in a furtive manner; they wore Prime military camouflage.

Jury was still out on whether they were actually Prime soldiers or not. Her vote was "not."

"What do you think, Nadia? Friend or foe?" asked Commander A'tem, a Volusian member of her training team and the chief engineer on her former ship, the *Starship Leonidas*. He was her partner for her third scouting mission of the day.

God, she was tired. The pain of her laser wound was a constant reminder of the potential of danger. There'd be no rest until she had a handle on this clusterfuck. Pushing her goggles up, she turned away from the scene below and focused on A'tem's emotionless face.

His pale blue skin glowed in the lowering light. His demeanor was calm and alert. But underneath the facade he was boiling mad; his anger had texture as it vibrated over her skin and made her itch.

Nadia snorted. "Foe until proven otherwise." She replaced the goggles and focused on the scene below.

Her team had suffered numerous casualties during the surprise attack just after sunrise. Three of her injured were in critical condition and fighting for their lives back at base camp. Someone had to pay. But who? That was the sticky issue.

The action reports from the less severely wounded had been divided as to whether the ones who'd shot them were

Prime or not. The bodies of the enemy dead—so far—had been non-Prime males dressed in Prime uniforms. That didn't mean the enemy soldiers who'd gotten away weren't Prime. She'd rather err on the side of caution.

"The only Prime I trust on this rock," she added, "are the ones assigned to Gold Squadron. Mel and Wulf vetted them all and weeded out potential rebels. Any Prime soldier on this piece of shit planetoid not a member of a Gold ship's crew is the enemy until proven otherwise."

The culling of the Prime soldiers who'd been merged into the Gold Squadron had occurred as the result of several treacherous acts. The last such act had occurred a little over two weeks ago. Nadia along with Mel Dmitros-Caradoc, her longtime friend and the *Galanti*'s co-captain, had been the victims of a kidnapping from the home of the treacherous aunt of the *Galanti*'s other co-captain and Mel's mate, Wulf Caradoc. The two women had been taken and roughed up by the Pure Blood rebels.

"I agree." A'tem's voice rang with certainty and his ire. His cousin was one of the severely injured being cared for by Lia.

Something in his voice had Nadia once again shoving her goggles up. She glanced at the Volusian with whom she'd served for many years in the Alliance Military. His normally silver-blue eyes were as dark as midnight, reflecting his tangible need for revenge. Volusians, like the Prime, were a warrior race. This sneaking around went against his nature and training. A'tem would much rather roar his family's battle cry and take the enemy head on.

She could relate. Her Siberian ancestors were all warriors and had managed to survive the twenty-first century Armageddon on Earth. Later they had been instrumental in bringing back stability to the remaining inhabitants in lower Siberia, often having to use draconian methods to do so. Tough situations had called for tough methods until the order of civilization had once again reigned. Her nature, her nurture, had led her to the Alliance military. And while she was a science officer, a job she loved, and spent most of her time discovering and documenting the secrets of the galaxy, she had no problem taking the fight to the enemy when appropriate.

That time would come soon.

Laying a hand on A'tem's tense shoulder, she squeezed. "Patience, my friend. We can't go on the offense yet. We don't know for sure who the enemy is and how many of them we might have to fight."

Nadia pulled her goggles back down and turned to continue to track the two prowling along the valley floor. "We go by the book. When dropped into enemy territory, we evade. Establish and defend security perimeters. Gather information. Take out any enemy straying into our protected area. Survive until help arrives. Then we go on the offensive."

"Agreed." A'tem's tone said he really didn't.

He wanted to rush down into the valley and kill the enemy. But he'd hold the line, follow orders.

To her astonishment, so far the Prime under her command had done the same. Her decision to send the scouting teams back to base camp earlier had saved lives. Her risking her skin to make sure her soldiers made it safely back to camp had earned her respect. She'd impressed the notoriously chauvinistic Prime—for now.

Prime warriors weren't used to following orders issued by a woman. She had the feeling she'd have to continue to prove herself worthy of their deference. The meshing of the Prime military into the Alliance was still too new.

"Who do you think the enemy is?" A'tem's piercing, navy-blue gaze focused on the valley. His Volusian vision was different than a Terran's—he could see the two furtive shadows without the aid of specialized goggles. A trait she'd love to have; the goggles were heavy and bruised her nose and cheekbones when worn for too long.

Nadia remained silent for several seconds. "Not sure. I suspect the real soldiers are either captured or dead. The ones who attacked us are probably mercenaries hired by the Pure Blood fanatics. They would love to cause a galactic incident and damage the new treaty between the Prime and the Galactic Alliance." *God, I hate fanatics.*

She angled her head toward the two men on the valley floor; they wandered up and down the dry riverbed in a standard search pattern. "Those two aren't Prime military, that's for damn sure. While they have some military training, they're searching the low ground when any Prime soldier who'd trained on Tarn would look to the high ground and the caves hidden among the rocks. They aren't familiar with this planetoid at all."

"I concur." A'tem turned away from the activity below and looked at her through narrowed eyes. "An Alliance or Prime-trained soldier also wouldn't have tipped their hand so soon. Instead, they should've lured us into the war games and annihilated us during mock battle. By acting prematurely, they've allowed us to gain the better defensive and ultimately offensive position."

"Exactly," Nadia said. "They hurt us, but we've recovered quickly due to superior training. With our better knowledge of the terrain, thanks to our squad's Prime soldiers, we'll be able to hang on until Mel and Wulf realize we haven't reported in."

Unfortunately, Nadia still couldn't radio for help. Whoever the enemy were, they had control of the military facility and had blocked all off-planet communications.

For a short, chaotic period after the surprise attack, Gold's com units didn't work. But once back at base camp, Joen had managed to overcome the com unit block. He was currently working on fixing the off-planet communication issue.

"We're lucky Commander Dakkin was scheduled for this joint training. If anyone can get the off-planet communications up and running, it will be him. Only Iolyn Caradoc could do better," said A'tem.

"Luck is all well and good, but Lady Luck's a fickle bitch. I'd rather rely on brains and training." Deciding the two clueless mercs in the valley were no danger to her people sheltering in the caves, Nadia turned to A'tem. "Let's finish setting up the perimeter alarms Aeron and I rigged. With any of that luck you mentioned, we might run across our missing team members."

Renewed grief—and anger—streaked through her. Nadia was missing six soldiers—two Terran females from the *Renard* and four Prime newly assigned to that particular Gold Squadron battle cruiser. They hadn't answered after the intrateam communications had been re-established. Nor had they made their way to base camp.

Remaining on her stomach so as not to skyline herself, Nadia wiggled her way off the cliff's edge. "If the fuckers make a mistake and attempt to search the high ground, they'll not leave alive. No more of our people will be harmed or go missing—we defend what's ours."

She and Aeron had incorporated some explosive surprises into their perimeter security. Aeron's choice of caves had proven to be serendipitous with the Prime military base's overstock of food, medical supplies, and explosives and other munitions. They could hold out for a very long time if they had to.

A'tem captured her narrowed gaze with his navy one. "No mercy to the traitors and their hired killers. It is a good policy—very Prime and Volusian."

"And very, very Siberian." Yeah, the Prime as a race underestimated Terrans and especially Terran women. This joint training should go part of the way toward dispelling that ignorance.

Nothing like getting dumped in head first, eh, Nadia?

Her arm throbbed as the local Lia had given her had begun to wear off. But she couldn't stop and rest, couldn't give in to the pain … she had her soldiers to protect. She also had a responsibility to represent all Terran female soldiers well. No pressure. *Yeah, right.*

Nadia let out a sigh and rubbed the back of her neck. Her head pounded so much she was forced to let go of the shields she'd built around a newfound psi ability; the energy she used to maintain the walls tapped into her reserves. She'd strengthened the mental walls two weeks ago when Huw Caradoc had held her naked against him after he and Wulf had come to her and Mel's aid. She wasn't only extremely sensitive to his emotions, but was also telepathic with him—and only him.

Since then, the stubborn ass, while always cordial and polite, ignored the psychic connection between them and the intense attraction they had for one another.

With Tarn at the outer edge of the habitability zone of the Cejuru solar system, Huw was over six standard hours away; he couldn't sense her—and she couldn't sense or feel him denying the bond between them.

Grow a thicker skin, Nadia Petrovich. The man has tunnel vision about mating a Prime female—and you ain't Prime.

The relief from lowering her shields was immediate. Her headache lessened, and she obtained a second wind.

Yet, as soon as her shields were down, some deep-rooted urge had her seeking the connection she shared with Huw.

All she found was a bleak blackness. The resulting pain was soul deep.

What did you expect? The man is hundreds of thousands of kilometers away on the main planet. He's at that party for Wulf and Mel—probably has some Prime sex surrogate on his arm. Later, he'll go home and have sex with her … she's Prime. You're not.

Jealousy. Anger. Grief. The emotions overwhelmed Nadia. She closed her eyes, well aware A'tem watched her curiously.

"Nadia…" A'tem's soft voice and light touch on her back brought her outside of herself. "You okay? You looked deadly there for a moment. I sensed … more rage in you than before. Then sadness … you were so deeply sad."

Dammit. I won't let whatever in the hell this connection is turn me into a weepy woman pining for a man.

"Not rage … fighting mad. There's a difference." That the mad was not only aimed at the enemy, but also at Huw "stubborn as a jackass" Caradoc and the thought of him having sex with a woman who wasn't her … well, A'tem didn't need to know that.

Her lips twisted into a parody of a smile. "I'm fine. Let's finish setting up the perimeter defenses. I could use some food, and my arm needs some further attention."

Nadia was back in control again. She didn't need to touch Huw's mind to do her job, to protect her soldiers. She was a goddamn decorated Alliance officer.

And soon the enemy, the Prime, and Huw "blind as a fricking bat" Caradoc would learn there was nothing more deadly than a pissed off Siberian female who could trace her ancestry back to the early days of Terran history when Attila the Hun had ruled all of Asia and parts of Europe.

CHAPTER 2

Cejuru Prime, Premier Caradoc's Ballroom

The ivory, gold, and black circular-shaped Caradoc family ballroom was crowded, so crowded that the yellow-liveried servants had opened the doors to the terrace that lined the outside curve of the house.

Mel inhaled deeply; she could smell the flowers growing on the terraced gardens that bordered one small arc of the porch. The same gardens she and Wulf's mother Lorinda had picked flowers from for tonight's dinner tables now had armed guards hidden among the blooms in case any of the rebel faction decided to crash the party. The rest of the terrace was built for defense and faced a deep drop to a rock-strewn river that swept to the distant moonlit ocean. It was a breathtaking view and one she'd like to enjoy with Wulf, but that was not what they were there for. Their job was to mingle with the tall Prime males in their dark formal wear and the few ladies in their brightly colored gowns.

She hated mingling, hated crowds. Crowds provided too many chances for people to shove up against you and stab you in the back.

No one, however, had managed to make it close enough to her to do any sort of damage. Wulf, her overprotective *gemat*, had scared most people off. He'd glared and growled more tonight than he had since he first pulled her out of his ship's maintenance tunnel traps.

"Melina," Wulf whispered against her ear, "let's leave. I must see what you have on under that dress."

Her Prime mate and the man she shared command with over the Gold Squadron, and the heir-apparent to the ruler of Cejuru solar system, slid his hand down her mostly naked back to cup her rear. His sharp inhalation made her smile. He now realized she wore nothing underneath the skintight creation.

"You are in so much trouble, *gemate lubha*." Wulf patted her bottom and slid his arm around her waist, where he massaged her through the thin, silky fabric.

"You love this dress." Mel turned into his big, warm, well-muscled body. He looked very handsome in his dark suit with a pristine white collarless shirt closed at the top with a jeweled pin featuring his family's royal crest. She traced the wolf-like creature on the pin and brushed a kiss over his chiseled jaw. "And you especially like it when I'm naked under my clothing. Admit it." She nipped his chin, then soothed the spot with her tongue, uncaring that others stared. "It took you all evening to figure it out, though. You're slipping."

Wulf eyed the room populated with Prime Elder Council members and their families and myriad members of the various branches of the Caradoc family. He growled low, in the back of his throat. She let out an exasperated breath. This was one of his kill-someone snarls, not one of the I-want-to-fuck-you growls. His aura read as jealous of male eyes on her—and of fear.

"Wulf?" She stroked the muscle pulsing in his jaw. "Are you sensing a danger I'm not?"

She opened her empathic abilities to the room and found no trace of a killing rage, just some low-level animosity, lots of curiosity, and a goodly amount of jealousy aimed in their direction. She shared her findings with him telepathically, but his tension remained. She attempted to access his thoughts through the psi connection that was a part of their unique battle-mate bond, but his prodigious mental shields were up. "Talk to me."

Wulf took the hand stroking his face in his and kissed her fingertips and traced her palm with his tongue. "Even though there is no direct threat in the room, I'm worried about your safety. The mood could change in a nanosecond. There are too many people here—most of whom I do not even like. Some of them would kill you without blinking an eye. My father's insistence on these fetes is insane."

"I'm fine. We're fine." She rubbed his chest over the area where the mark that made him hers could be found, soothing him in a way unique to bonded Prime mates. "The parties are necessary for political reasons."

Her efforts weren't working. "Stop growling. You're giving me a headache—and scaring the natives." She smiled at an Elder Council member who approached them. He eyed Wulf with fear and retreated.

The older man had good instincts. If the poor man had said one wrong word, Wulf would've exploded. Her mate's temper had been on an extremely short leash since her kidnapping two weeks ago.

"Two more days and all the parties will be over." Mel rubbed Wulf's back under his black evening jacket until the buzz-saw-like rumbling ceased. Tomorrow evening, there'd be another ball to introduce her as Wulf's *gemate,* and the first battle-mate since the Berean Wars, to the upper echelon of Prime society. And the day after, there would be a day-long, open-air festival to introduce her to any Prime citizen who wished to attend.

Her father-in-law Ilar Caradoc, the hereditary leader of the Cejuru solar system, was footing the bill for all the celebrations.

He and Lorinda understood the potential for danger, but had felt the Prime as a people needed to see Wulf and Mel.

For many Prime citizens, Mel, one of the Lost Ones, was a miracle, and the people were elated to celebrate her return. There was now hope other Lost Ones would be found when Gold went on their first mission with Wulf's Prime crews merged into the Alliance Gold crews.

The couple's bonding was also touted as the hope for a Prime resurgence in galactic politics.

Those who weren't happy with Mel's resurrection—the Pure Blood faction and certain distaff Caradocs—wanted her dead. The Pure Bloods hadn't wanted the closer ties to the Galactic Alliance. With her status as an Alliance officer and the new mate of the Prime heir-apparent, her appearance had made the situation worse in the fanatics' warped minds. For those Caradocs who weren't in the direct line of power, some wanted her dead before she could produce an heir.

"I hate parties," Wulf grumbled, echoing her earlier thoughts. "I'd rather be crawling around in the dirt on Tarn playing war games with our Gold team."

"So would I." She resumed rubbing Wulf's back with an occasional detour to pet his nice firm ass. She smiled at his low rumble of pleasure. She ached for privacy and their bed. But there was still a sense of worry underneath his desire and the worry wasn't all for her safety.

Mel touched his mind, now open to her since he'd confessed his concerns for her safety. She frowned. "You're upset because we haven't heard from Nadia and Aeron."

She withdrew her hand from his back and stepped around him to face him fully. Not caring about the shocked gasps from the people surrounding them and observing their every move, she placed her hand once more over the *gemat* marking above his heart. She sent him soothing warmth and all her love. The rest of the world could go hang. Wulf needed her and she could do no other than fill that demand.

"My mate. My heart. You give me such peace." Wulf's eyes blazed gold as he leaned over and sheltered her against his body. He circled her waist with his arms and pulled her closer. His breath whispered across her ear. "Yes, *lubha,* I am very concerned. They should have checked in before this be-damned party started. It is unlike them to miss a check-in." He kissed the tip of her ear and rubbed his cheek over the side of her face. "I had Iolyn attempt to contact Nadia after that interminable dinner. He couldn't raise her or the military facility on Tarn."

Mel laid her head on Wulf's chest. His body vibrated against hers, revving for action. She felt the increased energy flow along their mating bond. He'd restrained the need to fight … for now.

She tilted her face up. "Wulf?"

He must've read her concern, because his lips quirked slightly before he kissed the tip of her nose. "I'm fine, *lubha.* I won't let loose in my parent's ballroom. I promise. But I can't deny my instincts … and my instincts tell me we will need to leave and fight soon."

Someone had to be the voice of reason, and she guessed it would have to be her. "Maybe communications are spotty because of Tarn's extreme weather and electromagnetic interference."

What made the planetoid uninhabitable for common citizens made it great as a training ground for the Prime Elite military units. There were many planets in the galaxy with as harsh or far worse conditions. Soldiers needed to train for all potential dangers. In fact, several of the scientific experiments being conducted by the Prime military on Tarn were centered on how to predict the electromagnetic storms and create communications systems that could work during such events.

"The communication silence could be part of their war games," Mel added. "There could be all sorts of reasons why they aren't responding. We aren't leaving this party and embarrassing your parents because Iolyn couldn't touch base with anyone on Tarn."

"Everything you mentioned has gone through my mind also and is highly probable. But I would feel better if we knew exactly what was happening." Wulf kissed her forehead. "I think we should approach Father and advise him to rearrange the other two events for some other time. I want to go to Tarn as soon as we leave this party."

So much for her voice of reason.

She nuzzled his chest. "If it would ease your fears, then I'm in agreement … but only if your father says it's all right. He must consider the fallout from canceling the public appearances. We can't afford to alienate the general public. The rebels' slogans about keeping Prime blood pure could easily impress naive minds. The people need to see we aren't monsters." *We* being not just her and Wulf with their unique bond, but the Alliance military as a whole.

Wulf started to reply and stopped. His brothers, Huw and Iolyn, approached them. The few females in the room followed the two with greedy gazes. Mel had to admit, all of the Caradoc men were swoon-worthy; the fact they were dressed in formal wear just added to the effect.

Huw punched Wulf in the arm in lieu of a greeting. "Hey, you two, mingle. You are the guests of honor at this … this…" he waved an arm at the large room, "…whatever it is." Wulf's brother added under his breath, "Too many damn stuffed shirts if you ask me."

"No one asked you." Iolyn cuffed the back of Huw's head.

Mel laughed.

Wulf shifted her to his side and held her there. "Iolyn, have you managed to contact Tarn?"

Sobering instantly, Iolyn's lips thinned and his eyes held worry. "No. And no one at either Prime Military Command or the Alliance Military Command can get a response from anyone on the planet. It was as if no one was there. And there is no electromagnetic interference at the moment—I checked. Prime Command has also verified the climactic conditions through the long-range sensors. Something has happened to cut off all communications."

It went unsaid, but the only way communications could be cut off was by sabotage.

Iolyn joined Wulf in snarling, raising the hairs on the back of Mel's neck and probably scaring every civilian in the room.

Huw stiffened and looked from Mel to Wulf to Iolyn. "What's going on? And why am I just hearing about it?"

"Because you've been an irrational idiot lately," Iolyn said. "And Wulf asked me to check things out and keep it quiet until we figured out what was going on."

When Huw bunched his fists and growled, Mel rushed to stop the escalating animosity among the brothers. "Behave. All of you."

However, Iolyn was correct—Huw had been a proverbial ostrich since Mel and Nadia's kidnapping. And if the truth were told, he'd had his head buried in the sand since he'd first met her attractive friend. But the Caradoc ballroom was no place for a fistfight.

Mel turned to look Huw in the eyes. "We haven't heard from Nadia or Aeron since the Gold team was dropped off."

Huw's emotional response was immediate and strong. His anger, his fears buffeted her. She wondered if he even acknowledged the fears were for Nadia and her safety and not the team as a whole. She imagined not ... Huw was in extreme denial concerning what, Mel suspected, was a serious attraction between him and Nadia.

"Balcon's balls! I knew we should have gone with them." Huw paced around her and his brothers. The partygoers around them cleared even more space between them and the obviously on-the-edge-of-control man. Finally, he stopped in front of Wulf and snarled. "So? Why are we standing here in our fancy dress and not on our way to see what's going on?" Huw's hands were fisted at his sides.

"Because," Wulf said, "we just realized something really was wrong. Melina and I had already decided to ask Father to postpone the next two days of celebrations and leave for Tarn tonight. So, calm down, little brother, before I put your ass on the floor."

Wulf turned to Iolyn. "Ask the Alliance Military to send a drone from space dock to buzz Tarn. I want video intel of what is happening on the planet before we get there. Contact Nowicki and the other Gold captains and have them cancel all leave for the crew members who did not go to Tarn. Tell them to prepare for departure. We'll leave for the space dock as soon as Mel and I let Father and Mother know what is happening."

The Caradoc brothers bristled with the early stages of *batel rabia*, Prime battle rage. The energy they threw off affected all the males in the room. Their strong emotions had every Prime male in the ballroom rumbling in an instinctive need to join the battle. The low-level noise had everyone who wasn't a Prime male looking around in fear.

Mel's gut clenched, and her heart rate elevated as the Caradoc males' subvocalization stimulated her fight-or-flight response. Wulf's store of battle-ready energy now zipped from him to her and back, making her itchy and ready to kill someone—preferably the overreacting males in front of her. Instead, she used the excess energy to put some threat in her voice. "Don't go into full-blown rage in this ballroom or…"

Hell, she didn't know what she would do. The very air in the room heated from the energy pouring off every Prime male. Mel had never experienced *batel rabia* en masse before. No wonder the Prime defeated the Antareans time and time again. It was the scariest thing she'd ever encountered—and as an Alliance officer she'd faced down some fairly frightening things.

Mel stroked a shaking hand down Wulf's tensely muscled arm. "Wulf … please?"

"Sorry." Wulf rubbed her waist and throttled back his rage. Then he glared at his brothers who managed to do the same.

The women in the room seemed to sigh all at once as the other men in the room took their cues from the Caradoc brothers and calmed down.

"That was potent." She shuddered as the adrenaline-cortisol boost she'd gotten through the communal hormone surge pulsed in her bloodstream. She was pretty sure she could kick ass and take names against any two or three of the Prime males in the room. And since no Prime male was less than six feet in height and most tended to be solid muscle that was saying a lot.

"You okay, *lubha*?" Wulf's harsh whisper carried no farther than the four of them. He stroked her chilled naked back.

"Other than needing to kill something right now, I'm fine." The three males chuckled. She sensed the control they exercised for her—and for the safety of the people around them. But a small spark could easily set them off once more. "Let's hurry and make our excuses to your parents before you boys let loose with the Caradoc battle cry and start a civil war in the Caradoc ballroom."

"A very good idea, my *gemate*." Wulf placed her arm on his and began walking. His brothers headed in the opposite direction toward the exit.

Wulf guided Melina toward the table where his parents sat with two other members of the extended Caradoc family. His mother and father glowered at him. Well, why not? They had to have been affected by his and his brothers' reaction, just as everyone else had. It was amazing his father hadn't tracked them down and kicked their asses for ruining his mother's party.

Then he caught sight of who sat with his parents. His rage threatened to escape the box in which he'd shoved it. Darga

Caradoc! His father's cousin. The man had serious balls to show up at this celebration of Wulf's mating.

Melina rubbed her cheek against his arm. *"What's wrong? You blocked me again. Stop it. Who's that man sitting with your parents? I haven't been introduced."*

"Darga Caradoc."

"That's … awkward. Is he the reason your mother is distressed? Your father, furious?"

"Partially. But their anger is more because me and my brothers almost started a war in the ballroom. Father feels he has Darga under control by setting spies on him."

"I didn't know that."

"I can't believe the apayebo *had the nerve to come here after his sons attempted to kill you."*

"Wulf, I read him as embarrassed, but not sorry."

"He isn't sorry. He is a viper in our family, just as my aunt and her husband were."

"Do you really think he's behind the rebellion?"

Wulf pulled Melina closer to his side. He wanted her anywhere but here.

"Nothing surprises me any longer. I never would've guessed the animosity Father's relatives had toward him—and all for a matter of birth order. Darga's father, Lemi, was the middle son, three years younger than my grandfather. Lemi died a hero during the last major Antarean attack on the planet. Lemi's wife also died. She'd refused to leave with the other women and children. They would be shamed by their heir's behavior."

Melina hugged his arm closer. *"Who's the other man? He looks like your father."*

"That's my Father's youngest brother, Tenar. He never found a gemate *and devotes himself to documenting and writing about Prime history. Your Terran parents would've had much in common with him."*

"Father. Mother." Wulf inclined his head. "I apologize for earlier. We have lost contact with our people on Tarn and need to leave. Please cancel the next days' celebrations until after we come back from Tarn."

"I understand. We will definitely reschedule the celebrations. Our people are looking forward to meeting Melina." His father's stern face lightened as he smiled at Melina. "But before you go, I wish to introduce Melina to more of her new relatives."

Wulf grumbled under his breath, but a glare from his mother had him turning to the other two men at the table and inclining his head in greeting. "Tenar, thank you for leaving your mountain aerie to attend our celebration." He gently brought Melina forward. "*Lubha*, this is my Uncle Tenar."

Melina held out her hand, and Tenar gently encased it within his before releasing it. "Pleased to meet you, Tenar. Wulf has told me you're a historian of some note. I would love to sit and speak with you about the history of our people. Maybe after we come back from Tarn?"

Tenar smiled. "Any time, my dear. Wulf must bring you to my home. It has the most wonderful view of the capital city and the area surrounding it."

A snort from the other male at the table drew everyone's attention. "Ignoring me, Wulf? Have you no welcome for your cousin?"

Wulf gritted his teeth. "Uly and Donte attempted to kill my *gemate*. I think your presence here is inappropriate."

Darga nodded, his forehead creased into a scowl. "Would you hold the father responsible for the actions of his adult sons? I don't blame you for Uly's death or Donte's incarceration—"

"Donte will die for what he attempted to do on my ship." Wulf snarled. Only his parents' presence and Melina's calming nearness stopped him from picking the man up and throwing him off the cliffside of the terrace to his death a hundred meters below.

"Why would you even think of blaming Wulf?" Melina's voice was calm and yet authoritative. "*I* killed Uly after he'd drugged me and slaughtered a spa's entire personnel to get to me—not Wulf. And *I* spared Donte. I could've easily killed him and his friend when they entered our quarters and attempted to murder me."

Darga's emotions read as a wild mix of rage, embarrassment, and regret at his sons' failure.

"This is our enemy, lubha."

"He's our people's enemy," Melina communicated. *"But he doesn't seem to know we can read him. Doesn't he understand the connection between battle-mates?"*

"Darga wouldn't believe it. The man is hungry for power and wealth. He doesn't respect the past glory of the Prime—I wonder if the fanatics even understand what he's about?"

"We'll make sure they learn. But timing is everything, darling. Right now, he's a member of your family and on the Elder Council, yes?"

"For now—yes."

"Then we will bide our time, gemat."

His father broke the awkward silence which had Tenar glancing at them curiously, a glint of amusement in his sharp, dark amber eyes. "Wulf. Melina … take care on your journey. Keep me apprised of what is happening with your crew."

"We will. Thank you." Melina leaned over and kissed Ilar on the cheek and then turned to kiss and hug Wulf's mother.

Wulf hugged his father and whispered against his ear. "Be careful of Darga."

His father squeezed him back and whispered, "I am." Ilar said more loudly, "Go with the One. May he protect and watch over you and your people."

As Wulf and Melina made their way out of the room, he felt the dagger-like stare of his enemy aimed at his back. "Well, at least, we've confirmed who the real enemy is."

"But we can do nothing until we can get to the root of the fanatics who follow him." Mel smiled at her uncle, Tor Maren, who'd come to stand with Wulf's brothers as they waited by the ballroom's main doors. "Cutting off the head does not necessarily kill the treasonous roots—there are always others who'll step forward in the name of fanaticism. Your greedy relatives might've used the Pure Blood faction to further their own ends, but my gut tells me the reactionaries have spread roots of their own."

"I don't doubt that, my Melina. The fight has just begun."

Neither one of them mentioned they were afraid the next battle might've already begun on the planetoid Tarn.

CHAPTER 3

Cejuru Tarn

After finishing planting early warning alarms along the mountain pathways and cliffs leading to their sanctuary, Nadia and A'tem had also done some careful scouting around the military facility, gathering intel. They now entered the cave fortification. She was tired, hurting, and worried. They hadn't come across the missing six crew members. She feared her missing people were captured or, worse, dead. She also had even bigger worries after what she and A'tem had seen on their information-gathering mission. Whoever the enemy was, they had bigger plans than killing off her training team.

But she had a plan to stop them.

"There you are!" Dr. Lia Morgan accosted them. She was followed closely by Joen, who had appointed himself the comely doctor's protector.

Yeah, something's going on between those two.

"Nadia, your wound needs more attention. Now! No putting it off. Do you want an infection?"

The diminutive doctor didn't let Nadia get a word in edgewise and took her arm and pulled her along the path toward the smaller cave Lia had appropriated for her patients. Joen followed closely on their heels. A slight quirk to his lips indicated he found Lia's take-charge attitude amusing.

Nadia entered the cave. The most seriously injured lay about the small room, lying quietly on blankets found in the stores in the cave. The less injured helped by feeding or providing liquids to their brethren. The air reeked of blood and sweat brought on by fevers. The emotional atmosphere was one of stoic fortitude.

Anger surged through Nadia's tired body, giving her an extra boost of adrenaline. She practically vibrated she was so mad. These people, her responsibility, were injured on her watch. Hell yeah, that plan she'd concocted was an absolute go in her book. No one would talk her out of it—or take it away from her. Her people needed more care than Lia could provide here, and she would see they got that help and sooner rather than later.

"Lia, I'm fine." She shook off the strong emotions threatening to erupt. She *would* maintain her calm as an example to her soldiers. "Has the missing team checked in?"

"No." Joen frowned. "We'll continue to ping them over the emergency frequency."

"Damn. A'tem and I didn't see them either. We'll send out another search team."

Joen nodded.

She glanced at the still forms of the three most severely injured soldiers. "How are they, Lia?"

The doctor sighed and tears formed in her silver-colored eyes. "They aren't doing well. I need three regen beds ASAP."

Lia paused and glanced toward the doorway where Joen stood guard. Outwardly he appeared calm, but Nadia's empathic abilities had grown stronger since meeting the Prime or more specifically since meeting Huw. She read Joen's emotions as explosive.

Then Lia smiled at Joen, whose expression lightened somewhat, and continued, "Joen has done his best to get our off-planet communications back up and running as has Aeron. But they haven't managed it yet. So, I'll make do with what I have and keep the three severely injured men in an induced coma and alive for as long as I can." She pointed to a stone seat built into the room's perimeter. "Sit, Nadia—at least I can treat your laser burn. You don't want it to scar."

"Scarring is the least of my concerns." Nadia sat where Lia indicated and sighed at the relief of getting off her feet. The gear she wore was heavy, and she and A'tem had covered a vast amount of territory on their last outing. Her feet needed a short break, as did the rest of her.

At six feet two inches tall, she was now at eye level with the much shorter Lia. The doctor ripped off the remnants of Nadia's laser-shredded uniform top. The wound on her arm was raw and seeping. She winced when Lia tweezed some stubborn bandage remnants out of the burned skin and swabbed it with something that made Nadia's eyes water.

"Dammit, Lia. That hurt." Nadia blew at the wound in an attempt to calm the antiseptic down.

"Stop being a baby." Lia applied a soothing ointment and then wrapped the wound with gauze.

Nadia snorted and looked down at her torso. Shit, she was showing way too much skin for her comfort level. Good thing she'd worn a tank top underneath her uniform top instead of a bra or the crew members in the makeshift sick bay would've seen more of her than she'd like.

Even with the mostly adequate covering, Joen and a couple of the less severely injured soldiers had zeroed in on her full breasts. The Prime males showed their appreciation by the golden glow in their gazes. The last Prime male whose eyes had heated at the sight of her 36-Cs had been Huw Caradoc—and he'd seen them totally naked.

Her nipples tightened at the memory of Huw's arm touching the lower curve of her naked breasts as he'd held her nude body protectively against his. That had been two weeks ago, and she still felt the heat of his touch and his emotional aura. She'd relived the moments in his arms every night since then in torrid dreams. Unfortunately, Huw had treated her as just another crew member and with exaggerated courtesy ever since that day. He purposely kept her at arm's length when they were in the same room, but more often than not, he avoided her. The man's middle name had to be "denial" since whatever this connection was, the feelings between them were strong. And she knew he felt them also because the heat between them was as intense as a star going supernova.

No, she couldn't think of him now. It made her heart hurt and was a distraction. She had her crew to protect—that was the only thing she should be thinking of. *Good luck with that.*

Nadia raised a brow at Joen, whose gaze was still fixed on her breasts. He flushed slightly and shifted his focus to her face. "What is blocking our signals off planet, Joen?"

He entered the room more fully and took a seat beside her. "The jamming is definitely originating on the planetoid itself and not from any ship in orbit. Aeron and I can only conclude the enemy has taken over the communication control center at the Tarn military facility." He rubbed a hand over his face. "This shouldn't have happened. The communications center is manned at all times by highly trained Prime Elite soldiers. It is a secure, impregnable, and self-contained room within the facility. At the first signs of a breach, the men would've sealed themselves inside. It would take someone on the inside to let the enemy in and with the knowledge on how to shut off all communications. I can't believe any of the soldiers stationed on this planet are in bed with the rebels."

Nadia understood Joen's shock and disbelief, but facts were facts. "It would only take one or two well-placed traitors to let in the mercenaries. Much like what happened when the pirates took over the *Galanti*."

The previous treachery had occurred before the merger of Prime crews into Gold. The *Galanti*, then a Prime starship under Wulf Caradoc's command, had been escorting the new Prime ambassador and his party to finalize the Prime joining the Alliance. This had also been before Wulf had met and fully bonded with Mel, who hadn't known she was a Lost One.

Nadia winced in pain as Lia wielded the cold laser to a laceration on her shoulder she must've gotten while climbing. "No matter how it happened, Joen, the enemy has taken over the military compound and is in control of the communications center and the weapons systems."

"How do you know this?" Joen asked.

"A'tem and I did a little extra scouting while we were out." Nadia winced at the low, rumbling snarl Joen emitted. "My call, soldier. My call."

Joen nodded. "What did you see?" The resigned expression on his face indicated he was prepared for the worst.

"Lots of armed guards now surround the facility." They hadn't been there that morning, but that was because the enemy had been in the hills harrying her scouting teams. "Only a few wore Prime uniforms, but they didn't look to be Prime. I spotted several Terrans and even an Erian. Definitely mercs. We concluded the facility's soldiers, if they're still alive, are being held prisoner in the underground barracks."

"Yes, that makes sense. The underground barracks are completely defensible and an invader could easily hold a large number of hostages in them since there are few ways in and out." Letting loose his anger and frustration, Joen snarled several ugly Prime epithets. The emotional display shocked her and caused Lia's usually steady hand to shake as she worked on treating all Nadia's bruises and lacerations.

"Stand down, soldier," Nadia said. "We'll figure a way to get inside the military facility and see what's happened.

Besides needing to get off-planet communications back up, I don't want the enemy shelling our position and forcing us to move. We have too many injured." She turned toward the other side of the cave. "A'tem ... please locate Commander Ard and bring him here."

A'tem, who'd been sitting with his injured cousin and having some lacerations of his own attended to, stood and left the small cave room.

Joen's rage continued to bubble and roil under the surface. Lia went to stand next to him, and with a touch, his anger cooled enough that Nadia didn't feel like scratching the phantom itches on her skin.

When A'tem and Aeron entered the medical area, she could tell A'tem had briefed her second-in-command about their reconnaissance and their conclusions.

His first words confirmed it. "Your plan is sound, Nadia. But I will take a small team and infiltrate the facility, shut down whatever is blocking our communications signal and the weapons systems, and then free the loyal Prime soldiers imprisoned there."

Nadia glared at A'tem who returned her look with a blank one of his own. She'd have a talk with the Volusian later about loyalty and his misplaced overprotectiveness.

"That isn't your call, Commander Ard." Nadia's tone was harsh, but Aeron needed to understand—and trust— that she or any Alliance female, whether an officer or a soldier, could do this job. And he needed to back her decisions up or this clusterfuck would go even more tits up. "It's mine."

When Aeron opened his mouth, anger in every line of his face and body, Nadia slashed the air between them with her hand. "Not one more word."

The atmosphere in the cave heated up, and every Prime male in the room who'd been conscious enough to overhear the loud confrontation growled. The sound reverberated off the stone walls. "All the growling, snarling, and rumbling will stop now. That's an order."

Lia gasped, and Nadia looked over her shoulder at her friend. The good doctor wore a frown and radiated concern. Lia knew her well and had been present the last time Nadia had lost her temper. It didn't happen often, but when it did—well, heads rolled and careers had been lost. Nadia didn't appreciate when a male attempted to undermine her authority even when they did it with the best of intentions.

When the men had quieted down, she continued, "I'll take two men and lead them on this mission. Aeron…" she used his first name to soften her previous acerbity, "…as my second, you'll remain here to defend our base and continue to direct the search for the missing team and to work on establishing off-planet communications from this end."

Nadia looked first at Aeron and then at Joen who'd opened his mouth, probably to protest. "This is my responsibility, gentlemen—and, I repeat, my call."

"But you…"

She silenced Aeron with an icy glare. "Don't say what you're thinking. You don't want to piss me off right now. I'll have your respect and your cooperation." She swept a glance around the room at the avid observers. "That goes for every man and woman on this team."

Aeron stood tall and inclined his head. "You have both. I have complete faith in your abilities."

"Thank you." Nadia gave him a weak smile. "And I trust that if my team and I don't achieve our objectives and something happens that we don't return, you'll do what is needed to protect our people. You know the planet and can evade the enemy more easily than I."

"I should be present on this mission," Joen said. Lia's pained gasp drew his gaze, and he shook his head slowly. "Lia, don't. I'm the expert in communications. The enemy can block our off-planet communications for as long as they want. It's crucial we get a message out to Alliance and Prime military commands."

Yes, there was definitely something more than mere attraction going on with these two. Nadia wondered if it was anything like what she felt for Huw Caradoc when they were in the same vicinity. God, she hoped not for Lia's sake. If Joen held the same attitude about non-Prime women as Huw, Lia was due for a severe disappointment.

Prime males talked a good game about finding a non-Prime mate, but had very little follow-through. Men! Passive-aggressive assholes—no matter the race or culture.

"No, Joen. If something happens and I fail to return, you and Aeron together have a better chance of rigging something to get an emergency call out." Nadia looked at A'tem. "I'll take A'tem and one of the other Prime soldiers from our crew."

She sent a sideways glance at Aeron. "Two big, strong men from warrior races should protect my little female ass, don't you think?"

Aeron had the grace to look embarrassed. "My offer to lead the ... I never meant to imply you are ... weak."

Nadia let out a snorting laugh. "Yes, you did. It'll take a lot more than two weeks of team building for Prime males to accept that women can fight as well as a man."

She stood and rotated her treated shoulder. It twinged but moved smoothly and wouldn't impede her if she had to fight. "Those bastards attacked our crew on my watch. They'll learn that was a mistake."

She turned to A'tem. "Go with Aeron and find me a volunteer among our Prime crew members."

A'tem snorted, a smile in his startling blue eyes. "They're standing in line, Nadia." He angled his head at the one critically injured Prime male who'd pulled two injured female crew members out of the line of fire. The Prime soldier sustained multiple direct laser hits but had still managed to get the women to safety before succumbing to his wounds.

She'd already entered into her log he should be awarded the Alliance Medal of Valor.

"Every single Prime member of Gold is raging mad over what has happened. Prime turning on Prime is an act of treason," A'tem said. "They want to find whoever perpetrated this atrocity—be they Prime traitors or hired killers—and kill them."

"The killing will have to wait until we know what we're dealing with. We have no clue how many enemies are on the planet and where they're positioned. Pick me a soldier who has some familiarity with the Prime facility and in particular the underground area where the communications and weapons systems are located."

Joen spoke up. "If I cannot go, then Crewman Bram Tilga is the one you want. He trained under me. We've manned the facilities here as a team for many war games."

Aeron nodded. "I concur with Joen's suggestion. I'll take A'tem to Bram. He is a loyal and fierce fighter. When do you leave, Nadia?"

"Give A'tem and me a chance to eat something—and I need to find another uniform top, one that is a little less airy." She picked up her shredded top. "Give us thirty standard minutes."

Aeron inclined his head and left the room with A'tem on his heels. Nadia turned to Lia and angled her head toward the three most severely wounded. "Keep those soldiers alive."

The doctor nodded. "That's the plan."

Nadia grinned at the insulted look on Lia's face. "Once we gain control of Tarn's communication system, Mel and Wulf will be here as soon as they can with all the medical facilities you require."

"If they aren't already on their way." Joen moved to stand behind Lia and placed a hand on her shoulder. "I think our co-captains would be worried that they hadn't heard from us since we landed."

Joen's manner toward Lia was possessive and protective. It struck her they had already begun an even more intimate relationship than she realized. Joen had fully embraced his attraction for Lia. Their auras meshed in the same way Mel and Wulf's did. How that was possible was a question for another time and place.

Nadia was happy for the couple. And for a split second, she was optimistic that maybe she and Huw could find the same oneness.

Wanting what her two friends had, she reached for the intimate mind-to-mind link she had with Huw, the one that had made itself known two weeks ago on a Cejuru Prime mountainside as Huw's touch and scent awakened her deeply buried libido.

Unlike the last time she'd reached for Huw, the link was no longer buried in a deep well of blackness. But it was faint, still not strong enough to connect with him mind to mind or even read his emotions.

Either she was getting stronger or he was getting closer.

Why she reached for a man who continued to avoid her and deny this unique bond, she didn't know. It seemed to be instinctive in times of stress or other strong emotions. Not once had Huw tried to reach her.

What a glutton for punishment you are, Nadia. The man doesn't want you. You aren't Prime.

Nadia barely managed to beat down the need to try again. She dragged her mind back to the situation at hand. "I agree. They could already be on their way here. We missed two check-ins so far. Mel is probably having conniptions by now."

She walked to the doorway, paused, and looked back. Joen nuzzled Lia's nape. Lia reached back with one arm to pull his head closer. A pang of envy hit her hard. Damn Huw's stubborn Prime hide. They could have what Lia and Joen had found—she knew it deep in her soul.

Nadia cleared her throat, but Joen didn't let go of Lia. His blazing golden eyes dared her to call him out on the intimacy. She wasn't that petty. If shit happened, this might be the last time the two would ever spend together. "If Wulf and Mel are on their way, I don't want them rushing in unprepared for the extent of the perfidy. Those guards I mentioned at the Prime military compound?"

"Yes?" Joen's arms went around Lia as he sheltered her against him as if to protect her from an attack.

"They were manning the super-laser artillery."

Joen swore. Lia gasped and clutched at his arm. Every soldier who flew the galaxy had seen what super-lasers, part of most planets' defense systems, could do to space vehicles. No soldier ever wanted to be on a ship struck by the giant weapons.

"I don't want our people running into ship killers. Our people don't know the military facility has been compromised. They'd be sitting ducks. If I need backup, I'll communicate my needs to Aeron."

So many things could go wrong, but she had to do this because those were her peers and soldiers on the *Galanti* and the other Gold ships that would come to their aid. They could be killed. She'd do *anything* to keep them alive—even if it meant going on a suicide mission into the depths of enemy-held territory, even if it meant contacting the man who denied the bond between them, the bond which was her only means of warning them about the danger.

Deliberately, she reached for the psychic connection with Huw. He was closer—the *Galanti* was on its way to Tarn.

This time she blasted her message with everything in her and hoped he'd be receptive for once.

Careful, it's a trap!

On the Galanti, four standard hours away from Tarn

HUW STIFFENED AT HIS POST on the Command Deck. "Mel?"

His sister-kin turned. "Yes, Huw?"

"Did you just send me a mental message?"

"No." Mel frowned and looked at Wulf. "Wulf?"

Wulf shrugged and turned toward his brother. "You know such a communication is impossible, Huw. Melina can sense your moods, your emotions, but she can only speak telepathically with me. Why do you ask?"

Huw wished he'd kept his mouth shut. Everyone on the Command Deck stared at him. As much as he wanted to deny he'd heard a female voice he'd hoped was Mel's and not Nadia's, the warning could be important. "I received a warning. Tarn is a trap. To be careful."

Wulf approached Huw and leaned over to whisper next to his ear. "Was the warning from Nadia?"

Huw nodded, and his brother's expression turned pensive.

The One knew Huw hadn't asked for this preternatural connection with Nadia. He was far too attracted to her the way it was; there were times when he'd dream of her and expect her to be in his bed when he awoke.

Beyond the lust for her beautiful body, he liked and admired her. She was a strong, intelligent woman. But if he succumbed to this intense attraction and courted her ... what would happen later if he found his true *gemate* on their mission to seek the Lost Ones? If he found and marked his *gemate*, then he would hurt not only Nadia but also the *gemate*. He would dishonor the Prime woman who was destined to be his mate and the Terran woman he'd prematurely wooed.

Honor and fair play demanded he wait until after the search for the Lost Ones before he made any overt attempt to court Nadia. He'd made a decision after the rescue of Nadia and Mel two weeks ago to keep Nadia at arm's length until the mission was complete. But it grew harder and harder to maintain such a distance. The mental link between them, whatever it was, grew stronger each time he was near her. He'd begun avoiding her—and it had still grown stronger.

Maybe Nadia was a Terran witch or a psychic? He'd read about such anomalies when studying the cultures with which the Prime would come into contact once they'd joined the Galactic Alliance. This link between them could not be a sign of a Prime mating—Nadia was Terran, not Prime.

Mercenaries. Super-lasers. Danger. Mercenaries. Super-lasers. Danger. Mercenaries. Super-lasers. Danger.

Huw gasped and shot out of his chair.

"What is it, brother?" Wulf placed a hand on his shoulder, steadying him when he would have fallen.

"Nothing … no, not nothing." He couldn't deny the voice. The message was crucial to their safety. Nadia—and he had no doubt now it was her voice and mental touch—was trying to warn them. There was more than just a communication issue on Tarn. "I, um, keep hearing the same words over and over."

He lied. There was more than just the words, but he couldn't admit to his brother Nadia had drawn on him somehow for strength and energy. She was injured, exhausted, and in pain—and how in Balcon's depths had he sensed those things? And he definitely couldn't explain how he knew Nadia was leading herself and two others into what could be a suicide mission.

Fear struck him in the chest and he gasped for breath. He was too far away to help—to stop Nadia from walking into danger.

"*Diew!* We need to hurry." Huw looked at his brothers, Iolyn having come to stand by Wulf. Both of them sheltered him from the gazes of the command deck crew. "And we need to be careful. The training facility is in the hands of mercenaries—and they have activated the super-lasers."

Wulf grunted. "I believe your source." He mumbled so only his brothers could hear. "The telepathy must be of the same kind that occurs between me and Melina."

Huw shook his head. "No! This is different." It had to be. Nadia wasn't his *gemate* and that meant she couldn't be a battle-mate either. Nadia had to be a strong telepath. Huw thumped the area over his heart with his fisted hand. "I have no marking. This isn't what you and Mel have."

Mel had come to join them. She covered Huw's fist with her hand and squeezed gently. "Whatever this is, Huw, we'll trust it. The situation on the planet was suspect to begin with…" she stroked a comforting hand down his arm, "…we'll deal with whatever is happening between you and Nadia … later. Once we have her and our fellow soldiers back."

"There is nothing to deal with. She isn't Prime." Huw turned back to his station. "She's not my *gemate*."

"Stubborn ass," Iolyn muttered as he passed by.

"Shut up, *bak*." Huw snarled the epithet for a motherless son of a fucked bovine. "It's none of your business."

"*Ansu bhau!*" Wulf said. "We will discuss this later as a family and not on the Command Deck as we head into danger." Wulf stared at him until he had to look away from the anger and dominance in his older brother's eyes. "You and Nadia will have medical tests done. We'll send them to the Alliance Astrobiology lab on Oz in the Tau Ceti system for evaluation."

When Huw opened his mouth to protest, Wulf cut him off. "That is an order from your commanding officer. Right now," Wulf turned to glare at the fascinated command deck crew, "we are going to Red Alert. Maximum speed, Mr. J'ar."

"Aye, sir." J'ar programmed the helm and the resulting surge from accelerating from cruising speed to maximum vibrated the deck.

The alert was sounded. The Command Deck became a beehive of activity as systems were monitored and decks reported in. The *Galanti* and its crew were preparing for battle.

Wulf turned away from Huw and toward Mel. "Contact Nowicki on the *Leonidas* and bring him up to speed, tell him we'll have an intership com-conference with all section officers in five standard minutes. We have less than four standard hours to come up with a plan to land on the planet without being seen or shot out of the skies, locate and rescue our people, and take back control of Tarn's military facility."

Mel nodded and hurried to her command chair to begin relaying the orders.

"Iolyn," Wulf said, "notify Prime Command, Father, and Alliance Military Command of the situation as we know it." Iolyn shifted to the communication console.

Wulf took Huw by the upper arms and shook him. "Tell me the instant the message from Nadia changes. She's trying to warn us and using the only way she can. Do *not* be a stubborn ass! Open yourself up. Tell her we're coming. Understand?"

"Yes, sir!" Huw closed his eyes and concentrated on the fragile thread in his mind and found it not as fragile as it had been a mere week ago.

Diew, when had it strengthened? He'd avoided Nadia, blocked her attempts to communicate with him in this way, in the hopes distance and denial would make whatever *this* was go away. Obviously, he'd been unsuccessful.

"Hang on, Nadia. We received your warning. We're coming."

What he could only describe as relief came back at him. She'd received his message.

His brothers and Mel might think this was evidence of a mating of some sort, but he remained unconvinced. The connection could have no basis in biology. The medical tests would prove his case.

Still, even though Nadia couldn't be his mate, he didn't want anything bad to happen to her and would do all he could to avoid her injury or death.

"Don't die, Nadia. Stay alive."

"Hurry, Huw!" The feminine mind touch raised the hairs on the back of his neck. She was afraid for not just herself, but for the ships coming to her team's rescue.

"Wulf!" His brother paused at the open door to the Captain's Board Room. "We need to hurry."

Wulf, grim-faced, nodded, and gave the order to the helmsman. "Red-line it, Mr. J'ar."

"Aye, Captain." The Volusian programmed the helm to circumvent all engine safety measures to get the most speed from the ship. The *Galanti* surged forward even faster until the stars passed the bridge window like so many silver streaks. "Our ETA is now two point five standard hours."

"We're coming, Nadia."

Huw left the Command Deck at a run and headed for Engineering where he would keep the *Galanti* running at redline and beyond until they reached Tarn. He'd get everything out of his engines and his engineering techs or die trying.

CHAPTER 4

Night, Cejuru Tarn

With no moon, the only light illuminating the flat, arid landscape upon which the military compound sat were the stars and the perimeter security lights on the compound walls. Shadows upon shadows covered the scene below her team's vantage point. They'd taken a position near the back of the facility about one hundred meters away, hidden in the rocks that had tumbled from the foothills during one of the infrequent periods of tectonic behavior of the planetoid.

Nadia used the magnification in her night-vision goggles to zero in on the door that led to the subterranean communications room and from it to the weaponry control room. The target building was near the back of the military compound. Between them and the entrance was open space; they'd be seen by the mercenary guards before they'd made it five meters from their hiding place.

"Bram?" She turned to look at Crewman Bram Tilga, who like most Prime was huge, well-muscled, and extraordinarily handsome despite his somber demeanor. "Where are these maintenance tunnels you were telling me about?"

Bram pointed to a small, gray stone building that abutted the woods not too far from where they were hidden. "We can access one of the utility maintenance tunnels from that equipment shed. This tunnel will allow us to cross the open space without being seen. There is an exit onto the surface closest to the door we need." Bram's golden gaze was calm, and his voice even and emotionless.

But underneath his purposely blank exterior, she sensed he constantly evaluated her, testing her for weakness. Well, she hadn't expected complete trust from her new Prime crew members. They didn't know her yet.

"How close?" she asked as she turned back to the building and looked through her goggles to see if she could spot a trap door on the hard surface.

"Less than five meters from the back of our target. You cannot see it from here, Commander." Bram's voice held gentle amusement. "But the door is behind the stack of palettes near the building entrance."

Nadia slid down the rock upon which she'd perched to reconnoiter the situation and turned to face her team. "We'll make our way to the storage shed using the cover of the trees and rocks, take out any guards stationed there, and then enter and use the tunnel. Will you know which exit from the tunnel we'll need, Bram?"

Bram nodded. "They are marked."

"Excellent. Once we get to the appropriate exit, I'll go first and distract the guards. You two will take them out. Since A'tem and I have determined the guards change every hour on the hour," she checked her chronometer, "we have less than a standard hour window from now to get into that building."

"Not an issue, Commander." Bram's lips quirked into what might have been a smile. "I have the backdoor codes Commander Dakkin and I created when we trained here. I can have us inside in less than a standard minute."

Nadia grinned at the Prime. "Very good. Once we're inside, Bram, since you know the facility and the tunnel systems connecting the buildings, you will be on point. I want us in and out with communications and weapons under our control and not theirs as quickly as possible. If we manage not to alert the enemy upon accomplishment of those goals, then and only then we will scout to see if we can free the Prime prisoners." If they couldn't, the prisoners would be freed quickly enough once the rest of Gold arrived. "Agreed?"

"Yes, Commander," A'tem said. "What is the contingency plan in case we are discovered while trapped underground?"

Nadia hadn't created one. Her main goal had always been to get off-planet communications up and running so Joen and Aeron could contact Wulf and Mel and then fix it so no one could use the laser weaponry against the rescue ships. Without a lot of luck on their side, which she'd never counted on, she'd fully expected this to be a suicide mission. Both Aeron and Joen had understood that and that was why they had wanted to come in her stead.

Before Nadia could come up with an explanation as to her initial reasoning, Bram spoke up, "We will not be trapped, Commander A'tem. There are other ways out of the subterranean complex known only by certain Elite-trained soldiers with specific security clearances."

Bram looked from A'tem to her and back as if deciding whether they were worthy of what had to be Prime military secrets. He smiled. "I am one of those soldiers."

"And what are these other ways out?" Nadia asked.

"Once we are in the subterranean complex, I will point out a door closest to the communications secure room, leading to an escape tunnel into the mountains and the cave systems."

Bram's revelations sent a chill down her spine. "The enemy can get into the mountain caves from these escape tunnels?"

"Not the specific caves where our people are located, but into other similar cave systems," Bram said. "Commander

Ard suggested the cave system we occupy for its defensive capabilities and for the fact that not many know of the system outside of the certain Elite team members. Commander Ard told me to reveal facility security measures to you as needed. I have."

"Thank you, Bram. A'tem and I won't share the location of the escape tunnels with anyone else in Gold."

"Commander," Bram said almost gently, "I am sure Captain Wulf will reveal such secrets to his senior crew when he has the time. But you need to know all of your Prime crew members know of these tunnels and others like them in similar Prime military fortifications all across this part of the galaxy."

And from Bram's last statement, Nadia deduced every single Prime crew member in Gold was Elite-trained with the highest security clearance and the best the Prime had to offer. Wulf must've taken that into consideration when he and Mel vetted the Prime soldiers to be merged into Gold. She'd remember to thank him for that foresight later.

Her confidence level on surviving their particular mission had now gone from under five percent up to fifty. The fact A'tem had served in the Volusian military's elite squads before joining the Alliance military bumped the fifty percent chances of mission success and survival up to maybe sixty-five.

Another thought struck her. "Then why aren't we using these secret tunnels in the mountains to get into the compound?" Nadia scowled at Bram.

"Because the escape tunnels are meant to be exit only. They are booby-trapped against entry into the compound, but not against exit from it." Bram's tone was very dry and along the lines of "did you think Prime were stupid?"

Ignoring his sarcastic tone, Nadia let out a breath. "Bram, once we accomplish our primary missions, you remain on point to lead us out of the compound."

"Gladly, Commander." Bram inclined his head.

Of course, completion of their goals still wouldn't be that easy, which was why she'd only bumped up the chances of success to sixty-five percent. Once they were in the military compound's underground rooms and tunnels, they'd be like rats in a maze. And rather than trying to find their way to a piece of cheese, they'd be avoiding the entrenched enemy.

Plans in place, the trip to the storage shed and into the maintenance tunnel was accomplished easily and without trouble in under ten standard minutes.

She shoved open the lid of the tunnel, climbed out onto the dirt-packed surface, and then ran to the cover of the large pallets of boxes. A'tem and Bram, after replacing the lid over the tunnel opening, followed her quickly and quietly. She peered around the edge of their hiding place and spied the two large humanoid males who'd come on duty approximately fifteen standard minutes ago. They were alert and heavily armed with knives, laser pistols, and automatic laser rifles. They stood guard, one on either side of the only entrance to the building under which the communications room was located.

Nadia spoke, keeping her voice low and atonal so as not to carry to the guards. "We clear on the plan?"

The two men nodded.

She handed her goggles and laser weapons to A'tem. "Hold these for me. I have some men to distract. As soon as they are focused on me, make your move. I'll attempt to lure them closer to you and away from the door." She stripped off her borrowed uniform top under which she wore another garment—a lacy, sheer bra she'd borrowed from one of her female crew members who had a sexy lingerie fetish.

At Bram's sharp inhalation, she glared at him. "You never saw me like this, soldier."

Bram shut his mouth, which had dropped open, and nodded, but his fiery gaze did not budge. A'tem was unfazed since he was used to working with female soldiers who'd been trained to use whatever weapons they had at hand to defeat the enemy.

She coughed and the Prime had the grace to flush along his high cheekbones and shift his gaze back to her face.

A'tem chuckled quietly.

Nadia snorted. She'd have to remember to tell Wulf they needed to run some simulations with the Prime crew members to get them used to female soldiers using their wiles and attributes to defeat the enemy. Sex was a powerful drive, and when used appropriately had taken down many an enemy soldier. The strategy wouldn't be effective if their crew members were distracted right along with the enemy.

As ready as she'd ever be, she muttered, "Let's get these bastards."

She stood and stretched to her full height. Taking a deep breath in preparation to confront the enemy, she realized her breasts threatened to spill over the top of the low-cut bra. The cool night air had puckered her nipples, and they showed darkly through the translucent ivory lace.

Both A'tem and Bram stifled low groans and she shot them a narrow-eyed glance.

Bram's lust felt like fur brushing over her skin and her mind; the emotion had a taste—wine and chocolate. She shivered from a combination of the cool night air and the waves of feelings coming from her Prime teammate.

But she couldn't fault either man for their reaction. She wanted the enemy guards to react in exactly the same way— it was much easier to lead a man thinking with his dick instead of his brain. If this weren't a life and death matter, she wouldn't be caught dead in the bra that barely contained her full breasts—she looked like a Terran whore. Men, all men, no matter the race or culture, could always be distracted by a nearly naked set of breasts.

"Head in the game, soldiers." Her voice was harsh and cold.

A'tem recovered first and elbowed Bram. "Go, Nadia. We have you covered."

She ran fingers through her short, curly, blonde hair. The paleness of her hair and her cerulean blue eyes when set off against the golden skin of her Siberian ancestors gave her an exotic look. Licking her full lips, she slid around the protection of the stacked boxes and began the walk toward the soon-to-be dead enemy. She made an effort to put some sway into her hips, knowing her breasts would follow the laws of physics and move also.

She stifled a laugh when she heard Bram say to A'tem, "*Diew*, she is a goddess."

Yeah, she was a goddess. A goddess of war.

As she made her catlike approach, one guard noticed her almost immediately. His body stiffened as his gaze stripped her of her remaining clothing. She chanced a glance at his crotch. Oh yeah, he was alert all right. She sent him a sultry smile and then turned another on his buddy who'd moved to stand next to him. Both men concentrated on her breasts.

Nadia stopped about three meters away from the men. Chill bumps covered her exposed skin and she hugged her waist with both arms for warmth. This thrust her 36-Cs further up until her perked nipples threatened to spill over the top of the demibra.

She spoke haltingly in Prime, her two plus weeks of intensive language lessons being put to the test big-time. "You guys have an extra blanket or coat I could borrow? I'm cold." She fluttered her lashes and rubbed her hands up and down her arms, calling even more attention to her breasts.

Both men glanced at her face for a split second before turning their leering gazes back to her chest. After several seconds, one guy recovered enough to jab an elbow in his pal's gut and mumble something she couldn't hear.

The jabber walked toward her, his side arm at ready, and his eyes now focused on her hands. Looking for a weapon she didn't have. "Who are you? And where did you come from?" He spoke in standard Galactic.

She dropped her arms and waved a hand toward him. "Oh, I guess you aren't Prime. I thought everyone on this desolate rock was Prime." She replied in the same language, allowing her native accent to appear. "I asked if you had a blanket or a coat. It's cold out here."

"And I asked who you are and where you came from. Answer me, bitch." The man, with his comrade following closely behind, stalked toward her, narrowing the gap to less than one and a half meters. Close enough that she could smell the liquor they'd drunk wafting on the now brisk night breeze. They also stank of sweat and dirt.

"I'm ... um ... well it's embarrassing ... I'm really not the sort of girl who runs around in her underwear ... but this Prime soldier brought me here in a shuttle from Jump Station Ursa II and we've been..." she waved a hand over her exposed upper torso, "...um, you can probably guess what we've been doing."

Nadia backed away from them, slowly leading them toward the palette stack where her men waited. The minutes on her internal mission clock ticked away in her head. She needed to close the deal and get these two out of the way.

"The bastard was gone when I woke up. He'd taken my shirt and coat ... I couldn't find anyone..." She allowed her words to trail off and looked at them with what she hoped was a pleading look. "I could give you both a blowjob if you'd find me a coat."

The man who'd done all the talking closed the distance between them in several large steps. The brute grabbed her arm, jerking her up against him. She gasped at his action. Big mistake since it meant she also inhaled. She wrinkled her nose in disgust and breathed through her mouth. It didn't help. He smelled worse than a garbage scow.

The man muttered against her ear. His touch, his breath, made her skin crawl. He also continued to shove her closer to the palettes. "Oh hell yeah, a blowjob and anything else we want, you beautiful bitch. I've got dozens of friends on this rock who'd like that and more. You won't be needing a coat— we'll keep you warm."

Dozens of friends? She wanted to ask how many, specifically, but that would blow the plan. She sensed her men's rage at her being manhandled and their wavering patience. They couldn't attack while the man held her so closely with a laser pistol to her side.

His friend closed the distance and now flanked the man holding her so tightly. The other male's greedy stare never left her exposed skin. This was the best chance she and her men would get.

"I don't think so, *kozyol yobanniy*." She muttered the Russian for "fucked goat."

Letting her knees go weak, she threw the bastard off-balance. Using his momentum against him, she twisted to throw him over her hip. He crashed into his buddy and both men fell to the ground.

A'tem and Bram burst from their cover and broke the guards' necks with a strength and skill she admired.

Before his victim hit the dirt, Bram dashed toward the door to get them inside. A'tem dragged first one and then the second guard to the doorway Bram had opened within seconds. No alarms sounded.

Nadia picked up the guards' weapons and followed her men into the building, keeping an eye out for the enemy.

All was quiet. She wondered where everyone was. They'd seen one or two enemy scouts in the foothills who were easily avoided, but nothing like the dozens mentioned by the lecherous guard. They'd need to keep a sharp eye out; three against a dozen enemy soldiers weren't good odds.

Once all were inside the building, Bram closed the door and then did something to the locking mechanism, which began to flash orange and kept blinking.

"What did you do to the door?" she asked as he led the way deeper into the building and down a set of emergency stairs that paralleled an elevator tube.

"It is another one of those Elite safety features I was to tell you about." He flashed a grin over his shoulder. "I thought I'd just show you instead."

Nadia glared. "What safety feature?"

Bram stopped at the bottom of the stairs and turned. "I recoded every lock in the facility. Any of the enemy in a room with a door code is now trapped. And any Elite-trained Prime in such a room now knows he can get out at any time or stay safely inside until help has arrived." He smiled. "This will be a big help in eliminating some of those dozens of mercenaries the guard mentioned."

"How will the Elite soldiers know the door codes have been changed?" A'tem asked.

"The orange light blinks in every room where there is a door that can be sealed."

Nadia frowned. "But if there were traitors on the inside, they'll know we're here also."

"Agreed." Bram scowled. "But they do not know from where the alarm was set off. The alarm has disabled all the security monitors. Plus one must know the override codes to get camera visuals. Only certain Elite soldiers would know of these measures and if they have turned, well, we will deal with them as they come."

Bram turned to the door at the bottom of the stairwell and entered a code. A monitor popped up from the door pad. "It is clear on the other side."

Bram keyed in yet another code. A metallic-sounding *snick* echoed loudly in the stairwell. The light on the door turned green, and he opened the door. "Remember these codes." He repeated two alpha and numeric strings of numbers. "The first is the door code, and the second is the monitor code. You both are now in control of any door to a locked room in this facility."

Bram led the way into the hallway beyond and turned right. He walked briskly and kept scanning from left to right as he moved along the corridor. "The communications center is this way."

"I will bring up the rear, Nadia." Taking the enemy's weapons from her, A'tem handed Nadia her goggles, jacket, and weapons.

Following Bram, she shrugged into her cold-weather jacket, but left the garment unbuttoned. Who knew when she might have to use her secret weapons to distract the enemy again? After fastening on her side arm, hooking her goggles onto her belt, and slinging her laser rifle over a shoulder, she took one of the extra weapons from A'tem.

Bram waited patiently for them farther down the corridor. With Bram as a guide and the little fail-safes built into the Prime security systems, they might breeze through this mission and come out the other side alive. She mentally shifted mission success odds up from sixty-five percent to seventy-five—the other twenty-five was up to fate, luck, karma, or whatever you wanted to call it. The unexpected shit was what always got you killed.

CHAPTER 5

Nadia and A'tem crouched in the shadows while Bram scouted ahead. Bram's anger reached her before he did. His raging emotions scraped over her empathic sense like fingernails on slate. She choked back a hiss of pain and raised the psychic shields she'd perfected since her first encounter with Huw. She let out a relieved breath as Bram's ire now merely brushed across her shielded mind like a cobweb floating on a breeze.

"Nadia?" A'tem looked at her with concern. "What is it?"

"Did you feel it too?" Maybe the Prime's emotions affected everyone. Volusians were not known to be psychic, but their other senses and their skills at observation were sharper than most hominid species.

"Feel what?" A'tem frowned, a puzzled look in his eyes.

"I felt Bram coming. He's very … very angry." A'tem looked as if he might've probed for more information, but Bram turned into the small side hallway in which they waited. "What's wrong, Bram?" she asked.

The Prime soldier appeared shocked at her question. With him only inches away, she bolstered her shields to protect her senses from the volcanic flow of emotions coming from him. It was like a pyroclastic blast against her shields. She wasn't sure she could keep his emotions at bay.

A'tem touched her arm. "Nadia, what is it? You went ashen all of a sudden."

Nadia jerked her arm away from A'tem. His touch threatened what little control she had over her sensory intake. A'tem's eyes narrowed and worry lines formed on his forehead, but he gave her more space.

"Bram's anger is trying to breach my shields." Nadia ran shaky fingers through her hair. "My mental shields are weakening. It hurts."

A'tem nodded, his forehead smoothing out; he'd seen her empathic abilities in play before during battle. *Not like these new, improved abilities, he hasn't.*

Bram jerked in surprise. His eyes glowed with something akin to amazement. The anger beating on her psi senses dropped back to bearable levels. "Sorry, Commander. I didn't realize you were a sensitive. I slipped into the early stages of *batel rabia*, Prime battle rage. I will shield you as much as possible."

She'd experienced Joen's battle rage, but Bram's seemed stronger—or she had become more sensitive.

"Thank you." She took a few cleansing breaths and found she could think without pain. "What made you so angry?"

Bram growled under his breath, the sound vibrating the walls around them. "I checked the communications command center. It is manned by two Prime soldiers ... two men I recognized." He clenched his hands into fists so tightly Nadia could see whiteness appear around his knuckles. "They laughed and joked. The traitors."

"We knew someone on the inside had to have helped the mercenaries." Nadia's voice was gentle; even through her shields, she sensed his disappointment, his hurt, mixed in with his rage. She could taste the acridity of his emotions on the air. She would have to monitor her empathic skills and the sensory side effects carefully. If she needed to learn to construct stronger mental shields, she would. She couldn't allow the extreme emotions of any Prime soldier—friend or foe—to affect her in battle.

Bram scowled and nodded. "Yes, Commander. But one of them is my cousin. That makes it worse."

Yes, it would. Nadia's heart ached for the honorable man.

A'tem swore under his breath in Volusian and squeezed Bram's shoulder. "I'm sorry, my friend."

Bram clasped the Volusian's other arm and squeezed, a warrior's acknowledgment. "Thank you." He took a deep breath; his emotions disappeared as if encased in ice. He turned toward Nadia and inclined his head. "Commander, I will take the traitors out. They are Prime, and they should die as Prime traitors die."

Nadia made a mental note to find out what that was from Wulf. Whatever the method of killing traitors was, it wouldn't happen now. Bram didn't need that on his conscience and she needed to question the bastards.

Bram continued, "Once the room is secure, we can fix the off-planet communications and contact Captain Wulf and Prime Command."

"Bram…" Nadia reached for his shoulder and clasped it as A'tem had done. "We're in this together. You risk too much going in alone. I need you on this op."

Nadia let go of Bram and shrugged off her jacket. "I'll distract them. Same plan as before. We need to question them, soldier. They can stand before the Prime Military for their punishment later. Understood?"

Even in the throes of misery and anger, Bram couldn't avoid looking at her breasts. His lust lightened his despair for a brief moment before the acrid taste of his anger buried the wine and chocolate.

Bram took her jacket. "Commander, I will try. But if they make a move to harm you, I will kill them. They are not honorable."

"Bram is correct. One wrong move, the traitors will die." A'tem picked up her laser rifle. "Go. We'll be right behind you."

When she started to remove her laser pistol, A'tem said, "Keep that. You might need it."

"Who's the boss here?" Nadia was amused despite the mini-rebellion ensuing on her team. A'tem was her equal in rank; she was only his superior because of her command deck position as science officer and her position as head of the team on Tarn.

"I believe this is what is called a team consensus," A'tem said in a dry tone.

Nadia snorted. "Well, that *was* the underlying reason for the joint maneuvers."

She brushed past Bram. His low rumble and muttered words in Prime which she roughly translated as warrior-female-who-rules-as-a-goddess made her smile. She caught herself wondering what Huw would say if he knew another Prime male lusted after her. Now wasn't the time to be thinking of Huw. She had a job to do.

Nadia led her team down the hall. When she reached the door, she motioned for her men to stay back. "Let me get into the room about halfway before following me."

She entered the door code Bram had provided; the lights on the security panel went from red to green and the door slid silently into the walls. She strode into the room as if she owned it. The two men who lounged in front of the main communications control panel jerked upright in their chairs and swore in Prime.

"You two need to get away from the controls and surrender your weapons. The Alliance is taking over this facility." She spoke in Prime and hoped she hadn't asked for directions to the nearest restaurant.

The man to her left stood as the other reached for a control on the panel. She pulled her laser and stunned the man who'd reached for what she suspected was an alarm. She couldn't have that, even if Bram's changing door codes had secured part of the enemy in locked rooms, there would still be roaming guards who could respond.

The other man ran toward her, yelling a battle cry. He had a knife in his hand. Before she could stun him, the whine of a fully charged laser sounded loudly in the room. Her would-be attacker dropped to the floor; his body convulsed for a few seconds as his nervous system shut down—and then nothing. He was dead, every neuron in his body fried.

A'tem moved quickly toward the control panel. He secured the stunned man who writhed in pain on the floor with flex cuffs. "This one will live to talk."

"Good." She went back to the door and shut it, locking them inside. In her peripheral vision, she observed Bram move to stand over the man he'd killed. He spat on the dead Prime before going to the control panel. He sat and entered several commands.

After a few seconds, Bram grunted. "It's done."

Nadia wasn't sure whether he was referring to the death or the re-establishment of communications.

Bram turned away from the controls. He looked at her, a blank expression on his face, but the mixture of emotions underneath his skin threatened to overwhelm her once more.

"Bram, could you shield more, please?" She looked at the dead Prime. His battle blade was still clasped in his lifeless hand. "I'm sorry about your cousin."

"He would have killed you." A pained expression appeared briefly in Bram's golden eyes, and then his control strengthened, easing her discomfort. But not before she discovered grief tasted like ashes and felt like a gelid wind.

"I know. Thank you for acting so quickly." Nadia approached the communications array. "My jacket?"

A'tem handed it over.

Nadia shrugged it on and looked at Bram. "So? We're in control now?"

"Yes, Commander. All communications going in and out of the facility are under our control. With a little effort, I will be able to block the mercenaries' internal communications. I have programmed a search for their frequency." Bram's tone was brisk and all business. "What messages do you want sent and to whom?" He sat in the seat his cousin had used, awaiting her orders.

"Advise both Prime and Alliance commands of the current situation. Tell them we're in control of Tarn's communications now. Advise them any Alliance ships approaching Tarn to assist us should hold outside the laser cannons' range. We'll verify when we've shut them down."

Nadia looked at A'tem. "A'tem, can you handle the flow of communications and question this *apayebo*," she pointed to the bound man on the floor, "to get us a head count on the enemy and find out where they imprisoned the Prime military contingent? Then inform Alliance and Prime military commands of such."

"Easily, Nadia. You *are* taking Bram with you to shut down the laser cannons." It wasn't a question. A'tem took a seat at the control panel.

"Of course. Bram knows the facility the best. We'll let you know where to meet us." Nadia turned back to Bram. "Messages sent?"

"Yes, Commander. I also informed Commander Ard we're safe and that he can now contact Captains Wulf and Melina."

"Excellent. Let's go shut down some ship killers." Nadia retrieved her laser rifle from beside the doorway where A'tem had leaned it. Bram was on her heels. "A'tem, if you don't hear from us," she looked at her chronometer, "in twenty standard minutes, get the hell out of here."

Twenty minutes might be pushing it. But she figured the enemy had already realized something was wrong. With any luck, the majority of them had been trapped behind the coded locks. Those who weren't trapped behind secured doors would need some time to regroup and begin a floor-by-floor search.

Bram called out. "A'tem, if we do not make it back, the door to the escape tunnel for this section is at the end of this hallway and down a level. It is marked as AA567. Use the door codes I provided. The mercenaries should not know about the tunnel…" he scowled at the bound Prime soldier, "…unless one of the other traitors told them. My cousin," he spat the word, "and this one did not have the clearance to know of such. But I cannot guarantee there aren't other traitors who might have."

A'tem nodded. "I'll be fine. Now … go."

Nadia led the way out of the room and then allowed Bram to take the lead once more. "Where's the control room for the weaponry systems?"

"Three levels down, directly under the communications room. We go this way." Bram entered a door code into a key pad by a red door which led into a stairwell. "Allow me to clear the way, Commander."

"On your heels, Bram." She followed him down the stairs. When he stopped at another red door, she made a note that stairwell doors were all red in this facility. She hung back a second as he went through the door and followed at his hand motion.

"Bram." She whispered subvocally into her headset so as not to be overheard in an area probably rife with pissed-off mercenaries and traitors.

"Yes, Commander?" He replied in the same manner.

"If something happens to me, you get A'tem and get the hell out of here. That's an order."

Her reasoning was the mercenaries would be less likely to kill a woman. They could sell her and make a profit. She wouldn't think about what they'd do to her before they sold her.

"Sorry, Commander. Both Commander Ard and Commander A'tem told me you would say such at some point. They ordered me not to leave you or they would remove my reproductive organs. I am choosing to follow their instructions." Bram reached back and stopped her with a hand to her arm. "There are men ahead." His voice was a mere whisper across her headset. He signaled to retreat.

They drew back several meters and took refuge in a short side hallway dead-ending at a green door.

Nadia lowered her shields. Bram's emotions while simmering along the edges of her empathic senses weren't painful. She then sought outward and gasped. "Yes. Five of them. One is Prime. His emotions are the strongest. You sensed them … how?"

"My Prime battle senses are elevated for battle. I am trying to shield you and that has worked to our advantage since it has kept the traitorous Prime from reading my approach." He looked over his shoulder. "Are you in pain?"

"What you're doing is working. I sense you as a low boil and the enemy ahead as fearful, angry, and frustrated." This whole situation had already taught her to be more in control while working on a team with Prime, probably the best thing to come out of this clusterfuck.

She also suspected and couldn't admit to Bram that her stronger shields were also a result of drawing on Huw's strength as the *Galanti* came closer to Tarn.

"Huw! Don't get too close to Tarn. Tell Wulf and Mel—we haven't shut down the ship killers. Don't approach."

Bram gasped. "You are in communication with another Prime warrior. I feel the telepathic energy. It is very strong. You are a *gemate* … a battle-mate?"

So much for keeping her ability to contact Huw a secret. She'd forgotten Prime warriors could sense not only emotions but other psi energy when in close quarters. *Dumb, Nadia, really dumb. The Prime traitors will sense you also.* She tested the men ahead and found their emotions were holding steady. She let out the breath she'd been holding and shielded herself even more.

"No … no … just empathic and telepathic," *or so it seemed*, "I'm not Prime. I have no *gemat.*"

"As you say, Commander." He didn't sound or looked convinced. "How shall we proceed?"

Nadia sighed in relief. Bram was back to the business at hand. But she knew the topic wasn't closed. If they survived the next few minutes, the word of her abilities would get around. She'd deal with the fallout later. She handed him her rifle and then took off her jacket, tying it around her waist.

Sex as a distraction had worked the last couple of times; it would work again.

"We stroll in there arm in arm with our laser pistols hidden behind each other's backs. And in the short time they're in shock from our sudden appearance, we move apart and take them all out. Kill, not stun. We don't have time to mess with prisoners."

Bram smiled, a wicked twist of his lips. "My thoughts exactly. And since the entry to weapons control is what they are guarding, we are right on your schedule."

He came to her side, his laser pistol in his hand. He pulled her to him with one strong arm around her waist and waited until she had her pistol in hand and hidden it behind his back. "I hope your *gemat* never finds out I touched his woman's naked waist and back—or saw your breasts, uncovered as they are. I would be *dheu mete.*"

Even though Bram had the wrong idea about her connection to Huw, Nadia had to smile as she translated his words as "dead sustenance" or "dead meat."

"It'll be our secret," she reassured him. Bram's snort had her choking back a laugh. "Let's do this. I want to get back to our people."

"Yes, Commander." He squeezed her waist. "Let me take out the traitorous Prime."

"So ordered." Nadia understood his need for vengeance was mixed in with his sense of honor. She'd grant him that boon.

Bottom line, none of the five men would leave the hallway alive.

They walked into the main corridor and moved down the hallway in tandem. Bram's touch irritated her skin, but wasn't painful for which she was thankful. She didn't need the distraction. When they turned the corner leading toward weapons control, she spotted the group of five blocking a huge door.

The large Prime noticed them first; he seemed puzzled as he tried to place Bram. His gaze when it swept over her narrowed.

Nadia nudged Bram. He dove to the right as she went left. They both fired. The enemy hadn't had time to react. Five laser blasts, all kill shots, and it was over.

Well, not quite. Bram, trained as an Elite soldier, walked over and fired another lethal blast first into the Prime's brain and then into the other four's.

Nadia stepped over the dead Prime. She shuddered, suddenly so cold she clenched her teeth to keep them from chattering. She'd killed before and would again. No soldiers, if they were honest with themselves, ever got used to taking lives. She hadn't and had the nightmares to prove it. She and Bram were alive and that was what counted in the long run. Time enough later to deal with the emotions she'd buried deep inside her and encased in ice. There was still a job to do—and possibly even more lives to take before the night was over.

She approached the door and used the code to activate the monitor attached to the door code entry pad. The room appeared to be empty. She dropped her psychic shields a bit and found no emotions inside the room. The mercenaries had placed the guard only on the outside. Mistake on their parts. She entered the unlocking code and walked in as the door slid into the walls.

She ran toward what looked to be the main control panel. The monitor showed ships holding just beyond the ship killers range. Gold was here! Relief made her weak at the knees, and she held onto the control panel array to keep from falling.

The door swooshed shut behind her. "Bram. Our help is in a holding pattern. We need to get this system shut down, but I'm not familiar with all the Prime symbols yet. Which are the ship killers?" She waved a hand over the glowing symbols on the board's touch pads.

"Allow me, Commander." Bram came to her side, touched a sequence of pads, and keyed in several lines of code, which streamed over the monitors.

The facility went dark and silent. For a very long second, she stood frozen. Fear niggled in the primitive part of her brain and icy fingers walked up and down her spine. Her limbic system told her to run, but her higher brain told her the infinite darkness was momentary, that she was safe. Still, she breathed a sigh of relief when the emergency lights came on with a low whir.

"What did you do?" she asked the hulking shadow outlined in the orange glow of the dimly lit room. His eyes gleamed like a bonfire in the shadowy near-darkness.

"Shut down the power to the entire planet's weaponry system as you asked." Bram leaned over and looked into her eyes. "That is what you wished, is it not?"

Nadia laughed. "Yeah, that'll do. Let's get the hell out of here and meet A'tem at the escape tunnel."

"Gladly, Commander. Follow me." Bram walked back to the door, checked the corridor on the monitor, and then entered the door code.

Obviously, whatever power he'd cut off hadn't affected the security of the facilities' doors. The trapped enemy would still be trapped, but those wandering about would be more dangerous than ever. She, A'tem, and Bram were still not home free.

Nadia hit a combo of codes on her headset and connected directly to A'tem. "Weapons shut down. Notify the *Galanti*. They're currently in a holding orbit outside the range of the cannon. Bram and I will meet you at the escape tunnel he told us about."

A second or two passed before A'tem responded. "The *Galanti* is notified. I took the liberty of advising Commander Ard of the situation. He's sending a three-man team to the other end of the escape tunnel we're taking. He feared there might be enemy soldiers hiding in the caves. I'll see you soon."

"Good luck, A'tem. Watch your ass. Out."

"Same to you. Out."

Nadia switched her headset to monitor only. Any slight noise might apprise the enemy of their position once they were out of the security of the weapons center.

The path between their current position and the escape tunnel could possibly be filled with mercenaries hunting the saboteurs who'd plunged the facility into relative darkness, lit only by the low-level emergency lights.

Laser pistol in hand and set on kill levels, she put on her night-vision goggles and followed Bram as he hugged the shadows along the edges of the corridor.

CHAPTER 6

On the Galanti on approach to Tarn

Huw sat in his chair on the Command Deck and fumed. He'd pushed his engines into the danger zone and beyond to get them to Tarn as quickly as possible. But just as they were about an hour away, Wulf had slowed the ship to sub-light speed to make a cautious approach to the planet.

Yes, the planet had ship killers. Yes, Nadia had warned them about a trap ... but she—and the others—were down there with who knew how many enemy.

He looked up and found Mel standing by his chair. "Are you okay, Huw?" She stroked his arm. "You're whiter than Earth's ice caps. And your eyes have gone dark amber. I feel the emotions pouring out of you. Is it Nadia? Is she safe?"

"I can't contact Nadia, Mel." *Liar.* "Sometimes she connects with me. And the last telepathic thoughts I had were the ones about the ship killers. What has Ard said? Has he heard from Nadia's team?"

When the communications with the planet had been restored, Wulf had demanded a situation report. Ard gave a brief one on injuries, the safety measures taken to protect the Gold crew members in the caves, and, finally, relayed that Nadia planned to take Crewman Tilga and shut down the weapon systems.

Huw had wanted to rage and scream at the idiocy of the woman. *Ansu bhau.* She could've sent any of the men to do the job and stayed safely behind in the caves. She was an officer, not battle fodder.

Somehow, he'd managed to control his emotions and kept his mouth shut. He had already called enough attention to the unusual psychic connection between him and Nadia.

"Captains!" the soldier monitoring communications shouted. "Commander A'tem has sent a message. Commander Nadia and Crewman Tilga have shut down the weapons systems. We can move in."

The Command Deck erupted with shouts and battle cries. Something in Huw's gut eased—but not entirely.

"Where is Commander Nadia's team now?" Huw asked the communications officer.

"They are moving toward the escape tunnels into the mountains. Commander Ard has sent a team to meet them on the other end and aid them in getting back to their secured area."

Huw nodded his acknowledgment. He'd war-gamed many a time on Tarn as had all of Gold's Prime crew members. Tilga was following an infiltrate-sabotage-get-out scenario that all Elite-trained soldiers practiced many times. Huw would owe Tilga a drink or two for taking care of Nadia—and the other team member, of course.

Mel tugged on Huw's sleeve. She glared at him and Wulf who'd come to join them. "What escape tunnels? They weren't marked on the facility plans Nadia and I reviewed for the joint maneuvers. You Prime are still holding out on the Alliance, aren't you?"

His sister-kin was pissed.

Wulf pulled his *gemate* away from Huw and up against his side. He brushed a kiss over her hair.

Huw envied his brother such closeness. He thought of Nadia and wondered how soft her hair would feel against his lips—and then felt searing guilt. Until he'd proven there were no women who could be his destined mate among any Lost Ones they might find, he was not free to think of Nadia as anything other than a colleague.

"You *are* Prime, *lubha*. The information on these things is on a need-to-know basis." Wulf scolded Mel gently. "And now, you, Nadia, and A'tem know. The tunnels are extra lines of defense Prime have against internal and external enemies."

"Okay, fine." Mel huffed. "But once we're down there. I want to see them so I can compare them to the tunnel systems I've seen in other ancient Prime ruins."

Mel rubbed her cheek against his brother's chest. Huw sensed Wulf's love reaching for Mel; it surrounded her and calmed her ruffled feathers.

"I will give you a personal tour, Melina mine—once I am assured we are in complete control of the facility." Wulf turned his gaze away from Mel and looked Huw in the eyes. "I assume you'll want to be on one of the teams that go to the surface."

"Yes." Huw's tone was abrupt. He didn't appreciate the knowing look his brother gave him in return. His big brother paid far too much heed to the fact he and Nadia had some telepathic ability with each other. "I will contact Nowicki and coordinate the away teams from both ships. Security teams first, followed by medical and other support teams, correct?"

"Exactly. I'll let Iolyn know he has command of the squadron while we are on the planet. He can deal with anyone attempting to leave Tarn." Wulf walked toward his command chair, taking Mel with him.

As Huw rose from his seat, a feeling of fear and rage swamped him. His body reacted immediately. He reached for a weapon that wasn't there and looked around the Command Deck searching for someone to fight. Then he realized—they weren't his emotions, but were Nadia's.

"Wulf!" His brother turned, a question in his eyes. "We need to hurry. Nadia and her team are in danger."

Wulf barked out an order to the communications officer. "Call down to Ard and see what in the hell is going on! Huw, get those security teams down there … now."

———

On Tarn in the military facility

NADIA AND BRAM HAD MANAGED to avoid several men running toward the weapons command center. So far the path to the escape tunnel had been too easy. But they had yet to get to their destination. So she wouldn't count her chickens, as her farmer grandmother had always said, just yet.

She'd thought too soon. Anger. Fear. Pain. The strong emotions rode the air currents of the subterranean corridor. She upped her shields against the emotions coming from the direction of their ultimate destination.

Nadia pulled on Bram's belt, staying his movement. He turned and mouthed, "What is wrong?"

She signaled four men ahead and mouthed, "A'tem. Danger."

Bram's ramping up to battle readiness was evident in his aura—and oddly enough seemed to supplement her fight readiness. And then it hit her—Huw! She'd drawn on him without realizing it, using him to help her utilize the Prime battle rage Bram emitted.

Nadia moved to the corner and peeked around it. Her control over her emotions at the sight was tested. Bram touched her arm, holding her back. He whispered over her ear, "Steady. Plan."

She nodded and Bram let go of her.

A'tem was bleeding and down on the ground. His eyes were closed and his skin, pale, its normal blue now bluish white. For a split second, she'd thought him dead, but a frisson of his emotions brushed up against her. He was alive and pissed. He was waiting—he knew they would come and he played opossum until they did.

She turned to look at Bram and mouthed, "Not dead."

Bram's fiery gaze lightened. He pointed at her open jacket and the expanse of skin it revealed, a question in his eyes. Bram had learned quickly her female attributes were a boon in distracting the enemy.

Nadia thought for a second and shook her head. There were only three of the enemy, and A'tem was on the ground out of the line of fire. It would be quicker to take the bastards out all at once with a wide blast from the laser rifles. She slipped her rifle off her shoulder and set it for a wide blast.

Bram must've agreed with her strategy, because he mimicked her motions.

She hand-signaled one, two, and on three both of them surged around the corner with lasers blasting. The three mercenaries had no time to react—just die. This time she gave no additional thought to the dead men she stepped over. They'd hurt her friend.

Nadia went to help A'tem as Bram fired insurance kill shots into the heads of the three. "A'tem? How badly are you hurt?"

The Volusian allowed her to help him stand. He stumbled slightly before gaining control of his stance. He heaved a sigh and eyed the most serious wound on his upper left chest. He applied pressure to the wound with his hand. "I'm fine, Nadia. I'm thankful the enemy didn't have a rudimentary understanding of Volusian anatomy—or I would be dead."

Nadia was thankful also. The stab wound looked deep and was bleeding sluggishly, but was nowhere near A'tem's heart.

The Volusian heart's major chamber was centrally located behind a solid carapace of bone. The enemy had aimed for a Terran heart location. All the Volusians had in that position was muscle, bone, and fat. The wound would hurt like a bitch, but it wasn't life-threatening.

Bram joined them with the enemies' weapons in his arms. He looked A'tem up and down and smiled in grim satisfaction. "Well met, warrior. Are we ready to move? I will dump these weapons in the escape tunnel."

"How far are we from the entrance?" Nadia followed Bram as he took the lead. She stayed by A'tem in case he needed her assistance. But he moved just fine.

A'tem answered before Bram could. "Not far. I was at the door when the enemy attacked me. They attempted to drag me away, and I resisted. I knew you'd be coming along the corridor soon and figured I had a better chance of escaping if they didn't attempt to take me to their leaders."

"Did they call in your capture?" Nadia looked over her shoulder and found only empty corridor.

"Yes." A'tem chuckled and shook his head. "But Bram's trick with the door codes had locked up the closest backup which was why they started to drag me away. The enemy is now very shorthanded from what I overheard."

"That's good." Nadia would make sure the Alliance Command knew Bram deserved a commendation for his efforts. A'tem would get a medal also for being injured while engaging the enemy.

As a team-building exercise, this had been trial by fire. So far, Gold's crew members had proven they were the best of the best. She was proud to call these men her peers.

"We are here, Commander." Bram indicated the door that looked like every other door but was gray.

Nadia frowned. "Aren't gray doors waste disposal access doors?" She was sure that was what she'd learned while poring over building plans with Mel. But she now knew not everything about this facility was reflected on the plans, so the gray doors might've been a red herring also.

"Yes." Bram smirked. "No one likes to deal with what is behind them. This one leads into the caves and not the waste recycling system." He turned to the door and accessed the control pad and monitor hidden in the wall.

Bram's snarl of rage set the hairs on Nadia's body on end. A'tem stiffened at her side and emitted an answering low-level growl.

"What is it, Bram?" she asked. "What do you see?" But she knew. She could feel and almost see the rage. Red. Heat. Pain. Fear. Battle rage.

"The enemy had a unit," a unit meaning nine soldiers, "guarding the exit into the cave. Our people are under fire."

"Get us in there, Bram." Nadia signaled Aeron. "Aeron, the team you sent us is under attack. We're engaging the enemy."

Aeron's voice came back instantly. "Will send additional help."

When the door opened, the sounds of laser fire, yells, and screams blasted Nadia's ears. Yelling a Hunnic war cry handed down through the ages, she leapt into the fray. A berserker's rage swept through her, supplemented by the *batel rabia* from Bram and, through their link, from Huw. She fought her way into the mass of large male bodies fighting hand to hand and with knives.

With a Prime battle cry, Bram leapt into the battle. A'tem followed with a Volusian battle cry, his wound obviously not a problem.

For a fraction of a second, even though Nadia knew the two men were on her side, their cries and those of the three Prime Aeron had sent struck fear in her heart. Shaking it off, she let instincts as old as the galaxy and her training take over—and she fought, knowing in the back of her mind that Huw was connected and doing what he could to keep her alive by sharing his strength and knowledge. *God, what is this connection we have?*

CHAPTER 7

With Nadia and her team attacking the enemy from the facility side, the all-Prime team of three Aeron had sent surged forward from the cover they'd sought when first engaging the enemy. Fast and furious moments of fighting tipped the former standoff in favor of the Gold soldiers.

With four of the enemy on the ground, dead or dying, Nadia's crew surrounded the four still standing, who threw down their weapons in surrender. None of the eight were Prime, but were a mix of Terran, Antareans, and some who looked to be from the Umbraxi system. The Antareans were the most dangerous and she didn't have a damn dart gun. She kept her battle blade in her hand, just in case.

"Bram, shut the door behind us," Nadia ordered. He hurried to do so while she and A'tem kept the four remaining enemy under guard. The men Aeron had sent collected weapons.

"Secure them at wrists and ankles." Nadia threw one of the men her extra set of restraints as did A'tem. "We'll leave them for the Prime military to deal with." She counted heads and frowned. "I thought there were nine mercenaries."

"Commander." One of the three Prime crewmen, all of whom she recognized as *Galanti* crew members, spoke. She hadn't learned all the new crew members' names yet. "One of the mercenaries got past us and headed into the main tunnel which leads to the surface. He will bring others."

"If he attempts to make it back to the military compound, I'm fairly certain he'll run into the Gold rescue teams." The teams should've landed and begun to secure the facility not long after she and Bram had shut down the weapons system.

The three men bellowed their approval. Prime tended to be a noisy bunch when their battle hormones were elevated.

Nadia should talk; she'd yelled just as loudly during the attack. She clicked her com unit. "Aeron?"

"Nadia! Status?"

His concern came over the headset clearly—and it was more than concern for the general welfare of the men. Aeron had feelings for her. Too bad her emotions and heart were already tied to another man—one who was too stubborn to give up a pipe dream and accept what was in front of him.

"We're fine. The men you sent held their position and we trapped the enemy between us. One got away and is probably heading for the surface." She looked over the three-man team. "All wounds, but for A'tem's, are superficial."

A'tem protested. "And I'm also fine, Aeron. It's a minor chest wound for a Volusian."

Aeron came back. "Good. Make your way back. Gold has sent teams to the surface from the *Galanti* and the *Leonidas*. They are taking the battle to the enemy. They should make short work of it."

Nadia chuckled. "Should be like shooting fish in a barrel."

The trussed up enemy glared. But when her team eyed her as if she were crazy, she laughed and explained, "An old Terran saying which means the battle would be easy."

"Very colorful," Aeron said. "And true. Be alert. There could be isolated groups of the enemy on and in the mountains."

"We'll be fine." She looked at the three Prime standing over the downed enemy and then at Bram and A'tem. "I think the team-building aspect of the maneuvers has been very successful. I'm proud to serve with such brave and quick-thinking soldiers. We'll see you soon."

After she signed off, Bram came to her side. "Commander, you neglected to tell Commander Ard you are among the wounded."

"No, I'm not." She took a mental inventory and concluded she had no pain, thus she wasn't wounded. "It must be the enemy's blood."

"It's your blood." A'tem came to her other side. "A laser cut along your waist. Your uniform top is shredded and singed. Doesn't it pain you? It looks very deep."

Nadia looked down. "Well, damn. I don't feel it. Must be the adrenaline." Or Huw's extra-strength adrenaline coming over their connection. He was very close now—and raging mad.

A'tem pulled a small med kit from his waist pack. "Let's just make sure it continues to be painless, Nadia."

Before she could protest, A'tem injected a bolus of painkiller and then applied a smaller version of the healing cold laser to the deep laser tear at her waist. She shuddered as the icy numbness swept over her side.

"That should hold until Dr. Morgan can look at it." A'tem repacked his field medical kit and stowed it in the pack attached to his utility belt.

"Thanks, A'tem."

"Nadia! You are hurt! I am coming."

"I'm fine. Pay attention to your surroundings. No need to come. See you at the cave."

Huw didn't need to be distracted by her minor injuries while he was fighting off mercenaries, especially the Antarean ones. He could get himself or his men killed.

Gritting her teeth, she cut off the pathway to Huw. Cutting the connection, with him so close and his battle rage so strong, felt as if a piece of her soul had been torn from her body. Every one of her instincts demanded that she stay in touch, lend him her strength, monitor his health.

Also, with the mental connection now blocked from her side, the pain from her wound and her general exhaustion almost took her breath away. She barely managed to stay upright. Only the painkiller and ice laser treatment kept her from whimpering in pain. All she wanted was a warm meal, a good, stiff drink, and eight solid hours of sleep—but she knew she wouldn't see that particular combination of luxuries anytime soon.

Glancing at the concerned faces of her team, she shrugged. "I must've zigged instead of zagged. I'm fine." She waved a hand toward the exit from the small cavern in which they'd battled. "Let's get back to our people. Oh, and keep a look out for our missing team. They might've sheltered in this cave system."

The six entered the tunnel and used LED lights to illuminate their way. The Prime on point spoke up. His voice while low carried easily as it echoed off the stone walls of the narrow, roughly hewn tunnel. "Commander, the missing team came into the secured perimeter after you and your team left on your mission. They are all well. Just tired and dehydrated."

Thank God, they were safe. It had been a constant worry niggling at the back of her mind even as she'd dealt with all the other issues of keeping her people alive. No matter how successful she'd been—if she had lost those six, she would've failed.

"Thank you, Crewman…" She needed to stop thinking of them as Prime crewman one, two, and three. Plus, she was fairly sure the one who'd spoken was under her direct command in the science lab. He was her exogeologist. The merger had occurred so quickly, she was still attempting to put names and faces together.

"Science Technician Jod … Bre Jod." He continued to walk, shining his light from side to side. "And, Commander, we heard what you said to Commander Ard—and we are equally proud to serve with you. You fight like a Prime."

And coming from a Prime male—that was an extreme compliment.

"Thank you, Tech Jod." Nadia looked over her shoulder at the other two; the movement pulled her wound and made her hiss. *Dumb move, Nadia.* The two crewmen trailing looked a lot like Bre. Well, all Prime looked a lot alike, but these three more so than others. She suspected they were kin and using last names would become confusing quickly. "And your teammates, Bre? Would you introduce them, please?"

Bre looked over his shoulder. "Gladly. The one on your left is my youngest brother, Cred Jod. And the one on your right is the middle brother, Cas Jod. We entered the military and trained as Elite at the same time. Our mother has worried ever since."

Bre's brothers looked slightly embarrassed by their brother's words. She chuckled.

Mothers, got to love them. They even embarrass the most alpha of males.

"Nadia?" A'tem touched her elbow. "What's so funny?"

"Sorry, but Bre's words and his brothers' obvious embarrassment brought up a memory. I thought my mother would have a heart attack when she heard I'd entered the Alliance Military rather than go into research or teach at the university. Mothers never want their children in danger. But I bet Bre's mother is proud of her sons all the same."

"Yes, sir," Cas said from behind her. "She is."

Bre held up a hand. "We must be quiet now. The tunnel to the surface is near and it intersects with several other escape tunnels in this particular cave system. The *apayebo* who escaped could be lurking anywhere. I suggest you all stay here while I scout ahead."

The men circled around Nadia, awaiting her orders. The mood was one of confidence in her leadership, and for the first time since the Alliance had merged Wulf's crews into Gold Squad, she felt optimistic about a woman's role managing a mostly Prime crew.

"Do it, Bre. Click your com unit if you see the enemy, and we'll come to back you up," Nadia said.

The Jod brothers looked at her, the trio's eyes glittering like bonfires in the relative darkness of the cave tunnel. She read them as being somewhat in shock and wondered what she'd said to cause them to feel so strongly.

"Thank you for your trust in my judgment," Bre finally said. "I won't be long." Turning off the light he carried, he slipped into the darkness and disappeared.

"How does he see?" Nadia asked his brothers.

Cred grinned. "He doesn't. He uses his spatial sense. For some reason, our brother has one of the early traits of a Prime warrior. His abilities are similar to the Terran creature that flies and sends out signals. It is why he went into exogeology. He is in his element underground."

"The Terran creature is called a bat." Nadia couldn't stand any longer. Her knees were shaking and her body trembled with adrenaline drop. Plus, she kept fighting the instinct to drop her mental shields and check on Huw. She sat on the cold rough ground of the cave tunnel and rested her head against the rock wall. She took a drink from her water bottle and allowed herself a small sigh of relief. "Just before Bre left, you all seemed shocked by something? What was it? Did I misstep?"

"No, sir. We couldn't believe you accepted Bre's suggestion on how to proceed. Prime officers tend not to appreciate rank-and-file soldiers making suggestions," Cred replied.

Cas and Bram mumbled their agreement.

Cred sat by her side and placed his light on the ground. The way the light reflected around the tunnel reminded her of sitting by a campfire on the Steppes of Russia on hunting trips during her early childhood.

Bram and Cas sat on her other side and A'tem sat in front of her. Her men had surrounded her with the protection of their bodies, and she wasn't sure whether to be flattered or insulted. She decided to be neither; she was too tired.

"Then why did Bre take the chance of making the suggestion?" Nadia asked. "Is it because I'm a woman?"

"No, no, though any Prime male would wish to protect a female in their midst," Cas said. "Commander Ard informed us that in the Alliance military there is no 'I' in team. He said we must learn to work as units, big and small. That serving in Gold would be more along the lines of what we as Elite soldiers do on secret missions. Everyone's ideas and suggestions are important. Did he misinform us?"

"No. That's exactly what you're to do. The Alliance while we have chain of command has found team-building allows for more productive crews. Commander Ard was one hundred percent correct." Nadia paused and felt the need to add, "But an order from a superior officer is still an order."

"We understand the difference, Commander. We may have input, but we must follow orders," Bram said.

"Good. I wouldn't want you to get into trouble." Nadia patted Bram's arm and removed her hand quickly. It felt wrong to touch him, more wrong than a few hours ago. She had a suspicion it had to do with Huw being on planet. "Bram, you saved us precious time and lowered our risk of being captured or worse with your ideas and actions. I'll take your input anytime."

"Thank you, Commander." Bram closed his eyes. "I sense Bre's calmness."

Bram stood and offered an arm to Nadia. She took it, not wanting to offend him, but quickly let go. His touch resulted in an effect similar to spiders crawling on her skin.

Man, I'm in deep shit. Huw will never accept this connection. Will I ever be able to touch another man casually? Sexually?

"Thank you, Bram." She turned to look at Bre as he came into the light provided by Cas and Cred's LEDs. "We all clear?"

"Yes, Commander. At least to the surface exit. I suggest we stick closely together. The enemy has to be fleeing. They could choose to head to the caves, hoping to escape."

"I agree. You take point again, Bre. Cas and Cred, would you take the rear again, please?" The brothers inclined their heads and took up their positions.

Nadia moved out behind Bram with A'tem at her side. Soon they'd be safe and she would be alone to think over all the sensory and psi changes she'd experienced since she'd landed on Tarn. She needed to make a decision as to whether she should tell Mel, and maybe Lia, about what was happening to her. She was concerned the changes taking over her mind and body could affect her work.

Huw was one person she'd never approach on the topic. He'd made it clear she was a colleague and he wanted nothing to do with whatever was happening between them.

God, it hurt.

———

A RAGING URGENCY POUNDING THROUGH HIS body and mind, Huw had left his transport and led his team of five into the mountains. His team's primary mission was to check on the safety and condition of the Gold crews that had come to Tarn for military maneuvers and add to their security. While he'd much rather be in the thick of the fighting, his gut drove him to seek out Nadia and make sure she was safe. Not that he'd ever acknowledge that fact to anyone; though he was sure his brother's smirk indicated Wulf knew the real reason Huw had chosen securing the caves over fighting for control of the facility.

His team had met with one or two groups of fleeing mercenaries and had dealt with them easily. His bigger concern was where and what Nadia was doing now. Driven by a need stronger than his will, he attempted to link with Nadia along the path shining like a beacon in his mind. He found nothing. It was as if he'd hit a rock wall.

The mental pathway was there, but had been shut on her end after one short exchange assuring him she was fine. Nadia's strong shields went even further to convince him that she was merely a talented telepath and nothing more.

Just keep fooling yourself.

"Ard? This is Huw. I'm approaching your coordinates with a security team. What's your status?" He really wanted to ask if Nadia was safely inside the caves, but refused to expose his interest in her any more than he already had. It wasn't time yet.

Soon. Not much longer. After the mission to search for Lost Ones.

"A security team?" Ard's voice was calm, but Huw read sarcasm in his tone. "I don't need security. We have that under control. I need regen beds. Dr. Morgan has three severely injured patients who need more care than we can provide."

"Understood. But we can't risk the medical response teams until Gold contains the enemy. Medical teams are ready to hit the dirt as soon as Wulf gives the go-ahead." Huw gazed at the mountain where the entrance to the cave system Gold's training team had taken over was located. It was a rough climb about thirty meters or so above the canyon floor. "Any perimeter security I need to know about before coming up?"

"Yeah, Nadia and I whipped up some explosive surprises. I have a man on guard at the base. He'll show you the safest way through the security perimeter." Ard chuckled. "Don't want to blow up our crew members."

Huw snarled under his breath. He hadn't appreciated the way Ard had coupled his name with Nadia's. The *Leonidas*'s science officer had set his sights on Nadia since the first merger meeting on the space station. Huw had practically killed the *apayebo* last week in a training session when Ard had shared his plans to ask Nadia to spend leave with him on the resort planet of Tooh 2.

But you haven't claimed her … so why shouldn't Ard have a chance with her?

Because … before he could remind himself of his justification for postponing his courtship of Nadia, a Prime soldier dressed in an Alliance uniform stepped out from behind an outcropping of rocks and scrub and gestured his team forward.

Huw waved his men ahead and was about to follow when Nadia's shields slipped. Her anger, her fighting rage, her fear consumed him, almost driving him to his knees. She was in danger again. He sought her mind and found the red haze of battle hormones. But underneath the fighting spirit, she was exhausted, in pain. Her energy reserves were low and that was probably the only reason her shields had dropped, she needed all her energy to stay alive. Huw instinctively supplemented her strength.

"Nadia! Nadia!"

No answer.

"Ard, have you heard from Nadia's team?" Huw barked out the question as he turned in a circle in an attempt to hone in on Nadia's exact location. He wasn't sure how this psychic connection they had worked, but he knew he could find her if necessary.

It was necessary.

"About a quarter standard hour ago. She and her team met up with the team I sent to back them up. After a short, but successful, skirmish with a small band of mercenaries, they were heading in. Why?"

"What's the alternating com frequency you're using for intrateam surface communications?" Huw repeated the com codes for his team's benefit over the general Gold frequency. His team waited for his orders at the base of the mountain along with the guide. He keyed in the emergency frequency on his unit. "Nadia? This is Huw. What's going on? Answer me!" He waited a few seconds and got no response. "Ard, what was their last position?"

He tried the link they had once more. *"Nadia! Nadia!"* Still no answer, but he knew she was alive; he could feel her drawing on his energy.

"They were getting ready to exit the cave system that's connected to the facility's underground escape tunnels." Ard paused. "I can't reach them either. They might have run into the enemy fleeing our forces. The guide has the coordinates and will take you to their last known position."

"Good." Huw signaled to his team and the guide to head out and that he'd bring up the rear. "I'll let you know when we find them. Until then, I am going on monitor only."

"Understood," said Ard. "She has A'tem and four Elite-trained crew members with her. She'll be fine. The team I sent her has instructions to protect her."

Fear and dread ate at Huw's gut. The rebel faction's mercenaries would like nothing more than to capture a female Alliance officer and turn her over to the rebels to be used as a hostage to get concessions for their cause.

"I'll make sure of her safety myself. Out." Huw checked on Nadia again. Her emotions seemed caught up in the battle rage of her Prime team members; it was as if she rode the wave as any Prime warrior would. But she was not a Prime warrior; she was a fragile Terran woman no matter her training. Icy fear swept over him, chilling him to the bone.

Nadia was in deadly danger, and he was too far away to protect her. And yes, he was acting irrationally, but there was nothing rational about his feelings for Nadia.

CHAPTER 8

Outside the cave

As Nadia's team, with Bre still on point, exited the cave, the atmosphere seemed heavy, laden with the scent of ozone and charged with waves of pressure like an impending thunderstorm. But the night sky was clear, and it was the dry season on Tarn. Then she recognized the sensory impressions were the accumulation of the menacing emotions of mercenaries lying in wait.

"Down, down! Get down, Bre!" Nadia dashed forward and tackled Bre as intense laser fire strafed the area outside the cave entrance. Rolling off Bre, she found his alert, but pain-filled gaze on her. Behind them, the team laid down cover fire, forcing the enemy to take cover. "Come on, let's move."

Bre nodded, his breathing labored. He was wheezing ominously.

"Can you move on your own, or do I need to help you?" In less than a second, Nadia rolled him over and checked him out. His entire front torso had laser singes from multiple hits. She worried he might have taken a direct hit to a vital area of his chest or abdomen. Moving him could make it worse, but moving was their only option.

Another barrage of laser fire streamed over them. Nadia flattened over Bre's body, front to front, his breaths hot and moist against her neck. A burning pain streaked across her already injured shoulder. Her shields dropped, something in her forcing them down.

Immediately, Huw's searing hot mental touch swept through her mind like a solar wind, alleviating her pain, taking it down to bearable levels. She also managed to absorb a much-needed burst of energy; she had a feeling she'd need it before she got Bre to safety.

"Go, Commander! I will make it." Bre wiggled out from under her, rolled onto his lacerated and burned front, and turned toward the safety of the cave entrance. Then he stopped and waited for her to precede him.

"Unh uh, doesn't work that way. You go first. I'll cover." She shoved his ass with a hand. "Move, dammit!"

Nadia got up into a crouch and covered his retreat, placing her body between his and the enemy positions. Her team was doing a good job of keeping the enemy pinned, but she couldn't count on that much longer. She and Bre were sitting ducks, and she hadn't planned on dying now that the rest of Gold was here to back them up.

After less than a meter, Bre collapsed and buried his face in his arms. She snarled, "Move! That's an order, soldier. Move that ass! Or I swear we'll die out here together."

His face as white as Tarn's limestone rock faces, Bre grunted and once again pulled himself arm over arm along the rocky ground toward the cave entrance. His pain rolled off his aura in tumultuous waves and threatened to topple her control over her own exhaustion and stinging aches.

Bre's agony was horrific, even felt secondhand. Only Huw's constant stream of energy and support kept her going.

How Bre kept going Nadia would never know. But he did, and she'd do whatever it took to protect him. No Alliance soldier ever left a man behind.

One audacious mercenary stood and fired wildly at her and Bre. Nadia dove to cover Bre's exposed body. She was hit in the side by a chunk of rock sheared off by the laser fire.

Damn! The projectile hit the laser wound she'd received in the firefight in the cave. The added pain was excruciating.

Once again Huw responded, a seemingly endless reservoir of strength, encouragement, and faith, a surprising confidence in her ability to save Bre and stay alive. Greedily, she drew on his energy like a black hole sucking everything around it into its core. The surge of adrenaline and power across the psychic thread connecting them was astonishing.

"Go, Nadia. Go. Get to safety. We are close. We'll get the apayebote."

Using the extra spurt of energy while she could, she tossed her rifle toward the cave and moved to Bre. She screamed at her team. "Cover me, guys!"

Nadia dragged the injured soldier up by his shoulders, lowered her shoulder into his laser-lacerated chest and abdomen, and lifted him in a fireman's carry. She ran for the cave, propelled by fear, instincts, rage—and the strength of a bond that shouldn't have existed.

The other two Jod brothers came to meet her. Cred took his brother from her. Cas picked her up and followed the others into the shelter of the cave. Bram and A'tem fired their laser rifles to cover their retreat.

"I'm fine, Cas." She reassured the Prime soldier as he set her on her feet. He kept a hand on her arm, steadying her while the cave swirled around her and her knees threatened to give way. After several deep breaths, she adapted to the buzz of adrenaline and energy Huw shoved at her across the link.

"Ease off, Huw. You're giving me too much. I'm safe now."

Soothing warmth came over the connection; she classified the emotion attached to it as satisfaction. Then the energy decreased in amount, but wasn't cut off; Huw's energy now felt more like a warm massage of her senses, a healing heat.

"Cas." A'tem came to their side. "Help Bram keep the enemy pinned down. I'll take care of Commander Nadia."

"Huw and his security team are already on their way." Nadia realized she'd spoken too soon when both Cas and A'tem stared. Cas's eyes lit with interest and A'tem's, with questions she had no answers for. "I'm telepathic, remember?"

"Yes, sir." Cas bowed his head to Nadia and placed his fist over his heart. "I honor you, Commander. You saved my brother."

"We're a team … shipmates. He would've done the same for me. No thanks are necessary. Plus, it wasn't our day to die." Nadia reached to balance herself on the cave wall and winced at the pull on her wound. While her pain was not as bad as it could be due to Huw's psychic assistance, it still nauseated her. A small wave of dizziness swept over her again as the extra adrenaline continued to dissipate. She allowed A'tem to lower her to the ground. Cas assisted him before turning to help Bram.

"I add my thanks, Commander Nadia," Cred said as he worked over Bre's wounds with the healing cold laser.

"How is … *dermo*, shit, A'tem. That hurt!" She glared at the Volusian who'd torn away her borrowed, now-tattered uniform top and proceeded to clean the side wound, the most serious of her injuries. She examined the deep gouge, which had jagged edges from the rock that had torn through the seal A'tem had placed on the earlier laser laceration. "Any grit in that?"

Laser fire blared in the background. She sought Cas and Bram's emotional auras and found them immersed in the battle. Calm. No fear. They didn't need help. She touched Huw's mind and found him even closer to their location, fighting through small groups of fleeing mercenaries to get to them. He was immersed in *batel rabia* which, she now realized, started out as a fiery-hot, explosive buildup and then progressed into a collective icy heat of determination shared by his fellow Prime. Their common goal? To win at all costs.

"Much grit." A'tem's tones were clipped; his lips thinned with anger and concern. "That was very foolish, Nadia. You should've had one of us retrieve Bre."

"There wasn't time. I sensed the enemy before they fired. I was the closest. I wasn't leaving a man down to save my own butt." She shot him an icy glare. "I did what I had to do. You would've done the same."

"Yes." A'tem's touch became gentler. "Are you in pain?"

"Hell, yeah, but it's bearable." She glanced at Bre whose skin was ashy under his normal bronzed skin tone; he was unconscious. *Probably a blessing.* His front torso was a mass of laser burns and torn skin from pulling himself along the rocky ground. "My injuries are mild compared to his. Then I plowed my shoulder into him. God! That must've hurt. He made no sound—none at all. Cred?"

"Yes, sir?" Cred looked up from tending his brother. Worry and anger glittered within his golden eyes.

"How is he?" She winced in sympathy as Cred continued to tweeze grit from the deep lacerations marring Bre's sculpted abs. She ignored the fact A'tem was doing the same to her; she'd consigned her pain to the deep, cavernous well of Huw's borrowed strength. The constant pulse along their connection hummed in the back of her mind and tingled along every nerve in her body.

"He will live. I have given him a strong anesthetic and two boluses of the strongest painkiller we carry. He is not in pain."

"You're lying through your teeth, Cred." Nadia snorted which quickly turned into a gasp as A'tem turned the ice laser on her wound. "I sense his pain and so do you."

"Yes, Commander." Cred didn't express any surprise at her statement; the Jod brothers, like Bram had, accepted her preternatural abilities.

What they actually thought about her psychic talent was anyone's guess. She was pretty sure Bram had shared his theories concerning her and Huw. *Shit.*

"But pain is a sign he is alive," Cred continued. "This is a good thing."

"Yes, it is," Nadia agreed.

Still at their posts at the cave entrance, Bram and Cas were no longer shooting. But a massive increase in the sound of the laser battle could be heard outside.

"About time Huw and his security team arrived," Nadia said. She knew the battles Huw and his team had fought to get to them, but declined to share them with the others. They'd hear about them soon enough when all reports were filed. She'd already overexposed her ability to communicate with Huw. She refused to fan the flames of her men's curiosity even more.

Cred spoke up. "How soon will they get a medical team to my brother?"

"Protocol is to contain the enemy combatants before risking medical teams in a war zone." A'tem had chosen to answer and Nadia let him. "We should remain here and let Huw and the others take care of the remaining enemy. Captain Wulf will send a medical team as soon as he can. I sent a coded message to him and requested one regen bed for your brother."

A'tem removed his jacket and placed it around Nadia's shoulders. "Take my jacket. You're chilled."

She stifled the totally inappropriate laugh threatening to erupt. Of course she was chilled. She was practically naked from the waist up with the mere scrap of lace covering her breasts. None of the men had mentioned her near nudity and made Herculean efforts to ignore her exposure—after their first heated glances, of course. She appreciated their courtesy.

"Thanks." Nadia pulled the jacket, warm from A'tem's body, closer around her body, and shivered convulsively for several seconds. She hadn't realized how cold she'd been until he mentioned it.

"It is interesting Huw is leading the security team that relieved us," A'tem said.

Nadia almost groaned and made a note to kick A'tem's ass later. His curiosity was aroused—a dangerous mental state for a Volusian since they were known to dig until they received answers; it might be a great trait for an engineer, but not when it was used in idle conversation.

"Why interesting, Commander A'tem?" Cred asked, a frown marring his forehead.

"When I first alerted Ard about the surprise attack, Ard said Huw had already switched from his original mission to add to the security of our base of operations to come to us. That Huw knew about our danger before Ard did. Strange, yes?" A'tem shrugged, but didn't wait for a response or for her to kill him. "For some reason, Ard sounded ... displeased with Huw. But then Ard and Huw haven't gotten along well during this period of merger. My conclusion? Ard is allowing his dislike of Huw to color his opinion of Huw's current actions."

A'tem looked pointedly at Nadia. "I think you should be aware of this friction between them, Nadia." His "do with it what you will" implication was left unsaid.

"Ah, I didn't know they weren't mixing well." How could she? She rarely saw Huw. When she did see him, he treated her with all the respect and courtesy due to her as a colleague and left the room as soon as he could. He sure didn't chitchat about his interactions with other crew members. And during meetings of all Gold officers, Huw and Ard never sat together; she had no firsthand observations of the two men's dealings.

Until today's action, Huw hadn't bothered to acknowledge the psychic connection they had and blocked her mental touch time and time again—so she couldn't have gleaned his feelings that way either.

"Then it's a good thing Ard will be stationed on the *Leonidas*." Nadia turned and caught her Prime teammates' gazes on her. "What? You guys have something to add to this conversation?"

From his position at the cave entrance, Bram cleared his throat. "Commander Ard was particularly insistent you be protected at all costs."

Nadia winced. *Lord, save me from overprotective Prime males.*

Cred nodded. "We think he is jealous of Commander Huw. Commander Huw has been very vocal about Ard staying away from you."

Oh, hell! Nadia's cheeks burned. How had her private life become such a topic of interest? She didn't understand why Huw acted the way he did, and her crew was already speculating on a love triangle.

"I'll cut you some slack." She glared at A'tem. "Well, maybe not A'tem…" the Volusian had the audacity to grin, "…but the rest of you, because you're new to the Alliance. But it's not appropriate to talk about private matters on an op."

"We realize this and do not mean to be impolite or disrespectful, Commander Nadia," Bram said. "But we have few women on Prime and none in the military, so it is hard not to speculate. Many of us are very interested in how we will … what is the word you use when a man wishes to impress a woman and enter into a relationship? We have no such word since we mate by a genetic demand."

The man had a valid point, but she still intended to kick A'tem's ass for opening the whole can of worms. Since the sound of laser fire was still loud outside the cave and the enemy was well occupied by Huw and the other Gold forces, Nadia and her men were stuck here for a while longer. She decided to allow the conversation to continue. She might as well sound Bram and the others out about their views on the Prime male-non-Prime female dynamic.

Mel and Wulf would want to know the crew's feelings on the matter.

Before she could answer Bram's question, A'tem chuckled and replied, "Bram, I believe the word you want is 'court' although 'dating' usually precedes courting."

"This dating means the man approaches the woman, indicates his interest, and then they have sex, yes?" Cas asked.

Nadia choked and started coughing. A'tem handed her his water, she took a drink, and then a deep breath. "Um, it's not that straightforward." Every man's intent gaze was fixed on her. "In that instance, the man might get kneed in his testicles."

The Prime soldiers muttered under their breath. Their pained expressions and confusion were almost comical. A'tem began to laugh.

"Shut up, A'tem. It's not funny." She sighed and looked at the Volusian whose eyes glistened with the tears of his attempt to stop laughing. "I told Mel we needed a fricking class on dating dos-and-don'ts for our Prime crew. Now, I know we do."

Nadia beat back the increased pain throbbing in her side and shoulder; she now had a headache to go along with it. The stream of Huw's soothing warmth had slowed to a trickle. Worried that he and his team might have been overwhelmed and needed her and her team's help, she touched his mind. She shivered at the ice-cold rage she discovered as he fought furiously to protect her and her team. She sighed with relief. He was unharmed and had things under control. He didn't need her pain or exhaustion to distract him. She quickly withdrew her mental scan and slammed up her shields. The drugs A'tem had given her would eventually handle her pain; Huw needed his own reserves for the fight.

She attempted to smile at the curious, relationship-naive Prime. Well, naive as to dating and courting. She imagined they all had the same sex education Wulf and his brothers had had. Though, she refused to even think about the sex-surrogate thing. She saw red each and every time she imagined Huw going to one of the women Prime society provided to meet their males' sexual education and needs. She had no reason to be jealous. Huw had been politely scrupulous about not encouraging this … whatever-in-the-hell attraction they had between them, but hearts weren't rational most days. Hers sure wasn't.

Taking a deep breath, she plunged into what would be for her a very uncomfortable, but needed discussion. "I can see how speculation about who is courting whom would be a hot topic. So, until you attend the dating lecture, I'll be insisting Gold provide for its Prime crew members, let me state—it isn't proper to guess about relationships not publicly acknowledged by the couple in question. That's called *gossip*, and it is frowned upon."

Every Prime male there, including Bre, who had roused from unconsciousness, pinned her with a golden stare. She bet every word she uttered would be shared with their fellow Prime as soon as the men returned to their ships.

She continued, "Spreading such speculations could lead to hurt feelings, especially where the relationship doesn't even exist. When in doubt about whether a female crew member is seeing someone or not, it is appropriate to ask 'Are you dating someone?' As for dating protocols, sex is always something the woman can say no to, and the man must respect that or be considered a sexual predator. Understood?"

"Yes," Bram said. "Does this mean you and Commander Huw are not a couple?"

She had to choke back a laugh. Well, she had told them to ask. If she refused to answer, they'd think about this and talk it to death—and possibly draw conclusions that would be embarrassing to her and Huw—and hurtful. She needed to nip any further assumptions in the bud. Hopefully, these men would pass her answer along with tales of her actions and leadership in battle to the other Prime of Gold.

So, she answered, "No, we are *not* a couple." It was the truth. Huw didn't want a relationship with her. She wanted one with him—and it hurt.

"How about you and Commander Ard?" asked Bre, barely awake, but enough so to follow the topic of conversation. His voice was raspy with pain.

The tension in the cave escalated. The heat of it pulsed against her psi senses. *God, save me.* They were all attracted to her. Well, not A'tem, he was merely amused.

Nadia trembled at the intensity of the Prime soldiers' collective emotions and pulled A'tem's jacket more closely over her breasts, which felt even more exposed than before. She tasted chocolate and wine and felt fur brushing along her senses as the lust in the air grew thicker. "Commander Ard and I are *not* a couple either. We are colleagues. The time we spend together has to do with our job exchange and training."

But if she were truthful with herself, she had noted a romantic interest in Aeron's voice and attentions. What a mess!

She liked Aeron. But with the increase in strength of the unusual bond she had with Huw making itself known more and more each day, she could never be with Aeron or any other man. It wouldn't feel right—emotionally or physically. Because of this connection to Huw, she'd be forced to live as chastely as a nun unless the man gave up seeking a Prime female who might not even exist.

Nadia wasn't holding her breath on that last part happening. *There's always the vibrator in the bedside drawer and the simulation rooms.* So not the same.

At her denial of all dating relationships, the tension in the room left as quickly as it had built.

Bram smiled. "Thank you for clearing this up, Commander. Maybe you should let the two men in question know so they don't kill each other in training."

His suggestion was made in a gentle tone, but she sensed amusement underlying it. She would've called him out on his attitude except what he'd said had come as a shock. A'tem had alluded to mere friction between the two men; how had friction escalated to killing attempts?

"They tried to kill each other?" Nadia forced herself not to seek answers from Huw since the battle still raged outside. He couldn't afford the distraction; from the amount of laser fire and battle cries, it sounded as if the enemy had dug in fairly well.

A'tem coughed. "Bram exaggerates, Nadia. I was present. Aeron and Huw merely fought hard as warriors do during a training session. Neither was hurt." He narrowed his dark blue gaze at Bram who still guarded the entrance with Cas. "Bram should not have intimated such."

Cas snorted. "I beg to differ, Commander A'tem. I was also present. Prime warriors do not use some of the moves the commanders used during mere training. It took Commander Iolyn and Captain Wulf to pull the two men apart when time was called. Theirs was not typical training behavior."

When A'tem opened his mouth, Nadia cut him off. "Leave it, A'tem. Cas and Bram are Elite-trained. They should recognize what is and isn't Prime training behavior." She swept a stern glance over the men surrounding her. "I couldn't be the cause of their enmity, since I'm not involved with either man. This topic of conversation is at an end and won't be mentioned again. Clear?"

A chorus of "yes, sirs" came from her Prime team members. A'tem snorted.

Cas coughed. "Commanders? It has quieted outside. I see Commander Huw directing his team to check the bodies. It is safe to leave the cave now."

Nadia looked at A'tem. "Please check to make sure, A'tem." She couldn't talk to Huw right now to save her life; her voice would betray her chaotic feelings.

A'tem raised a brow in question, but nodded and spoke in low tones into his com unit. "Huw confirms all enemies are dead or subdued. Aeron also reports Wulf, Mel, and Royce's teams have retaken the military facility and released the Prime soldiers held prisoner. Gold teams are combing the area and the other caves for any lingering mercenaries. Medical teams are landing and one will be here soon."

"Good." Nadia stood and almost fell. A'tem steadied her with a hand to her elbow. "Thanks. I'm okay, just a little stiff from sitting on cold stone." The males' gazes were skeptical to a man, but no one called her out on the obvious lie. "Let's move into the light. This cave is cool and damp. It can't be good for Bre's condition."

Cas and Cred shouldered their weapons, lifted their brother to his feet, and then carried him between them.

A'tem and Bram stuck by Nadia's side. "I'm fine, guys. Don't hover."

"Please let us be assured of that, Nadia." A'tem kept his hand on her elbow and led her around a dead enemy lying right outside the entrance. "That was the slime-creature's ass who attempted to kill you as you carried Bre. Bram shot him as Cas and Cred came out to assist and I covered them."

Nadia shuddered. She'd been so concerned with getting Bre to shelter she hadn't realized how closely she'd cut it.

"Thank you all." She took a deep breath and forced herself to remain strong. She could deal with the mission's aftermath later in the privacy of her quarters with a glass of scotch and maybe Lia and Mel for emotional support. "I'm recommending you all for commendations and the appropriate medals."

Before any of her men could say a word, Huw stormed into view. "Nadia! You are hurt! Why are you standing? What happened?"

A'tem and Bram moved closer and braced her; each man placed an arm around her, taking care not to jar her wounds. She was happy to have their help. Huw's anger—and was that jealousy?—had hit her hard; it felt like an emotional punch to her gut. She sagged between A'tem and Bram.

"Back off, Huw!" A'tem snarled.

Nadia stared at her colleague in amazement. She'd never heard that sound from the normally calm—well, except in battle, that is—Volusian. "She's injured and doesn't need your attitude."

Huw stopped as if he'd run into a wall. Shock, hurt, anger, resentment, and some emotion he refused to name flickered through his mind. Then he truly looked at Nadia and felt all the color go out of his face. Why wasn't she unconscious?

His gaze burned across her body, categorizing her numerous wounds—two severe ones, one at the shoulder and an even more severe one at her waist, among a multitude of laser burns, bruises, and abrasions. His already chaotic emotional cocktail intensified. But it was the moment he realized her breasts could be seen by anyone looking hard enough that tipped him over the edge of any control he might have had.

The unnamed emotion, irrational jealousy, won out.

"You are practically naked under that jacket. A man's jacket." Huw's growl started low in his chest and increased in volume and power. He fisted his hands, clenching and unclenching them. He would kill the man or men who had touched her, looked upon her beautiful breasts.

"Stop the growling and tone down the emotional tantrum." Nadia shrugged away from A'tem and Bram, who'd pay for touching her, later in the training room. She started to approach him. "I was shot. My jacket was shredded." Glaring, she stopped less than an arm's length away and jabbed her finger into his chest as if to punctuate every word. "A'tem gave me his. End of story."

Her explanation and obvious anger directed solely at him did nothing to halt his rumbling. In fact, it became worse. So much so, the other Prime in the area stiffened and began to match him growl for growl.

"I order you all to stop growling." Nadia shouted the order in a voice that clearly said do-not-mess-with-me.

It was all Huw could do not to laugh and growl at the same time. She sounded like a furious she-cat. He'd always liked she-cats.

Huw attempted to use the psychic connection with Nadia to see what she really felt, but all he touched was blackness. The same blackness he'd felt near the end of the battle with the entrenched mercenaries that had caused him to panic and fight harder to get to her. He'd needed to see she was okay.

A'tem, however, did laugh and received a glare that could cut stone from Nadia. "You aren't helping," she muttered to the Volusian.

"Nadia," A'tem shrugged, "I'm not sure there's anything I can do to help."

"Commander Nadia." Bram spoke in a low, raspy voice.

Huw turned to stare at Bram and didn't like the look in the crewman's eyes. Well, he didn't like any of the other Prime males' gazes. The men, all of them, wanted Nadia.

Well, who wouldn't? She was a woman to be admired and treasured—and Huw would be happy to court her, claim her, as soon as the mission for the Lost Ones was complete. He refused to dishonor either his destined Prime mate, if she existed, or Nadia by moving too soon.

What if Nadia's unavailable after the mission? That was something he refused to address.

Huw snarled at Bram who ignored him and continued to address Nadia. "You obviously need my and A'tem's support, but Huw is losing control. His loss of control is inciting the rest of us. Are you sure you are not a couple? He is acting territorial. My father does this around my mother when he feels she is threatened by the presence of other males."

"Nadia, do you want me to stun Huw?" A'tem asked.

Huw recognized that the Volusian looked forward to doing just that. Why were all these men mad at him and acting as Nadia's champions? What had happened during the mission?

"No, I'll handle it." Nada looked up at him while A'tem and Bram remained close enough to catch her.

Ansu bhau! He wouldn't let Nadia fall. If anyone held her up, it would be him.

He hissed, snarled, and growled at A'tem and Bram. His warnings worked; they backed off.

"Huw. Behave." Nadia touched his chest and patted him in the area over his heart, the exact spot he'd had an ache since he'd landed on Tarn. Her touch was gentle and soothing, lessening the throbbing. "Calm down. I'm fine. We did our job—and we were successful. My team protected me."

His full-throated buzz-saw growl subsided to a low rumble deep in his chest. Huw took the hand on his chest and looked at it. He frowned and wiped a thumb over the dirt and bloody scratches marring her fingers and the back of her hand. His rumble threatened to escalate.

"I'm fine." Nadia continued to talk to him, her soothing voice the only thing keeping him from losing control. "A'tem took care of my wounds."

Huw swept a finger over the bandages at her shoulder and her waist. "Lia needs to check these out as soon as possible."

"I'm not the one who's seriously hurt." Nadia touched his face, swiping at something along his jaw.

He focused on the feeling of her finger on his skin—it elicited a warm and tingling sensation where she touched him. It made him want to smile.

"Huw?" Nadia's voice sharpened.

She was ticked off at him—again. He didn't like it. He began to growl again.

"What?" He wiped a smudge of dirt off her chin. She needed a nice long bath and her bed.

"Pay attention. Bre needs a regen bed." Nadia looked tired. "Did you make sure one would be sent our way?"

Huw's wildly erratic emotions settled at the exhaustion and pain in her voice. "Yes. Two are on their way. I knew you were in pain. I ordered two."

He couldn't handle even the smallest distance between them any longer. He pulled her into his body and held her gently against him. Her head nestled on his chest, her disheveled hair tickling his chin. He rubbed her back from the point where her shoulders met her neck to the top of her sweet bottom and back. "I am pleased you are okay."

Nadia felt too good in his arms, was too tempting. He could not with any honor court her properly at this time. So he didn't attempt to stop her when she shoved at his chest. He let her go. She stepped away. He watched her clench her jaw. She was in pain, but refused to let anyone know. He felt it sweep over her body; she might have shut off her end of their telepathic link, but her pain pounded his skin like thousands of fists.

"Nadia ... you need to lie down," he chided gently.

"Later. I need to make my report to Mel and Wulf." Nadia straightened to her full height; no sign of weakness betrayed her to the men. Huw's admiration for her grew. She was a warrior. She added, "I'm sure you can handle things here ... right, Huw? A'tem and Bram can help me to the field headquarters."

The warrior-woman needed a keeper; if she could walk more than two meters without collapsing, he'd be surprised. Courage and pride was one thing, but refusal to accept help was another. "Nadia, Wulf and Mel can wait on the report. You must have medical attention." Huw reached for her, but she stepped away. A look in her eyes pleaded that he not shame her in front of her team.

He grunted and inclined his head, honoring her unspoken request.

Nadia turned to A'tem and Bram. "Gentlemen, might I ask you for your escort?"

"Gladly, Nadia." A'tem came to her injured side and took her arm.

"It would be an honor, Commander Nadia." Bram took her other arm.

Huw fought the urge to tear her away from the men who touched her. He didn't have that right—might never have that right. The sooner the Lost Ones mission started, the sooner his questions, his honor would be resolved. And then, maybe, he could punch out A'tem and Bram for touching her. The thought gave him a small amount of pleasure.

"See you on the ship, Huw." She walked past him with A'tem and Bram assisting her. She paused by the Jod brothers and spoke, "I'll see you all later. Maybe once Bre is feeling up to it, we can dine together and discuss concerned mothers."

Huw couldn't help it—he snarled. Dinner? With the Jods?

The Jod brothers smiled and saluted her. Cas spoke for them. "We will be honored, Commander Nadia. Our mother will want to meet the woman who saved her eldest from sure death."

Nadia smiled at the three brothers with more than a hint of fondness. "I would love to meet your mother. We'll arrange it."

Huw clenched his fists as Nadia moved away. He'd just added the Jod brothers to his tentative must-kill list.

CHAPTER 9

Two Standard Days Later,
Alliance Training Facility on Cejuru Prime

The large gymnasium was filled with the sounds of bodies slapping on mats, the squeaking of bare feet on highly polished wood floors, and the grunts, groans, shouts, and taunts of men and women training in various forms of hand-to-hand combat.

Today, a select group of female soldiers were paired with Gold's Prime soldiers. So far the hand-to-hand fighting had been a lesson in futility. None of the men wanted to hurt the women and had been holding back.

Nadia had paired up with Bre to fight against Bre's brother Cas and Aeron. Even after their experience with her on Tarn, the men still held back with her also. She was pissed and gaining on going ballistic.

"Time out!" Nadia shouted.

Cas obviously hadn't heard her in time and his forward momentum took her out at the knees. She landed hard on her back and hit her head. For several seconds the huge fitness room spun around her.

As Bre and the other two went to their knees by her prone body, a roar of rage echoed around the cavernous room. *Huw!* Before she could sit up and assure everyone she was fine and merely had the air knocked out of her, Huw raced across the room from where he had been monitoring several groups, tore Cas away, and began to pummel him.

"*Dermo!* Shit! Help me up!" Nadia reached for Aeron and Bre who pulled her to her feet. She leaned against Aeron's supporting arm for a split second before shrugging him off. "I have to stop Huw. He'll kill Cas."

"My brother can hold his own," Bre assured her. After a day in the regen bed, the Prime was healthy again. He stood with his arms crossed on his chest and a grim smile on his face. "Huw has been asking for someone to put him on the ground all day. Let Cas have his fun."

She couldn't disagree with Bre's sentiment: Huw had been difficult most of the day, especially toward Aeron and the Jod brothers, but still…"Cas did nothing wrong. Huw's being an ass." Nadia added, "As usual" under her breath.

Aeron snorted. He'd heard her. Damn good hearing the Prime had. She'd have to remember that.

She approached the combatants with caution; all she needed was a wild elbow or foot to catch her. The men were on the ground and wrestling for superior position. Everyone in the training room had crowded around, yelling encouragement to their chosen warrior. But the fight went far beyond training as defined by the Alliance. A soldier didn't put choke holds on one of their peers.

Huw was trying to kill Cas.

"Huw! Stop it!" Forgetting all about her resolve to avoid getting clocked by a stray punch, Nadia straddled Huw's back; he was on top of Cas. She pinched a nerve on the side of Huw's neck until he released Cas from the oxygen-depriving hold.

When Huw turned and attempted to dislodge her, Nadia barely avoided the punch he threw at her throat. His fist hit her shoulder instead and spun her around, throwing her off-balance. She landed on her butt this time.

"Nadia! I didn't mean ... I never would ... are you hurt?"

Both ends of their psychic pathway had been selectively open since Tarn. It was as if he had to monitor her well-being, and she had to let him. Yet, he also hadn't physically approached or spoken to her in the two days since she'd walked away from him outside the cave. Which was why she chose to ignore the mental voice now; she wasn't sure her answer would be civil.

Aeron was at her side immediately. "That was one way to stop them. A Volusian nerve hold. Well done." He pulled her up and surrounded her from behind with his arms.

She wasn't sure why Aeron felt the need to protect her, but that was how she read the attractive science officer's emotions. *Shit.* He *did* have feelings for her. But his touch was wrong and made her skin itch.

"You okay, Nadia?" Aeron whispered against her ear. The sensation was like flicks of a whip and had her pulling away.

Conscious of Huw's narrow-eyed gaze of molten gold, she patted Aeron's arms. "I'm fine. Let go, or he'll attack you next." When Aeron didn't release her, she added, "Please."

Aeron let her go slowly as if to taunt the beast seething inside Huw who had risen from the floor. He stood less than an arm's length away from them, his hands clenching and unclenching and his lips twisted into a snarl. Damn, just what she didn't need—Aeron and Huw going all ape-shit territorial on her, especially when the first man, the wrong one, wanted her and the other just played at it.

"I'm not afraid of him," Aeron told her. "None of the men here are." He paused and came to her side and whispered, "Why do you think he attacked Cas? It was clearly an accident."

"Not sure," *liar*, "he must not have seen the whole thing." Nadia glanced at Cas who'd gotten up also. "Cas? Are you okay?"

"Yes, Commander Nadia. Did I hurt you?"

"I'm fine, Cas." Ignoring Huw, she addressed the soldiers who'd surrounded them. "In fact, I was stopping the fight to tell you men to cease holding back with us women. The Antareans, the Erians, the mercenaries, and the Prime rebels won't hold back. We women have to be able to go toe-to-toe with bigger males. We need to learn all the dirty tricks to take a bigger opponent down. That is why we're here today—help us learn! Understood?"

The men in the room shouted, "Yes, sir."

"Good." She turned to Huw who'd moved closer and stood in front of her. He snarled subvocally, but she could hear and feel it scratching over the psychic link with him. His dark gold gaze was focused on Aeron who'd remained close to her side. Goddammit, she didn't have the time or the patience for this chest-thumping shit.

Nadia nudged the science officer away. Thank God, Aeron took the hint. Huw's raspy snarling subsided and his breathing slowed.

"As for you, Huw." Nadia turned her muddled emotions on him; after all she was an emotional basket case because of his hot and cold treatment of her. "What in the hell were you thinking? You don't attack one of my teammates. Cas didn't hurt me. We were training. That's what we're supposed to do. We need to get you Prime males used to working and fighting alongside women. We aren't fragile flowers here. We're goddamned highly trained Alliance soldiers. Understood?"

"*You were hurt.*" His concern was real, and it swept through her like the leading winds of a thunderstorm.

"*Huw. I'm fine. The dizziness was due to the air being knocked out of me. My head is fine.*"

Huw looked her in the eye, nodded once, and then turned and walked away. His emotions, their link, locked down behind a frigid black wall.

Nadia's breath hitched, but she refused to let the watery sob emerge. He'd walked away ... again.

"Nadia, what's going on?" Aeron whispered against her ear, his body as close as he could get without touching. "Are you in telepathic contact with Huw?"

She angled her head to look at Aeron. She read anger and jealousy mixed with envy in his voice and aura, saw those mixed emotions reflected in his glittering gold gaze. "I've always been empathic." It seemed Bram and the Jod brothers hadn't spread the word about her telepathy, or if they had, Aeron hadn't heard about it. He was genuinely shocked. "And now it seems with some Prime I'm telepathic—and that's all I'll say on the matter."

Aeron's nostrils flared. Before she realized what he was about to do, he spun her around, tucked his fingers into the waistband of her pants, and pulled it down far enough to view her lower abdomen. His sigh of relief was audible in the oh-so-quiet room.

Nadia blushed when she noticed all the Prime males with a view looked and promptly began to spread the word. Her hearing was also good enough to hear the gist of the comments. "Commander Nadia is still available. No mark."

She punched Aeron's gut with a stiff-armed jab and shoved him away from her. "Don't ever touch me that way again." Her voice was low and ragged with her anger and shock. She felt feral.

She tugged her pants back into place. In a louder voice, she announced so all around could hear, "Terrans don't mark. I'm not Prime. Also, it is never, I repeat, never appropriate to stick your hands down a woman's pants in public. It is also not appropriate to do so in private without the woman's consent. Is that understood?"

A chorus of "yes, sirs" came from the males present and "damn rights" from the females.

"Now that the side show's over." She swept the assembled soldiers with a stern glare. "Let's get back to work. Pair up. And if I see any Prime male not giving his best effort when paired with a female, those men will be on tunnel maintenance for a standard month on their respective ships."

Mel had instituted tunnel maintenance as a punishment since she'd crawled and walked through some dirty ones on the *Galanti* back when she'd first met Wulf. No Prime male worth the name wanted housekeeping duty.

Her soldiers went back to work and soon the fitness room rang with the shouts and thuds of fighting pairs.

Nadia approached the two Jod brothers with Aeron following her. "Aeron, you're seriously pissing me off. I don't need protection."

"I think you do. Huw is still within earshot. He's outside the training room, watching us." Aeron placed his hands on her shoulders and turned her toward the side entry to the room.

Yep, there he was skulking in the shadows like some demented ghost in a gothic novel.

Get his hands off you, Nadia. Now.

So, now he lowered his shields. She ignored him for the moment.

"Aeron, I consider you a friend, but please don't touch me again. It sets a bad example for the men." Nadia stepped out from under Aeron's hands and looked toward the sky. "God, what have I done to deserve this?"

Dammit, Huw. You've caused enough disruption today. Go away. Find some other female to glare at. Hey? I've got an idea—why don't you go find your gemate?"

Huw's answering snarl traveled across their mental connection and made her shudder. He was furious. *Fine.* Let him be. She was mad also. He'd all but ignored her for two days and then he went all primitive on her as she did her job, which happened to entail working with men. If he didn't get his act together, she'd report him to his brother. Let Wulf handle him.

When she looked again, he was gone.

"Okay, that was fun." Nadia pinned the Jod brothers and Aeron with a narrowed glance. They'd surrounded her like the coastal mountains of Cejuru Prime hugged the capital city's bay, isolating her from the rest of the room. "Let's get back to training. I'm not holding back. You are not to, either. I'll use every dirty fighting technique I've learned in my years in the military and from my pre-military days in some of the seedier neighborhoods on Mars Colony—and I expect the same from you. We can share the techniques and decide which ones our female soldiers can use to their best advantage. Understood?"

Bre nodded, an impish grin twisting his lips. "Will you teach us the Volusian nerve hold you used on Commander Huw?"

Nadia grinned back. "Sure. Let's do this."

Huw slammed his way out of the training facility. Damn Nadia! She made him crazy. He was defending her and she turned it around so he looked like the bad guy. In front of the crew.

Adding insult to injury, she'd easily defeated him with one fragile, female hand.

And he was a sick man because he found that sexy.

Her touch. Her smell. Her beautifully muscled, long body. Her mental touch. All of those things had him stiffer than the titanium barrels on the ship's laser cannon. But he couldn't approach her—not until after the Lost Ones mission, and maybe not even then if he found his *gemate*.

Ansu bhau. He needed sex. Now. Nadia was a temptress, created by the One to lead him off the honorable path he'd set for himself.

Requisitioning a surface vehicle, he drove to the house of the sex surrogate his family had always used to teach the younger Caradoc males about how to make love to a woman and later ease all of the Caradoc males' sexual needs until they mated.

Susa would take away the gnawing pain in his balls and cock.

After parking in front of Susa's villa, he ran up the steps. Her door panel indicated she was home and receiving clients. He entered his code and waited for her to let him in.

"Huw!" Susa greeted him at the doorway, wearing only a sheer floating garment. Every line of her curvy, long body was visible. Her dusky rose nipples showed clearly as did her dark curls over her sex. "It's been so long. With Wulf mated, I have one less of my favorite Caradoc men to take care of."

She stood on her tiptoes and nibbled at his lower lip before kissing him fully. Her soft hands petted his chest, paying particular attention to his nipples.

He grimaced with discomfort when her hand brushed over a particularly sensitive part of his chest. He stopped her caresses by covering her hands with his and pulled away from the kiss. "Susa? Do you have time to give me a massage and ease my erection?"

"Always, darling Huw." She pulled on his arm. "Come to my bedroom. I will get you a Valerian whiskey and then undress you." She rubbed her cheek along the arm she held. "You do seem tense, warrior."

"Yes." He kissed the top of her head. "But you have always eased me well in the past. I expect no less of you now."

"It is nice to be wanted, needed. Many of my peers are afraid that if our men can procreate with other hominid females in the galaxy that we will no longer be needed to care for their needs."

Huw had never thought of that consequence before and was embarrassed that no one on the Elder Council had thought of how the merger into the Alliance and seeking compatible females from other planets would affect the women who had no *gemats* and had taken care of unmated Prime males' needs for several centuries.

"You will always be needed." Even to Huw his assurance sounded lame.

"Ah, Huw. None of us wish the men who find mates to be unfaithful to their chosen females. That would be immoral—such a bond, even though it is an emotional bonding and not a full mind-body-spiritual one, should be inviolate."

She went to fix him a drink. "We are thinking to ask Premier Caradoc if the Alliance Astrobiology Research scientists would look into the possibility of us sex surrogates mating with non-Prime males. Maybe what stops us from mating with our own kind would not be a barrier to let's say a Terran or Volusian male. What do you think?"

"I think that is an excellent idea." Also one that would make the Pure Blood faction crazier than they already were. "I will mention it to my father myself." He took the drink from Susa. "But tell your peers this needs to be kept secret for now. There are some…"

"Stop, Huw." Susa unzipped his uniform top and placed biting kisses down his chest onto his abdomen. Kneeling, she opened his uniform pants and looked up at him as she grasped his rock-hard cock. "We know the rebels would target us and any male we approached or who approached us. We can wait until the rebels are subdued. We've waited this long."

Susa licked the purpled head of his cock then took it into her mouth and suckled it before letting it out with a pop. "What first? Massage? Or me swallowing your seed?"

Huw wanted to say swallowing his seed, but her tongue and lips, which usually had him impatient to come in her mouth now made him cringe. Her touch was wrong, and he roared inside to realize that sex with Susa wouldn't help his dire need, but only make his sexual tension worse.

"Massage. A long one. I'm so tired. Tense." He would suffer through the emotional, almost physical, discomfort her touch brought him. He wouldn't insult her by leaving prematurely after he'd sought her out.

Susa nodded and stood up. "Whatever you need, Huw. I will try to provide. Just tell me." She stroked the side of his face with gentle fingers. "So many worries I see on your face. Let them go. Susa will soothe you."

Huw closed his eyes and nodded—but it wasn't Susa's face he envisioned or her hands touching him—but Nadia's.

The mental pathway between them was shut down for now—from both ends. Nadia was mad at him, and he was afraid she'd discover he'd left her and come to another woman. And why he felt as if he'd betrayed her, he would never know. Nadia was not Prime. She was not his *gemate*, chosen by the One. And why those facts made his head hurt, his heart ache, and his body cry out in need—he didn't want to touch with a meter-long battle blade.

CHAPTER 10

Filing into the meeting room were the leaders of this part of the Milky Way Galaxy: Admiral Nelson, the Alliance military commander for the outer spiral of the Milky Way Galaxy; General Arnat of Prime Military Command; and two representatives from the Prime Elder Council responsible for military and civilian security. Joining these leaders were Drs. Lia Morgan and Kerr Lenke, Chief Medical Officers of the newly merged Gold Squadron.

The meeting had been called to address issues which had arisen from the merger of Wulf's Prime squadron into Gold Squadron, the mission Gold would embark upon once joint training was completed, and the continued unrest caused by the Pure Blood faction and its hirelings.

Wulf had other things on his mind as he fondled Melina's thigh under the table, far more enjoyable things for a newly bonded couple to do than decide the fate of this small sector of the universe.

"Wulf," Melina whispered against his ear, "stop touching me, or I'll retaliate in front of all these important people. And you'd be very embarrassed."

He leaned over and kissed the hair above her ear. "No, I would be very proud—and all these important people would be very jealous. You'd be the one to blush."

His precious *gemate* growled, a cute little female version of his own snarl. They were a perfect match. Thinking about perfect matches had him frowning. "*Lubha*, have you noticed that since Tarn, Huw has gone out of his way to avoid Nadia? Kerr told me Huw even avoided looking at her during the blood tests I ordered. What's wrong? It is clear to me there's an attraction between the two of them."

"Your brother is a stubborn idiot. This is their personal business and we need to stay out of it."

"If it begins to affect their work, I will have to get involved. Until then, I will do as you suggest, *gemate lubha*." Wulf kissed her cheek. "Iolyn and I might have to beat our brother to a pulp for his actions, though. *Diew*, even Aeron went out of his way to mention Huw's behavior. There was an incident in the training room this morning. Huw attacked one of the Jod brothers and then stormed out. No one has seen him since."

"I heard." Melina sighed. "Unfortunately, someone spotted him. I was eating lunch with Nadia in the crew's mess on planet, and the whole room was filled with talk of the training incident. Then some loud mouth said Huw had gone to Susa's. The men in the room snickered." His *gemate*'s eyes flashed with anger. "Nadia asked me point-blank who Susa was. I told her the truth. Nadia paled, excused herself, and left the room. The Jod brothers were present at the time. Bre told the men who'd spread the gossip they were asses and that such private matters weren't for public consumption. I was ready to give him an additional commendation for his loyalty to Nadia."

Wulf sighed and hugged Melina. "It will be a rough period of adjustment for my Prime soldiers. They aren't used to male-female interactions in their workplace and will fixate on the relationships that do develop. It is a good thing the doctors planned so quickly to have the lecture on dating and social interactions with non-Prime women this evening. I am ordering Huw to attend."

"What if Huw doesn't?" Melina's brow wrinkled with concern.

"Iolyn will drag Huw's ass to it even if we have to beat on him a bit." Wulf wouldn't allow Nadia to be hurt by his brother. She was an excellent officer and a good friend to his *gemate*. His brother needed to get over his fixation on mating with a Prime woman and take the obviously compatible and lovely woman right in front of him.

And if he and Iolyn had to kick his brother every day until he woke up and realized the fact—they would do it. Their father was also on board; he had adored Nadia since the kidnapping. His father recognized a strong woman when he saw one—too bad Huw didn't seem to be as astute.

"I'll help beat on him if you need me." Melina rubbed her cheek against his arm.

"That is very generous of you, *lubha*. We'll let you know." He patted her thigh and left his hand there. The connection soothed him.

"The meeting will come to order." Ilar Caradoc looked around the table, a solemn look on his face.

Wulf sensed anger in his parent and wondered what else had happened since he'd last spoken with his father that morning.

"Thank you for taking time out of your very busy schedules to attend this hastily arranged meeting." His father made eye contact with every person at the table. His gaze lingered on Wulf and Melina for a split second longer than the others, and Wulf felt his father's pride and pleasure in their bonding. "Matters have come to my attention which concern Gold's upcoming mission to find any remaining Lost Ones. Another layer of duties will be added to that mission."

Wulf stiffened and unconsciously gripped Melina's thigh tighter. This was news to him. Melina covered his hand with hers and stroked until he loosened his grip.

"Wulf, I know this comes as a surprise … and I'll get to the additional duties in a minute. But, first, we need to address a more immediate concern." Ilar looked down the table. "General Arnat, please share your findings gleaned from the intelligence elicited during interrogations of the mercenaries and Prime traitors and your suggestion on how to handle what you've learned."

"Thank you, Premier Caradoc." The General stood and strode to the head of the table. "My adjutant is handing out the transcripts of the interrogations. Briefly, the mercenaries and the few traitors working with the rebels planned to use the joint training as a way to get their hands on female Alliance soldiers. The rebels would then have used some of these women as hostages to leverage their demands upon the Prime government. The women not so used would have been sold to the Antareans as sex slaves."

Lia and Melina gasped and the men rumbled angrily. Wulf wanted to kill someone; preferably the man he suspected had given the orders to the hirelings—his second cousin, Darga Caradoc.

"Therefore, I have advised Premier Caradoc it would be unwise while Gold is in space dock and the soldiers are on planet for training to allow the female crew members to walk about without extra protection. He has agreed. Thus, we wish to request the Alliance Military Command make it a requirement that the women of Gold Squadron have at least one male Gold soldier with them while out in public on planet at all times. The Prime Military Command will do what is needed to keep the peace on the planet and protect the

Alliance soldiers, but we cannot be everywhere. Thank you." The General returned to his seat and sat.

Wulf's father turned to Admiral Nelson. "Admiral, would you like to address this concern and our request?"

The Admiral stood, but remained at his seat. "After reading the transcripts and having sat in on some of the interrogations, I'm very concerned about the rabid tenor of the orders given to these thugs and traitors. I don't want any of my personnel, male or female, in the hands of these animals. I've been in touch with Alliance Command and my superiors have concurred. An order will go out at the end of this meeting. It requires *all* Gold Squadron soldiers to stay in pairs while on the planet. My order also further requires that our women will always have at least one male soldier with them. My soldiers will also be armed at all times with their hand weapons set on the highest stun levels. Do you have an issue with that last order, General?"

"No, I do not. I will make sure my people know this is authorized … with your permission, Premier Caradoc?"

"Granted. The female soldiers do not have the physical strength to take on even the weakest Prime male…"

Wulf had to smother a smile when Melina snorted.

Ilar paused and smiled at Melina. "Maybe with the exception of my daughter-kin, but, Melina, you are a Prime battle-mate and thus have an advantage."

"Acknowledged, Father-kin." Melina inclined her head in respect. "But I have several female soldiers whom I know could take down a Prime male—and have in training. But I agree with the Admiral, pairing the women with another male soldier and the addition of the lasers set on high stun should be a deterrent—and that is, after all, what we want to do, isn't it? Send a message?"

"Exactly, Captain Melina," the Admiral said. "And I've observed the women in question and am proud their Alliance training has stood them well. Keep up the good work. I witnessed a lot of respect from the Prime males who were put on their asses earlier today as I passed through the training center. And the sense of teamwork is coming across very well in the short two weeks since the merger."

"The Tarn situation was the turning point, Admiral." Wulf swept a glance around the table. "I have not had a chance to read the transcripts from the interrogations, but did any of the traitors provide us any leads as to whom they worked for?"

"No, Wulf." Ilar scowled. "They all had the same story. They joined a small cell and the instructions were provided in written messages, left in pre-arranged spots. And they burned the messages." His father snarled and shook his head. "There were never any direct voice communications that could be traced. The mercenaries were hired by the small cell leaders per instructions spelled out in the messages. We are at a dead end unless we can get someone undercover in one of the cells or the rebel leaders make a mistake and become more visible to their followers."

"They have made mistakes in the past, Father. They will again." Wulf hoped it would happen before anyone he loved was captured or killed. "How are you distributing the new orders to our crews?"

"A text message has been sent to all Gold crew members. And a scrolling notice is on the monitors in all barracks. And I will also ask that the good doctors mention the new orders this evening at the mandatory program on social interactions among Prime Gold crew members and non-Prime females." Ilar looked at the two doctors and inclined his head. "I applaud the doctors for coming up with this program so quickly. We do not want any misunderstandings during this crucial period of adjustment."

Wulf nodded. "Now, Father, what has happened that Gold's first mission's objectives have been altered?"

"I will turn that over to Admiral Nelson." Ilar sat.

"Thank you, Premier Caradoc." The Admiral walked to the front of the room, speaking as he moved. "The Alliance has had a request from two scientific outposts in the Iota Persei system." The Admiral stopped by an audio-visual panel and called up a galaxy map. He zeroed in on the part of the galaxy between the Perseus and Cygnus-Orion arms that was affected. "Mercenaries and pirates are raiding the outposts and the scientists need assistance. So far they've only lost supplies and no lives, but the head scientists feel they've just been lucky."

Melina's breath hitched and the hand she'd placed on top of his trembled.

"Melina mine, are you all right?"

"Yes, just remembering how helpless I felt when the Antareans attacked Obam IV—and killed my parents and their scientific team. We have to help these people."

"We will."

Ilar must have sensed their telepathic communication, because his eyes gleamed with sympathy as his gaze singled her out. "My daughter-kin can testify to the helplessness of the scientists who are not soldiers and are at the mercy of these marauders."

Admiral Nelson also turned a sympathetic eye on Melina. "This situation is very reminiscent of what happened with your parents' expedition. We hope to avoid another tragic outcome. Thus, Gold shall visit each expedition so threatened, resupply them, assess, and then bolster their defenses. Gold will also leave one battle cruiser per colony to remain on patrol and present a defensive posture to any would-be raiders."

"Will this be a permanent assignment?" asked Melina. "While I'm sure Gold can handle anything tossed at it, battle cruisers are the only large ships we have that can make a dirt landing. This might hurt us in a battle to protect other colonies."

"I agree, Melina," said Admiral Nelson. "Once you're back from the Lost Ones mission, we'll assign two more battle cruisers to your squadron. You'll then be able to rotate the duty to protect the scientific expeditions. The permanency of the assignment will be dictated by the expeditions' durations." He looked first at Wulf and then Melina. "Do you have any concerns about the Lost Ones mission and being down two cruisers?"

"It won't be a problem, Admiral," said Wulf. "My bigger concern would be a battle cruiser per expedition might not be enough if the Antareans chose to attack. Pirates are more easily handled. But Gold will be within twelve-to-twenty-four standard hours of the planets you've noted. So, I don't see a big problem. Our battle cruiser captains have the heavy air experience to go dirt-side and defend the scientists on the ground until we get there. Don't you agree, Melina?"

"Yes. I'd like to suggest the *Renard* and the *Picarus* as the two battle cruisers." Melina leaned into Wulf's body. "The captains of those two cruisers have the most experience at dirt-side defense."

"I concur. My Melina knows her captains well."

"Good. Inform your captains," Admiral Nelson said. "I'll request two new battle cruisers and crews from Alliance Military Command. They'll be here, ready for crew mergers with the Prime when you return from your mission. Good luck and God speed."

CHAPTER 11

That evening, an ocean-side bar, Cejuru Prime

"How do we know Prime males can mate with other hominids?"

"What do you mean by mate, Huw?" Lia eyed him curiously.

Dr. Kerr Lenke, her Prime colleague, nodded his agreement with Lia's clarifying question. "Be specific, Huw. Do you mean actual procreation? Because we know we can have offspring with Terrans—we did so in the distant past. There are family lines on our planet with Terran DNA, although it's recessive. I also don't expect too much of an issue with other hominids especially in light of Dr. Brianna Martin's successful gene-splicing work with the Volusians. Or, do you mean *actual* production of a *gemat-gemate* bonding?"

And wasn't that the million-credit question?

Nadia leaned back against the plush booth and surveyed her dinner companions, all of whom were focused on Kerr's comments. To her right were Huw and then Iolyn. To their right was Royce Nowicki. On Royce's right were Aeron, Kerr, and Lia. Sitting to Nadia's immediate left was Joen Dakkin.

The current topic of debate had begun during the required lecture for all Gold Squadron crews members: "Dating Dos and Don'ts." The early evening lecture had carried over post-class to this ocean-side bar. While the lecture had been aimed at educating the Prime males about non-Prime social interactions, Huw had broached the topic that had been the ten-megaton pachyderm in the room: would all this interaction produce what the Prime male desired the most— the mind-body-spirit trinity?

Nadia hadn't needed to attend the lecture or its aftermath to hear how Huw felt about the topic. From the heated discussion during and after the doctors' lecture, he seemed to be the only Prime male who cared about the bonding aspect all Prime had sought in the past.

Which sucked because she was attracted to the obstinate male. More than attracted.

Each time she saw or heard or scented him, her clit throbbed and her pussy flooded with her arousal. Since Tarn, she'd experienced a recurring, sharp pain on her lower right side, above her ovary. Of course, since Huw had made it his goal to avoid her as much as possible over the past two days, the physical reactions were bearable. It was her heart and head that hurt the most.

Sitting next to Huw, his scent overwhelmed her. She rubbed her lower abdomen where the phantom ache viciously stabbed at her womb. Though she was one hundred percent Terran on both sides of the family, she realized she was bonding with him in some manner. What that manner was? Was anybody's guess.

After the incident on Tarn, Kerr and Lia had taken blood and tissue samples from both her and Huw on Wulf's orders. Since the blood draw, Huw had become even more scarce than usual. The fact he was sitting next to her at all was after a sneaky move by Iolyn. After one short "hello," he'd studiously ignored her.

Jerk.

And dumb her, her heart ached for him even more. Whatever in the hell was going on in her body, she wished it would stop. If the strained relations continued, it could affect their working relationship. If that happened, she'd have to transfer away from Mel's crew, because she refused to endanger her crew members. Nowicki would take her back on the *Leonidas* in a flash. Aeron could go back to the *Galanti*.

While Nadia wasn't afraid of learning the truth about what was happening between them, Huw was.

If the results of the testing on their blood and tissue samples were positive for some sort of Prime-like mating and Huw denied the biological evidence, it would crush her, especially in light of their psychic connection and physical attraction.

A gal could only take so much rejection from the man she desired and, yes, had begun to love despite his stubbornness. Huw was exactly the kind of man she'd always been attracted to—big, strong, intelligent—and the sexual attraction between them was off the charts. When he wasn't ignoring her or denying the tie between them, he was fun to be with. They shared a lot of the same interests. Over the weeks she'd known him, he'd shown himself to be honorable, courteous, and very caring and protective of her well-being. His actions on Tarn had underlined some of those more admirable traits. She could envision them being partners in every aspect of their lives.

From the corner of her eye, she noted Huw's handsome face was flushed from the heat of arguing with the other Prime males at the table, all of whom were actively looking for a companion among the Terran and Volusian females in Gold. It was a good thing Mel and Wulf had responded so quickly to her suggestion about addressing dating and sexual etiquette before someone's feelings were hurt or a woman was approached sexually in an inappropriate manner. No one wanted the first foray into uniting the two fleets to be sabotaged by cultural misunderstandings over male-female relations.

Prime males tended to be autocratic and one hundred percent alpha. Terran, Volusian, and other hominid females in the Alliance military were strong-willed and used to kicking such high-handed approaches in the teeth. The potential for cultural misunderstanding—and bloodshed—would've been high.

Huw's low rumbling tones cut through her chaotic thoughts. "I still seek a *gemat-gemate* bonding."

Nadia mentally swore and bit her lip to keep from vocalizing angry words. *Damn his hide!* But he'd accept sex from a woman who wasn't his *gemate*. His visit to the sex surrogate Susa had proven that.

After hearing about Huw's visit to the sex surrogate, Nadia had toyed with the idea of going to another man in order to salvage her pride, but she wouldn't be able to endure his touch. And she wouldn't hurt another man's feelings or pride by rejecting him in an intimate moment.

A shard of pain sliced through her gut. Nadia gasped and quickly took a sip of her wine to keep from crying out like a wounded animal. She understood Huw's current words were a knee-jerk reaction to the other men's more logical arguments. But his lack of concern for her—and Lia's—feelings was inconsiderate to the point of being callous. His every word denying that a non-Prime female was a viable substitute as a life partner for a Prime male was like a knife to the heart.

Huw had made up his mind. Their dining companions were wasting their breath, attempting to convince him otherwise. If the existence of their unique psychic bond hadn't convinced him, why would mere words? It would take a major shift in his life view to allow him to date or court a non-Prime female.

Despite the pain he'd caused and continued to cause in the deepest levels of her being, she had the urge to soothe him, calm his anger.

She needed her fucking head examined.

"Brother, you are nuts." Iolyn shook his head and shot Huw a look filled with disgust. "Wulf finding Mel was a one in, well, a whole hell of a lot of chances. Face the facts. There are no unmarked Prime females of mating age left in the Cejuru system or even the galaxy—and fewer females are born each year and those tend to be mostly infertile."

Iolyn rubbed at his chest where Nadia knew he had a quiescent *gemat* marking; his mate was one of the Lost Ones. Hope was minuscule that the lost women or their grown daughters would ever be found—or, at least, found alive.

"I don't want to spend my life alone," Iolyn continued. "If I can have children with a Terran or another compatible female ... well, I want that."

"But we still have a chance to find others like Mel." Huw's sculpted cheekbones were highlighted red with his righteous anger.

Is that what he really thought? He was gambling that he might find the one perfect Prime woman during their upcoming mission? Nadia shook her head. Iolyn was correct—Huw was nuts. The odds were so small they were negligible.

Huw smacked the table with the flat of his hand, making the tableware jump. "It is possible some of the women and the female children survived and were assimilated into local populations just as Mel was. We could still find your *gemate*, brother."

Iolyn shook his head, sadness in his eyes, but said nothing. Huw wasn't in a receptive frame of mind and his brother was in a better position to know that than most.

Just her luck, Nadia was attracted to the wrong brother, the one who had pipe dreams and believed in fairy tales.

"It's also possible they all died." Royce Nowicki took a sip of his Valerian whiskey. "The destinations are located in some of the most isolated and dangerous sectors of the galaxy between the Perseus and Cygnus-Orion spiral arms. The fact the planets had at one time held Prime fortifications doesn't mean the planets were habitable at the time of the Lost Ones evacuation."

He gestured with his glass. "Hell, the ships probably didn't make it to their final destinations. Keep in mind, they were being actively pursued by the Antareans and taking on laser fire and torpedoes. Face it, Huw. Iolyn and the others are correct—find a lovely woman, court her, marry or mate or whatever you want to call it, and get a chance to have a family. It's a no-brainer to me."

Huw scowled into his whiskey. "The others can do what they want. There's still a chance some might live—and they are waiting for their *gemats* to find them. It should be a matter of honor and conscience that a Prime male eliminate that possibility before seeking a life partner among non-Prime women."

Nadia's heart stuttered. The fervor in his voice demonstrated Huw would never be happy with second-best—and she would always be second-best. The anguish was all consuming. She barely managed to stifle the cry erupting from her very soul. She inhaled sharply and grabbed at the knife-like pain in her lower abdomen.

"Nadia?" From her left, Lia leaned around Joen, her voice low. "You okay?"

Thank God, only Lia and Joen had noticed Nadia's pain. In the background, the others continued to dissect why Huw was crazy and why mating with non-Prime females would be good for the Prime people as a whole.

Nadia turned toward Lia and Joen. She wouldn't be surprised if her pain was etched on her face. "I … I ache, Lia."

Joen murmured something low; it sounded like "stupid Huw." He patted Nadia's shoulder. Sending the concerned

Prime a tortured smile, she shrugged away from his uncomfortable touch. His nostrils flared and he glared past her at Huw whose back was to them. "Very stupid Huw," muttered the communications officer.

Dermo. She needed to regain her composure; this was so unlike her to lose command of her emotions in front of peers. The calm, cool science officer of the *Galanti*, the "Iceberg," never showed emotion. She'd learned a long time ago to hide the tender, feminine part of herself in order to survive in the male-dominated Alliance fleet. She could almost hate Huw for what his careless words had done to her self-control.

Lia frowned. "Do you want to leave?"

Lia had doctored Nadia's wounds for many years as they'd served together in the Alliance and would know she was normally a stoic about pain.

Nadia nodded, afraid to speak for fear she'd start weeping convulsively. The emotional roller coaster she'd ridden since her feelings for Huw had first appeared were as devastating as the physical side effects.

Lia's full lips thinned, and then she turned to the others at the table. The men had gone silent at Lia's question. Huw's narrowed amber gaze was fixed on Nadia; he radiated concern. Too little, too late. She needed to leave.

"Nadia's ill," Lia said in her best I'm-a-doctor-don't-mess-with-me voice. "We'll head back to crew's quarters."

Rising from her seat, Nadia looked away from Huw's piercing stare. The other men stood; some voiced their concerns since she'd been injured during the Tarn attack and had sustained some bruises during fight training earlier that day.

Huw opened his mouth and immediately shut it. Instead of speaking, he took a sip of his drink. His gaze was now anywhere but on her.

The public sign of rejection even as he nudged her shields gently sent a chill down her spine. The courteous, caring Huw versus the uncaring, single-minded, I-want-a-*gemate* Huw were going to drive her over the edge of sanity. God, she might really have to switch ships. She couldn't work, live, like this.

Nadia trembled, cold to her core. Dizziness struck as she forgot to breathe. She staggered slightly and braced herself on the table to keep from losing her balance.

The much smaller Lia took hold of her arm, steadying her. "Nadia? Do we need to get ground transportation?"

"Move, Lia. I've got her." Joen had his arm around Nadia's waist and supported her easily until she regained control. She moved away from him and he released her immediately.

Did he suspect his touch felt wrong? Probably. Joen, she'd noticed, was very observant.

"No … no ground transportation! Lia, I'm fine. I can walk. The fresh air will help." She stiffened her spine and stood tall, willing her knees not to give out at least until she and Lia were out of sight. "Let's get out of here. Please?"

"I will accompany you, ladies." Joen tucked Lia's arm in his and left it up to Nadia as to whether she would take the other arm he offered. "No female Alliance soldier is to be out alone on the planet."

Ignoring the icky feeling touching his arm sent through her, she placed her fingers on his forearm. She refused to show a hint of discomfort in front of Huw. She'd keep her pride if nothing else.

"Nadia?" Lia whispered. "Do you want one of the others to come also? Mel and Wulf want every woman to have a male escort."

"It's okay, Lia. I think one Prime male for the two of us should suffice." Nadia attempted to smile at the darkly handsome Joen who towered over both women.

"I am a very lucky man to be allowed to accompany two such beautiful women." Joen winked at Nadia before leading them away from the table toward the exit.

As they moved farther and farther away from Huw, the formerly piercing ache in her womb lessened to a phantom ache such as when a person had lost a vital limb. If she looked back, she knew she'd find Huw glaring at them. He might not want her as she wanted him, but he noticeably fumed whenever she spoke to or interacted with a male crew member. The man had feelings for her; he was just too stubborn to give up his dream and admit it.

God, what am I going to do? She stumbled and only Joen's strong arm kept her from falling.

"I could carry you, Nadia." Joen's sincere offer brought tears to her eyes. "You are very pale. You are shaking."

"That's not necessary … I'm … just … um, sore from the hand-to-hand training earlier today … and tired and…" She'd let him fill in the rest of it however he wished.

"Don't believe her, Joen. Nadia's normally as strong as a Volusian ox-steer. She bounced back from the injuries she incurred on Tarn with barely a standard hour in the regen bed. Huw's bullshit hurt her. He made me so mad I wanted to spit."

Lia was very empathic, had always been so. It was part of what made her an excellent doctor. Nadia suspected the woman had the same psychic abilities as Mel—and as Nadia herself.

"I don't want to talk about it." Nadia prayed both of them would take the hint. Dissecting Huw's feelings and actions would make it harder for her to sublimate the pain.

Joen released their arms long enough to open the bar's heavy exterior door and allow her and Lia to pass through the exit before him. Once outside, he offered his arm to Lia with a sympathetic smile to Nadia.

Yeah, he knew his touch bothered her.

Joen was perfect for Lia. He was intelligent, even-tempered for a Prime, and a complete gentleman. The couple's emotional auras meshed even more now than a couple of days ago.

And, no, Nadia wasn't green-eyed with jealousy at her good friend's luck; she merely desired the same luck.

Huw kept an eye on the trio as they left the bar. He fought the urge to run after them and escort Nadia to her quarters himself, to make sure she had no lingering injury from Cas Jod's barreling into her earlier that day.

It was getting harder and harder to avoid showing his feelings for Nadia in public. But the mission loomed, and his words to the others about honor and conscience were what he had promised himself to abide by until it was proven one way or another whether any Lost Ones survived.

The others didn't understand his position; but then had they really thought it through? He had—and he could not openly court Nadia until he was sure he wouldn't hurt either an undiscovered *gemate* or Nadia.

After the door closed on the three, Iolyn hit him on the arm—hard. "You, my brother, are a fool!"

Rubbing the place his brother had punched, he turned and glared. "What was that for? What did I do?"

Royce snorted and leaned back in his chair, cradling his drink. His light blue eyes glittered angrily. "You insulted all women other than Prime ones, asswipe. And, if you hadn't noticed, we had two non-Prime women sitting at the table. Mel would've wiped the floor with your face if she'd heard the crap you were shoveling."

Huw frowned. "I told the truth."

Iolyn muttered under his breath.

Huw winced at his brother's furious, vulgar words.

"Joen likes Lia, you imbecile." Iolyn punched him on the arm again. "If you hadn't noticed, he's been courting the little Terran doctor for weeks. How do you think Lia felt hearing she wasn't good enough to mate with a Prime male?"

"That's not what I said or meant. Joen and Lia?" Huw opened his mouth and then shut it. "I didn't realize. I will, of course, apologize if that is how my words sounded."

"They sounded all right. Better apologize to Nadia while you're at it," Ard interjected, "on your knees."

"Why on my knees?" He didn't like Ard speaking so familiarly of Nadia. The science officer had displayed far too much interest in her.

"Because Nadia likes you, dick wad," Royce said.

At Huw's huff of disbelief, the captain of the *Leonidas* added, "A lot. She likes you a whole hell of a lot." Royce sighed. "Listen up, dumb ass. I've known and served with Nadia for over five standard years. I've never seen the Iceberg so emotional over a man in all that time—and that includes the anger she felt toward the guy who attempted to rape her."

At the mention of rape and Nadia in the same sentence, a chill swept down Huw's back. It was as if Royce's words conjured up an ill wind, a portent of things to come, rather than a memory from the past. Huw shook it off and rubbed the ache over his heart. He wasn't precognitive. In fact, other than the usual empathy Prime warriors displayed for strong emotions during battle, he'd never been particularly psychically sensitive at all.

Well, that is, not until the Tarn incident when Nadia had somehow projected her thoughts to him and vice-versa. But he could explain the unusual occurrence as her being telepathic and him being a sensitive receiver.

"Mel shared some information about the incident in Nadia's past." Iolyn broke the long and uncomfortable silence Royce's words had spawned. "Prime males do not rape or abuse women."

Choking on his drink, Royce coughed. "Um, what about those fanatics who took Mel and Nadia? The women were beaten, bruised … naked from what I read in the report. Are you telling me those filthy bastards hadn't planned on sexually assaulting them? Hell, Wulf's swearing fucking blistered the paint on the conference room wall when Mel made her oral report to the Admiral about the incident."

Royce gestured wildly, some of his drink sloshing over the edge of the glass. "And what about Tarn? The Prime who'd hired those mercs had given them carte blanche to torture our crew members—especially the women. You don't think the rebel leader didn't know the mercs he hired had been slavers in the past and would've raped our female crew members before they sold them to the Antareans?"

Rage burned anew within Huw at what could have happened to Nadia if she'd been captured on Tarn. He'd seen the room in the military facility the mercenary force had prepared for torture. While it had been intended for all the Gold Squad members, the women would have been particularly vulnerable to some of the devices they'd found. He and the other rescuers had taken great pleasure in smashing the torture devices to bits.

"Stop growling, brother, or you'll have me starting." Iolyn's anger had turned his tanned skin dark red. "Royce, those Prime *apayebote* are not indicative of the majority of Prime men. Women are cherished for the creators of life they are."

"Yeah, sure," Royce drawled. "I've read some Prime histories, including one by your Uncle, Tenar Caradoc. Prime have prided themselves on their ability to fight and survive. Well, war is hell—and often, in the drive to win, acts are committed which violate all rules of decency. The Prime's history in the galaxy has been one of imperialism and subjugation of the native people much as England did on Earth during the eighteenth and nineteenth centuries."

Royce turned to Iolyn and then Huw, raising one sandy-colored brow. "So, you two keep telling yourself that little lie about the all-so-noble-when-it-comes-to-women Prime male. But from what I've heard and later read in the interrogation transcripts, the Prime fanatics have threatened to rape, torture, and then kill any non-Prime female caught consorting with a Prime male."

The Prime males emitted low, angry sounds, scaring the other diners around them.

Royce's lips twisted in what Huw discerned as scorn. "Didn't read your communiqués today or listen when Kerr made the announcement at the end of the lecture, did you? I'm thinking Joen did, because he made sure the ladies had an escort. If he hadn't offered, I would've. None of our female military personnel is to be out alone while we're dirt-side. Those orders come from not only the Alliance Military Headquarters, but also from Premier Caradoc."

He took a drink and swept the table with a glance, his stern gaze finally settling on Huw. "But I digress. Bottom line, Huw, will you apologize to both women or not?"

"Yes." Huw took a drink of his Valerian whiskey, needing the heated jolt it gave his suddenly icy body.

The voiced threat to the women of Gold Squadron—to Nadia—chilled him to the bone. The announcement and orders must have gone out while he'd attempted to have sex with Susa; his anger at being forced to attend this evening's lecture had caused him to shut Kerr and Lia out. Shame and guilt had him kicking himself mentally.

Then something scratched and thudded against the wall of denial he'd built around the mental bond he had with Nadia. The skin above his heart burned. And over it all, a deep foreboding—much akin to what he felt when a battle had reached a critical point—swept over his body and roiled in his gut.

Huw glanced around the bar, but didn't see anything to warrant such battle feelings—and none of the other Prime at the table seemed overly concerned. But then they were too busy being mad at him.

He shook his head in an attempt to throw off the sensations and turned his thoughts back to the current topic of discussion. "I will apologize, because I was rude and inconsiderate. But you're wrong, Royce. Nadia doesn't like me. She hates me. She turned her back on me, both on Tarn and again this morning." He strove hard to keep the petulance out of his tone.

"God give me strength. Am I the only one who has noticed you've been avoiding and turning your back on her whenever she's around?" Royce's voice was filled with antipathy.

"He's correct, Huw," said Kerr. The others nodded in agreement. "You are the one who does those things and have been for over two weeks. Nadia must have understood your message and decided not to engage with you any longer. If you want my opinion, you have driven her away."

"Kerr's correct. Nadia was open to you in a way she's never been with any Alliance soldier," Royce said. "But then you started spouting off the Prime women are supreme bullshit all the time and treating her as if she had a contagious disease. She probably got tired of your crap."

Ard smiled, a sly look in his eyes. "If you don't want her, Huw, I would like to date her. Court her like the good doctors suggested in class. Nadia is strong and beautiful. Her skin and hair glow like starlight off the Cejuru Prime seas. She would give a man handsome, strong sons and beautiful daughters."

Huw turned to snarl at his soon-to-be former friend's provoking words when the door to the bar was thrust open with a crash.

A disheveled, bloody Lia stumbled into the room and collapsed to the floor. "Help them," she cried out weakly.

Kerr ran to Lia's side to check over her wounds. The other men raced for the door.

Huw beat them to it and was the first through. He dropped the thick wall he'd constructed around the connection to Nadia. Images bombarded his mind.

Fighting. Knives. Thuds. Groans. Heavy breathing. Fear … cold, icy fear. Nadia's pain. Her increasing weakness.

Everything that made him a dominant, protective Prime male roared to the surface. Without conscious thought, he sent his strength across the connection he'd never verbally acknowledged, willing her to hold on, to survive until he arrived.

And his soul screamed *"Nadia!"* in a looping crescendo.

CHAPTER 12

Minutes earlier, outside the bar

The heat of the day had vanished with sunset. A fog bank hung low over the breakwater protecting the capital city's wharf area. Fishing boats and pleasure craft bobbed gently in their berths.

The night air was refreshing after the too-warm bar. Nadia took a deep breath, allowing the salty smelling air and the sound of the surf hitting rocks to wash over her. Unfortunately, not even the peaceful beauty of Cejuru Prime's ocean could calm her inner turmoil.

"Nice night." Joen's voice was whiskey-smooth and filled with concern. His body was a solid warmth next to her, close but not quite touching. She shoulder-bumped him, a silent gesture of thanks for his attempt to maintain a sense of normalcy. She was lucky to have him as a friend.

"Yes, it is," said Lia, following Joen's lead. "I love this temperate equatorial climate. Hot during the day and cool at night. The fog bank reminds me of San Francisco Bay on Earth. Looks like it might rain tomorrow, though. The sunset was really rosy."

Joen chuckled. "This is not Earth, Lia. The rain will come tonight, but tomorrow will be another clear day. Would you ladies like to go deep-sea fishing with me? It will be a perfect day for it. We could catch some fish and have a ... what do you Terrans call it when you cook and eat outside?"

"A barbeque or picnic," Lia said. "I'd love that. We have the day off before we find out what the change in mission orders entails. Nadia, please say you'll come."

"No, you two go." She appreciated the fact they wanted to include her, but she refused to be an awkward third. Lia and Joen needed the opportunity to connect. Being a couple on a ship populated with mostly Prime males would be challenging. Private time would be limited. "Anyway, I'd promised Mel I'd prepare what the landing parties could expect to find on the target planets we'll visit during our upcoming mission. Some of the planets aren't geologically stable and others have had changes in atmosphere."

The Prime had searched for years and found no trace of the missing ships. But Mel's survival and changes in original routes noted on the data disks she'd brought with her had been the impetus for the mission. Nadia put the chances of finding any of the missing Prime women and children at less than point two percent. Mel's survival had been a miracle according to her adoptive parents' diary.

Yet, the Alliance felt the effort should be made as a goodwill gesture for their new signatory, the Prime. Plus, it would be a good way to shake down the merged Prime and Alliance crews, a test before taking on more deadly and dangerous missions.

Lia opened her mouth to say something when Nadia stiffened.

"Shh." Nadia touched Joen's arm as she reached for her side arm with her right hand. "Someone's out there. Stalking us."

Joen stiffened, his formerly relaxed mood gone in an instant. He hissed under his breath, "Yes-s-s-s, I sense them now."

Leaning into Joen, she used her peripheral vision and detected four hulking shapes hugging the shadows of the buildings opposite the shoreline. Their stalkers had begun trailing them a few meters back. She'd thought nothing of their presence at the time, but as the group had begun to close the gap between them, their violent emotions had assaulted her senses.

"Of course, Nadia, we'll go back and get your jacket." Joen spoke loudly, his words echoing off the buildings in the quiet night air.

She admired Joen's quick thinking. He gently herded her and Lia back toward the brightly lit bar. They hadn't come far, maybe three hundred meters or less. The bar was the closest place of safety and reinforcement; all the other businesses were closed for the night.

Nadia flicked off the safety on her weapon and rested her fingers around the grip, ready to pull and fire at a moment's notice. She slipped her left hand down her thigh and prepared to go for her knife in its sheath.

Swearing under his breath, Joen subtlety maneuvered away from her and Lia's bodies, giving him room to fight. All the while, they retraced their steps.

"If they attack before we get back inside the bar…" Joen's voice was low and monotonic, "…I want you both to run. Let me handle these *apayebote*." He surreptitiously pulled his weapon and held it along his thigh between his and Nadia's body.

"Like hell," Nadia muttered. "Lia can run and get our crew members. You saw what I could do on Tarn—don't go all protective Prime male on me now."

"You are unwell—and in training this morning you were hurt…"

"*Dermo!*" Nadia hissed in her native Russian, cutting him off. "I'm fine. I won't leave you. Deal with it."

The four men stalking them were closer now. They appeared to be large Prime males. Joen was a decent fighter, but he wasn't the kind of warrior to take down four bigger men.

"Nadia's correct. You need her." Lia released Joen's arm. "What a day to leave the com-devices in our quarters."

"Be ready to run, Lia *lubha*." Joen's free hand swept down the doctor's back, a tender, loving gesture. "Nadia, don't hold back."

"Didn't plan on it. Get ready, Lia." Nadia echoed Joen's order. "They're coming."

The chilly calm Nadia was known for swept over her conscious mind, shoving all other worries aside. The primitive part of her brain was on full alert and in survival mode. Adrenaline flooded her veins, preparing her for the coming fight. The piercing ache over her right ovary, always bothersome, subsided as if it realized now wasn't the time to distract her. She needed all her energy, strength, and concentration for battle.

In the back of her mind, the connection with Huw unshielded and began to seek him out as it had on Tarn. All she found was blackness. Again, he denied her. She shoved the feelings of hurt aside; she had no time for such useless emotions with a fight to survive.

The black-clothed stalkers went on attack and flowed across the narrow street like a living malevolent fog rolling over the land. Their angle of approach cut Nadia and her friends off from the bar. The men were armed with laser weapons, but didn't fire them. They obviously weren't out to kill but to capture.

The repercussions of Alliance officers using deadly force on planet, even on men who meant them harm, swept rapidly through her mind. The diplomatic nightmare and the potential for destroying the new alliance had Nadia leaving her sidearm in her holster. "No lasers until they use theirs."

"Smart call, Nadia." Joen mimicked her move.

His immediate agreement meant his mind had worked along the same channels as hers—this attack could be a set up to see how Alliance crews would react to civilian threats. The Alliance military couldn't be perceived as easily resorting to deadly force for every potential threat. The fact that several Prime—traitors though they were—had died on Tarn, and even earlier on the *Galanti* and on Tooh 2 at the hands of Alliance officers, had created a furor in the Prime Elder Council.

Until these four Prime used deadly force, she and Joen would meet the threat level on an equivalent level.

When she spotted the glint of knives in two of the men's hands, she pulled her serrated battle knife. "Knives, Joen. They have knives." Joen's battle knife made a swishing sound in the quiet night as he drew it from his thigh sheath.

As the four men circled the three of them, one of them made the mistake of leaving an opening big enough for Lia, freeing a path toward the bar.

"Run, Lia. Get the others!" Nadia shoved Lia through the gap and leapt toward the man who attempted to follow the doctor.

Joen beat her to her target, shouting, "Lia, *gemate*! Behind you!" He roared a battle cry similar to one she'd heard the Caradoc brothers use and threw his body at the man who'd threatened Lia's escape.

Gemate? Joen and Lia were bonded? Joen's concentration would be to protect his mate at all costs. The other three attackers had heard Joen's words. They bellowed and turned to attack Joen and Lia; the bonded status of the couple made them the primary target.

Nadia shouted the battle cry of her family and engaged the enemy. Her job would be to keep the other three off Joen's back as he battled like a demon to kill the man who would've harmed Lia and prevented her from obtaining help.

Calling upon years of training and experience, Nadia rushed into the fray. She swept her knife in wide arcs. As she made initial contact with the three men, drawing blood, they turned to face her.

One man jumped toward her, leading with his knife, testing her mettle. She slashed him across his knife-wielding arm with a backhanded move and danced away from him.

Thank God, she had long arms and legs; they made hand-to-hand fighting easier.

A sweeping side kick kept his two buddies away.

The attackers now realized they had a real fight on their hands. She continued to use her knife and legs to block them from going to the aid of their friend who wasn't faring well at Joen's hands.

The man she'd sliced initially charged her as she maneuvered to reposition and find her balance after a series of kicks. Reflexively, she arched away, backhanding him across the face with the fist clutching her knife. He bellowed his pain and managed to slice her shoulder as she twisted away. She forced the pain of the shallow wound into the back of her mind, imagining it sinking into a deep well of soothing water. The pain now blunted; she fought back even harder.

"Forget the other two. The leader wants this one!" one of the three said in Prime. "She is a friend of Wulf's woman and is worth much."

Not gonna happen, bastard.

Nadia parried and thrust at the trio who taunted her with jabs of their knives and their talk of what they'd do once she was in their power. Her agility and superior training were the only things keeping her alive.

She could feel the blood soaking the back of her uniform as the slice was unable to coagulate due to the movement of the fight. Not a good sign. The loss of blood would weaken her eventually, and the predators would swarm and overpower her.

Definitely not gonna happen.

Ignoring the bleeding and the dull, throbbing pain, she fought with a furious concentration, doing as much damage as she could. The sounds of Joen's grunts and swearing punctuated the background as did the sound of Lia's feet hitting the pavement fading into the distance.

Joen was still standing and her friend had gotten away. Help would arrive soon.

At the thought of reinforcements, she dug deeper into the little bit of extra strength all warriors held back to close out a battle. She let loose with another battle cry. A new surge of adrenaline infused her blood and she went on the attack.

Nadia slashed at the closest man, slicing him across the thigh and adding to the wounds she'd already inflicted. He glared and spat Prime curses. She smiled and gave him a vulgar Prime gesture Wulf had inadvertently used with his brothers during training. The assailant's look of shock had her chuckling, which served momentarily to throw her three attackers off their game plan.

One of the thugs yelled. "You dare laugh? *Sued-seuater! Karote!*"

Anger ate at her gut. Fear threatened as she grew weaker. She encased both emotions within a box of ice in her mind. Soldiers didn't allow their emotions to dictate whether they won or lost a fight. At times like this, training took over.

Her attacker wanted her to react crazily at the egregious insults; she'd refuse. Little did these men realize her crew members didn't call her the Iceberg for nothing. Better men than these bastards had tried to get a rise out of her.

Only Huw's continued rejection had the power to touch her; nothing these cowards said could unnerve her.

"You are mistaken, *apayebo*—bastard!" She ducked as a fist headed for her face. "I'm not a seed sucker or a whore."

She shoved the fist-bearing arm up and away using a forearm block. She followed with a front kick to the man's crotch, missing his groin and getting him instead in his lower abdomen.

Then, the three backed away; their gazes aimed over her shoulder.

Nadia sensed Joen's presence behind her before she heard him. The aura of his anger was like a column of flaming heat washing over her back. Now she realized how the Prime worked so well together in battle—they could sense one another's *batel rabia*.

"Nadia … at your back." Joen's rumbling voice sounded loud in the sudden break in the fight.

The night air was chilly, and the rain Joen had predicted had begun to fall in a light drizzle. Nadia's ragged breaths became little puffy clouds as they hit the cool mist. Joen's breathing didn't sound much smoother.

The only good thing was the three Prime labored also. They'd probably expected an easy victory against one Prime and two women. The rebels would soon learn—the Alliance fought until the last man was standing.

"Why aren't they using their lasers?" Nadia muttered.

"Too noisy. They don't want to call attention to themselves," Joen muttered back. "Plus, pride. Your reasoning for not using our weapons was sound. One man is down. Lia made it away. Help will be here soon."

While it seemed as if they'd fought for hours, it had only been a few minutes. In five standard minutes more or less, help would arrive. She and Joen could handle these three for that length of time—and if not, they didn't belong in the Alliance.

As the enemy circled them, she and Joen worked in concert, keeping the three men away with effective sweeps of their knives. A quick glance confirmed the man Joen had fought was down and unmoving; the rapidly spreading blood pool under the body glistened black against the wet cobbled street.

Happier with the odds, Nadia went on the attack. The man who'd cursed her had come too close, so she shoved him back with a vicious forward kick to his diaphragm. Gagging, he fell sideways onto the rough, uneven pavement, his leg slipping awkwardly on the mist-slickened surface. The sharp crack of a bone breaking sounded loudly amidst the groans and curses of the fighting. The downed man's litany of filth testified to his pain and frustration.

Good. The odds were better now—one attacker each.

"Good job, Nadia. Left one's mine." Following his words, Joen charged the man to his left and quickly forced the fight away from her, giving her room to use her legs, her strongest weapon when fighting a man larger and stronger than her.

"Ready for me, you coward?" She waved him on. "Come get me, asswipe." She purposely goaded him; she didn't want him running away now that help would be here any minute.

Stalking her next victim, movement from the man with the broken leg had her glancing his way. *Shit, shit, shit.*

He fired his laser pistol.

Guess he doesn't care about keeping things quiet now. Reflex had her moving to her right. *Should've broken his arm or at the very least disarmed him.* Her mistake could cost both her and Joen's lives.

His shot cut a line of fire across her left upper arm. If she hadn't moved, she would've taken a hit to her heart.

As if being stupid and getting shot by a downed enemy wasn't bad enough, the bastard she'd been about to attack took advantage of her momentary distraction and rushed her. He took her to the ground. It was akin to being run over by a laser tank. The fall jarred her wounded shoulder and arm.

Madder than hell and in pain, she roared and rolled away from the man who pummeled her with forceful body blows. Like an eel, she twisted and slithered until she was out from under him. When he attempted to grab her by the shoulders, she thrust the heel of her hand into his nose. A nasty-sounding crunch and a gratifying amount of blood told her she'd broken the fucker's nose.

Wiping away the blood, her Prime attacker swore and threw all of his body weight on top of her, his forearm braced against her throat. She grabbed his arm to move it, but the combination of his strength and the leverage he had proved to be too much.

But she refused to quit. As long as she had breath, she'd fight him. She wiggled and bucked to dislodge him, but he was too heavy. If she didn't get him off her soon, she'd pass out from lack of oxygen.

In the background, Joen swore and grunted. He had his hands full. No help from that quarter. She was on her own until the others arrived.

Nadia took as deep a breath as she could through her constricted airway and calmed her mind and body. She needed to conserve energy and find a way to get the hulking bastard off her.

Brains won over brawn in most fights. The key was to eliminate the fear. Lessons she'd learned through hard-won experience.

The brute breathed heavily as he leered down at her. He was aroused, and his erection shoved against her lower body.

Her mind and body froze, remembering the past, the feelings of helplessness.

No, no, Nadia. Brain in the now. Not the past.

She'd found a way to survive then—she would this time also.

The man felt her up with the rough, cruel fingers of his free hand. "Terran slut." His spittle hit her face, but she forced herself not to flinch or display one iota of fear. "You want a Prime male so much? Let's see how you like me, eh?"

Without moving the forearm he held against her throat, her assailant shifted his lower body to the side slightly and shoved one fat finger of his roaming hand along the notch between her legs.

She gritted her teeth and resolutely shoved away the persistent image of the last guy who'd attempted to rape her—and had almost succeeded.

Not gonna happen, buster. I won that round and am even stronger now.

Her attacker moved his arm off her neck and shifted to grasp her throat one-handed. His hand was big and easily spanned the column of her neck, one finger placed against her carotid. He laughed. "Just a little more pressure, Terran whore, and I can make you unconscious and do whatever I like to you. But I won't—I like my women to scream. You'll scream for me, won't you, *karote*?"

He straightened to sit more upright. His knees straddled her torso, his powerful thighs acting like a vise to hold her in place. His ass settled on her thighs. In this position, his free hand had more access to her body. And he used it. He ripped her thin, long-sleeved T-shirt and proceeded to pinch and knead her breasts through the sheer camisole she wore underneath.

His movement off her diaphragm now allowed her to breathe more easily. She took in more oxygen as the hand he'd had at her throat now joined the other in poking and prodding her nearly naked upper torso.

Confident he had her subdued and absorbed in his lust, he'd forgotten Nadia was a trained soldier. To him she was just another weak piece of ass.

Big mistake on his part.

Head cleared now, thanks to being able to breathe, Nadia snaked her hand up her side and gripped his balls through the thin stretch fabric of his pants. As she twisted his nuts, she thrust the stiffened fingers of her other hand into his trachea.

The bastard's eyes widened with shock. He grunted and choked as his hands reached to cup his abused testicles and his damaged windpipe at the same time.

Using his pain and distraction and the better leverage with his body more upright, she bucked him off her using her strong core. She rolled away. Then using her elbows and feet, she scuttled backward along the pavement like a fleeing crab.

Her attacker had murder in his eyes now.

Too weak to stand, too dizzy to run even if she could get upright, Nadia continued to scrabble away. Fighting back the pain from her shoulder and arm wounds, she struggled to pull in more oxygen and dig deep for another life-saving shot of adrenaline.

Her attacker stalked her. His eyes glittered with menace as he rubbed his balls. "You will pray for death." He eyed her body. "It will be enjoyable to see how many ways I can make you beg."

Dermo! She'd hurt him, but hadn't disabled him. Most men would still be on the ground, retching up their guts from the shot to the balls alone.

Note to self, Prime males have tough packages.

He easily caught up with her as she backed into a curb.

Shoot him, dummy!

Damn! She'd forgotten all about her weapon as she'd fought the man. Lack of oxygen must've affected her brain.

Her gaze holding the man's leering stare, she slid her hand down her side and prayed the gun hadn't become dislodged during the fight.

"No, you don't!" The Prime's meaty fist connected with her jaw. Her head bounced cruelly off the rough edge of the curb, stunning her.

Dazed and unable to move, she lay at his feet, gasping for breath and seeing stars. He pulled her laser pistol out of her holster and tossed it to the side.

At the same moment, Joen shouted something. The sound of an Alliance laser pistol and another laser returning the fire registered in her scrambled brain. She struggled to get up. The world whirled. She turned her head and vomited into the gutter.

Coughing, she sought to crawl away from the grate in the street, but her attacker's legs stopped her. She turned to lie flat on her back as she attempted to breathe through the pain and nausea. She had a concussion for sure, maybe a skull fracture.

"Nadia!" This time she registered Joen's shout, but couldn't answer.

Another round of laser fire. Joen's cry of pain chilled her.

God, she had to get up. Had to help her shipmate. She struggled to sit, but fell back. She retched once again into the grate covering a storm drain. Definitely, a concussion. Jury was still out on the fracture. She closed her eyes against the swirling world.

"Joen?" Her voice was weak and so unlike her.

There was no answer. God, was he dead? Pain and despair swamped her.

"He's out of it, *karote*." The Prime's raspy voice held a sound of triumph. The legs connected to the harsh voice straddled her body once more.

She slitted her eyes and watched as he ripped her uniform trousers open. He raised onto his knees just enough to shove her pants and underwear down to her calves before setting his ass on her naked thighs.

Underneath her mostly naked torso, the wet, cold stones of the street set her body to shivering.

"Pretty sex. Never seen light-colored hair before." Her attacker shoved two thick fingers into her dry opening. She made an effort to move away from the intrusion, but couldn't. With his other hand, he twisted a nipple through the camisole. She gasped in pain.

He ripped the camisole away. "Very firm. Nice breasts." He grunted, a sound of satisfaction. Pulling his fingers from her vaginal opening, he slapped her across the face. "Let's see how you suck seed, slut. I want to be good and hard before I take you."

Nadia closed her eyes. She didn't need the world spinning around her to distract her from the fight she'd have to mount to avoid being violated.

The only good news was that help had to arrive soon. All she had to do was survive.

Using the last of her reserves, she bucked against the man atop her in an attempt to dislodge him. It had worked before, why not this time?

But she was too weak. He didn't budge.

"Stop it!" He squeezed her jaw cruelly with one large hand.

The pain shot through her head into her neck and spine. She moaned weakly. The brute let go of her jaw and knee-walked up her body until his knees met her shoulders. Stripping open his pants, he grabbed her jaw and yanked her head up so she had a direct view of his erect penis and the purpled head with precum leaking from the slit.

"Open your mouth, *karote*!" He dug his nails into her face as he shoved the wet head of his penis against her lips.

She shook her head wildly, whimpering through another wave of teeth-chattering vertigo, and tightened her jaw even more. He cursed and grabbed her hair with his free hand and tilted her head back onto the ground at such an extreme angle that taking a breath was painful.

She mentally screamed for Huw. He had to open for her—she needed him. The strange instinct which had gained strength over the past two weeks urged her not to give up. She continued to beat at the black wall blocking her from Huw's raw energy—and suddenly Huw was there. A sense of rightness settled into her very soul. *This is the way it's supposed to be.*

"Nadia ... Nadia..."

The sound of her name screamed in Huw's mental voice sparked her to fight anew. Huw was coming.

Nadia reached for the connection with all that was in her and found a deep well of pure power unlike anything she'd ever encountered. This was stronger than what she'd drawn from him on Tarn.

"Nadia! Nadia..."

Using Huw's strong energy, she threw her attacker off to the side long enough to get her right arm free from his imprisoning thigh. Her head pounded like a bitch of a marching band. So, she closed her eyes and lay quiescent.

Even with Huw and the deep-rooted instincts urging her to get up and fight, she couldn't stand, let alone outrun the man. But she could defend in other ways. Slowly, so as not to call attention to her actions, she reached with her right hand for the laser pistol the bastard had tossed aside.

"Nice try, but you will not succeed, *karote*. Prime males are superior in all ways to females of any race." The bastard was immediately back on top of her. He was far too sure of himself and ignored her grasping right hand.

It would be what killed him.

"You are one surprise after another." He cruelly twisted a nipple.

Nadia moaned, pandering to his ego, and moved her hand another inch. She'd spied the pistol just before she'd closed her eyes against the crazy kaleidoscope the world had become. Her fingers scrabbled along the damp paving stones. God, maybe she'd just thought she'd seen the pistol.

"Arch into me. I like my *karote* vigorous."

The Prime attacker was damn proficient speaking Standard. She'd bet her next pay he was a member of the Prime military—and a fanatic.

Huw's strength continued to flood her, saturating every pore of her being. The seemingly infinite well of pure energy cleared her mind and dulled her pain, allowing her to plot, plan, and observe as if she were looking at the scene from outside herself.

The Prime's alcohol-laden breath wafted over her face, nauseating her. She swallowed the sickness threatening to take her over.

Once more, he held her jaw still, his fingernails biting into her tender skin. The tip of his cock touched her closed lips. "Take me in your mouth. Suck me off good, and maybe I'll keep you for a pet rather than kill you."

A man yelled something. It was Joen's voice. Another voice yelled something back. Joen was still alive and fighting. *Thank you, God.*

Then she realized the sounds of fighting had been going on all the while like white noise. It wasn't until now with her heart not pounding loudly in her ears that she could hear the low grunts and curses as Joen fought the other man.

Joen's war cry echoed off the buildings. He was fighting for his life. The only one who could help Nadia at this moment would be Nadia. She couldn't wait for the rescue. She sensed Huw nearing, sensed his desperation to save her—but knew he wouldn't make it in time.

So be it.

Her eyes closed. She lay quietly as if she were defeated, as if she were totally helpless. Her right hand was free and moving at a snail's pace in the search for the weapon that had to be there. All the while, she plotted and planned what to do if she couldn't shoot the bastard.

The man slapped her. "Open your eyes—watch as I take your mouth."

He hit her twice more. Her head protested the abuse, but her mind remained clear and focused. Her hand edged its way over another millimeter of ground.

"Unconscious. Weak Terran woman." He grumbled, muttered, and raged under his breath. Releasing her jaw, he moved down her torso. His intent was obvious—if he couldn't have her mouth…

So not going to happen.

Fighting the need to tear off his dick with her bare hands, she forced her body to remain motionless. Then she found the butt of her laser pistol. She grasped the sidearm and felt for the safety. The man was too busy fumbling to notice. He leaned over. His foul breath touched her face.

She clutched the gun, getting her fingers around it more firmly. Safety was off. Power was on the lethal level.

Nadia moaned and fluttered her eyelashes. Through the curtain of her lashes, she found his attention was fully on her face.

He leered. "Ready for a real man, *karote*?" He grabbed her face to hold her for a biting kiss.

She brought the gun closer and fired the weapon into his thick upper body. The angle wasn't perfect for a heart shot, but it blasted him in the torso hard enough to roll him off her.

Nadia rolled onto her left side. She brought her weapon up and located him through blurred vision. He'd fallen only a few feet away. Somehow, he still moved. He lay on his side, facing her. He glared. He'd kill her if he could.

"Die, *apayebo*." She smiled grimly as she fired a full stream into his head. He fell onto his back. This time there was no movement, not even a fricking twitch.

Pain and nausea drove her to the ground. Breathing in gasps and moans, she curled into a ball, her laser pistol still clutched in one hand and clasped against her stomach. The cut on her shoulder, the laser gouge on her arm, and the damage to her head sent waves of pain throughout her body. She gritted her teeth against the need to scream and scream and scream. She could smell her blood mixing with the rain on the wet streets. She was cold and miserable and all she wanted to do was black out.

But she couldn't let down her guard until she knew all of the attackers were dead or contained. She wasn't sure she had the strength or the vision to hit anything else, but she'd damn sure try if someone else attempted to assault her.

Nadia groaned low in her throat, an animal-like sound, and hot tears streamed down her icy face. She'd survived; her attacker hadn't. At the end of the day that was all that counted. Anything he'd done to her body could be healed with time and a regen bed.

All sounds of fighting had died away. The sounds of the rain on the street, the surf hitting the breakfront, and some waterfowl calling to one another were the only things she heard. Then a thudding sound startled her. After a few seconds, she identified it as the sound of running footsteps coming closer and closer. Was it the last Prime attacker coming to finish her off? Had Joen fallen?

Nadia dug for the strength to uncurl and prepare to fight yet again. Huw's masculine energy was still there—a strong, beautiful, vital tunnel in her mind—waiting for her to call upon it.

"Nadia ... Nadia ... hold on..."

And then she knew, the sound of feet was Huw and the others.

Nadia smiled at the knowledge this would be all over soon and was shocked at how much energy it took to curve her lips. She was weaker than a newborn and wasn't sure even Huw's energy supplement would help if a halfway determined predator came upon her.

"Joen?" Her voice was weak, a mere croak, practically soundless. She turned her blurred gaze toward the sky, obscured by the rain clouds. Had it only been minutes ago Joen had predicted the rain?

A roar came from somewhere beyond her body. She recognized the sound as the Caradoc battle cry. Huw and Iolyn were near.

Joen's answering cry was music to her ears. He was alive.

Assured she was now safe and rescue and medical attention were close at hand, she curled back into her ball. They'd done it. They'd survived. Finally she allowed the laser pistol to drop to the ground.

"Nadia?" Joen grasped her hand and massaged it with gentle, trembling, and very hot fingers.

She swallowed once then twice before she managed to croak out, "You okay?"

"Yes, thanks to you. You Terran women sure are lethal." He chuckled as he gently checked her head with his other hand. She winced and hissed. "Sorry. You have a nasty bump back there."

She laughed weakly and regretted it as nausea swirled within. "I know. Concussion." Running feet came ever closer. "Cover me up. Don't let H—uh, him see me like this. I don't…"

"Shh, Nadia." Joen alternately growled and swore as he carefully, almost tenderly, checked her for other wounds. When he reached her exposed lower torso, his whole body stiffened and his growling crescendoed. He let loose a roar. Yet, his anger didn't affect the gentleness with which he pulled up her trousers and fastened them.

Something warm covered her trembling body and she realized he'd given her his jacket. Men always seemed to be giving her their clothing. She tried to say thank you, but her teeth chattered too much.

"Huw's a fool." Joen paused and looked over his shoulder. "But he sure looks as if he would like to kill somebody— possibly me or his brother."

"Why?" Nadia scrunched her forehead and wished immediately she hadn't. Even that small effort set her head to hammering.

"Iolyn is visibly restraining Huw from coming over here. Lia just pointed her finger at all of them. She is warning them all off." Joen chuckled. "My woman wants us all to herself before the crowd descends upon you and me."

His face lit up as Lia approached. "*Lubha*, you are all right?"

"I'm fine, love. Move aside." Lia looked Joen over carefully.

Nadia could tell Joen wasn't hurt too badly by the relieved look in the doctor's eyes.

"You'll do for now." Lia stroked a finger over his bruised and bloody face. "I'll take care of your wounds later. Now go and help the others hold onto Huw for a while. We gals need some privacy."

"Yes, Lia love." Joen got up.

Lia took his place next to Nadia and began checking her over with gentle probing fingers. She swore upon discovering the lump on the back of Nadia's head. "Joen, tell them we'll need transport for Nadia. I want to get her to the Prime medica, stat."

"I'll see to it, my *gemate lubha*. Thanks for covering my ass, Nadia." Joen patted her good shoulder.

"It's what … what we do." She ventured to lift her head to seek out Huw whose voice still called along their connection. She gave up when white dots and sickening waves of heat forced her to lie back and remain still.

Carefully, she turned her head to the side and watched Joen approach the other men. Even that small movement proved to be too much. "Dizzy, Lia. Sick to my stomach."

"You took a good knock to the head and look as if you've gone ten rounds with an Antarean. So, yeah, I'd say you have every right to feel like crap."

Nadia laughed weakly—well, it sounded more like the croak of an anemic frog. "Such a genteel bedside manner."

"You want genteel, become a civilian." Lia grimaced and muttered as she probed Nadia's jawline. The doctor's fingers were warm as they traced the places where her attacker had gripped her face. "Finger marks. Nail marks. The fucking lowlife, scum-sucking amoeba."

Nadia snickered and groaned. "Don't make me laugh. It hurts."

Lia got into Nadia's direct line of sight, concern etched in every line and angle of her face. "Iolyn and the others are losing the battle to contain Huw. So, before he comes storming over here, did the *apayebo* rape you?" The doctor's tone was worried and angry.

"Just fingers for a second or two—his lust … I used it as a distraction … had to get my weapon back. I killed him."

"Good. But we'll give you something in case any semen entered you."

Nadia whispered, "Just fingers. No need." She needed to close her eyes. Her vision went in and out and the pounding in her head was deafening.

Lia stroked the bruises on Nadia's jaw and shined a light in her eyes. "Regen bed for you, sweetie. Your pupils are constricted. You definitely have a concussion. And I want to make sure it's not anything worse than that. So we'll be scanning your brain. You also lost a lot of blood from the knife cut to your shoulder. How in the hell you stayed conscious to kill the son of a bitch I'll never understand."

"Let me in." Huw's demanding voice held concern and something more. His energy preceded him like a warm, wooly blanket, enveloping her. It felt and smelled and tasted familiar.

"Dakkin, you asshole." Huw growled. "What were you doing while Nadia was getting beaten to a pulp?"

Nadia gasped. Her eyes flared open to glare at the man whose connection undoubtedly had saved her life. But right now, she wanted to punch him. "Joen took out two men. I broke the leg of one, disabling him—and killed another. Two each."

She paused and gasped for breath. Lia grasped her hand and squeezed gently and shot Huw a nasty look.

"Teamwork. We did our jobs. We covered Lia. Took out the enemy. So, shut the fuck up, Huw. You weren't here. You know nothing." Nadia closed her eyes and turned her sore head to the side. Her teeth chattered from anger and cold.

"Jesus, Nadia." Lia re-examined the lump on her skull; it felt as big as the *Galanti* under Lia's small fingers. "It's swollen worse than a few seconds ago. Where's the medical transport? They coming by way of fricking Mars? I need a portable regen bed now! She's got a possible skull fracture."

Huw knelt by her head. "*Diew*. Nadia ... I'm sorry. I wish I'd been here." He stroked a trembling finger over her bruised jaw.

And a miracle occurred.

His touch soothed her, more so than it had on Tarn just forty-eight standard hours ago. Her aches subsided as if they'd whirled down a preternatural drain.

All of a sudden, she was sleepy. A warm, dark cloud of protective energy swaddled her within its strong masculine confines.

As she lost consciousness, she had an epiphany—this last battle and Huw's response to it fully confirmed her bond with him, mentally and emotionally. Only the physical connection remained to seal the trinity of mind-heart-body. But this bonding was an ass-backward Prime mating without the mark. In reality, it should've been impossible, but wasn't.

One thing she'd learned this evening—Huw cared, but he didn't understand why; maybe he was afraid of his feelings. The bond was there, waiting to be completed—but Huw might never accept it.

God, I'm so fucked.

"She's unconscious! Do something, Lia." Huw rubbed his thumb gingerly over Nadia's bruised face and swollen lips. His anxious gaze checked out each and every mark, cut, and laser burn he could see under the dim light of the street lamp. "Did the bastard ... was she ... raped?" He choked at the thought.

No one answered.

Huw stroked a shaky hand down her body and noted the jacket covering her was not hers and her pants were not fastened properly. He'd never felt such anger before. If he could resurrect the *apayebo* and kill him again, he would. "*Ansu bhau*, Joen. Where were you when Nadia was being assaulted?"

"Shut up, brother." Iolyn's voice came from behind him. "Nadia told you. They each took out two. She held up her end of the battle. Don't take her battle pride from her."

"So help me, Huw," Joen said. "If you make her out to be a victim, I will beat you until you are a bloody heaping pile of flesh. Nadia is a true warrior. I am proud to have her as a fellow crew member."

Joen's words struck Huw, shaming him.

Diew, what was wrong with him? He didn't want to hurt or insult Nadia, but it seemed that's all he had been doing lately.

Nadia had proven herself time and time again. She was a soldier—he knew that, respected that. So, why did he want to shield her from all harm? Why did he want to plant his fist in Joen's face for touching her? And why did he want to carry her away and care for her himself?

His gut gave him the answer. *You care for her.* He did, but there still might be a Prime female waiting for her *gemat*— and that *gemat* might be him. His honor demanded patience for a little while longer.

Royce approached and knelt behind Huw and looked over his shoulder. "Shit, the bastard really did a number on her. Nadia's a scrapper though. She regularly hands me my butt in hand-to-hand, but taking down two Prime hulking assholes … well, I'm damn proud of her."

"She should not have had to." Huw couldn't keep the words from escaping. His voice rumbled low, a growling tone he'd heard Wulf use around Mel when she was in danger or hurt. He controlled the sound, but couldn't keep from adding, "She could have been killed."

"She wasn't. So get over it." Royce squeezed Huw's shoulder, a painful grip that had him ready to lash out at the blunt Terran captain. "Besides, the only reason she left the restaurant was you. Nadia couldn't stand listening to your dumbass arguments any longer so she left before we could leave as a group."

Huw winced. The truth hurt.

Iolyn added, "Royce is correct. These four would never have attacked if we had left as a group. The attack proves the warning issued by the Alliance Military Command was accurate—the fanatics are targeting Terran women seen with Prime males. We'll have to take additional precautions to protect our female soldiers."

Huw stroked Nadia's cold, damp forehead. Touching her soothed him, and at some level he knew his touch soothed her. Whatever the psychic connection between them was, it was stronger each time they touched. It would be hard, but for honor's sake, he would have to keep his distance from her until after the final destination on the Lost Ones' mission. If there were no Lost One survivors, he'd begin his courtship of Nadia on the trip back to Cejuru Prime.

If someone else doesn't take her first.

A primal snarl reverberated inside his head; the more primitive part of his brain didn't like the idea of anyone touching Nadia but him.

Diew, he was fucked as the Terrans said.

"Mel and Wulf are on their way with the transport," Joen said. "Lia, Kerr, and I will stay with Nadia. Someone needs to deal with the Home Guard. They're here demanding answers. They'd probably take the report better from a Caradoc united front."

"Come on, brother. Let's keep the locals away from Joen and Nadia. Mel and Wulf need to hear their report before the Guard. With two dead Prime soldiers in civilian clothes and two badly injured ones, there will be damage control to be done before the Elder Council hears about this incident."

Reluctantly, Huw left Nadia's side. She moaned and grimaced as he stood and walked away.

Why did it feel as if he'd had his heart torn from his chest? He rubbed the aching spot above the organ in question.

Without looking back, he strode toward his brother who'd engaged the very angry local police. Each step tore the gaping wound in his soul wider.

CHAPTER 13

One standard hour later, on the Galanti in space dock

Huw stalked into the reception area of *Galanti's* Sick Bay and took a quick glance around. Mel sat along the wall, staring with some concern at Wulf who stood at the viewing window to the triage room. Anger and frustration poured off his brother in violent waves.

"Why was Nadia brought here?" Huw asked Mel.

"Wulf and I felt it necessary—safer." Her demeanor radiated Wulf's anger but was tinged with worry; the combination poured off her in crashing waves. "All Gold Squadron crews have been ordered back to the space station and their ships until further notice."

"Understood." He left his sister-kin and joined his brother.

Through the window, Huw observed Lia and Kerr working over Nadia's pale, motionless body lying on the regen bed. Joen sat on a nearby treatment table, his wounds being seen to by a tech.

Joen's gaze never left Lia as she worked on Nadia with fierce concentration. Yeah, he could see it now. The others had read the Communications Officer correctly—Joen was involved with the little Terran doctor.

"Why is Nadia so still? Why are both doctors still working on her? *Diew!* Lia told me Nadia would be fine." Huw aimed an angry glance at his brother before heading toward the triage room's door.

Huw had only taken two steps when Wulf grabbed his arm and held him back. "Just stay put. Nadia has a skull fracture, deep knife wounds on her upper back and shoulder, a second-degree laser burn on her arm, a couple of broken ribs, and various internal injuries. The doctors are stabilizing her injuries and prepping her for several days of healing sleep in a regen bed."

"*Ansu bhau.*" Huw snarled and twisted away from his brother's grip. "I'm going in there." It was crazy and he had promised himself to stay away from her until after the mission—but everything in him needed to touch her, smell her, listen to her breathing.

"No." Wulf shoved him toward a chair. "Sit. That's an order. The doctors don't need you interrupting. Nadia doesn't need it, either."

Sitting next to Huw, Wulf glared. "Now, what's going on between you and Nadia? Royce said you insulted her and she left the bar with only Lia and Joen for escorts. Didn't you get the orders about our female crew members being armed and escorted by at least one warrior-class soldier at all times while dirt-side?"

"No. Plus, Joen is warrior-trained." Huw hated the defensive tone in his voice, but couldn't help it. His brother very rarely used the commanding officer card with his brothers. That he chose to do so for the second time within a week meant Wulf was positively pissed.

"Joen is a Communications Officer." Wulf sighed and ran fingers through his hair. "*Diew*, Huw. The man hadn't had updates on his hand-to-hand and weapons training until these past few weeks. And he was *never* rated warrior-class, just warrior-trained. The fact he and Nadia held their own against those men—who *were* warrior-class—is a miracle."

"Wulf," Mel touched her *gemat*'s arm, drawing his attention away from Huw and diminishing the tension between the two brothers at the same time. "Cut Huw some slack."

Wulf lifted her hand and kissed the tips of her fingers. "You are right, *lubha*." He turned toward Huw. "I am sorry I yelled, brother. But I'm concerned after the incidents on Tarn and this attack that the rebels have infiltrated more of our military than we'd previously thought."

"Which is why," Mel turned to Huw, "we'll move all training to the space station. Later, if we need on-planet training, we can use the Alliance military facilities at Tooh IV. Right now, we have one standard week to whip the merged crews of Gold into shape before we embark on the mission to find Lost Ones."

"The time table was moved up. Why?" Huw's senses went on high alert. Had there been a sighting of some Lost Ones' ships by the drones sent to check the routes and the planets?

Wulf's next words dashed that notion to pieces.

"There have been attacks on two Alliance scientific teams in the Iota Persei system. We'll be stopping and leaving a battle cruiser at each planet to assist with their protection."

"I am glad we're leaving soon." A combination of anticipation and pain swept through Huw. This trip would end his turmoil; at the end, he would either have a Prime *gemate* or would be free to court Nadia. Not many knew, not even his family, but the only reason he'd followed his brothers into the military was the off chance he might find his mate while policing the galaxy.

A sharp ache had him gasping. He stood and walked toward the window. "Nadia's in pain. Why aren't they giving her a bolus?" He turned to catch Mel and Wulf exchanging a pointed look. "What is it? What aren't you telling me? Is Nadia dying?"

"No, no. She'll be fine." Wulf grabbed Huw's arm and stopped him once again from entering the treatment area. "Let's find Iolyn and have a drink. We'll ask Royce and the other captains to join us. We need to put together contingency plans in case the pirate activity in the Iota Persei system is worse than Alliance Military Command has heard. Melina will stay here and provide updates on Nadia. Okay?"

It wasn't okay. A primitive feeling in his gut urged him to stay and protect Nadia, but his higher-level reasoning told him she was safe among her crew. He would humor his brother for the time being.

Later, he'd return and sit with her. Anyone telling him nay would get their face punched in.

Once Wulf and Huw had left, Mel entered the treatment room and approached Joen. "You okay?" She swept a hand down his tense back. He'd been cut several times, defensive wounds, and burned by a laser. Like Nadia, he looked as if he'd gone through hell.

"Yeah." He nodded toward the outer room. "Huw wanted in, didn't he?"

"Yes. Wulf convinced him it would do Nadia no good at this point for him to be here. They're going to get a drink with Iolyn and the other captains and discuss the upcoming dual missions."

Joen nodded and his gaze traveled back to Lia as she hovered around the regen bed tending to Nadia. "You know I'm more than attracted to Lia?" His voice was pitched low so only Mel would hear.

She nodded, but noted Lia's head had jerked at Joen's words as if she'd heard him clearly.

"What you don't know is—Lia and I are fully mated—in the Prime way." He pulled up the hospital shirt and showed a marking over his heart. "Lia and I weren't going to share this until she'd gotten some test results back from Dr. Martin. She sent our blood and tissue samples when she sent Huw and Nadia's. No matter what the test results say, the markings are positive proof."

"Lia has a marking also?" Mel sent a searching glance at her friend who turned and solemnly nodded. Obviously, the increased sensory perception Prime mates gained with the marking was in effect. "I'm shocked, amazed and genuinely happy for you both. But how? Lia's one hundred percent Terran." She shot a quizzical look at Joen. "And why *are* you telling me now?"

He nodded toward Nadia. "Somehow she overcame a skull fracture, severe wounds, and blood loss to defeat the warrior-class Prime who had her on the ground … helpless. Her pain decreased while Huw was near, both on the planet and just now. Even in regen sleep, she sensed him near and called out his name as he left the outer room."

"Shit, just as Wulf and I suspected after the kidnapping—they're bonding in some way. But we never suspected … how could we?" Mel rubbed a finger over a sharp, nagging ache in the middle of her forehead.

Immediately, Wulf so attuned to her every mood sent her healing warmth. She sighed as the pain lessened and sent him a "thank you."

"So? You think Nadia is in some stage of a Prime mating with Huw? But where are their marks? A Prime mating…" Mel's words trailed off; she wasn't sure what to think or say next.

"Yes. Nadia is showing the same signs Lia experienced in the early stages of our relationship. At first, we were intensely attracted. But unlike Huw, I didn't fight it. We've been seeing each other and keeping it quiet, because we weren't sure what was happening." Mel nodded, silently encouraging him to continue. "Kerr knew because Lia wanted an objective medical mind looking over the symptoms she was documenting. As we were around each other more, we noted increasing symptoms of the Prime mating bond."

"What kind of symptoms?" Mel asked.

"First, it was the attraction. I liked the way Lia looked and smelled. Then I became aware of her emotions and could practically read her thoughts." He looked over at Lia who nodded and smiled. "Then we found we could communicate telepathically—that happened on Tarn when we were thrown together in a stressful situation, a survival situation."

"Those types of things happened to me *after* I met Wulf the first time, but I already had the marking." Mel absently rubbed her lower abdomen and reassured Wulf mentally she was okay as his worry over her disordered emotions came across their link.

"Yes, it seems backward." Joen rubbed his chest, and Lia let out a low moan that carried across the room. Kerr startled, but smiled. "We developed the markings after…" His voice trailed off and he looked at Lia again. His golden eyes glowed with heat.

Mel recognized the look—it was sexual. She'd seen it enough in Wulf's eyes.

"After what?" Mel asked. No good guessing; she needed Joen to verify what she suspected—the marks appeared after the two—a Terran female and a Prime male—had sex for the first time. This could impact all future such couplings and tests would have to be done to determine if any or all Terran-Prime couplings would produce *gemat-gemate* couples. The fanatics would go crazier than they already were.

"After we had sexual intercourse." Joen's lips turned up in a smile of dominant male satisfaction—another look she saw a lot on her mate's face.

"And the markings appeared how soon after you two had, um, intercourse?" She damned her red face, but talking about the sex life of two people who were her friends and subordinate crew members wasn't usually in her job description—the Alliance had counselors for that sort of thing.

But she needed to know. Because if Nadia and Huw were mating, there could be some serious issues, not the least of which would be Huw's continued denial of the whole process.

Mel recalled the separation from Wulf after she'd first discovered she had a mate. She'd been not only in physical, but also mental and emotional pain. Nadia was already going through some of that now with Huw's overt rejection of her.

"The marking appeared immediately, but then darkened with the next couple of intimacies until it looks as it does now. Lia suggested it was as if our bodies were acclimating to one another."

"That sounds ... definitely different ... from my process." Mel had always had her mark, but it had faded and had only come to life when she had first heard Wulf's voice.

"Lia and Kerr—and the Alliance researcher Dr. Martin—hypothesized some non-Prime women must have a latent Prime gene in their DNA. The doctors believe it exists, because Earth was one of the planets our ancestors used as a way station in their trips around the galaxy."

Mel nodded. "That makes sense. We knew the Prime intermingled with the native populations and most Prime family lines have mixed DNA. So, this latent DNA lies dormant and then is activated when brought into close proximity to whatever the gene responds to?"

"It's all about hominid neurochemistry." Lia joined them along with Kerr. Joen pulled Lia to his side and wrapped one arm around her waist.

Mel shot an anxious glance at Nadia who was now closed into the regen bed.

"She can't hear us." Lia had interpreted Mel's concern and answered the unasked question. "She's sleeping and will be fine. Actually, the pain alleviation while Huw was in the other room helped a lot. We may have to let him sit with her—it will hasten the healing."

"And hasten the bonding, if you're correct." Mel looked at the three. "You know Huw's in absolute denial. He's a stubborn Prime. And when you add to that trait the Caradoc bloodline, it makes him even more mule-headed."

Joen chuckled. He nuzzled Lia's neck and sighed. "Her scent is better than a pain blocker. And, yes, Huw will deny. But the more they're together; the harder it will be for him to continue to deny the mating dance. Prime selection will win out."

"What about Nadia? Does she know about your markings?" Mel waved a hand to encompass the couple as they leaned into each other. "I'm pretty sure she suspects something is happening between her and Huw. She said something to me when we were kidnapped by the rebels. And she said something again after the Tarn incident."

Lia nodded. "She suspects something is going on with us, but she hasn't said anything to me. She doesn't know about our symptoms or the markings. But we'll need to tell her. If she has sex with Huw and they develop the marks, I want her to know up front such an action *might* take the two of them down a path Huw isn't willing to accept yet." Lia frowned, sadness in her eyes. "Nadia has been hurt enough by Huw's rejection—forming the marks and him continuing to deny their bond would crush her."

Joen murmured soothing nonsense as he cuddled Lia and kissed her cheek. She sighed and visibly relaxed. "Nadia's open to a relationship with Huw and knows something is happening between them," Lia continued. "She confirmed as much to the three of us on the way to the space station. They spoke telepathically during the

Tarn situation. She heard him calling her name during the attack this evening."

Lia touched Mel's arm. "Mel, she told me she received a needed boost of adrenaline and what she called masculine-feeling strength to help her defeat the man who almost raped her. She admitted to getting a smaller dose of that masculine energy on Tarn when fighting the mercenaries."

"Shit—that's battle-mate behavior." Mel sent Wulf a shorthand version of the discussion to that point. He needed to know this. They also needed to make a decision if the Alliance Military Command and Premier Caradoc needed to know.

Wulf's shock and awe came across their link. *"I'll be there as soon as I can wrap up this planning session with our captains,* lubha."

The quiet in the room was only broken by the sounds from the computers and medical equipment. Then Lia looked at Joen and arched her brows—he shrugged.

"What aren't you telling me?" Mel frowned.

The other three exchanged looks.

Mel glared at the trio. "Okay, fess up. What's going on?"

"It's complicated—but in a good way … and almost unbelievable." Lia paused.

"Just tell me, Lia."

"Well, since Joen and I developed our marks, I've taken a lot of samples from both of us and have sent them to Dr. Martin. She checked them against Huw and Nadia's samples. One conclusion she's reached is Prime/non-Prime matings should be extremely fertile. So, children are a given."

Mel interrupted. "Not a surprise. That was why the Prime joined the Alliance to build social bridges to get at the much larger pool of fertile females. So, why is that complicated?"

"Bear with me, Mel. I need you to see how Dr. Martin arrived at the conclusions she did."

Mel waved Lia on.

Lia took a deep breath and let it out. "Dr. Martin has also found the lack of fertility on Cejuru Prime seems to be one-sided and only affects the females. Kerr was able to get a good sampling of Prime male semen during crew physicals. Dr. Martin tested the samples and found the semen across the board was rich with viable sperm."

Mel opened her mouth to demand what the fuck all this had to do with Nadia and Huw and the unusual complication.

Lia held up her hand. "Patience, I'm getting there." She coughed and continued. "Bottom line, a Prime male like most hominid males can smell when a woman is fertile. The Prime being one of the longest surviving races in the universe, their neurochemical process had mutated to where the male could scent his *most* optimal match, defined as the match that would have less chances of genetic defects. This scenting affects both the male and female and a neurochemical process produces the mark. With me so far?"

Mel nodded. "The Prime male can smell his mate, and he and his mate develop marks indicating a prime selection."

"Exactly. In light of my and Joen's mating and marking, albeit backward—and in light of Huw and Nadia's also backward bonding process we asked Dr. Martin to look at your and Wulf's DNA samples…"

"Whoa, wait a parsec. Mine and Wulf's? Why would you send her ours? I'm Prime and Wulf is Prime and we mated the normal Prime way."

"Well, for one, because of the fertility issue of Prime women. You, my dear Prime friend, are very fertile. Dr. Martin has concluded, and Kerr and I concur, something on the planet has mutated the Prime female's fertility. Also, whatever is hurting the Prime female's ability to get pregnant and carry to term isn't carried across the whole spectrum of Prime females since a few are getting marks and carrying healthy babies to term. We want to figure out what's causing the infertility in the majority of Prime women and how it can be fixed."

"Okay, I can see that." Mel frowned. "But wouldn't you need to test a variety of Prime women and see what's going on with their DNA?

"We did that," Lia said. "We sent Dr. Martin samples from some of the sex surrogates Kerr is acquainted with. Other samples came from women with no markings, and some from those who'd mated, but then lost their mates."

"And what did she find?" Mel was interested in spite of the long way around Lia was taking.

"She found that many of the women who acted as sex surrogates and the others who had lost mates were fertile," Kerr said.

"So, in theory, they should be able to conceive and carry a baby … if they had a compatible Prime male," Mel said.

"Exactly!" Lia almost bounced she was so excited. "We asked Dr. Martin to determine if the women who were fertile could mate with non-Prime males—or even a different Prime male. Remember I said the marking happened on the most optimal match—I didn't say the only possible match."

Mel groaned and sent an urgent call to Wulf. *"Are you getting this?"*

"Yes. I am coming, Melina. My father has listened to similar hypotheses from our genetic researchers. This is another reason we allied with your Alliance. You have more research capability in your Astrobiology research labs. We needed an objective observer and test results before we upset the whole of Prime society."

"Thanks for not telling me."

"I would have … we've been busy, lubha."

"Not that busy."

Lia continued, "No marked Prime female who has been widowed has tried to mate with another Prime. No one has ever demonstrated the women couldn't mate again. It was just ingrained culturally that they couldn't. Dr. Martin's conclusion is the Prime population crisis was propagated by not only a low fertility rate in some women, but also by a societal bias ingrained over thousands of years."

"Jesus Christ, Lia. Open a can of worms, would you? If it can be shown a Prime woman could mate with a non-Prime or another Prime male, you'd upset the whole cultural order of their mating ritual." Mel shook her head. "The Pure Blood fanatics will go wild."

"Captain…" Kerr drew her attention. "Dr. Martin wants to help the Prime have a future. I, for one, am thrilled she is dedicated to solving our problems. My sister is one of the women who lost her mate. Her *gemate* mark is fading."

Mel gasped and rubbed her mark.

Kerr nodded. "Yes, it is heart-breaking. She not only lost her mate, but is losing what made her his. When her *gemat* died, she had two choices: live a celibate life or become a sex surrogate. She chose celibacy. She is only twenty-nine standard years old. According to the tests, my sister is one of the lucky ones who are fertile. She should be able to conceive and carry a baby to term. I want this chance for her and other Prime women like her—and for the sex surrogates."

"I have no problem with any of that, Kerr. None. I merely stated a fact. The rebels will throw the planet into civil war over this if it's not presented properly."

"We agree, Mel." Lia smiled. "Which is why you—and I suspect now Wulf," Mel nodded, "are the only persons who know what is going on outside of the people in this room and Dr. Martin."

"Dr. Martin is all that is good," Kerr said. "She's running all the early tests herself, keeping the results under tightest security, until we give her the go-ahead to bring in more assistance. She is eager to travel to Cejuru Prime and set up a research lab here to garner more samples for her genetic and environmental testing and to set up a fertility clinic. She wishes to help the Prime women who are currently miscarrying and to assist the non-Prime women who mate with Prime males if their pregnancies run into problems."

"And I'm totally in agreement with all of that. So is Wulf and from what he told me, his father has had these same types of discussions with Prime geneticists." Kerr looked shocked, but pleased. Lia smiled. "But I still don't understand what this all has to do with Huw and Nadia, you two, and the *gemat-gemate* marking. What is the damn complication?"

"It's what Dr. Martin found in my and Nadia's DNA." Lia smiled at Joen who squeezed her waist. "I'm Joen's battle-mate. Nadia will be Huw's—once their marks appear."

"How can this be?" Stunned, Mel looked from Lia to Joen to Kerr.

"This is where *your* DNA sample comes into play. Dr. Martin isolated a gene in my and Nadia's DNA which is similar to one in yours—a Prime gene. On that gene, Nadia and I have alleles identical to ones you have. Dr. Martin then looked at Joen's, Huw's, and Wulf's DNA and found comparable alleles in their DNA. These alleles are what make us battle-mates."

"Are you saying all non-Prime women who carry this Prime gene with these certain alleles will form a battle-mate connection with a Prime male?" Mel asked.

"Yes, if the male carries the same set of alleles." Lia's eyes glittered with her excitement. "Joen has told me the history of his people. At the time they explored Earth and Volusia and several other similar planets—all Prime females were warriors and most were battle-mates to their *gemats*. Thus, the males having sexual relations with non-Prime women on the visited planets and impregnating them would pass both their maternal and paternal sets of DNA to the non-Prime woman. The battle-mate allele would be passed through the mitochondrial DNA, or MtDNA, the Prime male received from his mother." Lia laughed. "Isn't that amazing?"

"Amazing. Nadia has *definitely* shown battle-mate behavior." Mel frowned and eyed Joen and Lia. "Have you had such incidences?"

"Yes." Joen nuzzled Lia's ear. "We mind-talk all the time and shared energy on Tarn. Lia's touch alleviates my pain. We need the contact even if it is just mental—though physical is better. Don't you do that with Wulf?"

"Yes." Mel thought for a second and swore. "Huw could barely accept the telepathy. He keeps rationalizing it—saying Nadia has to be a strong telepath. But his feeding her energy— hell, he'll just deny it."

"Then he'll be fooling himself," Joen said. "Nadia definitely found extra strength in the fight on the docks. I saw her go limp. I couldn't get to her; my man was giving me fits. She struggled to get the bastard off her and then nothing. The next time I looked she had shot him and tossed him off her. She had to be drawing on Huw's strength."

Joen raised Lia's hand to his lips and nibbled her knuckles. "Huw will come around. Give him time, Mel. I'm not sure how I even existed prior to mating with Lia. I feel so … so…"

"Whole," Mel said. "Complete. Fully sensate for the first time in your life."

"Yes." Joen smiled. "All of those things—and loved. So very loved."

"And that, too." Mel shook her head. "Damn, this is an explosive situation. We can keep your marking to ourselves until Huw and Nadia become marked, but at that point, Premier Caradoc will have to know. He'll want to announce the discovery to the Prime population." She looked first at Lia and then Kerr. "For the time being, you two will need to keep an eye out for symptoms among our female crew dating Prime males."

"I know you are concerned about the fanatics, Mel, but the majority of my people will be elated," Kerr said. "It is only a few malcontents who'll be unhappy. The rebels behind those fanatics only want power. They could care less about pure blood." He snorted. "I can find non-Prime DNA, much of it Terran, in all Prime family lines. Lots of those early Prime travelers didn't just impregnate the native women, they brought them and the resulting children home to Cejuru Prime. Not one person on my planet is pure blood, not even the Pure Bloods. We wouldn't have survived all these millennia without fresh DNA in our gene pool."

"Yeah, but you're a scientist and logical." Mel sighed and shook her head. "The fanatics will believe what they want—and the rebels funding them will encourage those misconceptions in order to get what they want."

"We live in interesting times." Joen pulled a protesting Lia onto his lap and kissed her cheek. "But I would walk through a barrage of laser cannon to find what I have now. And once the men who have no mates realize they could potentially have the marking and the chance at a life with a woman and a family, they'll rally to our side."

"But at what cost?" Mel asked.

"Whatever the cost," Joen answered, "it will be worth it."

HUW SNEAKED INTO THE REGEN bed unit when Kerr had gone into his office to do charts. He pulled the screens around her bed, giving him a sense of privacy. He needed to figure out what was going on between him and the beautiful, strong, and fascinating woman lying so quietly in the regen bed.

All through the damn meeting with his brothers and the other officers of Gold, he'd mentally checked on Nadia's condition through whatever in the universe this connection they had was. Her night terrors had become his until he finally had to excuse himself and come to her side. His tension along with her fears and pain subsided as he neared Sick Bay.

Nadia now rested comfortably—but his mind was in chaos and a sharp, stabbing pain jabbed him over his heart, piercing his very soul.

He was a bastard.

There, he could admit it.

A stubborn ass.

He had hurt this woman who cared for him. Here … now … alone with her, he could admit he cared for her. Loved her. But he could not admit it out loud.

Until he eliminated all chances of finding his *gemate* alive, he could not voice or even hint at his true feelings for Nadia. If he was to have a relationship with this special woman, he had to come with his heart, mind, and body free to love her.

Huw leaned over the regen bed and lowered the shield until her face was uncovered. He kissed her forehead. "Heal, Nadia."

Closing the cover, he sat by her bedside, watching over her, willing her his strength. He'd stay here until somebody came and threw him out.

CHAPTER 14

Five Standard Weeks later, on the Galanti, orbiting Ursa 345

Nadia scanned the visuals sent back by the unmanned drone. The two ships on the surface of the planet called Ursa 345 were older-model Prime starships. She'd confirmed their identity with Prime Command—they were definitely two of the ships that had carried women and children off Cejuru Prime twenty-seven standard years ago.

Their condition indicated they'd crashed. The ships' main decks survived basically intact. The crews and passengers could easily have lived in the ships for quite a long time as long as the environmental systems hadn't been breached and the ship's fusion reactors had remained online. Food stores would've lasted them up to two standard years.

Lia and Kerr hung over her shoulder, checking out the images and the readings streaming across the bottom of the monitor.

"No carbon life-forms in either ship—dead or alive," Lia said. "The survivors must've found the old Prime fortifications."

"The atmosphere on this planet according to early Prime records was thin at the time of the first colonization and has even less of the needed oxygen-nitrogen mix now," Kerr said. "The fortifications could only have been underground with full environmental support systems."

"Like the ones on Obam IV where Mel lived?" Nadia asked.

"Exactly. But even with a liveable atmosphere, our ancestors liked underground facilities so they could remain hidden while mapping a planet and observing the planet's life-forms. The early reports on this planet indicated no higher-level life-forms, but that could have changed over the millennia." Kerr reached over her shoulder. "If I may, let's look at the subterranean scans."

The Prime doctor swiped a finger over the control panel until the ground sonar scans appeared on the monitor. He pointed. "See? There are the underground passages and rooms. They were reputed to be a natural phenomena and the Prime explorers merely adapted them. The entrance is at the base of a mountain not more than thirty kilometers from the ships."

"That's odd, Kerr. How did the cave systems form?" Nadia pulled up another screen. "My readings show no tectonic activity ... ever. The core of the planet is not and never was molten, but is instead a solid core of iron. This planet is more akin to a piece of a larger planet that had broken off and was pulled into the Ursa solar system as a satellite."

Kerr frowned. "I don't dispute the readings, Nadia. I'm just telling you what the early explorers said about the underground cave systems."

"Let's see if we can spot any evidence of carbon life-forms underground." Nadia entered the search code and the results were immediate ... and saddening. She glanced at Lia and Kerr. Their expressions of grief were a reflection of her own.

"They're all dead." Nadia refined the probe's parameters. Yes, the readings were indicative of decaying carbon life-forms. "We need to go to the planet and see if we can figure out what killed them. Plus, I know Wulf will want to transport the remains back to Cejuru Prime for proper burial."

Kerr's expression was grim. "Yes. We must take them home. I would like to be on the away team."

Nadia nodded. "You were my first choice. Lia can take charge of preparing one of *Galanti*'s storage bays for the receipt of the remains."

Lia moved to another station. "I'll contact several of the orderlies and we'll begin now. Let me know when you send up the first group of bodies. I'll consult with Wulf as to the proper Prime protocols for preparing the bodies for burial rites."

"Kerr?" He turned away from the monitor to look at Nadia. "Pick your medical team. I'll take the Jod brothers from my department and contact Aeron to have him pick his scientific teams. We're here, so we might as well document the current status of the planet. It doesn't look as if anyone has updated the planet's conditions since the Prime first visited here centuries ago and established this as a way station."

"What are the surface conditions?" Kerr asked.

Nadia switched to a live view of the planet's surface and accessed the probe's up-to-the-second readings. "It's the top of the day. The temperature is three levels above Standard zero. Atmosphere isn't breathable."

She hit several keys and another set of readings appeared. "The underground temps are warm enough. The facility's atmosphere is unknown. If the Prime technology has survived, we might be able to get it up and running so we won't need the survival suits underground. But we'll prepare for the worst and hope for the best."

Kerr nodded. "Will you ask Huw to come along? He is the best engineer we have in case the ancient equipment needs some work." His tone had definitely been tentative.

And why shouldn't it be? No one, least of all her, understood what was going on with Huw. The man blew hot and cold where Nadia was concerned—and his constant vacillation was wearing on everyone's nerves.

Immediately after the attack on Cejuru's dockside, Huw had remained at her side until she'd begun to recover. It was Lia and Kerr's opinion the connection between Nadia and Huw had helped heal her more quickly.

Nadia knew it had. Even unconscious, she'd sensed Huw pouring his strength across their connection. He cared—but he didn't want to—and that hurt.

For much of the time since then, he'd managed to avoid her. He stayed in Engineering and she stayed on Command Deck or in her labs. No one commented on the distance between them, but everyone watched them. But she'd sensed he always knew where she was and how she felt. One of the Jods had told her Huw had destroyed a punching bag in the fitness center after she'd made a trip to the *Leonidas* to visit Aeron.

Several times Mel and Lia had sought to talk to her about Huw, but she'd broken into tears. They'd comforted her and derided stubborn Prime males as a species.

The weeks confined to the ship had made her an emotional basket case. Huw's connection was omnipresent—simmering in the back of her mind, burning in her lower abdomen, and aching in her heart. She could smell where he'd been as she went about her duties. When he called up to Command to speak to Mel or Wulf or even the helmsman, his voice sent a frisson of awareness across her skin.

He was there, but he wasn't.

His side of their mental connection had been locked down since her recovery. So, she'd locked her side down also and mourned the loss of his mental touch, his energy.

But even with the telepathic lock-down, her empathy ran strong. Huw was hurting. She was hurting. *Damn him!* He hurt them both with his rejection and was too damn stubborn to see it.

"No, Kerr." Her tone was harsh. She patted his arm to show she wasn't upset with him. "Cas Jod has an engineering background. I'll take him and his brothers. We work well together."

"I understand." Kerr's expression was full of sympathy.

She suspected the Prime doctor really did understand her emotional state. She'd heard him curse several times under his breath about Huw being an idiot. That was the general consensus among all of the unattached Prime males on the ship. Too bad Huw wasn't listening to his peers.

Kerr continued, "The Jods have named themselves your protectors. They sing your praises to anyone who listens. There isn't a Prime crew member in Gold who doesn't know about your courage. They are calling you the 'Warrior Goddess.'"

Nadia blushed. "I told them to stop calling me that."

But deep inside, it had been that praise and support which had helped her move on as best as she could. She pushed away from the computer console. "I need to advise Wulf and Mel about our plans. They'll probably wish to send a security team. Until we know what killed the survivors, we'll need to proceed with caution."

As Chief Science Officer on the command ship, Nadia had sole control of what scientific missions took place on planets they visited. Even with that unilateral ability to say yay or nay, she always consulted with the co-captains as a matter of courtesy. "After Mel and Wulf are informed, I'll contact Aeron. Have your team suited up and in the shuttle dock in one standard hour. Will that give you enough time?"

"More than enough, Nadia. I'll have no live patients to triage, just dead ones. Determining cause of death and body identification will have to take place on the *Galanti*." He shook his head, his golden eyes dulled to the color of aged Valerian scotch. "This is so sad. Three planets with evidence of Prime landings. The last two, no one could have survived the crashes. This one, the ships hitting dirt-side had survivors, but none still live. With no more clues as to where any other Lost Ones' ships might have gone, we are out of options for finding the remainder of our lost women and children."

"Yes, out of options." A small, selfish part of Nadia rejoiced.

Finally, Huw would have no more excuses to ignore her. He would be forced to face what grew between them, connecting them more and more each day despite Huw's best efforts to avoid her as if she had a dread disease.

But had Huw's rejection already done too much damage to her heart? Could she trust a man who'd ignored the very real evidence of the bonding between them?

Did she have a fricking choice?

Hell, *she* had tried to ignore the bond—will it away—but without success.

Once the mission had begun, Nadia had attempted "dating" Aeron. Several times over the last few weeks, she'd taken a small transport to the *Leonidas* and had drinks and dinner with him in the Officer's Lounge. They'd even taken a walk on a Tooh 2 beach in one of the simulation rooms. When Aeron had kissed her, it had been a dismal failure on her side; gut-wrenching guilt had washed over her as if she'd been unfaithful. But the hunky Prime science officer had seemed pleased.

So, no, she had no fricking choice. The bond existed ... period. And she'd be damned if she lived the remainder of her life celibate and alone—childless. Huw would have to man up—and he needed to do so sooner rather than later.

Nadia shoved her personal problems to the back of her mental issues-to-be-resolved shelf and turned to the two doctors. "Let me know if you need anything else, Kerr. Lia, ask Wulf or Mel for whatever help you need." She left the lab's computer room and took the lift to the Command Deck.

When the lift doors opened onto the command level, her heart stuttered. She clenched her teeth in order not to cry out as a piercing pain traveled over her body and concentrated over her right ovary. It was all she could do not to hunch over with her arms wrapped around her lower abdomen.

The anguish wasn't even hers—it was Huw's.

He sat with Mel and Wulf. The trio stared at the forward monitors that displayed a magnified view of the two ships on the planet's surface. Grief. Anger. Frustration. Confusion. Guilt. An olio of emotions, all emanating from the man who denied the link between them.

Huw turned his head. He'd sensed her. His golden eyes blazed with some hard-to-nail-down emotion for a split second before he lowered his dark lashes and turned back to face the screen. The darker emotions overtook him once again, but became muted as if he knew he'd hurt her.

Dammit all! *Rejected again!* It hurt as much now as it had the first time he'd shut her out.

Mel swiveled in her seat and smiled, a showing of support and encouragement. Nadia was sure Mel would want to "talk" later about Huw and his "issues" once again. It was a talk Nadia didn't want to have. Both Mel and Lia had urged her to be patient—that Huw would come around eventually. She'd gotten the impression her friends weren't telling her everything they knew about the whole bonding process.

Fine. Whatever. Huw might "come around," but Nadia didn't want mere acceptance as if she were the consolation prize in some damn contest. She wanted him to love her—unconditionally.

Yeah, I'm stupid. Love sucks.

"Nadia? What do you have to report?" Mel asked, waving her closer.

Wulf and Huw turned their chairs, waiting to hear what she had to say.

Nadia concentrated on presenting a succinct report to Mel and Wulf and keeping her hungry gaze away from Huw.

Everything in her wanted to go to him and be held, comforted, and loved. Her head told her not to be silly.

"There are no carbon life-forms alive or dead on the ships themselves." Huw's feelings of hope at the news washed over her like a warm, gentle wave. "I located the underground fortifications."

Nadia moved to her station on the Command Deck and put the ground sonar images up on the monitor and paralleled a live view of the mountain under which the complex sat. "As you can see, the underground passages and rooms are quite extensive. The entrance to the complex is here, approximately thirty kilometers from the downed ships." She used the laser pointer and circled the area on the live surface view.

"Anyone alive down there?" Wulf voiced the question on every Prime-male-on-the-Command-Deck's mind.

Nadia took a deep, painful breath past the constriction in her throat. "No." Huw's low moan of pain became a sharp ache in her heart. "I'm deeply sorry. Just bodies."

Mel clasped Wulf's hand. He nodded. "Thank you, Nadia. It was too much to hope for. We must take the bodies home to Cejuru."

Nadia avoided looking at Huw although she felt him beating on her shields.

Now he wants to speak mind-to-mind.

Mel and Wulf looked between the two of them, frowning.

Shit, they felt Huw's telepathic attempts to break her shields. Let him try. She'd built them stronger over the past five weeks. The emotional hurt from constant rejection was a powerful building block.

"Dr. Lenke and I had already discussed that very topic," Nadia said. "His and my teams are preparing now. We'll bring the remains to the ship for transport home. I also contacted the *Leonidas* and asked Commander Ard to meet me on the planet with an away team of his own choosing. Aeron and I will do a quick mapping and assessment of the planet to update Alliance and Prime Commands' records—and of the complex for the Alliance Space Archaeology Institute. If all environmental systems are operational, the fortifications might be usable for military outposts in this region and definitely would be important to add to the study of early Prime space exploration."

"Yes, I agree." Wulf stroked a finger down Mel's arm. "We'll send a security team along—just in case."

"I anticipated that. While Aeron's and my people do the scientific assessment, Dr. Lenke's team will recover the bodies for transport to the ship and attempt to determine their causes of death and make preliminary identifications if he is able. Lia is preparing a storage bay for the bodies." Nadia left her station and walked to the lift. "I'm meeting my away team in the shuttle dock in under a standard hour. I'll stay in constant contact from the time we hit the surface."

"I'll go with the away team." Huw's low, rumbling voice echoed around the abnormally quiet Command Deck.

Nadia looked at Mel and Wulf. "I already have engineering covered."

"Who?" Huw moved to stand in front of her, his hands fisted at his side.

His aura read as angry—and jealous.

She allowed a tiny bit of satisfaction to cross her mind before shutting it down. Just because he'd shown jealousy over her trips to visit Aeron and over this situation didn't mean he'd changed his general mind-set about what constituted a real bonding.

"Cas Jod."

Huw snarled low in his throat and his eyes narrowed until Nadia only saw fiery gold slits. She winced and stepped away from his anger.

"Stop it," Nadia hissed. "Don't you growl at me. You have no right. Cas is a good engineer and has mining experience. He'll do fine. You're the head of engineering and don't need to be on an away team for what's merely a scientific assessment and a retrieval of bodies."

"She's correct, brother." Wulf had come up behind Huw and placed a restraining hand on his brother's shoulder. "She also has the authority to choose her away teams—and I'm not vetoing her choices—nor will Melina."

"But Wulf…" Huw turned to his brother and then shut up. Wulf's face was stern and had a do-not-mess-with-me look. "Fine. Just fine." Huw entered the now-open lift and closed the doors.

"I apologize for Huw, Nadia." Wulf touched her clothed arm lightly.

She pulled away, hoping he wouldn't take offense. He mouthed, "Sorry."

"Huw's attitude isn't your fault, Wulf." Nadia attempted to smile. "Thanks for backing me up."

"My brother is a fool." Wulf sighed and ran his fingers through his hair. "But when you told us all were dead, his grief struck me hard. He…"

"I felt it too, Wulf. He's in denial still." Nadia shrugged. *But … maybe he'll recognize I'm his mate and have been since we met.*

"Nadia…" Wulf's voice lowered. "Melina thinks you're bonding with my brother."

"She and Lia have discussed that with me." Nadia still wondered what Mel and the two doctors weren't telling her.

Wulf continued, hesitancy and quite a bit of discomfort in his manner. "My brother is highly attracted to you— possessive and protective. He is hurting and confused. His world view has been turned upside down. Please be patient with him. He is, after all, just a stubborn Prime male."

"Yeah, I get that. But constant rejection hurts." Nadia shook her head, willing the tears gathering in her eyes not to fall. Huw was making her a wuss.

Wulf touched a curl lying over her ear. "I understand. But can you live forever as you feel now? Lia and Joen have told me the pain they felt when they were apart in the early days of their courtship was unbearable. Melina and I could be apart, but it was a living death. To this day, we need to touch each other's mind for reassurance. The bond is like being one entity."

"I don't want to be apart from Huw." Nadia blinked back tears seeping from the corners of her eyes. "And I know I'll have to get over the hurt he's caused me, find a way to trust him not to hurt me in the future. I need him. I'm not stupid. I know what you and Mel went through … go through even now."

She took a deep breath past the lump in her throat. "But Huw has to make the first move." A few tears won and streaked down her cheeks. Through damp lashes, she looked Wulf in the eye. "He has to be a man and apologize. He has to tell me he accepts me, accepts this bond. I want the words, Wulf."

"He'll give you them, Nadia. Just give him time." Wulf swept the wetness off her face with a light, gentle touch. The lift opened behind her. "Go. You have teams waiting on you."

"Aye-aye, sir!" Nadia snapped a salute and entered the lift.

The door closed on a view of Wulf walking to Mel, pulling her into his arms, and kissing the top of Mel's head as she cried into her mate's chest.

Her friend wept for Nadia's pain.

Too bad Nadia didn't have time to join her. She sniffed back the tears that still dared to leak from her eyes. A good bury-her-head-in-her-pillow and a pint-of-double-fudge-ice-cream cry would feel swell just about now, but she had business to do. Thank God for work.

CHAPTER 15

Outside of Prime fortification on Ursa 345

Nadia stood alongside of Aeron as her team and his loaded bodies into the surface vehicles that would carry them back to the shuttles. Because the terrain near the entrance of the underground Prime complex was uneven and rocky, the shuttles sat on an ancient lake bed close to the two downed Prime starships. Part of Aeron's team combed the Prime ships for any data that survived the crashes.

Aeron's grief was etched on his face and swamped his aura. Even with her empathic shields up, his pain pummeled her psi senses. Nadia touched his arm lightly, giving what little comfort she could. "I'm sorry."

"Thank you for caring." Aeron picked up her hand and kissed the back of it. Nadia did all she could not to wince at the sweet gesture as a burning sensation arose where his lips had touched. "Security is now clearing the rest of the underground facility, looking for evidence of the beasts that killed the crash survivors."

The away teams hadn't had to go far into the underground complex to find the bodies; they were piled in a central room.

Certain areas of the victims' body parts had been eaten, mostly the soft internal organs. What was left were bones covered in desiccated skin, much like mummies found on Earth.

While the scene was now bloodless because microbes in the soil coupled with the extreme aridity of the atmosphere had eradicated the gore, the initial impact had been horrific. The survivors had had no chance against whatever the predators had been. None.

Upon seeing the remnants of the carnage, Nadia had called the ship for more security teams so her people removing the bodies would have protection. She didn't want to chance whatever had eaten the Lost Ones taking her crew by surprise.

"With any luck, the creatures…" Nadia gulped and hoped the bile she'd successfully kept down would continue to obey her will, "…that killed the survivors are also dead."

"The data logs kept by the survivors might have clues as to what happened." Aeron turned toward the entrance of the fortification. "Here comes Cas."

Nadia turned. Cas had volunteered to check out the engineering and technological systems, guarded only by one security officer. The teams would be able to work more freely within the subterranean complex without the cumbersome life support suits. "What did you find, Cas?"

"The systems are operable, Commander Nadia. I have them up and running. The power supply was fully charged even after all these years." A frown creased his forehead. "It seems the survivors had shut down environmental."

"Maybe to kill the beast eating them?" Aeron suggested. "But the act would also kill them. They wouldn't have had enough life support suits…" His words trailed off.

"God, they killed themselves rather than…" Nadia looked at what was left of a young girl as Kerr dictated a preliminary examination while scanning her lower right hip. The girl had a *gemate* marking; the mummification had preserved the mark perfectly.

Nadia moaned silently. She couldn't imagine the horror the survivors must have felt, waiting to die from lack of oxygen. But anything was better than being torn at and eaten.

A grim look on his face, Cas nodded, acknowledging Nadia's conclusion. "The security officer and I checked a room near engineering that had been closed off. There were ten bodies, all intact. They must have been the last of the survivors. There was a data journal." Her technician pulled a microdisk from his waist pouch and handed it over.

She took the disk and slipped it into her waist pouch. "I'll see that Wulf gets this. He and Mel are reviewing the data Commander Ard's team has already sent to the *Galanti*. We should be able to get a fairly accurate picture of what happened after they crashed. Not that it will help the poor souls any, but it might bring closure to their relatives back on the home planet." She didn't want to think of the men who'd grieve anew when told of what had happened to their mates on this godforsaken rock.

"Commander Nadia. Commander Ard." The *Galanti*'s head security officer, a Volusian by the name of Z'es, stood at attention.

"What have you found, Z'es?" Nadia itched to get inside the complex to continue piecing together the survivors' last days on Ursa 345 and to figure out how the caves had been formed and when.

The Prime records on this outpost were minimal; what were in existence were vague. The records found on other similar outposts including the ones in Siberia on Earth had been voluminous and detailed in the extreme. What was different about Ursa 345? And why had the captains of the two ships come here rather than one of the better-documented facilities?

"Commander…" something in Z'es's voice sent a tingle of dread through her body, "…we found desiccated remnants of two large creatures which seem to be a cross between a reptile and an annelid." Z'es like most Volusians normally didn't show a lot of emotion, especially not on duty, but a look of disgust and, yes, fear swept across his pale blue face. "They have large jaws that appear to unhinge in a similar manner to a snake's jaws—and very big teeth."

The Volusian swallowed audibly. He, like the others hearing his report, most likely recalled the missing soft organs of the dead. "Their bodies are segmented with no skeletal structures much like worms. Only the framework of their jaws eliminates them from that species. They're also not a carbon life-form, but are composed of silicates. My team is bringing out one of them for transport and study. To which ship do you wish me to send the creature's body?"

"The *Leonidas*." Aeron spoke before Nadia could find her voice. She had an aversion to giant worms and didn't look forward to examining even a dead one. Aeron must've sensed her emotions to jump in so quickly. "The *Galanti* has the remains of the survivors and more than enough to do. Is that all right with you, Nadia?"

"Yes, that's fine." Nadia could barely get the words out past the constriction in her throat.

"Nadia! You're afraid. What is it?"

Damn! She must've been putting off fear vibes like crazy if Huw could read her from the ship. *"I'm fine."* She bolstered her shields and took several deep breaths, willing her heart to stop pounding. What a liar ... she was anything but fine and the next words out of her mouth proved it.

"Are you sure they're dead, Z'es?" Her voice blessedly didn't crack though her limbic system had her ready to flee or fight. *What a stupid question, Nadia! Grow some balls.*

The security officer's eyes darkened to navy with sympathy. Z'es obviously recalled the last time they'd confronted a giant wormlike creature on a mission in the Prater system, long before the Prime merger into Gold Squadron. She'd hated her fear then and she hated it now. But, damn, giant hominid-eating worms were her worst nightmare. She'd rather fight an Erian hand-to-hand, naked, than face a giant worm.

"Yes, Commander." Z'es bowed his head. "We made very sure. No more surprises."

She assumed he deliberately left off the words "not like the last time."

"Nadia?" Aeron took her arm and turned her toward him. "Is there something I should know?"

Nadia let out a self-deprecating laugh. "Z'es and I had a run in with a worm creature which had been in a hibernation stage. It sort of took us unawares." *And nearly ate us.* She shuddered. She could still smell and feel the acidic slime eating at her clothing. Z'es had taken its head off with some difficulty since she'd been in the worm's body at the time. She'd avoided too-tight spaces ever since. "Needless to say, we're very careful with unknown species now."

She and Aeron turned as a gasp went up from the scientific teams waiting for security to give the all clear to enter the caves.

Ten members of the security team carried, no more like dragged, the body of a worm creature into the open. Its skin was light brown, but would've been darker with its natural secretions when alive. Its head had no eyes, but had prominent scenting slits above its mouth. Sometime after death, the mouth had fallen open, possibly due to deterioration of its supportive tissues; the teeth were in double rows, long and sharp-looking.

"God, it's huge!" Nadia's jaw dropped and her adrenaline ramped up another notch. Her hand hovered over her laser pistol. "This one's bigger than the one we dealt with in the Prater system. How big is it, Z'es?"

"We estimated between ten and fifteen meters when alive. In death, the creature has shrunk and curled in on itself, so it is hard to measure it accurately." Z'es shuffled his feet, an unusual sign of nervousness from the stoic Volusian. "I, um, took the liberty of locating the brains and placing a killing shot through both of the creatures we found, just in case. I didn't want to have a recurrence of the past. I'm sorry if that messes up the scientific aspects of studying the creature, but..."

"The safety of the ship and its crew is paramount," Nadia finished. "Considering our past experience, I would've done the same—and will if I see another one lying around." She wouldn't have stopped with the brain—she would've vaporized the damn thing.

The trio approached the creature, which the security team had stretched out to its full length. Two of her team took measurements and scanned the creature, dictating their findings rapidly into their recorders.

Bre Jod was one of the science techs. From his position by the creature's head, he glared at Z'es. "Did you have to destroy his brain stem?"

Nadia and Z'es said "yes" at the same time. Everyone, even Bre, laughed.

"I am sorry, Lt. Commander Z'es. I didn't mean to..." Bre stopped and looked at Nadia. "I have seen creatures like this before when I apprenticed as a geological engineer in the Umbraxi system. But they weren't as large."

"Is this particular specimen more annelid or reptile?" Nadia stooped next to Bre. She noted the dried out skin had no evidence of ever having scales.

"Annelid since the creatures have no exo-or endoskeletons. See? They are segmented." Bre poked at the creases which delineated the worm's segments and which were now cracked. Alive the creature would've been moist and supple. "You could cut them in half and they would still live and regenerate the lost body mass. Of course, they aren't exactly the same as the ones in the Umbraxi system since the Umbraxi giant worms are carbon life-forms. This creature is made up of silicates. I surmise it might live on the minerals in the soil of this planet."

Bre's forehead creased in thought. "I have heard of such creatures living in the Andromeda galaxy. This life-form could have been brought here by an asteroid from that galaxy and found a perfect environment to thrive."

"Interesting theory, Bre. One which I'll ask you to explore once you've finalized the examination." The science tech nodded and went back to work taking preliminary readings.

Nadia swept a glance over the teams standing around the dead creatures. "People, if you see one of these creatures alive—do not approach. Call security. If attacked, you can only kill them by a direct laser shot to the brain or by cutting their brain stem and cauterizing it so it won't reattach. Do you understand?" Or at least she hoped those methods would work; they had on the Prater giant worm creatures.

A chorus of "yesses" and "aye-ayes" swept through the crowd. And she had to smile when she heard a couple of "eeuws." She was so there with that sentiment.

She waited for the teams to go silent and then continued with her instructions. "Cas Jod has the complex's artificial environment up and running. The air and temperature should be suitable for working without environmental suits. No one is to work alone; work in pairs at a minimum. You all saw the condition of the bodies we removed. You've seen the remains of one of the creatures that killed them. Do not assume because the two giant worms we found are dead there aren't others. We have no idea of how these creatures live or hunt. I don't want to lose anyone because we weren't cautious. Understood?"

Again assent rippled through the teams.

"Aeron, will your teams handle documenting the facility, mapping it, and checking out the systems now that Cas has them running?"

"Gladly, Nadia. But what will you be doing?" Aeron replied, tension in every line of his body.

"Testing the geological soundness of the mountain over the facility and the strata under it." Nadia's narrowed gaze swept the rock-strewn area leading to the entrance. "I don't like the signs of rock fall I see. My readings from the ship indicated no seismic activity. There's no molten core. This planet unlike Earth or Cejuru Prime is a hunk of dead rock. And the substrata read as solid. I need to figure out how the caves were formed—we know your forebears adapted what they'd found here. So, what natural forces—or who—made the underground complex?"

Aeron inhaled sharply. "You don't think the..." he eyed the creature, "...the worms created the cave and passages, do you?"

"It's a working hypothesis and needs to be ruled in or out." Nadia walked to her team, which included the Jod brothers and four security people. "And I hope I'm wrong," she muttered. She had a bad case of déjà vu—because her encounter with the giant wormlike creature in the Prater system had happened in what had turned out to be the creature's underground home and not a cave formed by water or tectonic activity.

Damn, she hated giant worms!

Galanti Command Deck

HUW SAT IN THE CHAIR next to Wulf. Both men were transfixed by the sights and sounds coming from the surface.

"It is a pseudo-worm, then?" Huw turned to Wulf. "If it has a brainstem and teeth, it isn't a true worm, but without a skeleton it isn't a reptile either."

"We've seen such before, brother." Wulf's gaze never wavered from the screen. "I sense your tension. What's the problem? Are you worried about Nadia being underground and coming up against a living pseudo-worm?"

"Yes. *Ansu bhau*! She's scared out of her mind, and I'm not there to help her. She shut me out." He rubbed a hand over his aching forehead.

Wulf snorted. "And why shouldn't she? You've been denying her very existence since we began this mission."

"Yes … all right … I'll admit it … I care for Nadia. I-I love her, but…"

"There is no 'but.'" Wulf shook his head and growled. "Huw, I'm not sure what rod you have up your ass about mating with a Terran, but let's face facts—you are bonding with Nadia. You can't continue to deny the evidence. We all see it. You're hurting her, brother."

"I know." Huw grimaced. "I will make it up to her." He looked at his brother. "I could not approach her before now."

"What in Balcon's balls do you mean, you could not approach her before now?" Wulf frowned and his eyes held disbelief.

"I have cared for Nadia since I met her. I grew to love her courage, intelligence, beauty, spirit." Huw looked his brother in the eye. "But I could not offer her a relationship of any sort until I was sure I had no *gemate* waiting on her *gemat*. If I had, I would not only have dishonored my potential *gemate*, but would also have hurt Nadia when I had to leave her."

Wulf closed his eyes and muttered curses under his breath. Huw winced. "You mean to tell me you hurt Nadia's feelings and denied the obvious signs of more than a physical attraction between you on the off chance you might … might find an unmarked Prime female on this mission?"

"Yes." Huw firmed his mouth when his brother started to swear once more. "You found Mel when there had been no hope at all. Could I do less when there was even a small chance?"

Wulf shook his head and began to chuckle. "When you put it that way, I guess not." He laid a hand over Huw's. "You'll need to court her—and I suggest starting with an apology on your knees. You hurt her very much."

"I know. It hurt me also." Huw swallowed past a giant lump of regret in his throat. "It was like cutting off a vital part of me, but I felt I could do nothing else. I didn't want to tell her I loved her and then later have to reject her if a miracle happened."

"Tell her that." Wulf's voice was soft. "It might go some way to allow her to trust in your honor."

But what if she rejects you? Even after you apologize and explain your actions or lack of actions?

Failure was not an option. He'd have to woo her into his bed and bind her to him with sex. He needed to claim her openly, declare his intentions, and make sure no other man could steal her away. *That will not happen.* He would grovel if he had to.

Wulf punched him on the arm. "If I were you, I'd greet Nadia upon her return to the ship and begin courting. You have lots of ground to make up. But for now, you have the Command Deck. I will join Melina in the storage bay and help receive the bodies of our dead Lost Ones."

Huw nodded, not envying his brother the sad task. "Thanks for listening and your advice, brother. You will have a new sister-kin soon. I intend to do all I can to convince Nadia to be my mate, uh, my wife in the Alliance way."

A strange light entered and left Wulf's eyes and his lips twisted before straightening. Huw puzzled over his brother's expression—it looked a lot like a smirk. "Let me know if anything happens on planet that Mel or I need to be aware of." Wulf saluted casually and strolled to the lift.

Huw took the seat Wulf abandoned and donned the command headset. Iolyn came to stand next to him, a grin on his face.

"You heard all that?" Huw asked.

Iolyn chuckled. "Yes. Maybe you should invest in some knee guards for all the crawling and begging you will be doing in the near future. If I were Nadia, I would make you pay." Iolyn sat in the chair next to Huw and put on a com unit to monitor the oral feed from the teams on the planet. "You, brother, need to act quickly to secure Nadia's affections. She is a fine woman—and many members of the crew have their eye on her."

Huw growled. "They can find another woman. Nadia is mine."

He had to make a plan to get Nadia into his bed. If he couldn't seal the deal and make love to her, he didn't deserve to be called a man. He wanted her attached to him completely. Then he would do everything in his power to make up for his previous behavior for the rest of their lives.

And he had better do all of this wooing sooner rather than later, because the pain of denying Nadia's mental touch was getting worse every day.

CHAPTER 16

Ursa 345

"Commander," Bre Jod called to Nadia from a side tunnel off one of the main arteries of the huge underground complex. "Come see this."

Nadia abandoned her examination of what she'd concluded were man-made handholds. The grips carved into the solid rock wall should've led to an upper walkway hidden behind a waist-high curtain wall such as the ones found in the Prime complex on Obam IV, but didn't. Something had caused a cave-in and the upper walkway and any of the rooms off it were now buried under tons of granite.

The whole frigging planet was a solid ball of granite and iron, and the underground complex was definitely not natural. It had been carved out … whether by the Prime or a planet inhabitant was the question for which she and her team sought an answer.

"What have you found, Bre?" She stood next to the tall Prime and stared at the wall he indicated. "What am I looking at?"

"This tunnel is new." He traced the variance in coloration of the wall from top to bottom. "This rock has only been exposed to environmental conditions for the last ten or so standard years. Our people could not have done this."

"Theories, Bre?" Nadia's gut wasn't happy. She moved in closer and spotted etching in the granite. It took a lot to etch granite. A laser-cutting tool could do it. The ancients on Earth used chisels and hammers. Or…

"It was chemically hewn." Bre held up his analyzer. "Some strong acid. The chemical composition resembles nothing I've ever seen."

"Shit. Giant worms use acidic secretions to digest their food." She shuddered at the memories threatening to take her over. "What if the creatures on this planet also excrete strong acids?"

Bre nodded. "Very possible. Also, the bodies we found, though dehydrated, had teeth that were still intact and as hard as diamonds. The creature could also eat rock." He touched a pattern of scrapings in the tunnel wall. "These are very regularly spaced. It might use its acid to soften the rock and then it eats it and creates a passageway."

"But why kill the Prime crash survivors if its diet is mineral?" Nadia's stomach roiled at the thought of the women and children running from the creatures. "No, don't answer that. The creature must've felt threatened and killed them." And liked the taste and decided to eat some more. "God! I hope there aren't any live worms left. They have a taste for human prey now."

"Commander, the creatures must have been here when the Prime first landed and adapted the caves for their use. Why wasn't there a warning about this planet? Why would the Lost Ones come here?" Bre's face flushed dark red with his anger. "Coming here was a death sentence."

"Maybe they didn't have a choice. After we receive the report from the team examining the ships and study the survivors' logs, we'll know more." Nadia looked at the wall and followed it up. "There has to be an upper tunnel—and a room where the first Prime who came here left records. The upper walkway which the Prime added in the main hallway has collapsed." She led the way out of the side tunnel and back to the main passage.

Nadia pointed to the handholds and the Prime markings indicating the hidden walkway. "See? I've seen similar on Cejuru Prime in the fortification outside the capitol—and Mel reported on the ones on Obam IV."

"Then we should advise the other two-man teams to be on the lookout for such adaptations?" Bre asked.

"Yeah. Contact the others and tell them what we've found. I'll go farther up this tunnel and see if the upper walkway opens up." She left Bre at the tunnels' intersection and headed for what looked to be the main tunnel's dead end, about ten meters ahead.

As Nadia walked, she dictated her observations. "Ceiling height remains at approximately fifteen meters. Prime markings and handholds are evident all along this particular corridor. There is a distinct possibility there could be an upper walkway leading to storage and/or safe rooms."

She paused and touched Prime symbols, which she loosely translated as "climb up" and a letter and a number. "The Prime who adapted the tunnels labeled the lower and upper corridors with an alpha-numeric system. If the underground complex proves safe, it would be interesting to have a scientific team map the facility and compare it to other ancient Prime facilities documented in the galaxy. I know of three in the Steppes of Russia that remind me of this complex, but they weren't nearly as sophisticated."

Nadia reached a solid wall. "The tunnel ends abruptly with no markings." She ran her handheld sonar over the wall. "The dead end appears to be a collapse. I read an open space behind it. The fill is not loose, but is a block of granite as high as the tunnel ceiling and two meters thick."

Bre came up behind her. "Dead end? That makes no sense."

"There's an opening beyond. This block of granite either fell or was placed here." Nadia looked at the smoothness of it. "I'm thinking placed. To block out the creatures?" She looked at Bre whose lips were fixed in a thin, grim line.

He nodded. "That would seem logical. The Prime who came here many millennia ago might've tried to box the creatures out of the tunnels they'd taken over."

"The creatures would just eat through them." Nadia stated the obvious.

"Maybe the Prime didn't stay around long enough to know that. Ursa 345 was probably a way station infrequently used and they only needed security for short periods of time. These walls would slow the creatures down." Bre shook his head. "Or at least I would hope so."

"Then why hasn't one of the creatures eaten through this one?" Nadia asked.

"Maybe they didn't need to." Bre looked around. "If their major diet is mineral-based, they have a whole planet to eat."

"Too true." Nadia with Bre by her side retraced her steps. A grinding noise above them had them looking at one another and then up. Cracks appeared in the rock ceiling and widened at a rapid pace, sending a shower of dust and rocks on them. A hot smell of acid eating at rock permeated the air.

Holy hell! Nadia froze for a split second, but it seemed like an eternity. Her primitive brain forced her to move. She shoved Bre in the opposite direction and followed him. She yelled between labored breaths into her com unit. "Get everyone … out of the tunnels … and caves … now! There are still live creatures down here." They raced through the main tunnel and headed for the exit to the surface.

"Nadia! You're in danger?"

Nadia had sensed Huw's mental touch riding on the surface of the walls she'd constructed to keep him out. The shock of the creature eating through the tunnel ceiling, and her resulting gut-wrenching fear, had demolished her iron control. Her shields were down and Huw was inside instantly. *"Can't deal with you now, Huw."*

Huw remained silent inside her head, but his male energy rushed to supplement her own cortisol and adrenaline cocktail.

Behind her and Bre, more rocks fell as the jagged opening in the ceiling widened. Bre hung back, his weapon at ready, covering her ass.

Still running, Nadia looked over her shoulder. "Stop being a macho Prime. Get a move on! That's an order, mister!" She had her laser pistol in hand with the power set as high as it would go. "We leave together or not at all. If it comes after us, aim for the head."

"Yes, sir." Bre sprinted to close the distance between them.

Both of them looked over their shoulders frequently. It was hard to see if anything pursued them due to the cloud of dust emanating from the hole in the tunnel ceiling.

"Not too far to the entrance cave now, I see light." Nadia took a precious moment to pull her facemask down. The surface couldn't sustain oxygen-breathers for long. Bre did the same. When they hit the surface, they'd have to hoof it until they reached their team. Safety in numbers and higher firepower.

"Aeron!" she yelled into her com unit.

"Yes, Nadia." Aeron's voice was calm, but she heard the tension underlying it. "How can we help? Z'es and his teams are ready to enter and…"

"No! Keep everyone out. Take a head count. I don't want anyone underground. Be ready with the chemical grenades. I want to fire this thing up if he follows us out."

The chemical grenades would react with the acid in the worm and burst into flames; at this point, she wasn't a scientist interested in examining a potential new species. She was a very scared human not wanting to take a chance at the creature snacking on her teams.

"Commander, it's following us. I see flashes of glowing skin among the detritus." Bre's words were breathy from exertion, but his aura was calm. Her geological engineer was one cool customer. "It seems to be smaller than the dried hulks we found."

"I don't care." Nadia huffed as she climbed the last few steps to get out of the tunnel and into the large entry cavern to the complex. "It's a dead baby. I hate snaky, wormy creatures. And it's not safe to keep one alive."

"Agreed, Commander." Bre picked her up and threw her over his shoulder. "I can run faster and the baby is slithering along too rapidly."

"God!" Nadia's breath came out in gasps as she bumped up and down on Bre's shoulder.

"Nadia. Bre is touching you. Why?"

"Not now, Huw!" What a time for Huw to pick to be jealous. As if he had any right to be after the way he'd treated her.

Fear froze her next breath as she spied the creature chasing them and closing the distance. Man, that worm was fast. Huw's mental energy forced her to breathe since she seemed to have forgotten how.

Even if the pseudo-worm was a young one, the creature was still huge—and it was intelligent. She sensed its emotions. It read as hungry. Its mouth gaped and its body glowed a black green under the artificial lighting of the cavern. The worm left a trail of slime, which vaporized the rock floor. Its teeth dripped the same goo.

Ooh, ick! A phantom hand stroked her hair, imparting comfort as Huw's male energy calmed her stomach.

Placing her free hand on Bre's ass, she braced herself and raised her laser weapon. She placed three strong blasts into the spot between the worm's nasal slits. Most living creature's brains were centrally located in the heads. Most head shots usually did the job.

But not this time.

"Shit! It's still coming." Nadia yelled as they broke onto the surface.

Z'es's security teams were there to meet them. They let loose with their laser rifles.

"Aim for head," she shouted. "Get some men to the side and attempt to sever the head from the body. We're too close to use the grenades." And the creature moved too fast to put enough space between them and it.

Ten men and women shot at the worm, but it still slithered its way across the surface, literally eating up the ground as it came.

Bre reached their ground transports and tossed Nadia into the driver's side. She scooched across the seat and he hopped in behind her. Breathing heavily, they watched as the security team blasted the creature's head from its body. The body sans head continued to move forward. The head wiggled and squirmed where it had fallen.

"Shit!" Nadia knew such things happened, but she had never seen it before. "Z'es! Be careful. The creature is dangerous as long as its main nerve stem is synapsing. Do not touch it or its slime trail. The acid is strong enough to dissolve granite on touch."

"Yes, Commander Nadia." Z'es walked toward the head, but stopped at a respectful two meters away. "The head seems to track me. It's using its sense of smell to track us. What should we do? Can it regenerate its body?"

Aeron had come to stand by the vehicle in which she and Bre sat and replied in Nadia's stead. "I would say yes. We have sea worms on Cejuru Prime that can regenerate their bodies as long as their head is alive and their main neural system is mostly intact."

Nadia nodded. "Do we have pictures, Aeron?"

Aeron stifled a chuckle. "My astrozoologist recorded the mad dash you and Bre made. She was so excited, we have not only images, but also video."

"Good. Z'es … get everyone back and blow the head with the chemical grenades. I want the head vaporized. We'll vaporize the body once we get skin and tissue samples. We need to analyze the acid—if we can find a container to store it." She wouldn't allow anything on the ships that might endanger the crews.

"Gladly, Commander." Z'es gave the order and his team retreated.

The creature's head swiveled on the ground. It had already begun growing a new body. For a split second she could read its thoughts, its intent. It wanted to eat the tasty bipeds; it and its brethren had eaten the others—the Lost Ones—in the past.

Nadia shook off the empathic connection. "God, Z'es. Kill the damn thing. It's going to make an attempt to go for one of you."

Z'es took the chemical grenade launcher and aimed. The creature raised its head and acid dripped from its teeth, sending caustic gasses rising from the ground.

The shot was a direct hit to the head. The grenade exploded. A localized chemical reaction emitted flashes of bright green and white light and an almost instant incineration. Once the smoke cleared, all that was left of the creature's head was a dark greenish-black dust, which began to eat a crater in the granite ground.

"*Ansu bhau!*" Aeron turned a shocked look at Nadia and then back to the rapidly growing crater. "That is some strong acid. The grenade should've burned it up. The fact we have ash is amazing." The chemi-grenades usually left residue so minute it became dust motes floating in the atmosphere. "Maybe we should take a reading and not try to carry any of it to the ships. I would be afraid of the acid making holes in the ship's hull."

"We're on the same page, Aeron. Do it." Nadia swallowed hard. God, that creature had been one of her worst nightmares. Aftermath hit and she trembled, a full-body set of shakes that if she'd been standing would've taken her to the ground. Nausea threatened to overwhelm her.

A cool wind swept through her mind and calmed her. *"Nadia! Are you okay? Lubha, answer me! … answer me. Let me know you're all right."*

Huw's mental shouting was fear-filled and most shocking … caring. Loving.

He'd called her *lubha*? *Now he gets it?*

Well … he would have to wait for her response. She was busy and still needed to deal with her emotions from encountering the worm creature … ugh! Plus, she was mad at Huw. She couldn't believe the arrogant asshole. She'd endured weeks of his mule-headedness and to be honest, she didn't trust Huw's sudden about-face and wasn't quite sure how to respond. She needed time to think. What she did and said to Huw next would set the tone for the future of their relationship … because his mental touch today had proven beyond a shadow of a doubt there was a bonding.

Nadia slapped her shields back up and used her com unit to contact the *Galanti*.

Huw would hear her and know she was all right. She didn't want him to worry whether she was okay or not—but until she decided how to handle him, she wouldn't use the more intimate means of mind-talk.

"Wulf. Mel. Away teams are fine and all accounted for. Creature is dead. It has been preliminarily determined this planet is still inhabited by some of these creatures and is unsafe for habitation or use by the Alliance. The creatures are intelligent, deadly, and they have a taste for carbon life-forms now. I recommend this planet be placed on the Alliance fly-by list."

"Captain Wulf. This is Lt. Commander Z'es." The *Galanti*'s head of security stood over the dead creature, far closer than Nadia would've done. "I concur with Commander Nadia's assessment. This planet is a security risk."

That was for damn sure. Nadia couldn't stop another full-body shudder. If Bre hadn't picked her up and carried her out, she wouldn't have been able to slow the creature down with blasts from her laser pistol and they both would've been worm food. The creature had been that fast.

As it was, they'd barely made it to Z'es and his security teams. She and Bre could've lost their lives because of her initial moments of paralytic fear.

"Commander Ard also concurs, Captain Wulf." Aeron must've sensed her disquiet, because he came closer as if to take her into his arms. The heat of his body warmed her even through the layers of the survival suit.

Huw's antipathy to Aeron's closeness made itself known by his banging on her mental shields, giving her a headache. The fact he could sense what was going on, even with her shields reinforced, shocked her. She inched away from Aeron—and Huw's psychic temper tantrum ceased.

"Glad everyone is okay." Wulf's low, rumbling voice responded, pulling her back to the present situation. "Iolyn has already sent the fly-by order to Alliance and Prime Military Commands. Come home. Wulf out."

CHAPTER 17

Galanti Command Deck

Huw tore off his headset, thrust the data pad out of the way, and then stood up. "I'm going down there." He glared at his brothers. "Nadia is terrified out of her mind. She was almost eaten once by a pseudo-worm." *And Ard is making moves on my woman.*

He stalked toward the lift and was brought up short by a hand on his arm. "You aren't leaving this ship, brother." Wulf's tone wasn't that of a brother, but of the captain of the ship.

"I'm going." Huw shrugged Wulf's hand off and slapped a hand on the call pad for the lift.

When the doors opened, he entered and his brothers followed him on. "Shuttle bay," Huw ordered.

"Captain Wulf override. Fitness deck." Wulf glared at him. "Iolyn and I think you need an attitude adjustment and we're very happy to give you one."

"*Ansu bhau*, Wulf! Not two standard hours ago, you told me to court Nadia, to make her mine. Well, I am following your suggestions … Nadia is mine. She's scared, and she needs me to be there to care for and protect her."

"Protect her from whom?" Iolyn asked. "The danger from the worm creature is over. They're loading up and coming back to the ship. Where's the danger to Nadia coming from?"

Huw slammed his hand against the lift wall. The pain made the emotions simmering just underneath his skin come to a boil. "Bre had his hands all over her. Ard had his hands all over her. They caused her pain. I felt her pain. Even though she's blocking our mind-talking, I can still feel her emotions." He fisted his hands so tightly his nails gouged his palms. "Her fear, her pain, hurts my heart … she … she … won't … let me into her mind to help her."

Huw walked around the lift like a caged animal and ran agitated fingers through his hair. His emotions threatened to overwhelm him. If he didn't get away from his brothers, he might attack them. He needed to see, touch, smell Nadia. He needed to make sure she was well and whole. He needed … he needed.

"Calm yourself." Wulf halted Huw's pacing by gripping his brother's shoulder and squeezing. "I know exactly what you're going through. When Melina ran from me and I went after her, I sensed her emotions and her body's pain and weakness." Wulf paused and frowned. "Once you have wooed Nadia and regained her trust, she will find it harder to hide her thoughts from you … although I suspect as Melina does, Nadia will still try. These Terran women like their privacy."

Huw glared at Wulf. The lift door opened onto the fitness room. Huw stalked out and then turned. "I want to go to the surface and bring Nadia home." *And make her mine … now.*

"No. You have only one choice. Gloves or no gloves." Wulf shoved Huw onto the mats. "If I let you go to the surface, you'd attack Bre and Aeron—and possibly alienate Nadia. You can't confront her with all this pent-up anger and frustration."

Wulf stood over him, with Iolyn blocking from the other side. "Think, Huw. Get past the emotions roiling in your body. You've fought and rejected the attraction, the connection with

Nadia for weeks. You have built up all this tension. You need to cool down … release it … or you might hurt Nadia."

"I would never hurt Nadia." Huw struggled to his feet and shoved Iolyn out of the way. He turned to face Wulf.

"That's not true. You've already hurt her emotionally and mentally. And now you're in danger of hurting her physically, albeit unintentionally." Wulf threw a punch, which Huw managed to deflect with his forearm.

Huw retaliated with a front kick to Wulf's solar plexus. Wulf blocked the kick and Huw was forced to withdraw his foot before Wulf could knock him off-balance.

"You'll have to do better than that," Wulf taunted. "Shoes off. No gloves. You missed your chance to choose. Iolyn and I plan to beat some sense into you. The side benefit—other than it will make us happy to teach you a lesson for being an idiot—will be that you'll have let out some of your rage."

"You aren't keeping me from her." Huw stripped off his uniform top and tore off his boots. As soon as his second boot hit the ground, he dove at Iolyn and took him to the ground, putting him into a submission hold. "She's mine. I'll apologize for my past behavior … and uh…" he let out a grunt as Iolyn's elbow caught him in the jaw, "…then we can work on the physical part of our relationship."

Wulf pulled Huw off Iolyn and punched him in the stomach and followed it up with an upper cut to the jaw. "Huw! You can't just say 'sorry' and take her to bed."

Rubbing his jaw, Huw snarled. "Try and stop me." He used a jab and upper cut combo to drive Wulf away.

Emitting small growls, Wulf circled Huw. "Listen to me, you thick-headed ass. You need to woo her before having sex with her."

Iolyn came at Huw from the side and punched him in the ribs. Huw aimed a front kick at Wulf's crotch as he backhanded Huw across the chest. "Don't tell me how to claim Nadia."

"Try romantic dinners, walks on the beach in the simulation rooms ... you need to calm down and be nice to counteract the rude, cowardly ass you've been." Wulf hammered his advice home with an upper cut, just missing Huw's chin and clipping him on the ear.

Huw growled and let out a roundhouse kick to Wulf's head, circling into a front kick to Iolyn's thigh.

He didn't care what his brothers said. There would be time enough to woo Nadia after he'd made his claim on her. Everything in him that was primal male urged him to make love with her and put his scent on her. She wouldn't be able to run from him then ... and she'd thought of doing so. That one moment of connection with her on the planet's surface, when she'd been frightened out of her mind, he'd "seen" Nadia ... and understood her clear to her soul.

Everything she'd felt was there, an open book for him to see. She loved him, but didn't trust him. He'd hurt her, abused her trust. He'd been a dumbass. But he would make it all better ... he had to or he'd die inside if she left him.

Iolyn joined Wulf in a concerted attack and forced Huw to concentrate on putting his brothers' asses on the mat. He had to get to Nadia. The wooing would start tonight ... in his bed.

Ursa 345

Nadia turned to Aeron. "I'll go over the data I gathered and merge it with the reports from my team. I'll shoot you a collated report later."

Aeron smiled down at her and swept one of her errant curls behind her ear. "Come back with me to the *Leonidas*.

We can work on our reports together over a meal and some wine."

Suddenly Huw's extreme rage pounded her shields and distracted her from Aeron's words. She let down her shields and winced. He was fighting with his brothers. *Ow!* He'd just had his butt tossed to the floor. Her bottom and elbow throbbed in sympathy.

She slammed her shields back up. Damn, but she couldn't face his anger, jealousy, or fears right now. Plus, she suspected Wulf and Iolyn were fighting with him to hammer home some truths.

Huw was the only person on the ship who hadn't realized he was bonding with her.

"I'll go back with you." She smiled at Aeron. "It'll be nice to spend some time on my old ship. I miss poker games with Royce. He's such a horrible player."

Aeron laughed. "Yes, it's a good thing we only play for imaginary credits. Royce would end up paying us for the rest of his natural life."

Nadia turned to Z'es. "I'll go with Commander Ard's team. Tell Captain Wulf or Captain Mel I plan to spend the night on the *Leonidas*. They'll have Ard's and my reports as soon as we get them done."

She knew this would push Huw to confront her about their bond. She counted on it. Either he'd declare himself, if his last mental communication had been true, or he'd continue to ignore her. She was tired of playing the game his way. So, she'd use his jealousy of Aeron to tip the balance her way. Mean? Yes, it was, but desperate times called for desperate measures.

And if he didn't declare himself? She'd transfer to Blue Squadron.

"Bre, please put together the data our team gathered and shoot it to me on the *Leonidas* under Commander Ard's code." Nadia had a sneaking suspicion her tech knew what she was about. He had a slight smile on his lips and understanding poured off him in small, gentle waves.

"You're in charge of the lab while I'm off ship," Nadia said. Huw would get an earful from Bre if he went hunting for her in the lab.

Bre inclined his head in a traditional Prime salute. "It will be done, Commander Nadia." He turned to Aeron and inclined his head. "Happy to work with you again, Commander. Take care of my commander, please. She had a fright." He turned to organize their team.

Aeron helped Nadia from the *Galanti* ground transport. "Well, I've been told, haven't I?" He stared at Bre and his brothers; the three had their heads together. "The Jods have become your protectors."

"Bre feels he owes me his life. Though, after today, I'd say we're even." She looked back at the brothers. "Bre's mother has adopted me into the family. I never had any siblings. It's sort of nice."

"Just as long as the brothers remember you're their superior officer when on duty, I don't see a problem." Aeron kept a hand on her elbow as he guided her into the *Leonidas*'s ground transport for the trip back to the shuttles.

"They're always respectful, helpful, and obedient." Nadia pulled on her arm; his touch hurt more than ever. Aeron let go instantly. His gaze reflected concern. "You know why I accepted the invitation, don't you?"

"Huw contacted you." Aeron's expression was blank, but his emotions were anything but smooth. The air around them crackled with the intensity of the feelings he deliberately suppressed. "I felt the force of his telepathy—it felt similar to the emotion overflow a Prime soldier feels at the height of *batel rabia*."

"Aeron … if things had been different…" She turned to look up. "I…"

"Nadia, don't say another word." Aeron smiled sadly. "I know you're connected to Huw in a way similar to Prime bonding. The telepathy alone tells me this. Plus the asshole has said things to me from time to time that led me to believe he was possessive of you." He laughed at her gasp of shock. "I don't mind being used to hide from him. Besides, it will drive him crazy ... and it might take some jealousy to get through his thick skull."

"That's what I concluded. This time his mental touch was ... different ... more open... " Nadia trailed off.

She couldn't say "needy," "scared," or "loving" out loud, because it felt like a betrayal of the connection she had with Huw. Why couldn't Huw have been more like Aeron? Aeron would never have put any woman he was interested in through an emotional wringer.

"So, Aeron? Have you met anyone in Gold you're attracted to? Need an introduction?" She arched an eyebrow.

He chuckled. "Not yet. But I haven't met every female in Gold—and the one I wanted is taken."

God, he meant her. Her stomach clenched with pain and regret that she couldn't reciprocate this wonderful man's feelings. The fact he was being so nice and letting her use him to hide behind made her feel lower than a snake.

Aeron allowed her to enter the *Leonidas* ground transport first. "Royce is grumbling over one couple we suspect is bonding. They're technicians in my lab. The woman is a Volusian. I can't imagine what Royce would say if his Prime officers started bonding on a regular basis. At times, he has been very vulgar about the process, even though the couple is very circumspect in their wooing."

"That's Royce!" Nadia laughed. "You don't mind if we eat with him, do you?"

"Not at all. He'll want to hear our reports—and see the dead creature." Even the stalwart Prime shuddered. "I can't imagine what the women and children survivors went through."

"I'm sorry there were no live survivors." He might have had a mate among the dead. She would never ask if he had a marking; that was too personal.

"As am I." Aeron got into the driver's seat of the transport and waited until his lead tech did a head count. "As am I."

———

Galanti, one standard hour later

"WHAT IN BALCON'S BALLS DO you mean Nadia went to the *Leonidas* with Ard?"

Sore and somewhat out of breath after his earlier exertions, Huw stood over the workstation of Bre Jod in the laboratory. His hands fisted at his sides. The emotional release he'd obtained through the fight with his brothers was quickly history. His skin crawled and his gut churned with the excess of emotions surging anew in him. He clenched his jaw and could barely restrain himself from strangling the messenger.

His primitive brain reminded him this man's hands had been all over Nadia as he'd carried her out of the cave. Bre's quick thinking and fast feet had saved her, but Huw's higher-level brain was on hiatus for the moment.

"Just what I said, Commander." Bre's face displayed no emotion; his voice was calm. But Huw read animosity coming off the technician in waves.

Bre's brothers and the other lab technicians observed the conversation from their workstations. One technician was on the ship-wide com and the security alert alarm began to blare in the background.

Huw read the emotional temperature of the lab as fearful and shocked. The lab personnel were wary of him as if he were a wild beast. Bre's brothers feared for their brother's life. And rightly so. A primitive, territorial part of him wanted to kill Bre for ever being near Nadia.

"Nadia! Help me! I'm losing control."

"Commander Nadia ordered me to bring the team back to the ship and collate the data collected and send it to the *Leonidas* under Commander Ard's code." Bre continued in a tone of voice one might use with a crazy person. "That is what I have done."

Huw took a step back to keep from strangling the man. He *was* acting crazy and would continue to be on a short fuse until he had Nadia in his arms where he could keep her safe … from all the men who desired her. He took several deep breaths and willed his rage to the back of his mind where it belonged.

He needed information. Had Nadia run from him? Was she scared of him?

"Why in the name of the One did she go over there?" Huw's voice was low and raspy; he could barely keep back the growls wanting to be let loose. "Isn't this lab good enough for her?" He gestured at the room.

With his hearing made more sensitive by his increasing rage, he heard one of the other Jods urging Security to hurry. The Jods had been trained in the same manner as he. They recognized a Prime male on the verge of losing control. If Security arrived and saw him in his present state, he was in danger of being stunned.

A more rational part of his brain approved of the Jods' actions; the primitive part of him wanted to silence them.

Huw would like to assure them he wouldn't lose control, but he couldn't. He was walking a thin line and could fall off it at any time. It was as if he were preparing for battle—he recognized *batel rabia* when he felt it.

Cas Jod coughed and drew Huw's attention. "Commander Ard said something about dinner and wine and her spending the night, Commander."

And off the line he fell.

Flames of rage swept over him and engulfed what little was left of his sanity. Instincts as old as the Prime's existence pressed him to fly over to the *Leonidas*, kill Ard, and bring Nadia home.

"Nadia! Nadia!"

There was no answer. Her shields were solid, not even a crack. Yet, he sensed awareness. He sensed her pain. Was his anger affecting her?

"Nadia. I'm sorry … can't control … come to me. Help me. Forgive me … I need you."

No answer.

And why should she? He'd been a stubborn and sometimes cruel fool over the past weeks. Had he lost her? He growled, a low, rough rumble that set beakers and flasks to rattling on the lab shelves. The sound of breaking glass as shelves tore from the walls echoed around the cavernous lab.

The technicians ran for the exit … all except the Jod brothers. The men whom his Nadia had adopted as her brothers from what he'd heard through the ship's rumor mill. Men she liked better than him … loved even.

His next growl shattered the indirect lighting in the lab, throwing the room into darkness only broken by the red emergency lighting in the floor.

One of the Jods called to the Command Deck.

Huw glared. "Go ahead. Call my brothers. I beat their asses into the mats once already today. I can do it again."

A small squad from Security entered the room, their laser pistols in hand. He wouldn't get past them without a fight. Good. He needed to bash some heads in. They were keeping him from getting to Nadia.

"Commander, you need to calm down." Bre cast a narrow-eyed glare at Cas. "My brother's statement was vague and misleading. Commander Nadia is merely working on the report for Captain Wulf and Captain Melina. I think she plans on having dinner with Captain Nowicki and Commander Ard and then playing some poker with her former shipmates. There is nothing improper going on…"

Huw growled and raised his fists. Bre backed away. "Don't tell me nothing is going on! You had your hands on my woman. You hurt her. Ard hurt her. No one is allowed to hurt her!" He stalked around the lab, kicking fallen shelves and glassware out of his path.

Diew, he needed to gain control. But ever since the danger to her on the planet's surface, his emotions had spiraled out of control, only subsiding somewhat after the beating he'd given his brothers. He needed to see Nadia, smell her sweet scent … touch her. He needed to put his scent on her … mate her!

"Nadia! Nadia! Where are you?" He screamed at her mentally. *"Nadia … please come back to me! I need you. I'm sorry if I hurt you, lubha. Forgive me … please?"*

His telepathic shouts were ignored, bouncing off the titanium-strength wall she'd erected in her mind since the attack on the Cejuru docks.

Molten waves of anger surged through his body until he viewed the lab and the people in it through a red haze. He wanted Nadia back on the *Galanti* and he wanted her here … now! If he could see her … talk to her … she'd forgive him. Be with him.

"Commander?" Keeping out of Huw's reach, Bre spoke. The man looked concerned. "You need to control the battle rage before someone gets hurt."

"Don't tell me what to do—and stay away from my Nadia … she's mine!" He glared at Bre and the other Jods. "No one will keep me from her. No one!"

He ran at the Security team blocking his way to the hall and the lift that would take him to the shuttle bay. Three stunning blasts hit him midbody. He continued to run toward the men who'd shot him, barreling through them as if they were flimsy pieces of wood.

The hallway was crowded with more Security. He roared the Caradoc battle cry, because this was what it was—a battle to get to his woman. As he rushed the men armed with laser pistols, he was tackled from the side and taken to the floor.

"Huw! Huw!" Wulf's voice barely touched what was left of his rational mind. "Stop this! We don't want to hurt you."

Huw roared and twisted and attempted to throw his older brother off him. A stinging on his ass had him snarling.

"The tranq should calm him soon." Kerr's voice.

The damn doctor had drugged him. The anger swirling in him was soon buried under an avalanche of chemically induced ice.

"Huw! What have they done to you? I hurt. I'm cold. Huw?"

His consciousness wavering, Huw couldn't find the path to answer, to reassure her.

Diew! He didn't deserve Nadia. His denial of their connection had allowed his emotions to rule him—resulting in her pain. Now, the release of his jealous rage, his need for her, had also hurt her. He was a lousy mate. He'd hurt the woman he loved most in the universe.

As he sank deeper into the ice taking over his mind, he cried out in an attempt to connect. *"Nadia! I'm sorry. Forgive me."*

CHAPTER 18

Starship Leonidas, Captain's Quarters

Nadia jerked as a shard of freezing-cold pain tore through her. She pushed away from the dining table in Royce's quarters and then hunched over, her arms hugging tightly around her middle with one hand splayed over the knifelike pain centered over her right ovary.

"Nadia!" Aeron leaped up and placed an arm around her waist to prevent her from diving nose-first into her pasta.

His touch, normally uncomfortable, now felt as if iron bristles had been dragged over her nerve endings. With the overload of pain and discomfort, her thick mental walls tumbled down and Huw's voice, filled with so much anguish her heart hurt, shouted in her head over and over. *"Nadia! I'm sorry. Forgive me."*

"Huw! What have they done to you? I hurt. I'm cold. Huw?"

No answer. Only a thick, dark cloud of Huw's pain and torment met her mental touch. His pain had become hers. She struggled to stand and will away the referred pain.

She could handle the feelings—for now—but only because Huw's voice had dimmed and his pain had become buried under an unnatural bank of icy fog. The excruciating sensations were still there, merely camouflaged—an unceasing, knifelike agony scraping away Huw's sanity, clawing to take him over body and soul.

"*Huw? Are you there?*"

"*Dr-r-rug-g-ged. Sor-r-ry. Hur-r-t you.*"

"*Hold on,* zaychik. *I'm coming.*"

She sensed his immediate relief at her words. He needed her. And, dammit, she needed to be needed. Still didn't mean she wouldn't make him court her, though.

"*Dermo*! Shit! I have to go back to the *Galanti*! Something bad has happened to Huw!" Nadia headed toward the exit to Royce's private quarters. "I'll finish the report for Wulf and Mel later."

Royce stepped in front of her, placing a hand on her arm to halt her. "Stop, Nadia. You're as white as the Tooh 2 beaches. You're in no shape to fly a shuttle. Let me check on what's going on. If there's a *real* emergency, I'll have one of my crew take you back. But if it's Huw being Huw, why rush? It's not as if he's shown you any consideration over the past weeks."

Fury unlike any she'd ever felt before surged to her forebrain. She thrust away Royce's arm and got in his face. "He needs me. I can feel his pain. I can hear him screaming my name. He needs me … and I can't … can't…"

"Royce," Aeron spoke as Nadia broke into tears, "it's their bond. Nadia cannot ignore Huw's pain any more than he could ignore hers. And while he's been a stubborn idiot, he has gone to her side every time she has needed his nearness for comfort. Nadia can't not go … it's a biological drive."

"Shit!" Royce rubbed a hand over his face. "This bonding crap is going to upset discipline all to hell and back. We've got a couple of techs going through the same thing … and they've been inseparable. Hell, the Prime male involved practically killed one of the other men for hitting his woman too hard in training. It took four of us and some heavy-duty drugs to control him."

Aeron nodded. "A Prime male is very territorial during the bonding dance. He'll be under more control after he's assured his mate is his and only his."

Nadia stared at Royce. "Someone else is experiencing these hellish emotions? I knew Lia and Joen were … but…"

"The docs are watching and running tests on any couple showing signs. They said the mating would be in reverse order of a normal Prime mating or some such shit." Royce swept a finger over her wet cheek. "You're crying." He shook his head. "I've never seen you cry in all the years I've known you."

Nadia made an effort to smile, but failed. "I think Huw's unconscious now. I can sense him, but he isn't trying to reach me."

Aeron snorted. "Drugged for sure. Huw's been out of control since you ran from the giant worm. I spoke to Mel right after we reached the *Leonidas,* and she told me Huw beat the shit out of Wulf and Iolyn when they wouldn't let him come to the planet's surface. Mel had a feeling Huw's emotions would break through to you sooner or later. She wanted me to keep an eye on you."

The *beep-beep* of a communication from the *Leonidas's* command deck came through. Royce put it on speaker. "Nowicki here."

"Captain, Commander Nadia's presence is needed stat on the *Galanti*. She's to report to Sick Bay immediately per the order of Captain Wulf and Dr. Lenke."

Panic had her checking the connection with Huw. He was unresponsive … but alive.

"I'll let her know." Royce clicked off the speaker. "Sounds as if it's an emergency. What are you feeling now?" Her old friend looked curious despite his earlier indication he wasn't dealing well with the Prime mating on his ship.

Walking quickly, just short of a jog, Nadia left Royce's quarters followed by the two men. "Fine. I'm fine. Just feeling the increased need to be there when Huw comes out from under whatever they gave him."

"Nadia, be careful," Aeron warned. "Huw will still be in a rage."

"Why?" She frowned. "I'm not in danger now."

"That was most likely only a small part of what set him off." Aeron waved her and Royce into the lift and then followed them inside. "I suspect this outburst has been building for the whole time he's denied the connection between you. He sees you working every day, side by side, with other men. You train with them. You eat with them. Joke with them."

"Fuck me!" Royce said. "He's jealous and has been building up a head of steam."

"Yes." Aeron nodded and his lips thinned. "When Wulf wouldn't allow him to go to Nadia when she was in danger, Huw lost it. Only Nadia's presence, her scent, her touch, and the sound of her voice will soothe him. Wulf once told me he wanted to kill everything and anybody who'd initially kept him from Mel. He said it felt like full-blown *batel rabia* all the time—and he could barely keep it under control."

The three of them exited the lift on the shuttle bay level. The two men kept pace with Nadia's swift passage through the corridor as they escorted her to the shuttle dock. "So? Huw wants me because it's some biological urge … not because he wants me for me?"

Aeron hummed under his breath for a second. "I'd have to say yes and no. Yes, in the physical sense that there is a need to claim you … the bond for a Prime traditionally begins as a neurochemical attraction, and a physical claiming, a scent marking, if you will, cements it. No, in the sense that for a Prime male, a mate is a precious gift from the One. Emotionally and mentally, he needs you to make him complete, to fill a hole in his heart and mind. Once the bonding is complete, a Prime male is loyal and loving to his mate and only his mate."

Aeron closed his eyes as if in pain. "Every Prime male would give all he is to have such a bond—this is part of the reason why Huw held out so long. He thought he could only have such a mating with a Prime female."

"Obviously Prime males can bond with other hominid females," Royce said. "The couple on this ship act like Mel and Wulf did."

"Lia and Joen were very quiet about their bonding..." Nadia frowned, "...plus there's something they aren't telling people. Although both Mel and Lia were quick to tell me things would work out ... eventually. That Huw couldn't deny me for much longer, his instincts wouldn't allow it."

Aeron chuckled. "Well, I would say that has happened. Huw is definitely a Prime male in full mating rage."

"Fucking ass could've been dating her like a normal man all this time instead of being a slime creature's hind end." Royce snorted. "I remember when Wulf came to Tooh 10 and confronted me and the Admiral about where Mel had gone. The Admiral delivered a message from her to a very irate Wulf." He paused and scrunched his forehead in thought. "Her message went something like this ... *she was not a gift and that Wulf had to earn her.*"

Royce laughed. "Make Huw sweat a bit, Nadia ... make him court you."

"I was thinking that very thing before this breakdown occurred." Nadia shot Royce a look. "But first I have to help Huw through this rage. It hurts me as much as it hurts him. My body, my mind, my heart are crying out to go to him and fix the problem."

"I agree with Royce on this, Nadia," Aeron said. "Yes, do what you need to do to ease both yours and Huw's pain, but then make the *apayebo* court you. The courting stage of a Prime bonding is a much-needed period when the bond

238 · MONETTE MICHAELS

weaves itself into the heart and mind of the couple. It is in that phase the couple learns to trust one another to see to their partner's emotional needs."

"I think we don't know exactly what's going on with the Prime/non-Prime mating," Nadia replied. "I'm betting Kerr wants to get some samples before I go to Huw. We need to understand what's happening since it seems to involve strong biological urges and even stronger emotions."

Nadia entered a shuttle where a *Leonidas* crew member waited. She turned to look at Royce and Aeron. "We can't have mating couples losing control in a battle situation. We need to know if the mating couple is fit for duty."

The shuttle door closed on Royce swearing and Aeron frowning. Obviously, they hadn't thought about the long-term issue as far as it concerned military needs.

She'd bet Kerr and Lia had—and Mel and Wulf. Because if it was so easy to find a non-Prime mate, a woman who had the mind-body-soul trinity with a Prime male and merely lacked the marking—the Pure Blood faction would be all over this like the plague. Then what had happened to her, Lia, and Joen on the docks of Cejuru Prime would be minor compared to the future attacks against all non-Prime women in the Alliance, military and civilian workers alike.

CHAPTER 19

Nadia entered the outer room of Huw's suite and found Mel, Wulf, and Lia waiting on her. Huw's emotions buzzed over her skin like hundreds of crawling ants. His chaotic feelings hadn't been lessened by his unconsciousness; in fact, they'd increased the closer she came.

After docking, she'd attempted to go to Huw first, but Kerr had intercepted her and escorted her to Sick Bay. The taking of medical samples had been a lesson in control … and torture. Everything Kerr did exacerbated the pain of being away from Huw when he needed her. She'd even snapped at Kerr a couple of times. The prick had laughed and said her irritability was understandable because she and Huw were sharing a high level of sexual frustration.

As if she hadn't realized that fact on her own. Huw's thoughts, even while unconscious, were mostly about claiming, marking, and making her scream in ecstasy.

She was so ready for the claiming—had been for weeks. So she was happy he was finally on the same page. Screaming in ecstasy? She was on board with that too. Within the last few days, even her vibrator and the sex sims hadn't provided relief.

"What's going on?" Nadia moved further into Huw's quarters and looked at the two women she called friends. "Why are you here?" She inhaled sharply and glanced at the closed bedroom door. "Is Huw okay?"

"Huw will be fine now that you are here. Sit down, Nadia." Wulf gestured toward a small sofa across from where he and Mel sat. "Melina and Lia couldn't tell you any details prior to now, because the knowledge has been restricted. With Huw's display of rage at your danger and distance, most Prime on board this ship have guessed you are bonding and the bond is as strong as with an all-Prime couple. We can't hide the fact any longer that true *gemat-gemate* bonding is possible—at least with Terrans and Volusians."

Nadia ignored Wulf's offer of a seat and didn't completely process what he'd told her. Huw continued to call to her. She touched his mind and found him unconscious. He was still dreaming about taking her in every way a man could take a woman. Her knees went weak at one detailed and highly kinky image and she braced herself on a table by the door. She started for the bedroom door, wanting to be near him, but was stopped by Wulf.

"Nadia, wait." He led her to where Lia sat.

Nadia sank onto the buttery-soft gray leather sofa. Her hand covered the spot on her lower abdomen throbbing with need for Huw. "What about the marks?" She frowned and looked at Wulf. "You said something about a true *gemate-gemat* bonding." She glared at Lia and Mel. "I knew you were keeping something from me."

"Yes, we did. Nadia, look." Lia raised her top and nudged the top of her pants down just enough for Nadia to see a *gemate* marking.

"My God! Lia, you have a mark!" Nadia looked from Lia to Mel and then to Wulf. "How?"

Wulf chuckled. "Well, that's what we're asking. Dr. Martin has some preliminary theories, but would like to do more tests before we make any announcements to the Prime people. With Lia and Joen, you and Huw, and two other couples that seem to be bonding, we should be able to see what the common biological denominator is—and be able to test for it."

Nadia snorted. "You won't need to test. The couples will know."

Lia nodded and smiled her agreement.

"This thing between me and Huw was instantaneous. I just accepted the reality sooner than he did. It isn't comfortable, dammit, and that needs to be made clear. Staying away from the person connecting with you shouldn't be encouraged."

"I agree." Wulf braced his elbows on his knees and leaned toward her. "Huw wouldn't have lost control of his emotions and endangered himself and others if he'd accepted the courting phase from the beginning." Wulf leaned back against the sofa and Mel snuggled into his side. "My brother understands that now. He knows he's hurt you on many levels."

Wulf paused and what Nadia could only describe as a naughty grin crossed his lips. "I think once you calm him down and achieve the marking, you should make him pay."

Nadia choked, the sound between a laugh and a sob. "That's what Royce and Aeron suggested … I'd already made the decision to confront him."

"Ahh. And if he hadn't come to terms?" Wulf arched one dark brow, his amber-colored eyes glittering.

"I would have asked for a transfer to Blue Squadron."

Mel and Lia gasped. Nadia shuddered at the thought now, not sure she would've been able to go through with it … but she damn well would have tried.

Wulf nodded and hummed under his breath. "It wouldn't have worked, but it would have driven the point home. I chased Melina all the way from Tooh 10 to Obam IV. I would have followed her across the universe if I'd had to in order to make her mine. The urge was that strong."

Mel rubbed her cheek against her mate's arm. "And you took your damn time, too. By the time you found me, we were both hurting badly. I never want to feel that kind of torment again."

"God, Mel, when you first described that time to me, I didn't believe you." Nadia shook her head at the folly of it all now. "But this feeling ... of being separated from Huw, especially when he lost control and needed me ... well, it was like losing a part of me. I have this big hole in my heart. My mind can't seem to focus on anything else. The only thing that's keeping me in this seat and not going to Huw is I knew you were hiding something."

Lia touched her on the arm. "I didn't have the turmoil you and Mel went through since Joen made it his business to be near me as much as he could without drawing too much attention to ourselves." The doctor's lips twisted. "Joen was very inventive at finding ways of getting me alone. It was ... arousing ... fun. You definitely need to make Huw chase you. No moving in with him until you get to know each other."

"Okay, since we're all on the same page as to how Huw needs to chase or court or woo me ... would somebody tell me when the mark appears?" Nadia knew she sounded irritated, but they were jawing at her and she wanted to be with Huw.

"After sex, Nadia," Lia said.

They all laughed as Wulf snarled under his breath, "Be blunt, why don't you?"

Mel kissed Wulf's red cheek. "Lia's mark appeared after she and Joen had intercourse for the first time." She poked Wulf in the stomach with a finger. "My *gemat* doesn't like to discuss his crew's sex lives. Who'd have thought big strong Prime males were such wusses when it came to being frank about intimacy?"

"I'm not a wuss whatever that is," grumbled Wulf. "We're talking about my brother and my new sister-kin. Huw, for one, would knock me on my ass again if he knew we were discussing his sex life."

Nadia laughed. "I won't tell him." A thought crossed her mind. "Does Huw know about the mark?"

Wulf grinned evilly. "No. He had already decided to declare his interest in you when you returned from the planet. He told me his honor prevented him before this last stop on the mission. He didn't want to declare himself if there was a chance he would mark a hither-to-unknown Prime female. He didn't want to hurt you by beginning a relationship that might later have to be ended."

"He stayed away from me because of honor?" Nadia scowled. "On the outside chance he might find a woman he could mark?"

"Yes." Wulf's expression was solemn. "His reasoning was sound, but it was narrow-minded in light of the intense attraction between the two of you and the mental connection. He was so busy looking at the big picture, he missed all the fine details that demonstrated he had already found his mate."

Nadia huffed out a breath and touched Huw's mind, digging deeply and found that everything Wulf had said was true. Her thickheaded Huw had avoided her to keep from hurting her. And, he was right, dammit. If he had dated her, courted her, taken her to bed, and then later found a Prime female who took his mark, she would've been very hurt.

"I see his reasoning," she said, "but it doesn't make the pain of the last few weeks any less hurtful." She sighed. "Aeron told me Huw needed me for more than just the biological urges…"

"Aeron is correct." Wulf's eyes turned warmer; his expression became more gentle and understanding. "Nadia … sister-kin … Prime males desire and need their mates on all levels. Never doubt, you will be the center of his universe from now until death. No other will ever love you as he does."

Wulf sighed and frowned. "You need to understand why he reasoned it out as he did. My idiot brother has always had this skewed outlook about why Iolyn and I had markings and he, none. He felt lesser than us, wanted to be like us … so he searched for the perfect *gemate* and missed her when she was right in front of him. He forgot to listen to his instincts."

"And Prime males are all about instincts." Mel laughed. "Wulf is correct. Once that man beds you and completes the bonding, he'll want to be near you every second to make sure you're safe, happy, and well loved. You'll have to stand up to him and fight for your breathing space, or he'll smother you with his adoration."

"You're saying he loved me, instinctively, since he was first attracted? That to Prime males, attraction, biological or whatever it is, is the key to love for them? That the bond would've gone no further if love couldn't be found in the relationship?"

Wulf nodded. "There is an old Prime saying: The One does not make mistakes. The mating bond is considered a gift from the One."

Nadia stood and stared at the closed door to Huw's bedroom and then glanced back at Mel. "I've watched you and Wulf dance around for a level playing field since you've been together. I know what to expect. I can handle him." She shot them a naughty grin. "But can the big, bad Prime handle me?"

Wulf threw back his head and roared with laughter as Lia and Mel joined in.

Oh, yeah. Huw would have to dance to her tune for a bit—and it would be fun.

"When do you need us back on duty, Wulf?" Nadia asked. Her pussy tightened with need and flushed with dampness as she anticipated the hours of pleasure promised by Huw's thoughts.

"Forty-eight standard hours should do it. Aeron can handle the data from Ursa 345 and make the reports." Wulf stood and ushered Lia and Mel toward the exit door. "I can guarantee my brother won't want to leave his bed if you're in it. Plus, you could use a break after your encounter with the worm creature on the planet."

Nadia shuddered. "Don't remind me. Bre can assist Aeron with the report from our team and run the lab in my absence."

"That should work." Wulf paused in the open doorway. "My brother loves you, Nadia, never doubt it. He was devastated when he realized how blind he'd been, how much he'd hurt you." Wulf angled his head toward the bedroom. "We had to sedate him to keep him from hurting others in his drive to get to you. So, please, take that into consideration. Don't lead him on too much of a dance." He winked. "Prime males will only be led by the nose so far."

Nadia laughed. "I know. I've watched you and Mel, remember?"

"Then you won't make our mistakes." Wulf left and closed the door.

For all intents and purposes, she and Huw were secure in their own little world for the next forty-eight standard hours. Two days to come to terms with the physical side of the relationship and how they would proceed afterward.

Taking a deep breath, she opened the door and entered the bedchamber. The room was similar in layout to hers, but the colors more masculine, all navy blues and silver grays with chrome accents.

Huw lay on his back, his bare chest glistening with sweat from the excess of stress hormones undoubtedly flooding his system. While he was still deeply unconscious, his sleep wasn't restful. His mind was filled with intense sexual needs aimed at her and living nightmares of losing her. The strong emotions colored the aura she saw through their connection. Deep creases on his forehead confirmed the turmoil she sensed.

Nadia moved to the bed and sat on the edge. She soothed the deep furrows on his forehead with a finger. He inhaled and then sighed, "Nadia." All the tension left him like a deflating balloon.

Tears welled in her eyes. "God, Huw." Just a touch and all his rage was gone. For the first time, Nadia realized the power she had over this man. With such great power came great responsibility.

Then she noted all her pain was gone as well—well, not all. Her lower abdomen still throbbed. But this time the feeling was more sexual and akin to pleasure. The light skin-to-skin touch and his scent had her clit aching and her pussy flooding.

Since Nadia didn't consider herself easily stimulated, the quick and intense arousal scared her. Huw had a lot of power over her as well.

Trust … it all came down to trust. And it would be a learning process between two strong-willed individuals.

Huw turned his face into her hand, nuzzling it and then kissing her palm before settling into a deeper, more natural, and less restless sleep.

"No guts, no glory, Nadia," she muttered as she stood.

Stripping down to a tank top and panties, she climbed into bed with Huw. As she snuggled next to his arm, she realized he was naked from top to bottom. She gasped and tried to put some distance between them when his arm went around her shoulders and anchored her firmly against his side.

God, the feel of his warm skin against hers was aphrodisiacal.

She peeked at his face as she tested his mind. He was definitely asleep. His action had been instinctive. She rubbed her cheek against the light smattering of black hair on his chest and inhaled deeply. His scent was calming to her soul and heart while, at the same time, arousing to her body. She snuggled against him, one arm going under the pillow her head was on, the other over his chest. She covered the place over his heart where his *gemat* mark would appear.

Comfortable and suddenly sleepy now that the stress of the last few weeks had dissipated, Nadia turned her face enough to kiss his bare chest. "Sweet dreams, *zaychik*."

She snickered as she closed her eyes. Huw would freak when he found out what the endearment meant. "Little rabbit" was the loose translation of the Russian. Her mother had always called her father that … well, that or *sladkie*, sweetie. Huw wouldn't like that one, either. Tough, he'd learn to like them.

Nadia went to sleep with a smile on her face, thinking about him snarling over the too cute endearments.

CHAPTER 20

Huw woke slowly, his mind swimming through a thick, drug-induced fog. The rage that had overtaken him earlier was gone as if it had never happened. He felt … calm … at peace … and then he realized the reason why was the armful of sweet-smelling woman cuddled to his chest.

"Nadia?" he whispered against the blonde head lying on his chest. He raised a hand to cover hers covering his heart. "*Diew! Lubha*, you came to me."

Love unlike anything he'd ever felt saturated every pore in his body. The area of his chest she touched throbbed. His cock hardened as he breathed in her sweet female musk.

Huw pressed urgent light kisses against her silky, blonde curls. He battled the urge to kiss her entire body, to rouse her to the same level of sexual urgency he felt. He brushed her mind with a soft mental touch. She was completely open to him—and she was exhausted. He could wait. *Ansu bhau*, he deserved to wait after acting like an inconsiderate, blind brute toward her for weeks.

Settling her more closely against him, he idly stroked the arm holding onto him. He wallowed in the comfort holding her gave him and wondered how he'd ever existed without such closeness. A woman was a wondrous creature.

Nadia's first sexual experience with him had to be special, a merging of heart, soul, and body, and not the act of a dominant Prime male thumping his chest and claiming his mate.

A few more hours wouldn't make Nadia any less his.

Huw breathed deeply and took in her scent; the musk of her arousal overlaid with the sweet floral and vanilla fragrance of her skin made his mouth water and his loins throb.

Patience, asshole. She doesn't need to be awakened by a rutting male.

There was no denying the unique bond between them now—his body, heart, and soul had always known she was the one for him; it had been his damn thick brain holding him back.

Huw nuzzled Nadia's forehead. She lay against him so sweetly. "Sleep, *lubha*. I'll guard you and keep you safe ... even from my lustful self." He brushed another kiss over her brow and closed his eyes.

———

HUW AWOKE TO THE SENSATION of a mouth around his cock. He leaned up on his elbows and glanced down his body, and growled at a sight any red-blooded male would appreciate: his woman's head moving rhythmically up and down above his hips as she slowly sucked his cock.

"Ahh, Nadia," he breathed out her name. Her mouth was warm and luscious—and doing far too good of a job. He would come soon if she didn't stop. "*Lubha*, you..."

Nadia paused. His cock slipped from her mouth with an audible *pop*. "Yes, Huw? Am I doing it wrong, *zaychik*?"

"No … you're doing it too well. Would you have me shoot my seed before I give you pleasure?" He gently grasped her smoothly muscled shoulders and pulled her nearly naked body up his. He relished the feeling as her body rubbed against his steely member every inch of the way.

When he had her face-to-face, he tore her tank top off and then skimmed his hands lower and ripped away her panties. He tossed the remnants of her underwear to the floor. If he had his way, she would never wear underclothing again.

"Ahh, skin to skin is much better." He anchored Nadia above him by wrapping an arm around her waist. He smoothed a hand over her toned buttocks and back. Her purring response as she arched into him indicated she liked being petted. Good, because he loved petting her. Her skin was so soft, and though golden, so much paler than his bronzed skin—a light gold to his dark bronze.

Nadia's forearms braced on his chest, she lowered her face and nipped his chin. .

He inhaled sharply and then snarled. "You, my mate, are asking for trouble."

Her eyes, the pure blue of Cejuru Prime's midday sky, twinkled. "Have I found it?" She followed her words by taking his lower lip between her teeth and gently nipping it and then licking away the slight pain with her lushly pink tongue. "I hope so."

Nadia lazily nuzzled and kissed along his jawline until she reached his ear. She spent several long seconds licking the lobe delicately like a mother she-cat cleaning her kitten. When she took the lobe between her teeth and gently tugged, shards of pleasure shot straight to his cock.

With a patience he could not have managed hours earlier, Huw lay under her, enjoying her sensual ministrations.

"I ache, *sladkie*." She purred; her warm breath whispered over his now-sensitized lobe and caused him to shudder with pleasure. "Make love to me. I need your cock in me."

Huw couldn't stifle the animalistic growls rumbling from his chest. He rolled her over onto her back, careful not to hurt her. Now on top, he caged her between his forearms. His brain kicked in and he paused, his torso not quite touching hers; she'd been attacked not so long ago and he didn't want to trigger any bad memories. "You okay, *lubha*?"

"I'm fine, *sladkie*." Nadia smoothed a hand down his back. "Make love to me."

Huw touched her mind and found no fear—only desire. He breathed a sigh of relief and thanked the One as she opened her legs for him. He brushed a tender kiss across her lips. "You are my miracle."

"Damn right." She lifted her head and kissed one of his nipples as she stroked a hand down his flank. He shuddered and restrained the need to plunge his needy cock into her heat.

Instead, Huw settled more comfortably between her leanly muscled thighs; the sensation was that of being surrounded by warm, living silk. He groaned as she tightened her legs against him as if to hold him even closer. He caught a fleeting image from Nadia's mind of them making love with her long, strong legs hugging his waist, her hands gripping the headboard, as he took her fast and hard. He embellished her fantasy and imagined holding her legs toward her shoulders as he thrust his cock deeper into her tight, wet warmth.

Gritting his teeth, he fought the urge to move the few millimeters it would take for him to thrust inside her and make the images reality. He swore he could feel her clit pulsing with need against him. They fit perfectly as if they were made for one another.

It was pure joy having Nadia willingly under him. She freely touched her mind to his, showing him in thoughts and images what she wanted, needed … demanded from him as a lover.

A wide smile curved his lips. His little Terran was bold in her wishes and he would be more than happy to make them all come true. The rough taking his nature demanded and her fantasies desired would be for later. But for now, his mate deserved to be shown he worshipped her and cared for her feelings.

"Sweet … sweet … sweet." He punctuated the words with hot, wet kisses along her neck to her shoulder. He lightly bit the juncture, and she moaned her pleasure. "Nadia … *lubha* … I'm not sure I can perform all those adventurous … sex acts in one night…"

Nadia lifted her head and sank her teeth lightly into his shoulder, quickly soothing the bite with her tongue. "Lucky for you, we have more than one night. Wulf said we're off duty for forty-eight hours."

She wriggled her body under his and his cock moved even closer to her heat than before. *Diew*, she tortured him with her innate sensuality and he was a willing victim.

"I will have to thank my brother." Huw chuckled. He ran his fingers through her hair, enjoying the way the curls entwined around his fingers. "With two nights and a lot of enthusiasm on both our parts, I might be able to meet most of your desires. I, at least, can try."

"That's a good mate," Nadia whispered huskily as she petted his butt. "Nice ass. Why don't you put that big hard cock to good use … now." She slapped his buttock and the sting of pain translated to pleasure shooting up his cock. His precum now coated not only his cockhead, but also her mons.

"Patience." He nibbled along her jaw until he reached her perfect shell of an ear. He nuzzled her there and inhaled her unique scent—Prime passionflowers and the rarest of vanilla from the Tau Ceti system. "First, I need to explore this body. It is mine to pleasure." Huw snagged the hand with which she tickled his butt and brought it to his lips and kissed the palm.

"No touching, or this will be over all too soon. I wish to taste you first."

When she frowned, he nipped a fingertip. "Nadia, it is only fair—you have already tasted me." She scrunched her nose, but nodded. He released her hand after placing another kiss on its palm. Then he leaned over to kiss her mouth.

Her blue gaze fixed on his face had darkened almost to navy blue with her need. He brushed a kiss over her lips, still rose-colored and swollen from when she'd sucked on his cock. His nostrils flared as the heated scent of her arousal combined with his wafted on the air around them.

"So sweet. So responsive." He crooned as he brushed hot, moist kisses over her flushed face before seeking once again the sweetness of her mouth. He braced himself on one forearm and stroked her long, lean body with his other hand.

Nadia arched into him. He swallowed her moans and little cries. Her movements, her kittenish mewls, incited the animalistic side of his nature. He put more of his body weight on her, pinning her to the bed.

That had been a mistake. The movement forced his aching cock to slide in her juices. He beat back the urge to thrust and join them fully.

He released her lips, threw back his head, and prayed to the One to give him the strength to make this first time all about her. Gritting his teeth at the knifelike pain of his arousal, he concentrated on forcing his errant member back under his control. He wouldn't come inside her until after she climaxed.

Her whimpers and frantic movements to get closer touched his soul. She wanted him, and the One knew, he wanted her. It would be so easy to move and thrust and let his primal drives take over ... but this first time was special—and he would make it so for Nadia if it killed him.

"Shh, precious one ... hush, my *lubha*. I'll take the edge off your need." As he soothed her body with long, firm strokes of his hand, he touched her mind, soothing her in the even more intimate way of communication, showing her he only meant to give her pleasure.

She relaxed into the mattress. "I know you'll give me pleasure. I do trust you … not to hurt me … you aren't an attacker…"

She might not think so if he took her the way he really wanted … hard and fast and rough in the dominant Prime way.

"…you're my man … and I want you now." She wiggled her lower body and almost managed to notch his cockhead into her opening.

"Nadia, what am I going to do with you?" He kissed his way to one dusky-rose nipple and took it into his mouth, suckling it.

She moaned and thrust her breast further into his mouth. The guttural sounds coming from her throat added to his pleasure and soothed the part of him that needed to make his mate happy.

"Feels so good. Now will you make love to me?" she whispered, her voice husky with her desire.

He chuckled around the sweet bud he'd caught between his lips. Very single-minded and goal-oriented his woman. He let the nipple slip from his mouth and blew on it lightly. She shivered. "I am making love to you." He rotated his hips so his pelvis rubbed her hard, little clit. Another low guttural sound came from Nadia's throat as she closed her eyes and arched her head against the pillow. Her face glowed with her rapture. She was the most beautiful woman in the universe—and his, just his.

He couldn't resist the lovely length of her neck. He licked her pulse as it beat rapidly under her flushed silky skin and scraped his teeth lightly up her taut tendons. She mewled at his actions, so he repeated them again and again as the sounds coming from her became needier.

Braced on his forearm, Huw now kissed his way up her slender throat. With his free hand, he plucked one of her nipples between a finger and his thumb, alternating light and deep pressure. Her breathy sounds of pleasure were all he could ask for. She wrapped her legs around his thighs, holding him closely. Her legs felt as good as he'd imagined.

"I love you, Nadia mine. You are my calm in a chaotic universe. You *are* my universe." Huw took her mouth once more, thrusting his tongue deeply, mating her with his lips and tongue. She looped her arms around his neck and pulled him closer and tangled her tongue with his. Her taste and her eagerness shot pleasure up and down his body. Much more of this and he would fail in his mission to see to her pleasure first.

Keeping her pinned beneath him, he pulled away from the circle of her arms and kissed the inside of a convenient elbow before licking and nipping his way up her arm and then along her shoulder. His ministrations left love marks and chill bumps on her pale golden skin. Her cries and gasps of pleasure fed his arousal. He could pierce the ship's hull, his cock was so hard.

While he touched and worshipped her body, he shared his feelings along their mind link. And Nadia fed hers back. A continual loop of sensation that built both their pleasures exponentially. This was the way it should be between a man and his woman.

Leaving her shoulders, Huw kissed and licked his way to her breasts and to the nipple he'd already brought to a sharp, needy point. He cupped her full, teardrop-shaped breast and held it for his mouth. He suckled the nipple with strong, deep pulls of his lips, only pausing to add an occasional grazing of his teeth. She tasted wonderful, just like the vanilla of her scent.

"Oh, God! Hu-u-w!" Nadia's voice broke off on a low husky moan and he felt the ripple of pleasure wisping through her mind and into his.

A small orgasmic peak—he grinned. He could do far better than that.

Stroking her nipple with his tongue, he trailed a finger down her torso and found her sex wet and ready. He stroked a fingertip lightly around the opening, up one labia, over the clitoral hood, and then down the other side. Over. And over. And over again, he traced the sensitive tissues, varying the pressures and the path. He reveled in Nadia's sounds of pleasure and her body's trembling on its way to an even bigger orgasm.

"Huw…" Nadia's voice was raspy with her need.

"Shh, shh … I know what you need. You're almost there, *lubha*. Just feel." He gently inserted a finger into her opening and groaned at how the walls of her sex tightened to hold him there. He wished it were his cock instead of his damn finger. *Patience. Patience.* He kissed his way to her other nipple and paid the same loving, detailed attention to it as he'd done to its mate.

"Ooh, just wait until … fuck, oh God that's good…" Nadia arched as he added a second finger to join the first. "I get my mouth … ooh, do that again…"

Huw stroked the spongy flesh on her vaginal wall and rubbed the heel of his hand over her clit.

"Ohgodohgodoheffin'god … on your cock again."

Her threat didn't sound quite as effective when followed by a shriek as he applied pressure to her nipple and clit at the same time.

Another lazy ripple of pleasure flowed through Nadia's mind and up and down her body.

He inhaled the increased scents of her arousal. He needed to taste her. He would die if he didn't take her taste.

Letting go of her nipple after one last strong pull with his lips, he kissed his way down her torso, tracing her musculature and marveling at the strength in her womanly body. As he explored, he kept his fingers, now three in total, in her sex, scissoring gently, stretching, preparing her for the breadth of his cock. Nadia moaned and quivered as he lavished all his attention, his focus on her.

When he reached her belly button, he nuzzled it before tracing a path over her lower abdomen. One spot on her right side caused Nadia's breath to hitch. Every muscle in his body tensed and his heart pounded as he explored the area. He wondered over it, but idly checked it off as her pleasure coming to him over their mind-link.

Since it gave them both so much pleasure, he did it again. He lavished kisses and tender nibbles over the area and then laid his cheek over one particular spot. It was hot to the touch, far warmer than her normal skin temperature. He swore he could feel a throbbing against his skin; swore he could feel an answering heat and throbbing above his heart where a mark would appear if it could. *Strange.*

After placing one last, lingering kiss on the spot, he then licked his way to her clit. He removed his fingers from her vaginal opening, and at her whimper, he patted her hip. "Shh, *lubha*, I'm not going anywhere."

She moaned, and her body shuddered. "I need to come now, Huw."

"And you shall." Huw stroked her hip as he began to worship her sex with his mouth. He began slowly. He traced patterns all around her opening with his tongue as he'd done earlier with his finger. He suckled and teethed her labia, bringing the fleshy lips to a rosy-red color and making them swell. When his cock entered her, they would be sensitive to his every stroke and goad her pleasure higher, faster.

Purposely, he avoided her tightly budded clit as he prepared her for the joining.

When her hips followed the movement of his mouth and teeth, and the cries coming from her throat were low and raspy, and the feelings her mind sent to his scorched his brain, he knew she was ready.

He stroked three fingers back into her needy opening and pulled her clit into his mouth. As he suckled her, he began a shallow, fast rhythm with his thrusting fingers. Nadia's cries were constant now, breathy, grunting sounds as she reached for her pleasure. She was a creature of sensation in both body and mind.

Briefly removing his mouth from her sweet little nub, Huw growled out. "Come for me, Nadia." And he followed his order by grazing his teeth over her clit and then sucking it into his mouth. He thrust his fingers more deeply and applied pressure to the spongy bundle of nerves in her vagina.

"Oh God … Huw!" Nadia arched into his mouth and fingers and came with a guttural moan, breathy gasps of air, and a lot of creative swearing.

Huw chuckled around the throbbing bud in his mouth; the vibrations tipped his love over the edge. Nadia screamed and screamed and screamed as her orgasm reverberated through them both. Huw winced and forced his mind to focus on her pleasure and not the seeking of his. It was a battle, but it was one he was determined to win—for her.

As Nadia's climax wound down, he released her clit and nuzzled her mons and her thighs, soothing her through the smaller after-contractions. He slowed his fingers, drawing out the mini-climaxes until her body relaxed into the bed. Pulling his fingers from her carefully, he patted her clit lightly and drew another full body tremble from her.

Nadia's eyes were closed. Her naked body was flushed rosy and glistening with a light sweat from her orgasm.

Huw, the primitive Huw he had sublimated while he'd seen to his mate's pleasure, growled his satisfaction. He'd fulfilled his woman's needs and now he would claim her, mark her with his seed and scent. He wished he could mark her as a Prime—but realized mark or no mark, he was as bound to Nadia as he would have been with any Prime woman. Their mental link was strong and his heart, fully committed; they were already on their way to having the ideal mind-body-soul trinity. It was good—and he was blessed.

As Huw crawled back over her body, Nadia's pleasure-swamped brain re-engaged—sort of. Her eyes slowly opened. She gazed down his strong torso and found his cock, long, thick and oh so ready to rumble. "That looks like it might be painful."

God, her voice was a mere croak. All the screaming had done a job on her vocal cords. But it was a small price to pay to realize Huw cared enough to give her screaming orgasms—before he gave in to the primitive need she felt boiling just under his skin.

Huw grunted in response.

Nadia touched his mind and found a fiery space, all red heat and … hunger. Male sexual need that would no longer be denied.

"Huw?" Nadia stroked his face, traced his mouth. "It's okay, *sladkie*. Take me the way you need. I trust you."

Huw's eyes closed and his lips moved as if in a silent prayer. And when his eyes reopened, Nadia gasped. His golden eyes were dark, the color of Gliesian honey and in their depths, his desire raged and burned … for her. Plain old, Iceberg, Nadia Petrovich.

Then he lowered his head and took her mouth in a tongue-plunging kiss of ravishment. Her man couldn't talk, but he could kiss—and he did.

Her tongue tangled with his and she pulled him closer. He shared the taste of her and sent her images of how he wanted to pleasure her. She conveyed to him the words he needed, the answers to the questions her big strong, proud Prime male was afraid to ask.

"I forgive you for the last weeks. I want this. I want you. I trust you. I love you. You make me feel beautiful."

Some part of his brain processed every word, because a lightening of his spirit swept from his mind to hers. Freed from his fears of rejection, Huw conquered her mouth and stroked her body back to life, preparing her for his taking.

But her man needed to hear one more thing; the one thing that would allow him to be the Prime male he needed to be—and would be for the rest of their shared lives.

"Huw ... I won't break. Take me as you need. I want it. I want you."

Huw pulled away from her lips and nuzzled her cheek before roaring his acknowledgment of her surrender to his Prime nature. "Mine!"

He stroked her body with a sensual urgency as he kissed any part of her he could reach. Nadia moaned and gasped as her pleasure built up once more, aided by his feeding her his intense need, the need he'd restrained for her earlier. The man was a force of nature waiting to release its fury.

God, what had she gotten herself into?

"Won't ... hurt ... you. Die ... before I would."

"I know, love. Make me yours."

Huw stroked his fingers along her still-puffy labia, and a streak of pleasure shot up and down her spine. He growled and positioned his hard, hot cock to ride fully between her pussy lips. He braced himself over her and took her mouth in a quick, hard kiss. Then he zeroed in on a still-tender nipple. He scraped his teeth over and around the sensitive bud, pulled it into his mouth, and suckled.

"God, Huw…" Nadia had a mini-climax from the tenderly aggressive assault on her breast. Huw slid his cock along her slit and drew the pleasure out.

Nadia cupped the back of Huw's neck and forced his mouth against her breast. He took the hint and continued suckling her with deeper, stronger pulls. As he did so, he moved his hips in a firm, sinuous push-pull. His cock sliding over her clit and labia and the sensations on her breast pushed her quickly to another peak.

The resulting high-pitched squeal sounded nothing like her, but it must have made Huw happy because he growled, one of his sexy growls. The vibration of his rumbling tipped her into a full-blown orgasm.

She screamed and screamed until her voice was gone and she gasped for every breath. The pleasure—all heat and sharp shards—went on for frigging forever. Her mind and body attuned to Huw; she fed on the deep primitive needs of Huw to make her his, make her come and come again. God, he'd kill her with all this pleasure.

Huw released her nipple. He pushed up on his arms and positioned his cockhead at her opening. Then he roared, "Mine" once again and buried his cock inside her with one powerful thrust.

Nadia screamed as another climax swept through her with the speed of light.

Huw grunted. It sounded as if he said, "So good."

This was better than good. His cock buried in her was the best feeling she'd ever had in her life. He filled her and the pulsing of his cock made her body tremble in anticipation of how it would feel as he thrust within her.

Thrusting ... why wasn't he thrusting?

She squeezed him with her strong inner muscles. Huw snarled, and it seemed as if every muscle in his body tightened, but he still didn't thrust.

What had the fool man gotten into his head now? She touched his mind and almost cried even as she smiled. He wanted this first time never to end. He was savoring the moment—relishing the miracle of her. Tears streamed down her face. He loved her.

Huw kissed away her tears, wrapping her mind in soothing, sweet love. He controlled his animal side for her.

"Let go, Huw. Make me soar."

He nodded once and slowly pulled his cock out of her until just the tip was within the ring of her opening. She clenched her muscles to keep him in and felt him throb in response.

Huw nipped her lower lip. Then he pushed back inside her so deeply she could have sworn he touched her cervix. She tightened around him. He groaned. She grazed the skin of his chest with her teeth. He muttered something she couldn't hear and then pulled out and thrust back in. The sensation was incredible. Every ridge of his cock stroked her sensitive vaginal walls, sending tendrils of pleasure up and down her body.

Then he began to move without any hesitation, setting a slow rhythmic pattern her hips easily met.

His low grunts and groans told her of the strain on his body as he held back his rapacious need. The sweet man wanted—no, she read it as needed—her to gain her pleasure again—this time with him inside her. It was a primal drive as old as the universe.

"I'm close, zaychik. *Let go."*

This time he did. He began a punishing thrusting of his hips. All Nadia could do was hold on—and feel.

"Yes-s-s! F-f-f-f-uck! God! I'm co-o-ming!" Nadia screamed her pleasure to the ceiling.

Huw was all animal now. His mental touch swept across their link and took control of her mind just as his body dominated hers. All his thoughts now were of completion. Of how she felt under him. Of her hands gripping his arms. Of her legs wrapped around his waist. Of her sex milking him with her strong contractions.

When Huw ground his pubic bone against her clit, the pleasure bordering on pain flung her into another peak.

As he drove her to even greater heights, Nadia screamed. All higher language skills were gone.

Yet Huw still hadn't come and that would not do. Nadia lifted her head and bit his nipple and took it into her mouth, sucking him as he had her.

Huw let out a roar. For a split second ... for an eternity ... he hung over her, back arched, his gaze unfocused, and then he flooded her with his seed, a seemingly never-ending flow. As he shouted his orgasm, a pleasure-pain scored the skin over her ovary.

Nadia looked at Huw's sweat-soaked chest and gasped. A marking, all swirling colors, appeared over his heart. Tears streamed down her face—they were truly bonded and she'd never be alone again.

"Huw?" Nadia touched his mark. It was hot—and her mark pulsed in time with his.

Still riding out his orgasm and incapable of speech, Huw touched her mind. His awe, his happiness at the miracle of their mutual marking filled her with joy.

Then all hell broke loose.

The orgasm that swept over Nadia was the strongest one yet. It peaked and fell, again and again. Huw matched her climax for climax. Each orgasm seemed stronger and higher than the last, until the sensations became a joint orgasm weaving their minds closer together, binding their hearts, their souls, their bodies.

They were one now, marked for better or for worse, and nothing and no one, not even death would be able to tear them apart.

Huw held Nadia's still-trembling body against his, her head on his chest. He looked down at his chest; he still could not believe he had a mark. His brother, the *apayebo*, had known this could happen and had neglected to inform him.

Nadia, his *gemate*, was a wondrous gift, and one he would cherish and protect for the rest of his life.

He stroked his hand lightly up and down her lush, sleek body, pausing only to trace her marking gently from time to time. His touch made it glow and swirl and triggered an answering reaction in his.

"Did I hurt you, *gemate lubha*?" That had been one of his greatest fears. He had been very rough at the end.

"No…" Nadia pressed a kiss to his chest, very close to his mark, and he shuddered, "…it was very nice."

Huw tilted his head down and snarled into her curls. "Nice? I'm sure the whole crew heard your screams of pleasure—multiple screams of pleasure."

Nadia giggled and pinched one of his nipples. "I was teasing." She tipped her head and smiled at him, all her love glittered in the blue of her eyes. "I loved the way you made love to me. You had to know, you were in my head—just as I was in yours."

"You said you loved me." He kissed the tip of her nose. "While we made love … did you mean it?"

"Uh-huh." Nadia petted his mark. "Do you love me?"

"There are not enough words to express how much I love and adore you." He hugged her closely against him and rubbed her back.

She nestled against him. "Well, I had my doubts for quite a while."

Huw winced at her words. "I was an asshole. I am amazed you have forgiven me." He shoved back and looked down. "You did say you'd forgiven me? I heard you in my mind." If she had, he was the luckiest man in the galaxy.

"Sort of." She rubbed his chest in soothing circles.

What did "sort of" mean?

Just as he was about to ask her to explain, he was distracted by her hand encircling his cock and her lips nibbling his *gemat* marking. His mind turned off and his body took over—he'd ask her what she meant—but later. Much later.

CHAPTER 21

Nadia bent over her microscope and attempted to concentrate on the slide containing a section of skin taken from the desiccated worm creature. Aeron had sent it over with some other samples and his report, wanting her opinion on classifying the creature with similar ones in the galaxy.

While normally such a scientific exercise was right up her alley, this morning her mind was elsewhere—namely, back in Huw's bed with the man who'd marked her as his. She touched the *gemate* marking over her right ovary and it pulsed in response.

She'd awakened before Huw and realized if she remained in his bed, he'd expect it of her the next night and the night after that and so on. Since she'd already determined to make the damn man make up for all those weeks of ignoring her by courting her, she'd sneaked out of his room after a night of marathon sex. She went to her quarters and got ready for a normal day on the job. Normal would be good just about now, because the lovemaking she'd shared with Huw was unlike anything she'd ever heard or read about—and definitely beyond her past experiences. It was life-changing. Normal would be damn good for a while.

Unfortunately, her connection to him was stronger than ever. Huw was awake, and he was pissed.

"Commander?" Bre stood nearby. She'd been so involved in her thoughts of Huw she hadn't heard the man approach. "May I help you with something? You look perplexed."

"No … maybe." She looked into the tech's golden eyes. "You're a man."

Bre snorted back what sounded like a laugh. "Yes, I am."

"If your woman left your bed after a night of … well, you can fill in the blanks." *God, Nadia, blush why don't you? Why the embarrassment? The whole damn ship knows you spent the night with Huw.* "Would you be upset if the woman wasn't there when you woke up?"

To give her tech credit, he took some time to mull over the question before he answered. "If I hadn't damaged the woman's trust in me beforehand … yes. But since we're obviously talking about you and Commander Huw, I think you made the right choice."

Bre's lips twisted into a sly smile. "According to the good doctors' lecture on dating, a Prime male should appreciate and respect a non-Prime female who isn't easy. Women such as yourself need to know the man is serious in his intentions before you commit. This is a new concept for Prime men. Huw never dated or courted you properly though there was mutual attraction."

"Okay, that seems to be the consensus. Thank you." She let out a deep breath and looked up at the very sympathetic Bre. "So … why do I feel so bad? He's looking for me and is frantic." She touched her lower right side again. "I ache, because he aches."

Bre noted where her hand lay and his eyes widened. "You are marked? How can this be? Some of us surmised you and

Commander Huw had something akin to a *gemat-gemate*-type connection, but we never thought…" He looked at her hand once more. "He marked you last night?"

Face burning, Nadia could only nod.

"And you sense his moods, his thoughts, know where he is on the ship at this moment?" Bre's voice and words were rapid, breathless.

Again, she nodded.

"*Diew*! Commander, you not only have a true bonding…" He took in a deep breath and let it out, "…you are battle-mates!"

"Yes." Although Mel, Wulf, and Lia hadn't come out and said so, Nadia had made the leap to that conclusion on her own. Mel had told her once only battle-mates could supply the other with energy and mind-talk across distances. So, Nadia had figured it out early on whatever she and Huw had, they at the very least had a battle-mate-type of connection between them.

"This is amazing. Wonderful." Bre's face glowed. Her empathic skills told her he was overjoyed to the point of euphoria.

"And dangerous information in the wrong hands, Bre." Nadia was only too aware that if the Pure Blood faction heard a lowly Terran female could be marked and also be a revered battle-mate, the faction would accelerate their attacks on Alliance female personnel. Huw's and her connection would be proof the Pure Blood faction was wrong about everything they spouted.

"Yes, I understand. No one will hear it from me … not even my brothers." He frowned. "But it must be announced. If other Prime males find such a compatible mate, they'll need to know so they don't…"

"Act like assholes the way Huw did?" She grinned.

"Exactly." Bre chuckled. "But my answer to your previous question has to be modified. Yes, you needed to leave to make a point, but I'm not sure you should tempt the beast overly much. You didn't see Commander Huw when he was out of control while you were on the *Leonidas*." Bre shook his head. "As a Prime *gemat*, Huw will want to protect you and make your every wish come true."

"No, Bre. He'll want to smother me and dictate my every move." Nadia let out a short abrupt laugh. "And like Mel does with Wulf, I won't let him. It should be interesting to see how long it takes Huw to come to terms with my need for space."

Bre's face went blank, and he took several long steps away from Nadia.

Without turning around, Nadia said, "Good morning, *sladkie*. How did you sleep?"

"I slept just fine, my *gemate*." Huw stepped close behind her chair. He cupped her shoulders with his warm, large hands and massaged her gently. He leaned over and his breath brushed past her ear, making her shiver. "But I wasn't happy to find you missing when I awoke." He lowered his voice to a murmur. "We had another day to play before coming back on duty." He kissed her cheek.

His hands moved along her shoulder to her nape, his thumbs dug into the tense muscles at the top of her spine. "You're tight. How long have you been bending over the microscope, *lubha*? And I sense your hunger and thirst. If you'd stayed with me, all your needs would have been taken care of."

"*Including your sexual needs. You're aching, my Nadia. We'll need each other frequently in the early stages.*" He released her shoulders and straightened, but didn't move away.

Nadia shivered with pleasure as her mark flared with heat and tingles of remembered pleasure—and the promise of more to come. She turned to look at her lover, her mate. Huw had his hand over his heart; he massaged the area in small circles.

He was deliberately arousing her in her own damn lab!

"God, I'm in so much trouble," Nadia muttered. She rubbed her mark to assuage the ache, the need, but found it only exacerbated both.

Huw chuckled. "Come. Let me feed your needs … all of them."

Nadia shook her head. *Suck it up, soldier. Begin as you mean to go.* "Not all of them. I'll dine with you, but then I need to come back and do my job. I'm sure you can find things to do to occupy your time in Engineering."

Huw frowned. "We'll talk over food. We need to talk, Nadia." He placed a hand on her chair and pulled it away from the lab desk.

"Yes, we do." She stood and turned toward Bre. Then she noticed the whole lab had zeroed in on their conversation. *Shit.* Now everyone knew all about her love life. "Get back to work, people. Bre will be in charge until I get back from a meal break. You can com me if something important comes up."

Nadia allowed Huw to lead her from the lab, his hand on her elbow. When he headed for the lifts that serviced the officer's living quarters, Nadia dug in her heels, forcing Huw to stop also.

"What's wrong?" Huw looked down.

"We'll eat in the officer's dining room. Not your or my quarters."

"Nadia, we need to speak of personal things…"

"No, Huw, you want sex. I'm in your mind and the thing with you massaging your mark was low—you knew it would make my arousal worse." She shook her head. "At this moment, all I want from you is food and a conversation about how things are going to be over the next weeks—or maybe even months."

What a liar she was! She wanted Huw to fuck her until she was boneless with satiation; she'd been with him one hundred percent while making love—but someone had to be the rational partner in this bonding.

Huw's anger at her words washed over her skin for a mere instance before he got it under control. She breathed a sigh of relief when he nodded and turned toward the lifts that serviced the general areas of the ship. She wasn't looking forward to telling Huw they wouldn't be sharing quarters yet. She wanted to deliver that message in a public place so he couldn't use sex to persuade her to change her mind. She also thought a nice, stiff whiskey might help.

Her mark, her clit, her pussy, and her heart ached for him. But her mind told her the relationship while unbreakable and eternal had happened backward; they didn't wholly know or trust each other yet. She'd like her lover, her mate, to be her friend. They needed time to get to know one another while not living in each other's pocket.

Well, Nadia, if the experiment lasts a week, you should consider it a success. 'Cause do you think you can deny him anything now that you're more connected than before?

Probably not—but she had to try, had to make a point … had to show him how she'd like their relationship to be in the future. She wanted to be his partner … not his possession.

Huw walked alongside Nadia. Her fingers trembled where she touched his arm. Her thoughts were so chaotic she probably didn't realize her shields were down. As his brother had told him, she didn't fully trust him—she was afraid he would hurt her woman's heart again.

Damn his soul! He'd caused his strong woman unease. He should have wooed and courted her before he claimed her, proven he was a worthy male. But he had been so afraid she would be strong enough to turn away, to find another. He'd read such thoughts in her mind, and they had scared him. So he'd taken advantage of her sexual attraction to him and made her his. Now, she would make him pay. So be it.

He only hoped what she demanded wasn't too draconian since he didn't think he could tolerate not being with her. The sexual drive in early mating was strong—they both needed the physical touch, the closeness of the other to nurture the bond and to keep them rational.

Huw touched her mind in an attempt to soothe her and begin the wooing. Too much stress was not good for her. But she'd closed him off again! That had to stop. *Gemat-gemate* bonds thrived on the ability to touch the other's mind even more frequently than they touched skin to skin.

Ansu bhau! Now that he wasn't thinking with mostly his cock or through the filter of male hubris, he realized he and Nadia did more than merely touch each other's minds. They talked to each other, exchanged mental images, and shared strength, pleasure, and pain. Why hadn't he recognized that before? Oh, yeah, his head had been up his ass.

"We're battle-mates." He glanced at Nadia.

Her lips twisted with amusement. "I know."

Huw groaned. "The Pure Blood faction will try to kill you."

"You won't let them." Nadia put her arm through his and snuggled next to him, her free hand covered his mark. His pulse leapt and his cock strained against his uniform trousers. "I won't let them."

At least she trusted him enough to know he'd defend her to the death.

Huw covered the hand she'd placed on his chest. "That's correct. Together we're stronger."

He needed to drive the point home again and again. He wanted her to acknowledge the need to stay close and remain open with each other.

"I know, Huw." His little mate rubbed her cheek against his arm. "But that still doesn't mean I can easily forget you really don't know me very well, and I don't know you."

"We'll learn about each other, *lubha*." Huw promised. "Just give it time."

"That's the plan, *zaychik*, and what I wanted to talk about." The lift doors opened onto the officer's dining level. Nadia urged him forward. "Let's get a nice quiet booth and discuss this as partners should."

Huw wasn't sure he wanted to hear her demands—and that she would make demands he was very sure. He probably had Wulf and his sister-kin Mel to thank for this discussion they were about to have. He would be sure to kick his brother's ass later. Mel—he wouldn't touch since Wulf would kill him and rightly so. No man messed with another man's *gemate* and lived.

After they slid into a booth and ordered from the robotic server, Huw turned to Nadia and took her hand in his and kissed her fingers. "Okay, let me have it."

Nadia's laugh made his heart happy and his groin ache. "Huw … *sladkie*…"

He leaned over and kissed the smile on her lips. "What are these words *sladkie* and *zaychik* you keep calling me?" He grimaced. "Or do I really want to know?"

Nadia giggled and shock went through him. He had never heard her giggle before. *Maybe because you'd made her unhappy.*

"Russian words of endearment." Nadia leaned closer and lowered her voice. "My mother used them with my father."

Her blue eyes twinkled like the finest blue gemstones. He determined then and there he would buy her jewelry with such stones, but wasn't sure he could find any to rival her beautiful eyes.

"*Sladkie* means sweetie." She kissed his jaw.

He brushed a kiss over the tip of her beautifully elegant nose. "I like the sound of that. And the other word?"

She grinned naughtily and whispered against his lips. "It means 'little rabbit.'"

He thought for a second, trying to place what a rabbit was. Finally, he had a mental image—it was a small Terran rodent-like creature similar to a plains hopper. Rodents were considered vermin. He snarled. "You think I'm a little vermin?"

Nadia collapsed back against the booth and laughed until tears streaked down her face.

"I must be missing something," he muttered. He used the computer at the table to search for a description of Terran rabbits. The images that came up looked very cute and cuddly, not at all like a rodent and, in fact, were not in the same family at all. He looked up and found Nadia smiling at him with much affection. He touched her mind and found the same emotion, though she still guarded her thoughts. "You liken me to a little cuddly rabbit?"

"Huw, it's a term of affection that Russian women call the men who are special to them." She brushed a kiss over his clothed shoulder—the touch, even through his uniform top, had his cock leaking precum. Thank the One, the table hid his lower body. "You're special to me. You always have been … since the first day you butted into the conversation between me and Aeron."

Huw reached for her and pulled her closer to his side. He did not want the smallest distance between them. "I made your life difficult…"

"You made my life hell … but I understand what you were thinking now … and forgive you." She nestled closer. Her sweet-smelling hair tickled his chin as she laid her head on his shoulder. "Plus, you couldn't help it. You're just a man after all."

Huw groused. "What does that mean?"

Nadia angled her head and kissed his jaw. "It means you're a stubborn, dominant, alpha-male know-it-all who reacts sometimes instead of thinking."

And how could he refute her words? He couldn't—he hadn't been thinking. Well, he had, but wrongly. "You're correct. I'm sorry, so very sorry." He tipped her chin up so he could brush a kiss over her lush lips. "I didn't recognize what I felt was more than mere lust … not until…"

Nadia pinched his arm. "As I said, typical male."

"This reminds me of Mel and Wulf." He rubbed her back.

"What do you mean?" She looked at him confusion in her eyes.

"I need to learn to trust in your strength, your abilities. You want to be a partner." He stroked her arm, kissed the top of her head. Her blonde hair felt like silk to his lips. He couldn't stop touching her, kissing her—couldn't believe he had his heart's desire finally in his arms. He was truly blessed. So, he'd better not mess up the gift he'd been given. "When Mel came into our lives, I told Wulf those very things. You would think I would've listened to myself, eh?"

"Maybe my plan might not take as long as I'd thought." Nadia kissed his shoulder again. "Huw, look at me."

He turned his head and stared into her suddenly serious blue eyes. "What do you need from me, Nadia?" He braced himself for the worst and hoped for the best.

"I need time … space…"

"And what does *space* entail?" Huw was very much afraid he knew, but prayed he was wrong.

"You in your quarters and me in mine."

And he'd guessed correctly and hated it. He let out a low moan. "For how long?"

"A week?" Nadia scrunched her nose.

He couldn't resist—he kissed the tip.

"I was going to ask for a couple of months," she said, "but I think it wouldn't work." He nodded vigorously and she laughed. "Plus you're almost at the point I need you to be. As long as you keep listening to the very sound advice you gave Wulf, we should move right along."

Huw took a deep breath and exhaled slowly. "And during this week … we will do … what?"

Nadia petted his chest. "Don't worry, *sladkie*. We'll be together every day. Meals, walks on the beach in the simulation room, drinks in the officer's lounge…"

He cut her off by placing a finger on her lips. "Nadia, I … you … we cannot be without each other sexually for that length of time." Huw grimaced. "I would lose control again … they'd have to keep me sedated. If I could do this for you, I…"

Nadia kissed his finger and pulled it away from her mouth. She clasped his hand. "I know. We'll be intimate … as much as you … or I … need. But I'll sleep alone in my quarters and you, in yours, for a full week. I want the chance…"

He reversed the clasp of their hands and brought hers to his mouth. He kissed her palm, licking the sensitive center. He felt immense satisfaction at her shivering response. His woman, responsive only to him and no other—forever.

"No need to explain, *gemate lubha*. I agree to your week. Be warned, my beautiful one, I will do my best to persuade you to make love with me all over the ship and for as many times as I can convince you. You also have the right to seek me out for your needs—and trust me, *gemate*, you will have needs." He had to laugh at her look of consternation. "I'll endeavor to make your wooing an interesting one."

Their food arrived. "Eat," he said. "You'll need your strength, since I plan to find a place to make love to you as soon as we're done with our meal and before you return to the lab." He chuckled at her stunned silence and placed a hand over her marking. It throbbed with heat. "You need me now."

"Yes," she whispered. Her cheeks colored a pale rose.

He whispered a kiss over her hair. "I'll need you every time I see you for the rest of my days. I want to make you scream with pleasure." Through her uniform trousers, he rubbed her *gemate* marking gently in a circular motion. "You'll find we can climax just from stimulating one another's mark."

"Oh my God! What are you doing?" Nadia reached for her water and took a deep drink. "Stop it, Huw … for chrissakes … I'm ready to climax … right now, in the middle of the frigging officer's dining room."

Huw sensed her orgasm overtaking her. His own climax built in his balls and cock, racing to join her as he shared her ecstasy through their bond. "Nadia, kiss me … now!"

Nadia's blue eyes were smoky with lust. She angled her face and sought his kiss. As he thrust his tongue into her warm, eager mouth, he applied a deeper pressure with the heel of his hand to the heated, pulsing mark. He swallowed Nadia's scream of shocked pleasure. Her arms went around his neck and held onto him as if he were a lifeline. Holding her tightly against his body, he growled into her mouth as her climax triggered his.

Breathing heavily through his nose, he gentled the kiss and manipulation of her mark, bringing her down slowly as convulsive shudders swept over her body. Finally, she collapsed against him. Her fingers idly ruffled the hair lying on the nape of his neck. He swallowed her sigh of complete satisfaction.

Male pride swelled in his chest. He'd given her extreme pleasure and she had accepted it and returned the same. Of course, he now needed to change his trousers, but it was a small price to pay for sharing pleasure with his *gemate.*

Huw released her lips and brushed soft, loving kisses over her face and hair. "And that, my *cwen,* is why we cannot be apart for long. Newly bonded couples need frequent intimacy until the bonding has matured."

"Um, how long will that last?" Nadia gasped out the words as she leaned out of the shelter of his body and reached for her water to take a long drink.

Huw put his arm around her shoulders and pulled her back against him. "Varies." He gently rubbed his cheek over the top of her head as she nestled on his shoulder. "Wulf and Mel are still going through it. My father told me the 'honeymoon' period as you Terrans call it lasted him and mother almost ten standard…" He grinned at her shocked squeal.

"Months?" she asked, her voice quavering.

"Years, *lubha*. It took them ten standard years before they could be away from each other for more than a day or two. And when they weren't able to touch physically ... they touched mentally ... constantly." He stroked a finger over her forehead. "No more shields. If I cannot sleep next to you, I need to touch your mind to assure myself of your safety. You will do the same with me. We need the touching ... it is instinctive."

"Okay." She dropped her shields.

Huw hugged her. "Thank you."

"I'm afraid to ask ... but did your father talk about how often, um, we'd need to have..." Nadia blushed and gestured with her hand. "Um, you know."

"Sex? Yes, he had that talk with all us boys. You'll be a very happy and satiated woman, Nadia Petrovich-Caradoc, because we'll have sex two or three times a day when possible."

At her moan, he laughed. "And I expect that after our honeymoon period fades away, I will still want to make love to you that often. So eat ... we haven't even started for the day. And I want to begin satisfying the list of wants and needs you let slip as we made love."

"I didn't say anything." Nadia took a bite of her eggs and chewed.

"I read your mind, battle-mate. And I enjoyed every single image ... especially the one with me behind you, loving you, and your creamy golden ass all rosy pink from my hand."

Nadia choked and then coughed violently. Huw rubbed her back. "Be careful. With my plans for the day, we don't have time for you to visit Sick Bay."

CHAPTER 22

Five Hours Later

Nadia entered Sick Bay on a run and immediately sought out Lia.

Lia looked up from her computer monitor and smiled. "Nadia! How are you?" The doctor's smile faded as her gaze zeroed in on Nadia's face. "What's wrong?"

God, did she look that bad? She glanced at her reflection in the glass window that overlooked the treatment area of the medical facility from Lia's office. Yeah, she looked that bad—pale and exhausted … and with good cause. The cause's name was Huw "Sex Machine" Caradoc.

"Hide me! Quickly!" Nadia checked over her shoulder. "Huw's hunting for me. I can't … just can't…" She pressed a hand over her pulsing mark, her need increasing as Huw came closer and closer. She groaned low in her throat and felt her face flush red. "The man is a freaking sex maniac!"

Nadia collapsed into the visitor's chair next to Lia's desk. The doctor stared pointedly at Nadia's hand and chuckled. "Don't laugh, Lia. It's not funny. I can't get any work done. I'm exhausted. Sore—and still so horny I'm about to scream."

Lia swiped at the tears of her laughter with the back of her hand. "Nadia … I hate to ask, but how many…?"

Nadia shuddered. "Five times since breakfast and that doesn't count the orgasm he gave me while we had breakfast." Her voice increased in volume as she gestured wildly with her free hand. "In the Officer's Dining Room, Lia! He made me climax in public just from manipulating my mark. If he continues at this pace, I'm not sure I'll survive." She turned pleading eyes to her friend. "Do you have any energy bars? I'm starved."

Lia opened a drawer and handed her a protein bar. "Here. Eat. Now, tell me about the sex … does he initiate every, um, meeting?"

"Yes. I sense he's trying to accelerate the week of courting I'd asked for, so I'll move in with him sooner." Nadia gobbled the bar in three bites, chewing and swallowing as if she hadn't eaten for days instead of an hour ago at lunch. After which, Huw had taken her in a maintenance closet over the back of a workbench. Her ass still burned from the slaps he'd given it before he plowed her pussy from behind. It had been the second time that day for rear entry.

"I love your ass, *lubha*," he'd whispered into her ear as she came screaming into the hand he'd held over her mouth. After his climax, he'd tenderly wiped away their combined fluids from her sex and thighs with a soft cleaning cloth and then kissed every single inch of the heated skin on her bottom, soothing what he'd reddened.

She groaned at the memory of his words and actions. *Dammit!* She wanted him to take her again, and soon—in just that way. She was a sick, sick, sick person to want him again. Yet, though she desired the sexual intimacy, she couldn't do it. Physically. Could. Not. Do. It. She was sore, and her sex felt raw.

Huw nudged at her mentally and she rebuffed him. *"Go. Away. Work. I'm tired."*

"Nadia ... cwen ... lubha ... I love you. Let's take a nap."

"I need a nap ... but we'd do it again. You can't help yourself, and neither can I ... I can't handle more sex right now."

"I promise to hold you. Just cuddling. On my honor ... I need your skin next to mine. I have to have your scent on me, surrounding me. Stay with Lia. I'll be there soon."

"That's what I'm afraid of. Huw ... gemat ... I love you. But if you try to put your cock in me again ... I'll punch your lights out. I swear it."

Huw's low rumble of amusement sent shivers over her skin, making her even hotter. *"I promise ... just a nap."*

"Lia, I've had more sex today than I've had in the last three years! I hurt." Nadia leaned over the desk. "He's coming for me. Please tell me this isn't how it's supposed to be. How did you and Joen survive this? And is it still going on?"

Her friend smiled, a dreamy look in her eyes. "Joen and I had sex several times a day and still do, but we're always mentally touching. The mind link seems to fulfill a basic need of the Prime male." Lia lowered her voice. "Are you blocking him mentally? I knew you were when he was being an asshole."

"Not any more. Are you telling me this nonstop sex is because I kept him out of my head for the last couple of weeks? That he's making up for lost time?" Lia nodded. "Well, hell..." Nadia shook her head and snorted with disgust, mostly at herself. "I guess I need to give in on the moving-in thing, then, huh?"

Lia's gaze was filled with compassion and understanding. "Yeah, sweetie. I think at the very least you need to allow him to be with you physically as often as he can, even if it's only sleeping next to each other. By doing so, Huw might be able to cut back on the number of sexual interludes during the day. Your presence in his quarters, your scent on his clothing and his bed, will comfort him and help depress the sexual urgency. It's a marking of territory and possession instinct."

"Okay, that makes sense. With my sleeping next to him all night, he'll get the reinforcement his genetics needs." Nadia sighed and tears welled in her eyes. "Look at me! I'm an emotional mess. I never cry, and all I want to do now is cry."

"That's okay. Huw needs to see he's hurting you." Lia patted Nadia's arm. "Trust me, he'll bend over backward to make it up to you."

"He promised me just a nap this go-round." She sensed Huw gently touching her mind. His reaction was instantaneous, and his sorrow swamped her.

"Huw? Why are you sad?" God, she hated his unhappiness almost as much as she hated her own.

"You're crying. I don't like it."

Huw was near; she could sense him. And she didn't run. Speaking to Lia had centered her and shown her the overwhelming emotions were normal—and that Huw felt them also. It helped knowing this was mutual—he needed her as much as she needed him—and he wouldn't shut her out again. Because underlying her panic had been the fear Huw would take away his love and affection—and she wouldn't be able to survive such isolation again.

Huw strode into Sick Bay and hugged her from behind. "I will always be with you, always be what you need, *lubha*." He nuzzled the pulse beating rapidly in her neck. "Wherever … whenever you need me."

His words rang with sincerity and truth. With both sides of the mental connection wide open, she understood he'd cut off his arm before he hurt her.

Nadia patted the arm holding her. "I'll still cry from time to time. I'm female and hormones dictate crying when hurt or sad. You can't fix everything."

"I can try." Huw kissed the tip of her ear. "Hello, Lia. Thank you for speaking with my *gemate*. How are you and Joen doing? I understand that you and Joen are also marked and battle-mates."

Lia's smile lit up her face. "Joen and I are very happy. We'd like to invite you both to join us for drinks and dinner in the Officer's Lounge. We can compare notes about the intensity of being a newly mated couple. Since we're going through this at the same time and as the first Prime/non-Prime matings, Kerr has asked me to note what the stages appear to be. We want to educate the Prime males who find non-Prime mates about how the process differs from the traditional Prime mating."

Nadia looked up at Huw, who watched her intently, even as his mind soothed her erratic emotions. "I'd like to do that, Huw. We could help since we haven't had the smoothest of matings. I expect there'll be variations in the process, depending on the male and female involved."

Huw frowned and kissed the tip of her nose. "The roughness of this bonding was my entire fault. You, my *cwen*, have been wonderful from the start."

"It's in the past, *sladkie*. We move on from this point." Nadia swept a finger over his lower lip, and he sucked it into his mouth. She inhaled sharply at how the smallest touch made her pussy throb. "What does *cwen* mean? You've called me that several times today."

Huw released the finger he suckled and smiled. "It has no direct equivalent in Standard, but means something very similar to 'wife' or 'my woman.'"

"Well, thanks for that definition, Huw," Lia said. "Joen just smiled and wouldn't tell me." The doctor straightened and stood up. "Before you leave Sick Bay, I need to record your markings for the Prime database. Kerr had sent messages to your com units, but I guess you both have been too busy to check."

Huw snorted out a laugh. "Yeah, we've been very busy. So much so I haven't provided the appropriate aftercare for my mate's physical well-being."

He massaged the tense muscles at the base of Nadia's neck. Gentle, healing warmth permeated her body from head to toe. The rawness in her sex melted away.

"Is that better?" Huw whispered against her cheek. His warm, moist breath made her shiver.

"Yes." Nadia rubbed her cheek over his. "I see another advantage to the constant mental touch. Your energy transfer can heal any soreness you cause."

"That is true. As battle-mates, we have that extra ability." Huw moved away from her and helped her to stand. "You're not to be hurt in any manner. I'll always fix what I can or see that you receive the medical assistance you need."

"And I can do this for you, also?" Nadia turned and placed her arms around his neck and nestled her head onto his shoulder. She took in a deep breath. His unique scent made her happy and calmed the remnants of her earlier emotional upset.

"Yes. Battle-mates aid each other in battle and keep their partners from suffering pain from battle wounds. Soothing my woman's soreness is a simple matter compared to the pain from a battle blade or laser wound." Huw rubbed her back with his big, warm hands.

She sighed and leaned into him. All she wanted to do now before they met Lia and Joen for dinner was to lie down and take the nap he'd promised her. No sex, just the comfort of her man's big, warm body engulfing her, protecting her.

"We'll do just that … after Lia takes the images of our marks." Huw whispered against the hair over her ear.

Considering what she and Lia had discussed earlier, Nadia had one more order of business to complete. "Do you want me to move in with you? Or do you want to move in with me? We can make the move after supper."

The shock and then the joy which crossed from Huw's mind to hers pleased her. He hadn't anticipated her offer … even considering his now constant presence in her mind. So not everything she thought or did was sensed by him. She had some privacy.

"When did you make this decision?" He caressed her face with a gentle finger. "At breakfast you were so fixed on the week-long…"

She touched his lips, silencing him. "I made the decision a short while ago. Lia said you needed the physical closeness—and so do I. But I'm not cut out for nonstop sex. So I'm compromising with you." He laughed. She traced the smile on his mouth with the tip of her finger. "You were surprised. You didn't read my mind?" She wanted to confirm her hypothesis.

"No … I don't need to go deeply into your thoughts unless you're threatened in some way. I'll rest my touch on the surface of your mind. I thought you understood that from speaking with Mel about these matters."

Nadia shook her head. "Nope, no one mentioned that. Not even Lia," she shot her smiling friend a nasty look, "told me."

"Nadia," Lia said. "You wouldn't have believed me if I had. You thought a mental touch meant a mental digging. You needed to learn this truth about the connection yourself."

"Next time, share."

Lia laughed and nodded.

Nadia turned her face into Huw's neck and rubbed her forehead against his pulse. "Let's get the pictures done. I'm falling asleep standing up. It's been a hard day so far."

Huw laughed and picked her up as if she weren't a six-foot two-inch, strongly muscled woman. He then carried her out of Lia's office toward the medical lab.

"Huw!" Nadia slapped at his shoulder "Put me down. I weigh too much for you to lug around."

"You, my little *lubha*, are a delightful armful and weigh nothing to a Prime male such as me."

Nadia sniffed. "And you, my big, strong Prime male, are full of crap … but I love you saying so. And you can carry me any time you want. I like it." She snuggled into his arms and luxuriated in the sensation of being carried.

Several hours later, Huw's quarters

THE BLARE OF SIRENS INDICATING a yellow alert woke Nadia from the soundest sleep she'd had in weeks. She tried to sit up and reach for her com unit, but Huw's arms held her. "Rest on me, *cwen*. I'll check to see what's going on."

Nadia relaxed back into his body as he spooned her. His naked skin was hot and comforting against her back. His cock was semi-erect and lying along the seam of her ass. She wiggled into him and had to choke back her laugh at his swearing.

"You'll pay for that action later." He nipped at her ear. "Now, behave, while I speak to my brother."

"Wulf? Why are we on yellow alert?" Huw stroked her hip as he listened to his brother for several minutes.

Her man multitasked too well. She was aroused and wanted him.

"Nadia and I can be at our stations immediately if you need us. We are rested—Fine. Let us know."

Dammit, duty calls. Nadia willed her libido to calm down; there was always later.

Huw reached over her body and placed his com unit back on the bedside table. She turned over and plastered herself against his chest, her arms looped loosely around his neck. "What's up?"

"Emergency call from the two cruisers we left in the Iota Persei system. One outpost is reporting they are under attack by pirates. The *Picarus* went to back up the *Renard*. They took on heavy laser cannon fire and had to land. Now they are defending the best they can by using their cruisers' cannons as planetary defense. They put out a general call for help—and we're the closest." He kissed her forehead. "We'll be on red alert in about two standard hours once we near the besieged planet. Wulf wants us back at our stations at that time. There's nothing we can do now."

"Are our people okay?" Nadia frowned. Going dirt-side had meant the enemy had severely damaged the ships. Grounded cruisers could only do so much against a determined enemy.

"The captains reported minor injuries. Currently, they are holding their own. But the longer they have no backup, the more danger they'll be overrun by the pirates."

"Are they sure the attackers are mere pirates?" Nadia rested her head on his shoulder, kissing his skin, loving the taste of him.

"Captain V'ro of the *Renard* reported the pirate fleet looked to be cobbled from Volusian and Terran military rejects," Huw hesitated, "but he also told Wulf the enemy fought too well to be just a bunch of opportunists looking to rip off easy loot from some scientists."

Nadia frowned and looked into Huw's molten gold eyes. "There's been an increase in pirate attacks in this part of the galaxy on jump gates and traders. Could it be the Antareans are behind all of these attacks?"

"That's what Wulf and Mel think. They've sent word to both Prime and Alliance Military Commands. Blue Squadron is coming to back Gold up. But Blue was on patrol in the Gliese system and has farther to come."

"Well then, I think we should get up and get dressed and eat before…"

"*Lubha*, we'll do all those things … we have time … but first, if you aren't too sore, I need to be in you again." He brushed soft kisses over her eyes, cheeks, nose, and finally lips. "Only if you want me, that is."

"Oh, I want you. Your healing of me and the nap helped immensely." She brushed her lips over his. "This time, I'll make love to you. Just lie back and enjoy…" She lowered her voice to a growling murmur. "I intend to."

Nadia shoved him onto his back and straddled him. "But this time I'm on top." Rolling her hips forward, she pressed her swollen clit and pussy lips against his stiffened cock and rubbed herself up and down his length, spreading her moisture, marking his cock as hers.

Huw's intent, golden gaze fixed on her face; he opened his mouth. She caught the protest forming in his mind and leaned over. Cupping his face with her hands, she kissed him, swallowing his words.

Damn his alpha-Prime-male hide. He wanted to be on top. Obviously, the sex surrogates who'd taught him how to do the deed were all meek and submissive. She was not meek, and her peers and enemies could all attest to the fact she sure as hell wasn't submissive.

She broke off the kiss and Huw inhaled. His body tightened under her as he prepared to roll her over and take control. "Enh. Forget all that crap about always being in control. We're partners in everything now and that goes for our sex lives also. Let me show you how a battle-mate makes love to her *gemat*."

His body still tight with suppressed sexual urges, Huw said nothing. He lay quiescent and looked at her, his hands idly stroking her ass. His touch made her shiver. Yeah, her man was dominant as hell. The images in his head made her pussy clench and her clit throb. She readily admitted to herself she didn't need to be on top all the time.

But this time, she did. Her man had to learn she could hold her own and had her own fantasies. One was riding him, controlling all that male potency even for a short time. And, God knew, she could only do so if he allowed it. Huw could overpower her at any second—and they both knew it. Whatever control she had, he consented to. And wasn't that what being partners was all about? The ceding of control?

His mind-touch stroked along their connection and he smiled. A sexy, shit-eating grin which told her he'd once again picked up on some of her fantasies. He squeezed an ass cheek with one big, hot hand. "We'll definitely try that later. I love your ass and am more than happy to give you what you need. Claim me, Nadia. Show me what it is to be your man." He slapped her butt. "Since I'll be the only man who ever has you in his bed."

Nadia released his face and began trailing biting, sucking kisses along his neck and shoulders. "My only man."

She slid down until her lips found his *gemat* marking. It glowed and swirled in a hypnotizing pattern of gold, red, black, and white. She traced the intricate pattern with her tongue. Her own marking heated, and she imagined it mimicking the colors and motion of Huw's.

Huw groaned and swore under his breath, but did nothing to stop her. She touched his mind and found a predator lying in wait, ready to pounce. Well, the prey wasn't ready to be taken yet. The predator would have to wait his turn.

"Huw, am I too heavy?" Her body lay upon his full length, her legs lying between his, her arms bracing her slightly above him, and their lower abdomens skin to skin.

"No. Your weight is nothing. Why?" He stroked her back from the nape of her neck, down her spine, to the top of the crease in her bottom. His hand lingered, teasing and tantalizing her butt before he trailed his fingers back up to her nape. Over and over he petted her, slowly and surely driving her arousal ever higher.

Nadia shuddered and scrambled to find the words to answer. She had a plan and his stroking wouldn't dissuade her from its successful execution. "Because I intend to be on top of you for a while."

She pinched a male nipple and smiled at his sharp inhalation of breath. "So, that means, you're not to take over unless I tell you to." She scored his nipple with her teeth. "I want to lick and bite and touch you all over. It's my turn to arouse you until you scream my name."

He frowned and lifted her chin, forcing her to look up. "I always shout your name when I come."

"Not the same, big man—" Grinning, Nadia rotated her hips on top of him; she felt both their pleasure at the move zing along their mate-bond. He growled; the powerful rumble expanded his chest and she rode the motion like a sea creature rode a wave. "Because by that time, you've already had me begging for release and screaming your name many times and—"

"And swearing with words I've never heard before." Huw raised his head, nipped her lower lip, and then kissed away the hurt. "You, my *cwen*, are very foul-mouthed when you come."

"Never before you." At his look of shock, she explained. "No man has ever made me come as hard as you have. Only you have driven me to the point of begging and swearing. Only you." She brushed a light kiss over his mark. It pulsed against her lips.

Huw's immense pleasure at her admission was a living, breathing thing inside and all around her. His emotions wrapped her in a golden, hot glow until she couldn't separate her essence from his. It was the same feeling she'd had the first time they'd orgasmed together and cemented their bond.

"Take what is yours, my *gemate lubha*. Show me how you love me." Huw placed his hands by his head, a motion of surrender in most cultures in the galaxy.

Tears of joy teased the corner of her eyes. She knew what it had taken for Huw to cede control. She read it in his mind, sensed it in his still-taut muscles. He fought the primal need to claim—for her.

"I do love you, Huw." She undulated her body along his. "With my body, heart, and soul."

Huw's eyes glittered, but he said nothing. His molten hot gaze traced her body. His lips tightened, and he emitted a low rumble like a giant cat's rough purr. He asked to be stroked and stroke she would.

Nadia turned her attention back to his chest. It was a wide expanse of muscle covered in bronzed skin and a light dusting of dark hair. His nipples were puckered into tight peaks and his mark was sizzling and swirling like a kaleidoscope in nonstop motion.

Her lips twisted into a slight smile. *Mine. All mine.*

Bracing herself on one elbow, she rubbed her cheek from nipple to nipple, occasionally pausing to nuzzle and kiss the warm smooth skin. Turning her head slightly, she licked a male bud delicately, making it wet, before taking it between her lips and suckling it. He tasted clean and spicy, something uniquely Huw; it reminded her of the pure sea salt found only on Earth and some citrusy herb.

Leaving the one nub, now reddened from her lips, she nuzzled her way to the base of his throat and inhaled again. His scent had made her pussy ache from the first time she'd met him. She licked the hollow at the base of his throat. More salt. More citrus. And something earthy, musky.

"God, you taste so good. So hot." She licked her way from his throat to the neglected male nipple after making a quick lick over his marking. She suckled the other nipple until it was as red as its mate. "Do you taste this good all over, hmm?"

"Why don't you find out?" Huw purred the words. His body twitched under her, and his heart rate increased as she licked around his *gemat* mark without touching the mark itself.

"Does my mark look exactly like yours when we're aroused?" Nadia pushed up from him until only her lower body was meeting his.

Huw's gaze zeroed in on her *gemate* mark. His nostrils flared and his constant low purr turned into a louder, more guttural buzz-saw growl. She looked down and was amazed at the sight of her marking moving and glowing just as Huw's was.

Before she realized what he was doing, Huw brought one hand down to cover her mark, the heel of his hand massaging it.

"Huw!" Nadia pulled away from the incendiary touch. She took his arm and shoved it back toward his head. "No touching. Not yet—and especially not like that. I could come from that touch alone."

Huw's lips twisted into a naughty grin. "That's the point. I can make you come—you can make me come—at any time just by rubbing the marks that make us one. Prime"—his voice lowered to a sexy murmur—"are very sexual creatures with their mates."

"I'm getting that message." Nadia ached like a son of a bitch. She sensed Huw could come at any time. But she didn't want either of them to gain pleasure until she'd reached the one goal, the ultimate destination in her master plan to be on top of this magnificent male creature who was her mate. "But it might be nice to try another way, a Terran way to reach the same goal."

Huw's forehead creased. "What way is this?"

Nadia smiled. "Let me show you."

She slithered her way up Huw's body again and then retreated, brushing her body all along his until her face was in line with his thick erection. All through the hours of sex they'd shared, she'd felt his cock in her, but hadn't had the chance to explore it in all its glory.

"Your cock is the most beautiful cock I've ever seen." She breathed hot moist air over the tip of his cock as she fisted his base in one hand and cupped his balls in her other. Precum glistened on his purpled glans. "Like that?" She licked the pearly fluid away, cleaning his cockhead thoroughly. His cum was salty and sweet like a taffy she'd once had on Mars.

"Oh, *Diew*! Yes-s-s-s!" Huw's words came out on a sibilant hiss of pleasure. "More … please."

"Oh, baby, this is what I've wanted to do ever since I felt you in me the first time." She ran her teeth lightly down the heavily veined column of his cock. "I love sucking cock."

A stream of Prime words flowed from Huw. Nadia couldn't understand most of the words, but suspected they were both foul and praising. She took him in her mouth and hummed. Another spate of words. His hands were on her head, holding her. She sucked him in and out of her mouth using only her facial muscles.

Huw used his hands to force her to move more vigorously on his cock. She let him since it was what she wanted to do.

Hunched over his loins, she fondled his balls with one hand, balls so big she could barely hold onto both of them, and fucked his cock with her mouth. Huw set the rhythm, but when she sensed his balls tightening to come, she released his balls. Then she squeezed and pulled at the base of his cock, stopping the climax.

Huw roared above her head. "What…?"

She released her grip on the base of his shaft and began the rhythm Huw had shown her once more. This time her other hand stroked the seam running down his ball sac with little forays to his perineum. And as he was about to come, she stopped him again.

Huw's growls were now mixed with groans. In between the sounds, he muttered, "Please, *lubha* … good, *Diew*, it is so good … *ansu bhau*, Nadia, just wait…" His words disintegrated into streams of Prime words and her name.

Smiling around her mouthful of cock, Nadia dared to tempt the beast lying under the surface of Huw's iron control. God knew her man was being so good. Time to let the beast roar. Her own arousal was near boiling. Every time she'd stopped Huw's pleasure, she'd stopped hers.

Both of them needed release—and she'd made her point. Each of them had the right to tease and pleasure the other. Sex was a mutual endeavor, a rarefied balancing act of dominance and submission.

Suckling him strongly, she slipped a finger wet from the saliva coating his cock and balls into his ass.

Huw bellowed and withdrew from her mouth. The room swirled as he flipped her over and placed her under him. With an arm braced by her shoulder and one hand under her ass, he lifted her hips up and plunged into her wet and ready sex with one firm thrust.

And then they came.

Nadia arched up and into his pounding hips. She would later swear her mind and soul soared into the outermost reaches of the universe. Huw shouted her name as he engulfed her essence within his, anchoring her. They floated on a solar wind of pure pleasure as they came and came until neither could come any longer.

She must have slipped into sleep, because the next thing she was aware of was Huw nuzzling her neck just below her ear. His words of apology had her jerking awake. She tilted her head and looked down at his dark head as he nibbled his way along her shoulder. "What are you apologizing for?"

Huw raised his head. "For taking away your control. For taking over."

She looped her arms around his neck and pulled his head toward hers until they touched nose to nose. "You took nothing, my *gemat*. My love. I gave. Each of us took and each of us gave. That is love Terran-style."

Huw rubbed his nose gently across hers. Even that touch transmitted to their still joined bodies. "I adore you, Nadia Petrovich-Caradoc."

Nadia would've replied in kind, but her man stopped her by taking her lips with his and beginning to make love to her all over again.

CHAPTER 23

Red Alert on the Galanti

Amid the bustle and white noise of the Command Deck, Nadia sat at her station and began the task of fine-tuning the ship's long-range sensors. Her end goal was to determine the exact types of power sources the enemy ships used. If the energy signatures proved to be of the correct type, the beta-protean weapon could be used against them.

The weapon had been recently tested and proven reliable after an attack on the *Galanti;* it interrupted the engine function of the enemy ships and, as a result, cut all power to the weapon systems and shields. The beta-protean weapon didn't affect stored energy, and thus, backup battery systems would still be effective to power basic emergency systems and preserve life. Unfortunately, the weapon only worked on certain types of nuclear fission power sources which were used primarily by freighters, passenger ships, and older, decommissioned military ships.

Luckily for the Alliance, the pirates tended to fly fission-powered ships, because they were more easily bought or stolen. Only the home guards of signatory planets to the

Galactic Alliance, the Alliance Military, and now the Prime Military, who'd recently upgraded their fleet, had the newer fusion-powered ships.

"Nadia." Mel stood behind her. "Have you been able to lock onto any of their ship's engines yet?"

"No." Nadia swore under her breath. "There are extensive modifications, and the power sources are well shielded. We need to get closer. The long-range sensors aren't powerful enough to break through the physical shields the enemy has in place."

"Well, hell. Let us know as soon as you get a lock." Mel hurried away. With the recent increased sensitivity in her hearing, Nadia heard her friend relay the information to Wulf.

"Sound battle stations, Commander Dakkin," Wulf ordered. "Advise the rest of our ships I want six fighter ships from each starship to harry the enemy so the *Galanti* can get in close enough to lock onto the enemies' energy signatures."

"Aye-aye, Captain." Joen sounded battle stations.

Nadia recalibrated her sensors and attempted to zero in on the enemy battleships attacking the planet where the *Picarus* and the *Renard* had gone to ground. The ships profiles read as Volusian C-class battle cruisers and should have fission engines.

As the *Galanti* neared the action, she cursed softly. The enemy had not only made physical mods to the three C-class ships, but they had also upgraded their engines to fusion. How they'd acquired such military technology and the wealth to do so would be for the brain trust in the Alliance Military to figure out.

"Captain Wulf! Put some distance between us and the enemy, sir. The three ships attacking the planet are reading as possessing fusion engines. I recommend evasive maneuvers until I double-check my data. Hold on, sir. I'm getting something else." She fiddled with her sensors and found echoes of other power signatures. "Sir, I believe the enemy has other ships in orbit around the besieged planet. They should be coming onto the screen in the next standard minute."

The low murmur of shock which swept the Command Deck was understandable. Three ships in a pirate fleet was about one ship too many; most pirates didn't play well with others and worked alone or in pairs. To have additional ships orbiting the planet was so far out of the norm to cause a high degree of concern and a re-evaluation of whether these were actually pirates or whether they were mercenaries acting under orders—or were they Antarean ships disguised to appear to be pirate ships?

As Wulf ordered evasive action, Nadia sent her data to Huw and then connected with him mentally.

"Huw?"

"Yes, Nadia."

"Check the shielding and energy readings I just sent you on what seem to be decommissioned Volusian C-class battle cruisers. Do you see what I see?"

For several seconds she heard only silence along their connection and was barely aware of the white noise of the activity around her as Wulf and the Command Deck crew took evasive action and fired at the enemy. Then Huw swore and her heart fell into her stomach. He'd seen what she had. Damn!

"Yes, they've upgraded their engine systems. Have you checked the other ships coming into sensor range yet?"

"Just now. The other ships are smaller light battle cruisers that our fighter pilots can take out. I wanted to stop the larger ships dead in space with the beta-protean weapon if we could."

"I understand. But if the smaller ships possess older engines it will save our fighters and the planet's inhabitants some grief."

The smaller light battle cruisers were now strafing the planet's surface since the three larger enemy ships had now turned their attention to the *Galanti* and the rest of Gold coming to the planet's rescue.

"I'm checking the light battle cruisers' energy signatures now."

"I'm here if you need me, gemate."

"I know." She felt the love he sent her along their connection and returned it in kind.

"Report, Nadia," Wulf said.

"Huw has concurred with my conclusions—the enemy's large battle cruisers have advanced engine technology. We can't use the beta-protean ray. I'm running the sensors over the enemy's light battle cruisers now. We might be able to use the weapon on them."

"Let me know as soon as you have finished your scans." Wulf turned to face the monitor, which showed the three large vessels approaching in standard V-attack formation. In the background, the planet was under attack by seven smaller cruisers.

Nadia got back to work. Her fingers flew over her panel touch screen as she listened to the co-captains' discussion.

Wulf said, "Melina, please advise our fighters to concentrate on taking out the weapon systems of the three lead enemy ships and weakening their shields. Also, order our light battle cruisers to harry the smaller enemy ships keeping them occupied until we can…"

"Captain Wulf?" Nadia turned to look at her captains. "Pardon, sir. All the smaller enemy ships are reading as the older technology with no unusual physical mods. We can take them out en masse from the *Galanti.*"

Wulf grinned. "Excellent. Melina, please advise the *Leonidas* to have their light battle cruisers assist the fighter pilots in damaging the battleships heading for us. Advise our light battle cruisers to continue to engage any enemy ships that attempt to strafe the planet's surface. I will advise Gold's remaining starships to create a perimeter. We won't let these *apayebote* escape."

"Yes, Wulf." Mel turned to issue his orders.

Nadia turned back to the monitors. She inhaled sharply. Where in the hell had that ship come from? "Sir. We have a large battle cruiser coming up on us from behind. It must have hidden behind one of IP 568's moons. It has armed and locked onto us."

"Throw all power to the aft shields. Take evasive maneuvers. Fire the laser cannons and keep those other three bastards back." As the crew responded to his orders, Wulf split the view monitor to show 365-degree-views of the *Galanti*. "Report, Nadia. Power signature?"

Nadia scanned and assessed data as fast as she could type. Huw was in her head and duplicated her actions on his own panel. "Huw and I have concluded … fission energy pattern." The sigh of relief on the Command Deck was audible. "I've sent the reactor coordinates of the ship coming on us from behind to Weapons for a firing solution."

"Weapons, once you have locked onto the enemy ship's engine fire the beta-protean ray. Get that fucker off our ass."

"Aye-aye, Captain." The weapons officer programmed the data both Nadia and Huw had sent to his station. He only had to adjust for speed and trajectory of the *Galanti*'s evasive maneuvers. "Firing." He touched the Go button.

The release of the ray shook the ship.

Nadia held onto her station, her gaze locked onto the large view monitor in front of the co-captains' chairs. The resulting explosion made her wince. But the blinking out of the lights on the enemy's ship gave her a warm feeling in her stomach. One less enemy to worry about.

"Direct hit, Captain." The weapons officer announced.

Nadia checked her monitor and relayed the readings from the darkened ship as it floated without power along a trajectory away from the *Galanti*, a path forced upon it by the explosion. "Engines are dead. Shields are down. Weapons systems are dead," Nadia reported. "They're losing environmental. They don't seem to have any emergency power. They're drifting away from us very slowly."

"Estimate as to when the ship's environment will become lethal to the crew?" Mel asked.

Wulf continued to direct Gold's attack on the rest of the enemy as Nadia fed the dead enemy ship's specs into her computer along with the number of carbon life-forms her sensors advised were on the ship. "They have maybe two standard hours before the ship's air becomes toxic. Temperatures will fall rapidly over that time period and should be just above standard freezing. They'll be within range for a tow within the same time period."

"They'll keep then," Wulf said, his gaze never leaving the battles playing out on the monitor. "If we can't take out these three battle cruisers in the next two hours, we don't deserve to be patrolling space."

The crew on the Command Deck murmured their agreement.

"Nadia," Wulf said, "coordinate with Weapons' Control and feed them the data on the smaller enemy ships' reactors. Let's freeze them in space and make the odds even better for us."

"Anticipated your order, Captain. The enemy ships' engine room coordinates have been fed to Weapons. I took the liberty of programming the firing solutions from my station. Weapons can fire at your order."

"Weapons has them, Captain. Permission to fire?"

"Fire."

The big ray fired seven times in as many seconds. The ship vibrated with the echoes of the potent streams so much that Nadia's teeth ached from the energy transmitted through the titanium framework of the *Galanti*.

"Status?" Wulf asked.

"All direct hits, sir," the weapons officer stated.

Nadia scanned the smaller ships. "All engines are dead. Shields are down. Weapons systems are down. Emergency backup is active in all seven ships. Carbon life-form activity indicates panic on at least two of the seven ships."

She turned to look at Wulf, who grinned like a fierce beast ready for a meal. "Sir, I think some of the crews have decided to mutiny against their captains. There are indications of elevated body temperatures and heart rates akin to combat conditions."

"Well, good, maybe those rioters will tell us something about who hired them to attack Alliance scientific outposts." Wulf turned back to the view screen. "Because these aren't pirates—they have to be mercenaries masquerading as such."

Gold's fighter ships and light battle cruisers concentrated on attacking the three enemy ships left mobile. Nadia winced at several near misses by the enemy ships' light cannons.

"Melina," Wulf spoke in a conversational tone, "please advise our ships to back off."

Nadia smiled in anticipation of Wulf's next order. While the beta-protean ray wouldn't work against the modified battle cruisers, the *Galanti* and the *Leonidas* had ship-killer laser cannons with one hundred times the firing power of normal light laser cannons. She gave Wulf the information he needed before he asked for it.

"Captain, I will confirm that according to my sensor readings, the three remaining enemy ships do not have ship killers." It went without saying if they had, they would've used them by now. But Wulf would want documented data, not gut feelings. "With full-shielding, we should be able to get close enough to do some serious damage without any to us."

Wulf chuckled. "Are you reading my mind now also, Nadia?"

Nadia smiled. "No, sir. Just my training."

Wulf nodded and made a call over intership communications. "Captain Nowicki? Did you hear Nadia's conclusions?"

"Yes! Ard concurs with Nadia's conclusions. What are your orders?"

"Once our ships are clear, use your laser cannon on the ship closest to you. *Galanti* will take out the lead two. You back us up if we miss one of our targets."

Nadia knew that wouldn't happen as did everyone else, but Wulf was smart to cover all bases.

"No one gets off those three battle cruisers." Wulf's voice was stern.

"Aye-aye, sir." Nowicki's voice sounded as if someone had awarded him a million credits, all the women he could want, and a resort home on Tooh 2.

"Nadia, how far away do we need to be to survive if we happen to hit one of their fusion reactors?" Wulf asked.

She winced as did every other command deck crew member. She'd be careful with her coordinates so that really bad scenario would not occur, but then again … shit happened.

Nadia did a calculation. "With full shields, we should fire from a distance of at least five hundred kilometers."

Nowicki's voice. "Ard concurs."

"Weapons, engage full shields and then lock onto the coordinates Commander Nadia will provide." Wulf looked at Nadia. "Plot in the coordinates for the closest enemy ship's weapons control. That should be amidships. With their weapons cut off and a big hole in the middle, the captains will have to surrender or die. Do the same with our second target."

Nadia allowed a slight smile to twist her lips. Weapons control was close enough to the engine room to cause collateral damage, but not create a fusion explosion. "Aye-aye, Captain. Coordinates and firing solution are at weapons control."

"Weapons control is ready, sir."

"Fire." Wulf turned to watch the laser fire hit the first and then the second ship. The percussion of the energy wave hit the *Galanti*'s shield along with debris.

Nadia checked *Galanti*'s status. "Shields holding. No damage reports."

"Status of the enemy ships, Nadia?" Wulf idly caressed Mel's nape as he focused on the view screen.

"All three ships have lost weapons control. There's extensive damage to their fusion reactor engines, but they don't seem to be in danger of exploding. All three ships have auxiliary engines online. Environmental is down to fifty percent on all three, due mostly to the large holes amidships." Nadia switched to life-form sensors. "Those alive are moving to areas where I would assume they have escape pods or small shuttles, Captain."

"This is Captain Wulf advising all Gold ships. The enemy is attempting to escape the three battle ships. Watch for launches of escape pods and smaller transports. Stop them. Do not allow them near the planet's surface."

Acknowledgment came in from every ship.

"Commander Dakkin, advise our crews on the planet of the current status and have them watch for anyone escaping our net."

"Done, sir," Joen said. "Captain V'ro from the *Renard* asked me to advise you some of the enemy had landed prior to our arrival and have dug in. He also has reported our crews and the scientists have suffered injuries, some of them life-threatening. Both our battle cruisers are dead on the planet, having taken on too much damage in space and from strafing runs after landing. He wishes to know when assistance might arrive."

"Advise Captain V'ro assistance is forthcoming within the next standard hour. Get the coordinates of where the enemy has dug in. We'll send in our light battle cruisers to take them out from the air. Have the Engineering Chiefs of our downed ships coordinate with Huw about their needs to get those ships flying again. I'll advise medical to get their teams ready to leave the ship once we are sure it is safe for them to land."

"Captain V'ro has been advised and is relaying your orders to the *Picarus*, sir," Joen said.

"Permission to go dirt-side with engineering, Captain." Nadia stood behind Wulf and Mel, staring at the monitor and the results of the bloodless-on-their-side battle. Her gut kept reminding her that danger was still viable. Who knew how many more enemy ships were playing opossum behind another of IP 568's three moons?

Huw would be going down there, and as his battle-mate, she wanted to be there to cover his ass.

"Huw will be fine, Nadia. I need you here monitoring the ships we hit with the ray. I don't want our boarding parties to be surprised." He turned to look at her and smiled. "Stop worrying. You'll get some couple's time on Tooh 2 for R&R after this mission. Now, go and check for the numbers and types of life-forms on all the dead-in-space enemy ships."

"As in Antarean carbon life-forms in particular, Wulf?" Nadia arched a brow. "You think the Antareans are behind all the attacks?" That had been one of her hypotheses.

"I think the fact the supposed pirates had military technology on decommissioned Volusian ships points to someone hiring and supplying a bunch of mercenaries to attack Iota Persei 568. If the Antareans are behind it, they'll have a presence on board the three larger ships. No Antarean would completely trust a hireling not of their race to follow through completely."

A chill swept down Nadia's spine. "You think they're using the facade of pirate attacks in a renewed attempt to take over the Milky Way?"

"The Antareans have never stopped attacking. They just slowed down for a while." Wulf shook his head. "Now, they're escalating. It's still early in the new alliance between the Prime and the Alliance. They want to take us out and get a foothold in the Perseus arm or lose their chance forever."

"They see the inhabitants of our galaxy as a threat?" Nadia frowned. "The Milky Way is not all that close to the outer edges of Andromeda. Why do they feel the need to get an even larger buffer?"

"I've never understood it. They're acting on some tunnel-visioned instinct—and like all fanatics, they are paranoid. You can't reason with them or begin to understand their reasoning. You have to accept their actions and react accordingly." Wulf nodded at the screen. "We're in control of this particular enemy. Go do your work, Nadia. We'll let the politicians make the ultimate decisions. It's our job to gather information and protect the inhabitants of our galaxy."

"Aye-aye, sir." Nadia went back to her workstation, but kept a small part of her brain monitoring Huw. She'd not breathe easily until her man was back from his mission to the planet's surface. She always kept in the back of her mind that FUBAR was a corollary to the laws of military engagement.

Two Standard Hours later on IP 568

HUW STRODE THROUGH THE MESS that used to be the engine room on the *Renard*. He stopped at a blackened control grid and turned to one of his engineering techs. "Communicate with Commander Iolyn on the *Galanti* and have him send down a replacement grid. The power source wasn't hit. We should be able to get this ship up and running with a new unit and a day or so of work."

The tech nodded. "Aye-aye, Commander."

Huw turned and walked out of the engine room and headed for the bridge of the vessel where his counterpart from the *Leonidas*, Commander A'tem, checked over the control panel connections for the helm.

As he entered the emergency stairwell, he felt a sharp prick on his neck. He turned to defend himself, but lost his balance and fell.

Hard cruel hands gripped him and an unknown raspy voice snarled in a language he couldn't process at the moment. He didn't need to understand to know that some of the planet's attackers had managed to sneak onto the damaged Alliance ship. He raged at his rapidly weakening body and the increased fuzziness of his mind. Before he lost consciousness, he instinctively reached for the connection to Nadia. *"Enemy on planet. Warn the other away teams. They have me ... send help."*

CHAPTER 24

Officer's Lounge on the Galanti

With the airspace around the planet under the control of Gold's ships, the away teams in the process of securing the planet, and a fresh command deck crew monitoring the situations in both places, Nadia and the other senior command deck officers had gone off duty and decided to share a meal in the Officer's Lounge.

Letting out a sharp gasp, Nadia sat upright in the booth. Her exhaustion washed away in a flood of adrenaline. "Huw!"

"What's wrong, sister-kin?" Iolyn asked. "What's Huw done now?"

"He's been taken by the enemy … on the planet. I've lost contact with him…" She looked at Mel and then Wulf, who'd joined her and Iolyn for a drink before dinner. "I can feel him. Touch his mind. But he can't respond."

"He must be unconscious. Keep trying." Mel looked at Wulf. "She should be able to find him … as long as the enemy doesn't take him too far away." Mel turned back to stare. "Do you get the impression he's being taken away from the planet?"

"No." Nadia shoved her way out of the booth. "Get me down there. I'll find him." She now understood how Huw had felt when she'd been in danger. It was a horrible feeling akin to an essential piece of herself dying. She shot a grim look at the other three. "The enemy has probably taken others of our away team hostage. If I find Huw, I'll find them all."

The enemy had no way of knowing about battle-mate capabilities. Hell, she had no way of knowing all she could do … she was on a steep learning curve and a short clock.

"Captain Wulf! Captain Melina!" The head of security rushed into the lounge area. "We have a report from Commander A'tem that an enemy team infiltrated one of the downed cruisers and have taken Commander Huw and his engineering team hostage. The enemy is demanding a ship and free passage off the planet and away from the Iota Persei system."

"Is that their only demand?" Wulf asked.

"No, sir." Z'es's scowl grew darker. "They stated if we don't meet their demands within the next standard hour, they'll kill one hostage each half hour until we do." The security officer looked at Nadia. "They said they would start with Commander Huw."

Nadia pressed a trembling hand over her *gemate* mark as it throbbed with pain. "Like hell they'll kill my *gemat*."

"Get a transport ready, Z'es. We want two full security teams on board and ready to go within the next ten standard minutes." Wulf led the way out of the lounge. Nadia and the others followed. Z'es was on his com unit relaying Wulf's orders as they rushed to the lift which would take them to the shuttle bay.

Feeling lost, alone, barely controlling the firestorm of emotions threatening to erupt, Nadia yelled, cajoled, and pleaded with Huw over their bond. *"Wake up, Huw. Now! Dammit!"* She was scared she was about to lose her man. *Not gonna happen!* She ramped up her calls; she'd nag him awake if it was the last thing she ever did. She refused to lose him.

"Is he responding?" Mel winced and rubbed her forehead. "You're putting off enough psychic energy to vibrate the lift."

"No. He's out of it." Nadia closed her eyes and concentrated on examining his vital signs as best she could. "He's alive, but his heart rate seems low. They might have drugged him. Is there a way I can help him flush it out of his system?"

"Yes. Stop controlling your anger and fear," Wulf ordered. "Use your emotions to pump up your adrenaline and cortisol levels ... then share the resulting energy with Huw. It will help him metabolize and flush whatever they gave him out of his system. Be careful you don't succumb to the *batel rabia*. Seek it. Harness it. Share it. Use it ... as battle-mates do."

"I'll try." Nadia shuddered. She didn't know what in the hell she was doing and had no time to learn.

"Don't try. Do!" Wulf's low growl swept over her.

She nodded and let go of her ice-cold control. Her heart beat rapidly, her breathing grew erratic as she allowed her anger—and yes, fear—to take her over. She built her rage, heated layer by heated layer, until she swore she breathed fire and saw red. Her body hummed and vibrated with the surge of emotions sweeping through her. Then she felt Wulf, Mel, and Iolyn pull her into an icy cloud of controlled rage. The psychic connection was similar to what she felt with Huw, but then not. The collective psi pressed on her and showed her the way to focus her emotions so they would be productive and not destructive.

"Good. Good. Your aura shows the cold rage of a Prime warrior." Wulf slapped her on the back. "Now shoot it to Huw, pull him into the *batel rabia* ... he needs to be ready to react when we move in."

Feeding Huw her energy was easier than she'd expected; she merely pictured the unbreakable link connecting them and focused her energy across it. Less than a nanosecond after her thought, his jolt of awareness was a streak of lightning across their bond.

"Huw. Thank God you're back! We're coming, gemat. Pretend to be unconscious. Feed on the collective strength. Get the drug out of your system."

"Nadia. Stay away. Let my brothers and security handle this."

"Don't be stupid. I'm your battle-mate. I won't let some mercenary take my man from me."

"Not mercenaries. Antareans. Four of them."

Nadia followed the others to the waiting shuttle. "Huw says the hostage takers are Antarean. There are four of them."

Z'es nodded and ordered his security teams to load dart weapons onto the shuttle. The weapon had been developed by the Prime specifically to kill Antareans with fast-acting poison darts, which pierced the thick hides of the pseudo-reptilian species.

"Can Huw tell us where they're being held?" Wulf strapped in to pilot the shuttle.

The security teams and Iolyn strapped in behind Nadia as she took the copilot seat. Mel had remained with the ship to provide support from above if needed. With an Antarean presence confirmed, there might be more Antarean ships on their way to the planet to back up their compatriots.

Nadia relayed Wulf's question to Huw who appeared to be more alert than mere seconds ago. She turned to Wulf who took the shuttle out of the *Galanti*. "Huw was unconscious when he was moved. And since he's still playing at appearing that way, he can't question his team." She stared out the front port. "Don't worry. I'll know where he is. Just get me to his last known position. They can't be all that far from the downed ships."

"The four crashed on the planet when one of our ships took out their craft," Nadia informed Wulf and the others. "They need a ship. They're desperate."

"How do you know these things, Commander Nadia?" Z'es asked.

"Huw's feeding me their words, their emotions. He wants me to know they're lethally dangerous." She looked over her shoulder at Z'es and his teams. The Prime members nodded their heads; they understood what was happening. The non-Prime males looked confused and then shocked as quickly whispered explanations were provided by the Prime. "My *gemate* has ordered me to stay on the ship and away from the enemy." She snorted. "Like hell."

Beside her, Wulf chuckled. "My brother still hasn't accepted your strength ... and the full range of your connection has he?"

"Oh, he knows my strength and the connection is what's making him all bossy." Nadia snorted. "He just wants to tell me what to do. This relationship if it's to succeed needs to start out the way we'll continue to go."

"And that way is?" Z'es's voice was filled with fascination.

"As equal partners. As a battle-mate." Nadia looked at the men surrounding her, all Prime and Volusian males. The most dominant and alpha males in the galaxy. "Mel accepted no less and neither will I." She smiled grimly. "And if I have to pound that into my mate's head, I'll do so every time he tries to shunt me aside as a weak and helpless woman."

"Give him time, sister-kin." Wulf brought the shuttle into a perfect heavy air landing next to the damaged *Renard* and *Picarus*. "It's a steep learning curve. And even Mel and I haven't conquered it yet. Since there have been no battle-mates since before the Berean Wars, we must learn how to deal as we go."

"I'm sure Huw will learn." Nadia unstrapped herself, reached for the dart weapon lying at her feet, and then stood. "He has no choice. He's stuck with me."

"Not stuck, cwen. *I love you. Worship and adore you. But if you get one scratch on your body rescuing me, I'll think of new and arousing ways to punish you."*

"That's not scaring me, sladkie. *And the same goes for you. Don't attract undue attention to yourself. You're Prime. They'd love to kill you if your value as a hostage depreciates."*

She stalked to the shuttle exit and opened it. She walked down the ramp and was met by A'tem, the rest of Gold's away teams, and the crews from the downed Gold battle cruisers.

As Wulf received a sit rep from A'tem, Nadia turned in a full circle. She sought to triangulate Huw's position through their connection. During the first sweep, she could discern no specific direction. She swore a blue streak. There were too many emotions in the air around her.

Building semipermeable mental walls around the collective *batel rabia* psi, she tried again. This time, she followed the line to Huw more easily while still using the battle rage of the others to strengthen her focus. Huw was frantic. His fear for her and, yes, his anger and frustration bombarded her. His position was fixed in her mind now—she could find him on a pitch-black night if she had to.

"Wulf!"

Her brother-kin came to her. He placed his hand on her shoulder. "Have you found my brother?"

"My *gemat* is about one point five kilometers in that direction." She pointed toward a small mountain range covered by a dense forest. "And about twenty meters above the surface of the plain we're standing on. The enemy will have eyes on us."

Nadia turned and looked at the crowd surrounding them. "We don't have much time." She found a strange face and approached him. "You're part of the expedition here?"

The man nodded. "My name is Dr. Peters, and I'm in charge of the geological survey of this planet."

She took Dr. Peters firmly by the shoulders and turned him in the direction where Huw was. She pointed. "See the dark red shadow about twenty meters up? It's the only spot on the side of the mountain that has no trees. What is that place? And how do I get to it without the Antareans seeing me?"

"Without *us* being seen," Wulf interjected. All the soldiers grunted their agreement.

Nadia sighed. "Yes, all of us." She looked at Dr. Peters who had a look on his face between concern and bemusement. "What's up there?"

"A small lab which we use to test core samples we've taken from the caves."

"Is there another way up there besides scaling up the side of the mountain?" Nadia asked, taking control from Wulf who didn't complain. They all wanted the same result: Huw and the team back. Wulf would understand the instincts driving her better than most. He, too, was a battle-mate.

"Yes, you can get into the cavern system and come out behind the lab. I'll lead you," Dr. Peters said, picking up a pack and shrugging it on.

"Let's go." Nadia followed Dr. Peters. The security teams along with Wulf, Iolyn, and some of the other crew members from the downed cruisers followed. Wulf placed Commander A'tem in charge of continuing to communicate with and stalling the Antareans.

After they'd traveled about a kilometer, she spotted a path leading to a dark hole in the side of the mountain. Nadia grimaced. Before she could help herself, she asked Dr. Peters, "Are the caves safe? Are there any dangerous creatures we need to be aware of?"

Visions of giant, blonde-eating worms sent chills down her spine. Instantly, Huw was in her mind, soothing her, sending her warmth, sharing his faith in her courage and her leadership abilities. Her fear dimmed as Huw's strength became hers. Yeah, this bond had its advantages.

"The cave system is completely safe." Dr. Peters spoke over his shoulder as he traversed the well-worn path that led into a thicket of giant trees, dense ground-level bushes, and tall grasses at the base of the mountains. The terrain reminded her of the Caucasus mountain range on Earth. "The planet's core is cooling, and there is little tectonic activity left. The only life-forms in the caves are bacteria, fungi, some insects, small frogs in the underground streams, and some flying mammals similar to Terran bats. Mostly harmless."

"No giant worms." Nadia could've kicked her own ass as soon as the words left her mouth. So much for the boost of confidence Huw had provided. Phobias backed by real life experience were hard to put away. The only good news was none of the men with her snickered or teased her.

In fact, one soldier close by muttered, "Hope to hell not."

Dr. Peters visibly shuddered. "No, thank the Lord. I had a bad experience with one in the Umbraxi system."

Well, join the club, doctor. Maybe I should start a club and have secret handshakes for the members.

"Never want to meet one again." He turned and swept a glance over them all. "But if you see something glowing in moist areas…"

She nodded.

"Don't touch it. The only dangerous life-forms underground are several varieties of anaerobic bacteria. Nasty stuff."

The men grumbled—they'd gotten the message.

"Thanks for the warning, Doctor," Wulf responded and then gave orders to his team. "Cover all parts of your skin you can. We'll decontaminate in the *Renard* and *Picarus* decontamination chambers before transporting back to the ship."

As they continued to follow the doctor, the men pulled on gloves and balaclavas to cover their necks and faces as much as possible. Nadia pulled hers on as well. She didn't want a lecture from Huw about being careless. His masculine grunt of approval vibrated through her body.

They finally reached a dark hole in the side of the mountain. This was the adit or opening to the cave system.

Dr. Peters stopped and waited until all had gathered around him. "Stay close to me. Do not go off into any side tunnels. Many of them drop off unexpectedly and others dead-end. We have mapped the cave system and coded all the tunnels using standard mining symbols."

"How far to the hut where they have our people," Wulf asked, retaking his leadership role.

Fear for Huw and disquiet about entering yet another unknown cave system had struck her dumb. But her fears, though real, wouldn't keep her from doing what she needed to do. She'd let Huw comfort her ... later once they were safely locked into their quarters.

"I'm here, gemate. I'm fine. You are all that is brave and beautiful. I will give you all the comforting you need."

"I love you, Huw."

"And I, you, my battle-mate. Be careful, lubha. The Antareans are very nervous. They suspect something."

"About a five-minute walk ... single file." Dr. Peters attached a small red LED light to his hat. "I'll lead you and then get out of the way and allow you to do what you need to do."

"Hurry, Wulf," said Nadia. "The Antareans are getting antsy according to Huw. My gut tells me they won't wait the full hour before they kill a hostage." Huw's danger increased with every second they wasted.

Dr. Peters must have sensed time was not a luxury and walked into the opening. The inky blackness quickly swallowed him up. Turning on her LED light, Nadia hurried to follow.

"Huw. We're coming. Be prepared to distract your captors on my signal."

"Take care of what's mine, Nadia. I'll be fine."

Huw pulled at the bindings on his wrists. The cuffs slick with his blood now had some slight give.

He felt the battle rage building among the Prime on the planet; he fed on it, as did the other Prime hostages as they waited to make their move on their captors. But it was the connection with his battle-mate, her fear for him and his for her, along with his rage at being taken by the hated Antareans, which gave him the extra strength to weaken the bindings. He paused, breathing shallowly, sublimating the pain of fighting the restraints; his eyes slitted as he followed the movements of the enemy.

The two guarding him and his engineering team were paying more attention to their peers who watched the low-lying plain from the cliff.

"Nadia, we're outside on what looks to be a bluff overlooking the plain. Be careful, they're watching."

"We aren't coming up the front. We're coming through the caves."

"The guards are very lax. I almost have my bindings off. I'll be ready when you signal me."

"What about the rest of your team?"

"They're riding the batel rabia. *They'll be ready."*

Huw turned his head. His team members watched him as they also worked on their bindings with lesser success than him. Having a battle-mate was an added advantage.

When the two Antarean guards turned to look at them, all movements ceased, only to begin again when the enemy turned its backs. The lazy *apayebote* would deserve all that happened to them. Prime and Volusian soldiers, even captured and bound ones, were still deadly—as their hostage takers would soon find out.

Nadia was closer. Her energy was strong, pure, and filled with love and the instincts of a *gemate* battle-mate to protect her *gemat*. He'd read the epic tales of battle-mates, but as many of his generation had, he'd believed them to be merely fantasies.

Now he knew the truth. Battle-mates acted as one unit.

Even now, Nadia took the pain of his bloodied and torn wrists and muted it so he could break free. Her adrenaline and cortisol production increased to aid his and flush the drugs the enemy had used out of his system. As she neared, she continuously relayed what she saw and heard, keeping him informed of the rescue team's progress.

He also sensed her hatred of the tight spaces she traversed, but knew she would have faced her worst fear—giant worms—to get to his side. She was an amazingly strong woman. He was honored to be her mate and would tell her, show her exactly how special she was—once they were alone and in their bed.

The four captors huddled and spoke in hushed whispers.

Huw's hearing was ramped up by the hormones flooding his bloodstream. His understanding of the Antarean language was shaky, but he understood enough to decipher the four were desperate to get away. The Antareans were tired of negotiating. They had decided to kill Huw and his men and take their chances in overwhelming the Gold forces on the plain in order to steal a shuttle. They expected help from their brethren orbiting the planet.

Too bad there was no ship capable of assisting them. He'd gleaned the fact from Nadia's mind. Good thing the kidnappers didn't know, or he and the other hostages would already be dead.

"Huw, we see you. Where are the Antareans?"

"They're grouped by the edge of the cliff. They're thinking of killing us and taking the battle to A'tem and the others."

"Too late for that. Let us handle them. We outnumber them four to one."

"I'm almost loose … as are the others. Just get us some battle blades…"

"Sladkie—no need for hand-to-hand. We have dart guns. Just stay low."

Huw had no intention of getting between the poison darts and the enemy, but he'd be damned if he lay still while his woman fought. He hand-signaled his men to stay down and to wait for his next signal. He figured they'd know what to do when the time came.

One of the Antarean guards turned and raised his head as if sniffing the air. Damn reptilian senses. Smell was their best defensive weapon.

"Nadia, cwen, *they smell you coming."*

"Stay down!"

Huw roared the Caradoc battle cry as the rescuers poured from a seam in the mountain. The high whine of the dart guns as they sent their small, but deadly projectiles at the enemy filled the air.

The one Antarean who'd turned to face the mountainside dove for Huw with a chilling hiss of rage.

Huw rolled away, kicking out with his legs. The battle rage filled him and helped him escape the Antarean's sharp-clawed grasp.

Before Huw could get to his feet to fight the bastard, Nadia was there. She waved her knife, keeping the enemy away from him. Using her fragile Terran body and one small blade, she protected him.

Bellowing with rage—and fear for Nadia, Huw surged to his feet. He swept an arm around her waist and shoved her behind him while removing the battle blade from her hands. "My fight, *cwen.* Stay back."

He noted the other three Antareans were down, unmoving—dead from the darts.

The Antarean menacing him and Nadia was too close for the dart guns to be used safely. The poison was as deadly for hominids as it was to pseudo-reptilians.

"Huw, come with me. Step away, love. Wulf has him in his sights." Nadia's voice was calm, but he sensed her underlying fear … for him. She loved him and that made him that much stronger.

Huw laughed. *"Gemate lubha,* if I can't take down this slime, how could I call myself a man?" Keeping his body between Nadia and any danger, he circled the Antarean whose basilisk-like stare never wavered from his prey.

Nadia snorted. "Stubborn ass. You're my man … and there's no need to endanger yourself to prove it."

"Nadia, come here. Now!" Wulf ordered. "Brother. We want him alive. We need the intelligence about the attacks in this area."

"My thoughts exactly, brother." Huw grinned widely as he moved in a deadly dance designed to lead the Antarean away from the others—from his Nadia. He gestured with the knife. "Come on, you scaly, fork-tongued *apayebo*. See if you can fight me now that I'm not drugged."

The Antarean's lidless eyes glistened darkly. His split-tongue tested the air. Something akin to fear came and went in his reptilian eyes. "This-s-s cannot be." His Standard was stilted but fluent. "You smell as she does. You are … one?"

His opponent sought out someone behind him. Nadia! The bastard was staring at Nadia.

"Wulf, get Nadia out of here. He's fixated on her." Huw moved to cut off the enemy's line of sight. "*Gemate*, go back into the cave."

"No. He's not any danger to me. He has three dart guns aimed at him. He moves toward me … he'll die." Nadia's words and tone were a threat. A quick glance confirmed she held a dart gun in one hand and a battle blade she must have taken from one of the downed Antareans in the other.

The Antarean stood still. His gaze was defiant as he looked from Huw to Nadia, who now stood to his side and slightly back to give them both fighting room. "She is-s-s your mate, Prime?"

"She is my battle-mate, Antarean." Huw again blocked the pseudo-reptile from staring at Nadia. He didn't want the enemy even sullying his mate with his leering looks.

"This cannot be. We killed many, many of your women. Two whole generations-s-s of progeny were los-s-t." The Antarean shook his head. "She is-s-s Terran. You are Prime. This-s-s cannot be."

Nadia stepped to Huw's side. She ripped his already torn shirt the rest of the way off, revealing his mark. Before he could stop her, she peeled her pants down enough to display her mark. "We're one, Antarean. There are others."

"They lied to us-s-s." The Antarean's eyes turned livid with his rage. "They offered a pact ... they lied!" He attacked.

Huw slashed at the Antarean's chest. His mate went for the Antarean's legs with the unusual battle blade she'd appropriated. She aimed for a hamstring.

Both found their targets.

The Antarean dropped like a stone, bleeding from multiple wounds and regenerating with every breath. Huw and Nadia couldn't let down their guard. A wounded Antarean was as deadly as a healthy one.

Wulf ran forward and dropped to his knees near the downed enemy. He held a knife to the pseudo-reptile's jugular. "Who offered the pact?"

The Antarean's lipless mouth turned into a parody of a smile. "One ... of yours-s-s ... Prime. One ... of yours-s-s." Then he laughed weakly and impaled his throat on Wulf's knife and twisted, severing his carotid artery.

"*Ansu bhau!*" Wulf leapt back from the arterial spray.

The Antarean bled out quickly, dying with a sneer on his slitty lips.

Huw kicked at the body. "*Diew*, Wulf. The fanatics are working with our most hated enemy."

"That's what it sounds like." Wulf wiped the enemy's blood from his arms with a shirt one of the soldiers handed him. "He wanted to die, knowing we'd be frustrated at his last words."

Scowling, Huw turned toward his brother. "Well, it worked."

CHAPTER 25

Six Hours Later, on the Galanti

Huw gently urged Nadia from the lift into the corridor leading to his, now their, suite of rooms. She felt the olio of emotions coming from him: anger, love, fear, and oddly enough, amusement. The fact he maintained a calm facade and a gentle touch soothed her; however, she read his need to chastise her for placing herself in danger.

Nadia smiled and managed not to snicker at the images in his mind for the planned punishment—all the scenarios had them naked and on the bed. She couldn't wait; she needed him with an unceasing ache. He could've died on the planet, and that was unacceptable.

As soon as they entered their quarters and the door swished shut behind them, Huw had her turned, her back against the door, and her pants ripped off within seconds.

"Never." As he tore her uniform top off, he breathed the word against her ear before nipping the lobe sharply. "Ever. Again."

He fumbled with the placket of his trousers and then shoved them down his thighs. With one hand on her ass, he hoisted her up until her wet and aching pussy was level with the tip of his massive erection.

She wound her arms around his shoulders as Huw held her head still for his rough kisses and nips along her jaw, down onto her throat, and then along her shoulder.

"God, Huw! Up! Up!" She sent him an image.

With his eager cooperation, she toed off her ankle boots and managed to wrap her legs around his waist. She let go of one massive shoulder, tightened with his tension and lust, to grasp his cock and slide it through the copious juices moistening her slit.

"In. In." She attempted to line up her ready opening with his cockhead.

"Hush. Not yet." He muttered the words against her shoulder. "Hold onto me. Both arms. Now."

"But Huw..." Her vaginal opening clenched and unclenched, needing his thick, hard penis inside to send her over the slim precipice she balanced upon. The man had gotten her so hot, so quickly that all she wanted to do was come ... not rehash what had happened on the planet.

"Shh. Not. One. Word." He licked along her right shoulder, pausing to teeth the tendon running to her neck. Then he followed the same path in reverse with his tongue. "Don't ever," he squeezed her ass tightly, "ever scare me like that again." He bit her shoulder lightly. "I died a thousand times in those seconds. He could have..." he slid into her hungry heat with one solid thrust of his hips, "...killed you with one swipe of his hand."

Huw muttered in Prime as he peppered feverish kisses over her cheeks, eyes, lips. "Then I'd be forced back into the solitary darkness I dwelled in before I met you."

"I was scared ... too." Her head slid up and down the door as he steadily pumped his cock into her throbbing depths. She stared him in the eye and slapped his shoulder. "You could've ... died!"

"Never." His voice was thick with fiery lust and loving devotion. "I've just found you, *gemate lubha*. I'll never leave you alone." He paused, fully embedded within her.

She counted the beats of his heart in the pulsations of his cock. She tightened her vaginal muscles, fisting him. Her body screamed for release.

"Shh, sweet, I'll take care of your need. All of your needs." Huw withdrew his penis slowly; its thickly veined surface rubbed her sensitive nerve endings, heightening her arousal.

She moaned low in her throat. "So good. So good, *zaychik*. Take me. Hard. I need you so much."

"No more than I need you." Huw slowly, torturously pushed back into her.

She hissed, a mixture of pain and pleasure, as she felt every single blessed millimeter of his length drag across highly sensitized tissues. He was so big and filled her so full … and he was being too frigging gentle. Gentleness could come later when they were in their bed and the edge was off. She wanted the heat that had him shoving her up against the door.

"Huw … is this your punishment? I need to come, my *gemat*. Do I need to beg?"

He brushed a gentle kiss over the tip of her nose before bracing his forehead against hers. "No, you never need to beg me for your pleasure. Patience, *lubha*. I need you to understand…" He set a rhythm of deep, firm push-pulls, keeping her on the edge of orgasm. If he'd meant to punish her for placing herself in danger, he was doing a good job of it. "If something had happened to you—my people would have had to kill me to keep me from hurting others."

Never halting the movement of his hips, he tilted her chin until her gaze met his. She had never seen his eyes so dark before; they were almost brown with the pain and fear he didn't bother to hide. His emotions poured off him in great, rolling waves, pounding against her mind, her heart, her body. He truly believed what he'd said—he would've been dangerous if she'd died protecting him.

"I didn't know…" she soothed the tense muscles along his shoulders and at the base of his neck with gentle touches, "…I knew Prime males were protective … but not to the extremes you're describing." She kissed his lips lightly, gently to soothe the ravening beast inside him. "I promise not to knowingly place myself in danger without telling you."

When Huw growled angrily in the back of his throat, she nipped his lower lip. "This time you hush. I'm a starship officer. I'm a soldier. I'll encounter dangerous situations … you know that. You have to be willing to cut me some slack in the execution of my duties."

His hips increased in speed and forcefulness. His cock reached ever more deeply within her, giving her the most pleasurable type of pain.

"Stepping in front of me as I face an Antarean is not one of your duties." Huw's words were barely more than a guttural sound.

"Huw…" She shook her head. He kissed her, cutting off her scold.

"Hush, *cwen*." He nipped her bottom lip with his teeth. "I understand your point … but that doesn't mean I like it or accept it blindly."

His lingering rage was translated into harder thrusts into her body, lifting her so her back slid up and down the door's cold surface. "I can't help it. You…" he rotated his hips on the up thrust, "…in danger … not allowed."

He gripped her hips harder, holding her for the rapid pounding of his hips. "Each and every time you're in danger … I'll reinforce my claim … in the most primal way … as hard and fast as I can."

"I don't want you to fear me when I do."

He was afraid he'd hurt her. She trusted him more than he trusted himself. *"I like you wild, my gemat. We'll have a very full and vigorous sex life ... because such situations will happen again."*

"*Hold onto me,* lubha. *I need to take you.*"

"*And I need to be taken. Don't hold back,* sladkie. *I don't break easily.*"

"Diew, *I love you.*"

Huw buried his face into the crook of Nadia's neck and shoulder and thrust harder, faster, driving them both higher and higher. He fed her his love. Bared his soul and revealed the deep, voracious need for her to live and be safe. Admitted the fact she was the only being in the galaxy, the universe, who could drive him over the edge of reason into insanity.

"Huw ... Huw..." Nadia held his head to her with both hands as he took her roughly against the door. "Come for me, *sladkie.* Fill me with your seed. Take what's yours ... only yours, my love."

As Huw bellowed his completion against her neck, he shared his pleasure with Nadia. She screamed her release to the ceiling, her hands clutching his shoulders tightly. The tiny dig of her nails, the squeezing of his cock in her tight heat, had him shouting as yet another explosion of pleasure erupted up his spine.

"God, Huw ... hold me ... I'm ... flying." Her hands fluttered on his arms as she seemed to lose all strength. Her body arched and her head thrown back against the door, she screamed again and again.

Huw held her securely and plunged into her hot, tight sex over and over, nurturing what had become a seemingly infinite climax. Then Nadia went completely lax and fell against him, her head lying weakly on his shoulder.

Concerned he'd hurt her, he stopped thrusting and began to pull away.

Nadia twined her arms loosely about his neck. She dug her fingers into the muscles at the top of his spine, kneading like a she-kitten he'd once owned as a child. "No ... don't leave me. Stay ... stay in me."

She moved her hips in a small, circular motion and clenched his cock, holding him to her with her vaginal muscles. He groaned at the sensation; his cock somehow found even more semen to jet into her depths.

A small tremor shook Nadia. "I'm not done with you yet, my *gemat*." She licked the seam of his upturned lips. "Do you think you can get us to the bed this way?"

Huw chuckled. "Nadia, my flower, you are as light as a cloud and I'm a big, strong Prime male. Of course I can." He settled her more closely against him with one arm holding her hips to him and the other went around her upper back. "Nestle your head on my shoulder, *cwen*. Let me do all the work."

"Good." She snickered into his uniform top. "Someone is still clothed."

"I was in a hurry." He kissed a dainty ear that peeked out of her soft, blonde curls.

She turned her head and licked his neck, little swipes of her tongue that promised to drive him crazy. His semi-hard cock jerked and stiffened again within her heat.

"Nadia ... don't start something you might not be able to finish."

As he walked them into the bedroom, she lifted her head and scrunched her nose. It was so cute he had to stop and kiss the tip and then took her lips in a leisurely kiss. He ate at her mouth, dipping his tongue inside to play with hers. He groaned and pulled away. "Behave, little she-cat. You go to my head too quickly."

Nadia snickered and tightened her inner muscles around his revived erection. "I'd say I go to the little head also."

Huw laughed. "Both my heads, then."

As he resumed the walk to the bed, which seemed like light-years away rather than a few meters, Nadia ran her fingers through the hair at the nape of his neck. He shuddered and chill bumps pebbled his skin. When she traced his *gemat* mark through his shirt, he swore under his breath.

Nadia giggled. "When Mel first told me the marks were erogenous zones, I didn't believe her." Her body shuddered against him. Nadia moaned and shoved at his uniform top. "We need to figure out how to get your clothes off without your penis slipping out of me."

"We'll figure something out. And if the worst happens and I slip out for a second or two, I know how to put it back in you." He assured her in a husky voice. "The One knows I could live inside your body. All that sweet heat bathing my cock is the closest thing to the Eternal I can think of."

Nadia nuzzled his neck. "Being compared to heaven is a good way to get a lot of sex out of me, *gemat*."

"I plan to compliment you frequently and compare you to all the deities of all the religions in the galaxy if it will keep you close to me."

Huw lowered Nadia to the bed and followed her down; he managed to keep his cock fully inside her. The motion had them both groaning.

"Relax, now." Huw braced himself on his forearms above her. "Let your legs fall to the bed." He hadn't understood how she'd kept them around him as long as she had.

"I don't think I can."

Huw reached back and carefully pulled her legs off his hips where she'd locked them around him. She groaned and winced. "Cramps?" he asked.

She nodded.

Huw pushed up and sat back on his knees. His cock twitched, complaining at the loss of her tight heat. Ignoring his little brain, he picked up one of Nadia's long, sleek legs and massaged it. "I love your legs."

He lifted her foot to his lips and kissed her arch as he kneaded her calf. As he moved his fingers up her leg to her thighs, he kissed her ankle. Then he repeated the actions to the other leg.

"God, that is so good." She shuddered delicately under him. She peeked at him from between her thick, dark lashes so in contrast with her pale hair and golden skin. "I miss you, Huw. I need you in me again." She reached for his erection and slid the tip of one finger up and down his turgid length. "Bring that here."

Nadia left his cock and moved a finger to sweep through the glistening, blonde curls on her mound. When she thrust her finger inside and pulled it out, he captured the finger and suckled it, cleaning it thoroughly. He loved the taste of her sweet cream.

"Huw … please?" Nadia arched off the bed, pushing her hips up as she pulled his cock to her.

"One moment. Patience, *lubha*." Huw wanted skin-to-skin contact this time. He kissed the tips of her fingers and then placed her hand on the bed. "Patience."

His gaze never left her as he tore his shirt from his body and rose from the bed long enough to get his boots and pants off. When he came back to her, he slid into her welcoming arms and pussy.

Their mutual groan said it all. They were home, safe for now, in one another's arms. Safe enough to spend what remained of their off-duty hours to make love, sleep, and make love again. He didn't think he would ever tire of being with his woman in this way.

Nadia raised her head and nipped his chin. "Move those hips, Caradoc."

A fierce love soared within his heart and mind and soul. Her receptive body and amorous touches and thoughts told him all he needed to know—she loved him. Adored him. And needed him to take her to the heights of pleasure once more.

"My *gemate* has only to ask…" he leaned down to rake her lower lip with his teeth, "…and I will provide." Bracing himself, he gave her what she asked for. A pounding, hard rhythm that moved her body up and down the mattress under him.

She clasped his upper arms and arched into each thrust, matching the demanding pace he set. With each push, she groaned, and with each pull, she mewled. "Harder. Harder. I want to fly … make me fly."

"Mine!" He took her lips, his tongue mimicking the thrust and retreat of the sexual dance.

Nadia curled around him, clutching him to her with arms and legs. He touched her mind and found her climax was close; he fed it with his own impending pleasure. She clung to him tightly; she was afraid he'd leave her before she climbed the precipice and fell over the edge.

"*We'll fall together, lubha. I won't leave you.*"

"*God, Huw, harder. I'm so close … so close.*"

She drew on his tongue with a frantic suction that had him rumbling deep in his chest. But when she scraped her short nails down his back to sink into his buttocks, he came. He growled his pleasure into her mouth and willed her to come. She screamed her climax into his hungry mouth.

The waves of pleasure flowed over and through them, building upon one another's feelings until Huw could've sworn their souls left their bodies and joined the Eternal for a nanosecond before falling back into them.

As small aftershocks caused their bodies to tremble against each other, Huw vowed to the One—nothing and no one would ever take this woman from him. And if something should, he would follow her into the Eternal.

CHAPTER 26

One Standard Week later, Tooh 2 Resort

From a shady poolside table, Huw turned his head to glance at Nadia, Lia, and Mel as they sunned themselves closer to the pool's edge. The trio looked tanned and happy as they sipped some fruity, pink alcoholic concoction from large glasses decorated with fresh fruit. He was pretty sure they all had a buzz going on.

His Nadia was damn cute and amorous when tipsy. He couldn't wait to take her back to their hotel suite to make love in the huge sunken tub again; they'd practically drowned each other the first time they'd tried it. He thought he had the logistics worked out now.

Stretching his legs in front of him, he surreptitiously rearranged his cock which had gone from what was a constant semi-erect state since mating with Nadia to fully erect at the thought of his naked, slippery, golden-skinned *gemate* covered in bubbles and sitting on his hard-as-titanium cock.

"Down, Huw." Wulf chuckled from the chair to his immediate left. "Or resort security will ask you to leave for indecent exposure."

Joen who sat on the other side of Wulf laughed.

Huw shot the two men an ugly glance. His brother grinned and aimed an amused glance at Huw's crotch.

When Huw looked down, he swore and pulled his shorts' waistband up and shoved his cock sideways so the purpled tip didn't peek out over the top.

"Not funny, brother." Huw nodded at Wulf's lap. "You seem to be having the same problem—but mine's bigger."

Joen snorted his drink out his nose and broke out laughing and coughing at the same time.

Wulf glared at the communications officer and slapped him on the back—hard—several times. Their women all turned and looked at them. Probably wondering what was so funny.

"We know what's funny. Really, Huw, we just had sex an hour ago. And you know as soon as we hit the hotel suite to dress for dinner, we'll have more sex. So suck it up, zaychik."

"Behave, brother," Huw said to Wulf. "The ladies think we're sex addicts."

Joen saluted the three women with his glass of Valerian whiskey. "And the little darlings would be one hundred per cent correct. It's nice having a *gemate* to be intimate with … on all levels."

Wulf raised his glass. "I'll drink to that. My life was empty without my Melina."

Huw and Joen tapped their glasses to Wulf's and then took a drink.

Huw was grateful to the One for giving him the chance to have such a beautiful, brave, and intelligent woman in his life. He wasn't at all surprised the other two men felt the same way—for a Prime male of their generation a *gemate* was a miracle.

He took in and let out a deep breath of the fresh, salty sea air. *Ansu bhau.* It was nice to relax with his brother and his friend and not have to worry about being attacked by pirates,

Antareans, rebel fanatics, and assorted giant worms for a short while. It was more than nice to have a suite of rooms on one of the most beautiful planets in the outer galactic spirals and to have nothing to do but eat, sleep, have sex with Nadia, and repeat the same for the week of leave they'd been given by Alliance Military Command.

After securing the situation on IP 568, the Gold crews had taken the captured mercenaries and Antarean crews and their ships back to Tooh 10 for the Alliance Military to deal with, reported to everyone who needed to be reported to, and then were given leave time before the bulk of Gold went back to policing the outer spirals.

The *Galanti*, on the other hand, would be traveling in the opposite direction, toward the center of the galaxy. Their destination was the Tau Ceti system and their mission was to pick up the Alliance astrobiologist and geneticist, Dr. Brianna Martin, and her team, and bring them back to Cejuru Prime to set up a reproductive research lab.

"So?" Wulf asked after taking another sip of his Valerian whiskey. "Do you think we'll have to carry our women back to our rooms? Or can they hold their alcohol?" His question was precedented on the fact the very helpful poolside waiter had brought the three ladies another round of drinks.

Joen laughed. "Lia is the smallest of the three. So it is safe to say I'll at the very least need to offer her an arm. My little doc has no capacity for liquor." He hummed happily under his breath. "But I think I might just carry her anyway. I love carrying her—she nestles and nuzzles my mark. By the time we make it to our room, we end up on the floor, making love." He beamed proudly as he eyed his mate. "We haven't made it to the bed yet—well, for the first round of sex, anyway."

Wulf saluted Joen with his whiskey, a smile twisting his lips. Huw could tell his brother had had the same experience with Melina. As had Huw with Nadia. His poor *cwen* had bruises from being taken against the wall, door, floor, over the backs of furniture, and once on the dining table in their suite.

As a good Prime male, he healed his woman after every round of sex, which led to slower and even more lingering sex. Life was good.

Well, then again, not always.

Huw stiffened in his chair as he noticed three enlisted Prime soldiers staring at the women. His low growl had Wulf and Joen joining in. After cautious and scared glances at Huw and the others, the three unattached males beat a hasty retreat.

"Father just had to go and announce to the Prime people that some Terran women were capable of developing a *gemat-gemate* relationship," Huw said. "It's been like open season ever since."

Huw glared at another male, this time a Volusian, who stared at the girls' hips. The barely there bathing suits did nothing to cover their *gemate* marks. And with him and the other *gemats* within calling distance, the *gemate* marks on the women were in varying stages of arousal. The markings glowed and whirled, putting on quite a show for the casual onlooker.

Huw covered his mark with his hand and rubbed as if that would help calm it down. But the only thing that would effectively ease his mark was Nadia, and he drew the line at public sex acts.

"It's as if we're animals in a zoo." Wulf glowered at the clueless Volusian. "Everyone, no matter the race, wishes to see the markings."

"Be reasonable, my friends. We couldn't keep it a secret any longer." Joen spoke calmly, the voice of reason among the three males. "We now have ten Prime-Terran couplings in Gold Squad—all with markings resulting after the first sexual intercourse. And all the couples so far are displaying battle-mate symptoms. According to my little doc, there are twenty other couples, some of them with Volusian females who are indicating an ability to mark also, under observation on three of Gold's ten ships. The phenomenon is like a wild beast in the room. People can't help but notice."

"Well, some people had better stop staring at my Nadia." Huw uttered a low, nasty snarl. "Or I'll take the *bak*'s blue-skinned head off."

Nadia looked over at Huw, alarm in her eyes. *"Huw? You're projecting rage. What's wrong?"*

"The Volusian apayebo *sitting two lounges away is staring from your breasts to your hip and slobbering all over himself."*

Nadia laughed, drawing curious glances from the other two women. She pointed to their men, and the women smiled and nodded. Huw could tell his brother and Joen were also communicating with their *gemates*. The air all around their table shimmered and hummed with the telepathic communications.

"Come to me, sladkie." Nadia waved him over. *"Give me a kiss and then glare at him. That should handle it … don't you think? Although, the growling in surround sound scared the three Prime males handily enough."*

"The Volusian can't read a Prime male's batel rabia *as easily as another Prime."*

"Huw … no fighting." Nadia sent him cool, calming energy, taking his heated emotions down just enough so that he wasn't vibrating with the urge to castrate the idiot Volusian who probably was completely unaware he was close to death.

Her sweet touch didn't last long when the Volusian rose and approached the women.

"That does it." Huw shoved out of his chair and was quickly followed by the other two men. Their primal growls echoed around the pool area.

Nadia met him before he could travel two more steps. Mel and Lia intercepted their men just as quickly.

"Huw, *sladkie*…" Nadia stroked a hand down his arm and blocked his forward movement with her body, "…my man does not kill stupid people."

She nuzzled the side of his throat, nipping his shoulder before she relaxed into his body. He encircled her with his arms, rubbing his jaw over her blonde curls. He glared at the man who now beat a hasty retreat.

"Stupid Volusian," Huw said. "The Alliance needs to send out a memo to all soldiers about staying away from Prime *gemates* … or there'll be bloodshed, especially with the Prime males in the early stages of courting."

The doctors still didn't know if the Terran women could break the bond by staying away from a Prime male or not. So far, all the mating couples wanted to be mated. Getting Dr. Martin and her people to Cejuru Prime and starting a more comprehensive testing of the mating process was more important than ever. "I wanted to kill a lot of men who looked at you before I marked you." Huw kissed an errant curl touching Nadia's cheek.

"But you didn't." Nadia brushed a kiss over his tense jaw. "I'll sit with you in the shade. I've had enough sun."

Either the other two women had made the same decision or Wulf and Joen had convinced them, since all six of them now sat at the shady table.

"I'm hungry." Nadia shot Joen a nasty look when he snickered. "For food, Joen. Get your mind out of the bedroom. It's not as if you men were suffering…" She shook her head and Huw had to smile at the look of consternation on her face.

"*Cwen*," he took her hand in his and nibbled her fingertips, "we can do nothing but think of making love to our beautiful women."

Nadia rubbed her cheek over their clasped hands. "Well, once we're back on duty … you've got to give us a break. I have work piled up and I can't drop everything to meet you for sex every freaking three hours or so."

"More like every fricking hour," mumbled Mel.

Wulf laughed and kissed Mel's cheek, which burned bright red. "That's because we're on vacation, *gemate lubha*.

We men have some control—and you women have all the control. You just say 'not now.' We're not animals to take you when you don't want to be taken."

Lia snorted delicately. "But you men will attempt to change our minds." She added under her breath, "Been there, done that."

Joen leaned over and nuzzled her ear and whispered something not even Huw could hear with his more than excellent hearing. Whatever the man had said had Lia turning to kiss him on the mouth ... and tongue was involved.

Nadia laughed and turned to Huw to say something. She then stopped. Her frown had him turning to see what had changed her mood from amusement to worry.

Iolyn and Mel's uncle, Tor Maren, walked toward their table. Both men wore scowls. Huw sensed the auras preceding the two. Something was up and he feared the lovely vacation on Tooh 2 was about to end.

Iolyn spoke first. "Our leave is canceled. The *Galanti* needs to leave space dock within the next twelve standard hours. I've recalled the crew."

"What happened?" Wulf asked. He had his arm around Mel's shoulder as if he anticipated an attack on her.

Huw for some reason did the same with Nadia. Something was up; the vibes coming from the two men had affected all the mated males in the same way.

Iolyn sat, picked up Wulf's whiskey and finished it in one gulp, then picked up Huw's and did the same. Something was very wrong here—and it affected Iolyn.

Tor sat and told the hovering waiter. "Gliesian white wine for me and the ladies. Whiskey for the men." The waiter hurried off. "Since Iolyn is attempting to get drunk, I'll relay what has happened."

Iolyn snarled and grabbed Joen's almost empty glass and tossed it back.

Cold fear struck Huw's stomach. Iolyn had never been a big drinker. Nadia leaned into Huw and soothed him as only a mate could.

"I received word from Admiral Nelson at Alliance Command Dr. Brianna Martin has been threatened … someone attempted to kidnap her," Tor said. "She managed to escape and went into hiding. She put a call out to the Alliance to come and get her."

"That's terrible. Of course, we'll go get her and make sure she gets to Cejuru Prime safely," Wulf said. "But why is my brother attempting to get drunk?"

Tor sighed and shook his head. "Dr. Martin is a Lost One … and she is…"

"My mate!" Iolyn pounded his fist on the table. "She sent an image of her marking to the Alliance. She asked that her mate be found and told. She asked that he come to get her." Iolyn stood up and paced angrily around the table. "I'm clear across the fucking galaxy while my mate had to fight off an attack and run and hide." He threw his head back and roared the Caradoc battle cry to the skies.

Huw stood as did Wulf; they went to their brother and enveloped him within their arms until he quit shouting. His brother was in full-blown battle rage and would be in lesser stages of it until he had his Brianna in his arms.

"Huw?" Nadia came to him and placed her hand on Iolyn's shoulder. "How can we help?" He noted Mel had come to stand by Wulf and also touched Iolyn.

Tor, Joen, and Lia used their bodies to ward off the curious glances of the understandably shook up bystanders. The Caradoc battle cry had turned many an enemy's bowels to water.

"We get to Dr. Martin as quickly as possible."

EPILOGUE

The man behind the Pure Blood faction sat and listened as Ilar informed the delegates of the Council about Dr. Martin's attack and the revelation that she was a Prime Lost One. Through his sources at the Alliance Command, he'd discovered her mark had been verified as a match for Iolyn Caradoc.

He swore silently. *Ansu bhau!* The damn Caradoc direct line would not die out and disappear as he'd hoped and planned. Who knew the sons would *all* find potentially fertile *gemates*? And one of them was a Terran!

It looked as if he would have to incite the Pure Blood dupes even more.

His lips twisted and he suppressed the urge to snarl. He had some contacts on Tau Ceti where this Martin woman had gone to ground. He had no clue who had targeted her and made her run and cry for help. But he would be sure his hired killers got to her first and made certain she never made it to Cejuru Prime. He'd double their usual rate to give them extra incentive.

And if his agents failed?—Well, he had other mercenaries and even an alliance with a subfaction of the dreaded Antareans. Accidents could be arranged. Space flight was, after all, wrought with danger.

THE END

PRIME IMPERATIVE

Adopted and raised by Terrans, Dr. Brianna Martin never quite fit in. She's thrilled to learn she's a long-lost female of the Prime race. And that she has a mate living somewhere on the planet Cejuru Prime—one genetically destined to be hers alone. Before she figures out how to approach him, she's attacked in her research lab.

Iolyn Caradoc is stunned at the news that his mate, matched to him soon after birth, still lives. Even more amazing, she's a research scientist on the verge of discovering why the Prime race is dying. But Pure Blood fanatics are trying to kill her and she's on the run. Every primal instinct in him insists he find, claim, and protect his mate. But the woman won't stay put.

When Bria finally meets Iolyn, she's thrilled. He's everything she could want—physically strong, highly intelligent, and … the other half of her soul. Yet, he's also an overwhelmingly dominant and stubborn Prime warrior who wishes to protect her from everything—including her own Prime nature. As a Prime battle-mate, she has newfound instincts and skills—skills that will make her a true warrior. Skills she fully intends to learn and use.

If she manages to survive.

Tooh 2 Resort

"OUR LEAVE IS CANCELED." IOLYN Caradoc strode toward his brothers, Wulf and Huw, and their mates, plus Joen Dakkin and his mate Lia, as they lounged around the resort pool. Tor Maren, the Prime ambassador to the Galactic Alliance, barely kept pace with him. "The *Galanti* needs to leave space dock as soon as possible," Iolyn said. "I've recalled the crew."

"What happened?" Wulf had his arm around Mel's shoulder as if he anticipated an attack.

Huw did the same with Nadia.

Iolyn sat, picked up Wulf's whiskey and finished it in one gulp, then picked up Huw's and did the same. He knew he was putting off battle vibes, but he couldn't help it. He'd never felt such fear before and wasn't handling it well.

Tor, who was like a second father to him and his brothers, sat and told the hovering waiter, "Gliesian white wine for me and the ladies. Whiskey for the men." The waiter hurried off. "Since Iolyn is attempting to get drunk, I'll relay what has happened."

Iolyn snarled, grabbed Joen's almost-empty glass and tossed it back.

"I received word from Admiral Nelson at Alliance Command that Dr. Brianna Martin has been threatened...a man stalking her attempted to kidnap her," Tor said. "She managed to escape and put a call out to the Alliance to rescue her."

"That's terrible. Of course we'll go get her and ensure she arrives at Cejuru Prime safely," Wulf said. "But why is Iolyn attempting to get drunk?"

Tor sighed and shook his head. "Dr. Martin is a Lost One. And she is..."

"My mate!" Iolyn pounded his fist on the table. "She sent an image of her marking to the Alliance and Prime Commands, asking that her mate be found and told. She asked, if possible, that he come and get her." He stood and paced angrily around the table. "I'm clear across the fucking galaxy while my mate had to fight off an attack." He threw his head back and roared the Caradoc battle cry to the skies.

Huw and Wulf rounded the table and held onto him until he quit shouting. *Diew*, he was in full-blown *batel rabia*, the Prime battle rage, and would experience lesser stages of it until he had Brianna in his arms.

Nadia joined them and placed her hand on Iolyn's shoulder. "How can we help?"

Mel also joined the huddle, lending her support. Their combined presence calmed him a bit. He wasn't alone in this; his brothers and their mates would see him through the horrible hours until he could be with his *gemate*, the mate fate and the One had chosen for him.

Tor, Joen, and Lia used their bodies to ward off the curious glances of the understandably shaken bystanders. The Caradoc battle cry had turned many an enemy's bowels to water.

"We get to Brianna as quickly as possible," Iolyn growled.

36 Standard Hours earlier
Galactic Alliance Astrobiological Research Lab
Planet Oz, Tau Ceti system

Dr. Brianna Martin eyed her target and took careful aim. She nailed the male figure right between the eyes.

"Yay! See if you can beat that, my friend." Bria happy-danced her way toward the life-sized, pseudo-reptilian male anatomy chart and pulled her scalpel from the kill zone in the frontal lobe. "Did I forget to mention I was med school scalpel-throwing champion three years in a row? Looks like you get to buy dinner."

There was no response from her research assistant Cheri Stafford. Instead she heard a gasp and the sound of Cheri moving quickly away from their impromptu contest venue.

Primordial instincts Bria rarely had to rely upon in the medical world went on alert, sharpening her empathic abilities. Something dangerous headed their way. It smelled like a hot, fierce wind off a desert. She tasted the dustiness of it on her tongue and felt it flaying her skin. She hurried toward her friend, who stood in the entrance to the lab. "Cheri? What's wrong?"

"Red alert!" Her friend growled the words as she made a move to cut off whoever approached.

Bria peered around her friend and saw her nemesis, Jotak M'tali.

Jotak, the chief of security for the research facility, strode down the long corridor in his ruler-of-the-planet, owner-of-all-he-surveyed mode.

"Really? Now? Doesn't that...that..." *freaking, scary, creep-a-zoid* "...man understand the meaning of the word *no*?" As in never, no way, no how, ever in the infinite future of possibilities.

Cheri paused outside the doorway and threw a commiserating grimace over her shoulder. "I'll venture a guess and say *not*. He hasn't seen you yet. So hide. I'll get rid of the slime-sucking bottom-feeder. He won't get a chance to touch you again."

"No!" Bria grabbed the arm of her loyal and well-meaning friend, the sister Bria had never had because she'd been adopted into a family with six boys. She pulled Cheri back and whispered, "He can smell me. He knows I'm here. Go...get help. Preferably someone who isn't susceptible to his Dornian hypnotic abilities."

"But...but...he hurt you last time." Cheri's eyes filled with angry tears. "And no one did anything about it."

The incident Cheri referred to had occurred about a standard week ago. Jotak, tired of her holding him at arm's length, had become more aggressive in his pursuit. He'd cornered her in the research facility's storeroom, forced a kiss on her...then attempted to rape her.

Bria shuddered and swallowed hard against the sickness threatening to erupt. She still bore bruises and claw marks from his rough handling. If a janitor hadn't happened by, Jotak would've succeeded in assaulting her. Her rudimentary self-defense skills hadn't even made a dent against Jotak's superior strength and training.

The janitor had backed her story when she'd filed the complaint with local authorities, but then the poor man had gone missing. Using his mesmeric abilities, Jotak had persuaded the local law officers that the alleged attack had been a mere lovers' tiff. Her bruises were ignored.

So, until she had security footage of an attack or eyewitnesses who couldn't be *persuaded* to say otherwise—

or she was severely injured enough for medical treatment—no one would believe the Chief of Security was stalking and threatening her.

"If he smells you, he smells both of us," Cheri hissed as she reversed Bria's grip and held onto Bria's arm. "Come with me. We can both get away."

"No, he'll hunt us down." And he'd hurt Cheri, because he had no use for her. "Dornians love nothing more than to chase prey." And to kill them. Killing and hiding a body were as easy for a Dornian as putting on clothing in the morning. "It's me he wants."

And he wouldn't kill Bria. He wanted to breed with her.

Not. Gonna. Happen.

Bria gave her friend an urgent shove. "Go out the back. Now." Her friend hesitated. "Cheri, please go...and hurry! Bring back help."

Cheri cast one last angry, fear-filled glance at the six-and-a-half-foot pseudo-reptilian stalking toward the lab and then ran out the back exit.

Bria turned and blocked the lab's main entrance, giving Cheri extra time to make her escape. Realizing she still held a scalpel, she placed the hand holding the lethally sharp instrument alongside her leg. If he got too close, she knew just where to cut him, to force him to take the time and energy to heal himself as his kind did. She might've been raised by pacifists on a communal farming planet and was, by choice, a healer, but she believed in self-defense.

"Brianna! What is-s-s this-s-s-s I hear?" His low voice carried down the hallway as he decreased the space between them. His voice had an eerie, sibilant hiss due to his genetics and made the hairs on her body stand on end. She shivered and tried to ignore the primitive response of prey. "You will *not* leave Oz. This-s-s-s I will not permit."

Jotak had no rights over her, no matter what he thought in his screwed up, alpha-dominant, narcissistic brain. She'd made the point clear many times...and would again and again until he processed the truth—she'd never be with him.

"Good afternoon to you, too, Jotak." Despite her vow to remain calm and in control, her voice trembled from fear and all the adrenaline speeding through her system.

Of course, her subtly sarcastic reprimand on his lack of manners swept over his head like a solar wind.

"Explain, woman." Jotak loomed over her in full alpha-male-intimidation mode with his fists on his hips and a frown on his practically lipless mouth. Some women might find his six-foot six-inch muscular body, pale green skin, dark-green, almost-black hair, and golden eyes attractive in an exotic way.

Bria found him irritating and very, very menacing.

"We had this discussion almost s-s-six weeks ago. We agreed you were not going to Cejuru Prime."

Jotak spoke the name of the home planet of the Prime race, a recent addition to the Galactic Alliance, as if it produced a foul taste in his mouth. His Dornian race, a nomadic people that ran con games and hired out as mercenaries to the highest bidder, was a distant cousin to the Antareans, the Prime's archenemy for millennia. The antipathy must have been bred into their pseudo-reptilian genes.

While choosing to work within the structure of the Galactic Alliance had made Jotak an outlier within his race, he was no less criminal or less dangerous. The Dornian heritage which made him a good con man and warrior were lousy for just about everything else, including his current job providing security for a bunch of brainiac research scientists.

Whoever had hired and then promoted the man should be shot.

"*You* said I wasn't going," Bria pointed out with a calmness she didn't feel. The raw energy coming off the large and powerful male frame had her hominid primitive brain urging her to run—and another little used and more violent part of her congenital makeup urged her to fight.

For the moment, she chose a higher brain response and attempted to reason with him. If that tack didn't work, she'd use the scalpel on a vital artery and then run like hell.

"If you recall, I didn't agree." Slowly, she moved sideways, further away from his body, toward the rear exit of the lab. Just in case diplomacy didn't work.

During a normal encounter, Jotak had absolutely zero respect for personal space, but his current maneuver of crowding her was aimed at bullying her into submitting to his will.

Bria wouldn't succumb, but that didn't mean she didn't feel threatened...because she did. She'd had up close and personal experience with how quickly Jotak went from a simmering anger to a roiling rage.

For now, Jotak mirrored her movements, stalking her like the predator he was, while closing any gap she created. Then he stopped. His head swept from side to side as his split-tongue tasted the air. His slitted yellow eyes flared. He'd noted Cheri's lingering scent.

Thank the One, her friend was long gone, out of Jotak's reach.

"Someone is-s-s here?" He pinned her with his basilisk stare. It didn't work on her.

"We're alone." Bria placed her workstation between her and the large male. "Now, say what you have to say and then go. I have work to do before I can leave for the day."

He flicked his tongue, quickly tasting the air once more, and then emitted an almost orgasmic guttural sound. His body seemed to grow another inch in height and breadth. His thin lips twisted upward. If she were brave enough to look, she knew she'd find evidence of his arousal. He was feeding on the smell of her fear, and like the apex predator he was, he liked it.

Why had she ever thought she could be "just friends" with this man? She must've been nuts.

"If you wish to leave Oz, Brianna, I will take you wherever you wish to go. We can join my parent's space caravan."

"I am leaving Oz to do my job. I have no desire to wander the universe—"

She left "with you" unsaid.

"Wrong ans-s-swer," he hissed.

Her gut told her an attack was imminent. How long had it been since Cheri left? Five standard minutes or less? It seemed like hours.

Hurry, hurry, hurry.

———

Prime Imperative is currently available as an e-book at Liquid Silver Books, Amazon, B&N, iBooks and other on-line retailers. And will be available in print at Amazon in early 2015.

Interested in finding out about other books by Monette Michaels? Follow her at FaceBook or visit her website.

WWW.FACEBOOK.COM/AUTHORMONETTEMICHAELS
WWW.MONETTEMICHAELS.COM

ABOUT THE AUTHOR

Monette Michaels is the pen name for a multi-published author of suspense/thrillers. She's been married to the love of her life for far longer than she cares to remember. Her home is in Central Indiana.